## MERCILESS

"Convincing detective lingo and an appropriately shivery murder venue go a long way."
—*Publishers Weekly*

"Burton just keeps getting better!"
—*RT Book Reviews*

"Terrifying . . . this chilling thriller is an engrossing story."
—*Library Journal*

"Mary Burton's latest romantic suspense has it all—terrific plot, complex and engaging protagonists, a twisted villain, and enough crime-scene detail to satisfy the most savvy suspense reader."
—Erica Spindler, *New York Times* bestselling author

## SENSELESS

"Stieg Larsson fans will find a lot to like in Burton's taut, well-paced novel of romantic suspense."
—*Publishers Weekly*

"This is a page-turner of a story, one that will keep you up all night, with every twist in the plot and with all of the doors locked."
—*The Parkersburg News & Sentinel*

"With hard-edged, imperfect but memorable characters, a complex plot, and no-nonsense dialog, this excellent novel will appeal to fans of Lisa Gardner and Lisa Jackson."
—*Library Journal*

"Absolutely chilling! Don't miss this well-crafted, spine-tingling read."
—Brenda Novak, *New York Times* bestselling author

"A terrifying novel of suspense."
—*Mysterious Reviews*

"This is a story to read with the lights on."
—*BookPage*

**Please read on for more rave reviews!**

## DYING SCREAM

"Burton's taut, fast-paced thriller will have you guessing until the last blood-soaked page. Keep the lights on for this one."
—*RT Book Reviews*

"A twisted tale . . . I couldn't put it down!"
—Lisa Jackson, *New York Times* bestselling author

## DEAD RINGER

"Dangerous secrets, deadly truths, and a diabolical killer combine to make Mary Burton's *Dead Ringer* a chilling thriller."
—Beverly Barton, *New York Times* bestselling author

"With a gift for artful obfuscation, Burton juggles a budding romance and two very plausible might-be perpetrators right up to the tense conclusion."
—*Publishers Weekly*

## I'M WATCHING YOU

"Taut . . . compelling . . . Mary Burton delivers a page-turner."
—Carla Neggers, *New York Times* bestselling author

"Creepy and terrifying, it will give you chills."
—*Romantic Times*

## Books by Mary Burton

I'M WATCHING YOU

DEAD RINGER

DYING SCREAM

SENSELESS

MERCILESS

BEFORE SHE DIES

THE SEVENTH VICTIM

NO ESCAPE

YOU'RE NOT SAFE

COVER YOUR EYES

BE AFRAID

I'LL NEVER LET YOU GO

VULNERABLE

**Published by Kensington Publishing Corp.**

# COVER
# YOUR
# EYES

## MARY
## BURTON

**PINNACLE BOOKS**
Kensington Publishing Corp.
www.kensingtonbooks.com

PINNACLE BOOKS are published by

Kensington Publishing Corp.
119 West 40th Street
New York, NY 10018

All Kensington titles, imprints, and distributed lines are available at special quantity discounts for bulk purchases for sales promotions, premiums, fund-raising, educational, or institutional use. Special book excerpts or customized printings can also be created to fit specific needs. For details, write or phone the office of the Kensington sales manager: Kensington Publishing Corp., 119 West 40th Street, New York, NY 10018, attn: Sales Department; phone 1-800-221-2647.

PINNACLE BOOKS and the Pinnacle logo are Reg. U.S. Pat. & TM Off.

ISBN-13: 978-0-7860-4579-2
ISBN-10: 0-7860-4579-5

First Zebra printing: November 2014
First Pinnacle printing: January 2021

10  9  8  7  6  5  4  3  2

Printed in the United States of America

Electronic edition:

ISBN-13: 978-1-4201-3212-0
ISBN-10: 1-4201-3212-1

*October 13*

*Sugar!*

*You made me laugh today! Not a snigger or a giggle but a belly-clutching hoot! What a complete shock! I'd expected you to be stuffy and humorless but you had me chuckling all the way home.*

*You are right about me. When I sing my heart swells and the melodies fill the hollowness lurking deep in the pit of my soul. You are the first person ever to notice. Next time I am on stage, know that the dumb-luck joy in my voice is all for you.*

*Thank you again for dinner, but I'm not so sure another date is wise. Nashville is a small town and gossips gnaw on whatever morsels they can find. I wish you the best.*

*A.*

# Prologue

Dixie Simmons's pink cowboy boots, tipped in silver and embossed with glittering stars, clicked against the rain-soaked pavement. A rainstorm had flashed through Music City hours ago and left the air crisp, colder than normal and heavy with moisture. Burrowing deeper into her fringed leather jacket, she shoved chilled hands into her pockets, fingering the roll of wrinkled one-dollar bills from the night's tip jar. The brisk air snapped at her bare thighs but didn't slow her on-top-of-the-world gait or spark a bit of remorse for her choice of attire. The black miniskirt wasn't warm but it showcased her long legs, always a crowd-pleaser at Rudy's honky-tonk.

Tonight she'd been the last to sing at Rudy's bar, the centerpiece of Lower Broadway's four block stretch of honky-tonks and restaurants. The one a.m. time slot was not the best spot on a Thursday but considering Rudy hadn't been expecting her, she'd appreciated the spot, the chance. Some singers might not give one hundred percent to the late-night crowd, but not Dixie. She'd sung as if her life hung in the night, Momma had begged Dixie to take the secretary job in Knoxville, but Dixie had refused.

Dixie wanted to be a star. Wanted everyone to know her name. Just needed the right break.

*Worth following.*

Maybe, she'd finally paid enough dues. Maybe soon she'd look back on tonight and recognize the exact moment her life changed.

Her chest puffed with pride as she imagined people wanting her. She liked being wanted.

As she rounded a corner and headed north, a group of men on the opposite side of the street passed going south. They wore jeans, blue jackets, and collared shirts that popped up in a collegiate kind of way. She guessed they were students at Vanderbilt University. The men slowed their pace and a couple stared at her with wolfish gazes.

The flicker of pride grew brighter. She liked male attention almost as much as the stage. She savored the feminine power she brandished, knowing it could derail any man's train of thought right off the tracks.

Dixie paused and bent forward to adjust a tassel on her boot. One of the boys whistled.

She grinned and waved, her excitement building. She'd have crossed the street, maybe suggested a party, but tonight another man waited.

She tossed the boys a wave, and when they called her over, she pouted and shook her head no before hurrying toward her car parked a half block away. The boots bit into her little toe.

Dixie fished her phone out of her purse, dialed a familiar number and waited. The phone rang once. Twice. Dollar store bracelets rattled on her wrist as she untangled a blond hair extension from a silver feather earring.

The phone kept ringing.

Sugar used to pick up on the first ring. He'd be breathless

balance, or better, that a talent-hungry music producer sat in a darkened corner. She'd been spot-on tonight, quickly forgetting about the gig's mix-up while singing Patsy Cline's "Crazy." When she'd switched to a Taylor Swift song she'd energized the crowd who soon were hooping and hollering. Applause followed her when she'd left the stage, her black mini swishing around her thighs. The rush of excitement had rivaled great sex.

The club's owner Rudy Creed had watched her from behind the bar, clearly pleased by the way she'd roped the crowd's attention. He'd stopped her on the way out and had said there'd been folks asking after her. "They think you're good. Worth following," he'd said.

*Worth following.*

Lordy, but she wanted to be worth following more than the breath she took. She'd been on the music circuit for three years—a long time to be waiting tables, knocking on closed music executive's doors and sinking every extra dime into publicity stills and demo CDs. One record producer had shown interest months ago, they'd slept together but lately he'd been dodging her. However his *no's*, as far as she was concerned, were warm-ups to a *yes,* so she'd kept after him. She'd finally gotten him on the phone days ago and he'd been pissed by her persistence. *"Yeah, you got talent but stay the fuck away from me."*

All she'd heard was *you got talent.*

The metro buses didn't run this late so she'd been forced to walk west on Broadway and past the hotels before turning on the tree-lined side street where she'd parked her car. Her cute pink boots cramped her toes and dug a blister on her heel.

Momma would have complained about the walk, the cold, and her feet. Momma understood hard work but she didn't understand dreams or the cost of fame. Just last and excited as if he'd been waiting anxiously for her call. But lately, *if* he answered, he let the phone ring five or six times and his *hello* carried less anticipation.

Four. Five. Six. He picked up on the seventh ring. "Dixie." He'd wrapped her name in a honey-flavored bourbon, his drink of choice.

"Hey. Want some company tonight?"

Hesitation and then, "Not tonight, Dixie. I've an early morning."

Jealousy scratched as she imagined another blond lying beside him in his bed singing sweet songs in his ear. He liked blondes that could sing. The sound of a woman's voice crooning in his ear made him hot. The first song she'd sung to him had been "You're Still the One."

"I thought you wanted me to come by tonight." No missing the pout underscoring the words.

He yawned. "I know, but I'm tired. It was a long day."

In the early days, he'd never been tired when she called. She'd been his tonic. His muse.

His rejection amplified her craving for attention. She nestled closer to the phone imagining she could touch him. "Sugar, I can wake you up. That's a promise and a guarantee."

"Not tonight, Dixie. In a day or two." The soft edges hardened.

Rebuff coupled with cold and sore feet stripped her of patience. "Why're you doing this to me? I thought I was special."

He sighed into the phone. "You're special. But enough is enough. We need to take a break. People are watching."

Ducking her head, her long hair curtained off her face. "Who?"

"People. And that's all you need to know."

"You have names. I want them."

"It doesn't matter."

They'd been careful to never be seen in public, opting

for hotels on the outskirts of town. She recalled there had been a hotel clerk who had eyed her as if he were trying to read her thoughts. Did he put the pieces together? "It does to me."

"Let it go, Dixie."

*Let it go.*

What an ass. He'd promised her the moon and now he was kicking her to the curb.

Dixie peeked back toward the group of boys, now half tempted to double back. A party with them would teach him a lesson. "You'll be sorry."

"I'm not now but I could be real sorry. I've a lot riding on the next thirty days. I don't want trouble."

He'd given her the boot and still she clung. "Are you going to call me soon?"

"Sure. Sure." He hung up.

Dixie stood for a moment, the phone still pressed to her ear not really believing he'd ended the call. When the dial tone buzzed in her ear, she pocketed her phone.

As much as she wanted to imagine him begging for forgiveness, she'd travelled this road enough times with other men to know the score. When men like him lost interest, it was over. And if any lessons had stuck in her twenty years on this earth, it was to cut her losses and move on to the next opportunity.

After a successful gig, she was juiced and full of energy and the idea of going home and staring at her four walls didn't top the option list. She wanted a man. Her skin tingled and she conjured up the man at the bar who'd glared at her hours ago with burning desire as he'd pressed the napkin with his phone number into her hand. He'd not say no to her.

At her car, a twelve-year-old black Buick with silver chrome wheels, she unlocked the front door and tossed her purse inside. Those boys were almost out of sight but she figured if she drove she could catch up to them. If they went to Vanderbilt they might have a bit of money. And money always made the time pass faster. Thunder rumbled, promising rain.

Moistening her lips, she smiled at the sound of footsteps behind her. The boys had returned. Running her tongue over her lips so they glistened, she drew in a breath and turned. "Hey."

For an instant, she registered a dark hoodie and a face hidden behind a hockey mask, but before she could scream a metal rod whooshed through the air and struck her on the side of her head.

Intense pain stole her breath. She staggered and fell to cold concrete, which tore the naked flesh of her palms and knees. Her cell phone jostled out of her pocket and hit the ground hard enough to pop off the back.

She blinked once and then twice trying to regain focus. She'd been hit before, but never like this. She raised a trembling hand to her cheek now slick and swelling with blood. *Oh, God. Not her face.*

A cold metal rod pressed against her shoulder and she collapsed against the ground. "Scream and I'll cave in your skull."

Jesus, was she being mugged? She'd been mugged before. It sucked to hand over hard-earned tip money but sixty bucks seemed a fair trade for her life. "My pocket. I've money. Take whatever you want."

Black booted feet moved within inches of her face. "I don't want your money."

Dixie groaned. Not a mugging? Then it was rape. Another indignity she'd survived. Her shattered cheek throbbed reverberating lightning bolts of pain through her entire body.

She moistened her lips, bracing. She'd not beg or plead. She was tough. She would survive.

But the attacker stood there, staring, watching, gloating.

Dixie drew in a deep breath, curling the fingers of her hands. Tears pooled in her eyes as she waited to be flipped on her back and her skirt tossed up. She grit her teeth. "What do you want?"

"Nothing. You're a whore and a harlot."

"I don't want to die."

In answer, the attacker quickly raised the rod and brought it down hard and direct against her shoulder. She gasped in a breath, the pain so blinding she couldn't make a sound as she rolled on her back. Her vision blurred into black splotches. She wanted to fight, but couldn't string two thoughts together. Whatever was gonna happen, it wasn't going to be good.

"Why?" she gasped.

"Whore. Harlot. I've had it with watching you parade your pert little ass around. I've had it. You've hurt too many people."

Dixie blinked her vision into focus and glimpsed dark eyes staring at her through the mask. The tire iron rose. She braced hoping against hope she could mitigate the blow's damage by tensing.

"No mercy," the stranger said.

The next blow struck her temple and in a flash her vision went dark.


Baby exhaled, breathless and excited.

An hour ago Dixie had flickered bright on the stage, swishing her skirt and flirting with the crowd. Now Dixie's crumpled body lay on the cold, damp ground in a pool of blood.

Four well-placed blows had obliterated the sweet, seductive siren's high swipe of cheekbones, full red lips, creamy skin and thick eyelashes into pulp. No whore deserved to go into the next world with her looks. That smacked of injustice in Baby's book. A beautiful whore could well strike a deal with the Devil and then return to the earth to haunt.

The idea of Dixie returning had Baby gripping the cold iron high and slamming it on Dixie's face in another crushing blow. Blood splattered. Bone crushed. Again and again the tire iron struck until finally, Baby, breathless and blood-soaked, stopped.

Stepping back, a satisfied smile curled at the utter ruin and destruction of one once so beautiful.

Dixie Simmons wouldn't be parading her tart ass around town anymore or singing those songs designed to ruin men's lives.

Dead and gone.

*October 18*

*Sugggar . . .*

*You are a dirty little man. You shocked me but good when you whispered those bad boy words that swirled in my head like a merry-go-round. Each time they pass my knees go weak. You've got me curious. So forget all that I said about good and evil. Come on by after the show tonight. You might find I'm ready to play.*

*A.*

# Chapter One

Rain dripped from Detective Deke Morgan's jacket as he pushed through the doors of the Tennessee medical examiner's office, his shoulders tense with fatigue and a headache hammering his eyes. His latest homicide call had come after three thirty a.m., minutes after he'd polished off his second beer and scrawled his name on papers dissolving his second, and what he'd sworn would be his last, marriage. Conditioned by fifteen years on the force, he'd swapped regrets, faded jeans, and a Titans T-shirt for purpose, a coat and tie, and strong coffee.

With rain falling and thunder rumbling in the distance, he'd arrived at the murder scene by four thirty, greeted by the swarm of cops and news vans. "Driver's license says Dixie Simmons," said a young uniformed officer, eyes watery and troubled. The license showed the face of a pretty woman, thick lightly colored hair and eyes bright with amusement.

As the media had been corralled on the opposite corner and were firing questions at Deke, he'd donned gloves, passed the pallid faces of more uniforms, and ducked under the yellow crime-scene tape. When he had lifted the bloody sheet, he'd found an unrecognizable mess, which he'd studied with a clinician's eye. As he'd left the scene he had heard whispered comparisons to his cop father, also known for a fearsome detachment that had made him as efficient as he was untouchable.

At the medical examiner's security desk, separated from the lobby by a thick glass wall, Deke tossed the dregs of a fourth coffee into the trash and dug his badge from his pocket. With an all clear from a burly guard, the locked side door clicked open and he wound his way into the building.

Assistant medical examiner Dr. Miriam Heller had texted him a half-hour ago and told him his victim would be autopsied in exam room two. Outside the double doors, he put on a gown and gloves and then pushed inside the exam room.

Dr. Heller stood at the head of a stainless steel exam table, the body of Dixie Simmons covered in a clean white sheet.

Standing at five-foot-ten, Heller was a slim woman in her midthirties with a smooth olive complexion and long dark hair she kept twisted in a tight knot. Dark thick lashes framed blue eyes with a slight almond tilt. She rarely wore makeup and favored skinny jeans, flats, and sleeveless blouses. Caring and compassionate, she also possessed a dry sense of humor that kept most of the cops on their toes.

"Dr. Heller."

She peered around the computer screen. "Detective Morgan. Where is your partner in crime?"

Detective KC Kelly had five days remaining until Department retirement. With thirty-two years on the Nashville Police force, he'd worked with everyone who'd been on the murder squad, including Deke's father, the late great Detective Buddy Morgan.

Deke stretched the kinks from his neck. "He'll be here soon."

She tsked. "Short-timer? Less than a week to go but he's already quit."

KC now talked constantly about sailing the seas with his new girlfriend, who'd given him renewed purpose after his wife lost her life to cancer last year. "No. He's still hitting it hard. He was interviewing witnesses at the murder scene when I left."

"He doesn't like my office. Calls me Morticia behind my back."

"No offense intended, Dr. Heller." KC was a good cop, but could run his mouth. "He doesn't like the ME's office."

Eyes flashed with a mixture of annoyance and curiosity. "Then why choose homicide?"

"I never said he was sane."

"Which one of you on the squad is?"

"Point taken."

The Nashville homicide team had five members, Deke and KC, Ian McGowan, Jake Bishop, and Red Dickens. All solid cops and, except for KC and Deke, under forty.

"Is he having a big retirement party?"

"So I hear. I kicked into the kitty but haven't paid much attention to the plans. When I'm told where to go, I'll go."

She adjusted the overhead microphone to within inches of her mouth. "Still working on that house?"

"Getting around to unpacking last night."

A dark brow rose. "You've been out there what, six months?"

"There about. Never a fan of chores." Unpacking amounted to accepting failures and a new life that still didn't fit right.

Dr. Heller cut through the small talk to the heart of the matter. "If you want to sell, then do it. No law says you have to live in the family home."

"The Big House is wrapped around a lot of family history. Got to give it a try."

His mother had inherited the white plantation style house set on thirty acres from her parents and she and Deke's father had moved into the showpiece right after they'd married. The four Morgan children had been a tight-knit pack thanks to their mother who'd served dinner nightly at the big table. Buddy took his place at the table often enough to regale his children with wild cop tales and to infect each child with the law enforcement bug. When their mother had died twelve years ago, the family tapestry had frayed and when a heart attack had claimed Buddy six months ago it had unraveled. Though all the Morgan children lived or worked within miles of each other they saw one another only when their jobs demanded it. The Big House was the last bit of Morgan glue.

Deke touched his dark necktie. "Tell me what you know about the victim, Doc."

Dr. Heller pulled back the sheet. The body had been stripped of clothing, and exposed pale skin made the bruising and dried blood all the more obvious and grotesque. "Assuming the driver's license did belong to this victim, Dixie Simmons was twenty years old, stood five-foot-two, and weighed approximately one hundred and ten pounds. There're no defensive wounds. The first blow likely caught her by surprise. All her blows, except two, were sustained on or about the head and each would have been crippling."

Deke studied the misshapen, crushed face. "He destroyed her face and her identity."

She cradled the fractured face in her gloved hands and rotated it to the right to display a shattered cheekbone and eye socket. "She was hit eight to ten times on her face."

He studied the carnage. "One blow would have been

enough to kill her but to keep hitting her face . . . that feels personal."

"I've seen drug abusers commit great violence that wasn't personal."

"Her purse wasn't taken. None of her jewelry was taken and there're no signs of sexual assault, correct?"

"I've not done a thorough examination but so far no bruising on the inside of her legs, which would indicate rape."

"Now it's my job to figure out what whack-job in Dixie Simmons's life hated her so much."

The double doors to the exam room swung open and KC eased into the autopsy room like a man facing a rattler. He'd shaken off his jacket but his near bald head glistened with rain. "Five days to go. I was saying last night to Brenda that if I never saw the inside of this place again, it would be too soon. No offense, Dr. Heller."

She smiled. "None taken."

He took extra time to tug on gloves before approaching. He stopped several feet from the body and studied the victim's face. Sadness deepened the craggy lines etched around his eyes. "I won't miss this."

Deke shook his head. "I'll give you two weeks before you are back hanging around the station. Brenda's nice enough but not working is gonna drive you insane."

KC shook his head. "No damn way. I put in my time, and I'm retiring before the job kills me."

He stopped short of saying Buddy's name but they both knew the force had taken its toll on Buddy's heart. Eyewitness accounts had said Buddy had risen from his favorite booth at the diner after a hearty breakfast of bacon and eggs, winced, and dropped. He'd been dead before he'd hit the floor. "Before you take off, tell me what you learned. Witnesses have information?"

From his pocket, KC dug out a battered small notebook exactly like thousands of others he'd carried for years. He flipped through the pages until he'd reached the middle section. "I talked to a group of men who passed the victim about three o'clock in the morning. They said she grinned at them as she dug her cell from her purse. One of the boys whistled. She smiled but kept walking."

"No one was following her?"

"They didn't see anyone."

"What's their story?"

"Students at Vanderbilt on their way to a party. They said the party was a dud, which was why they left early and passed the crime scene at four a.m. I went to the party house and banged on the door. A not-too-happy kid answered. He verified that the boys had been at the party. The four had played video games, drank a beer, hoping girls would show and when the girls didn't materialize the witnesses left."

"Anyone else?"

KC flipped a page in the book. "A woman who lives a block over reported hearing a car backfire about the time of the murder. And we did find the victim's cell phone. Back of the case was knocked off and I'm thinking she had it in her hand when she was attacked. Dropped, hit the sidewalk and back popped open. Forensics bagged it and will search for data."

Frustration burrowed under Deke's skin. "No one saw anything?"

KC shook his head. "I knocked on twenty doors this morning. Woke up a lot of people and messed with several morning routines. No one saw the murder."

He shoved out a breath. "Did the uniforms find the murder weapon?"

"It would be long and thin judging by the injuries. Like a pipe or a tire iron," Dr. Heller said.

KC again shook his head. "No sign of a weapon and the uniforms have been beating the bushes."

A search of the victim's purse at the crime scene had produced a napkin with a number scrawled on it. The logo on the napkin had read RUDY'S, which he knew was a honky-tonk on Broadway. The place was a local institution where the best of the aspiring singer-songwriters played hoping to get noticed by a record producer. His baby sister Georgia had been trying to get a spot on the evening lineup but so far, no luck. Georgia, unlike her three older brothers, could carry a tune but like her brothers had joined the force. She worked forensics.

If Dixie had been singing at Rudy's then she'd had some talent.

"I'll swing by Rudy's this morning," Deke said. "He might remember a customer who'd shown interest in the victim."

KC stepped back from the table. "I can do that if you like. Rudy's is my watering hole."

His partner favored the tried and true police techniques. He'd gladly knock on doors before doing a computer search. "If you run the victim's cell phone records, you can leave now. I'll observe the autopsy and tackle Rudy's in a couple of hours."

KC grinned. "Deal."

Dr. Heller reached for a set of bone shears and snipped them. "You don't want to stay?"

"Sorry, Doc. Sacrifices have to be made." KC turned, then stopped as he fished in his pocket. "By the way, Deke, I came across this flyer when I was wandering around Vanderbilt."

Deke accepted the rumpled paper and smoothed it open. His mood soured instantly at the headline that read: JUSTICE FOR JEB JONES. "What the hell?"

KC shrugged. "Don't shoot the messenger."

Tension, like molten metal, seared his muscles. "She doesn't know when to quit."

Dr. Heller raised her brow. "And she would be?"

"A troublemaker," Deke said.

KC's demeanor toughened. "She is Rachel Wainwright, a local attorney who is wanting to reopen one of Buddy's old murder cases. Look up Pain-In-The-Ass in the dictionary and you'll see her picture."

"How old is the case?" Dr. Heller asked.

"Thirty years." Deke balled up the flyer. "She wants the DNA on the murder weapon tested."

Dr. Heller watched the wadded ball sail across the room and bounce off the trash can rim. "Thirty years ago would have been before DNA testing. Hers is not an unreasonable request."

"We didn't need DNA to prove this guy was guilty of murder. We had a solid case," KC said. "Wainwright is trying to make a name for herself."

Deke picked up the wadded paper and dunked it hard in the trash. "She's got a legal right to ask for the test."

KC snorted. "She's looking for her fifteen seconds of fame so she can build a book of business. The guy we sent away got what he deserved."

Deke adjusted his tie, ignoring the temptation to loosen it. "She's got a legal right."

KC stripped off his gown and tossed it in the trash before reaching in a pocket for a stick of gum, Brenda's current substitute for his preferred cigarettes. "Fucking ambulance chaser, if you ask me."

"No one's asking, KC," Deke said.

The attorney was out to cause trouble for trouble's sake, but bitching and moaning wouldn't stop her. "Didn't you say you had work to do?"

"Yeah." KC studied the body and took a step back.

"Talk to you soon." The swinging doors soon whooshed behind him.

Dr. Heller reached for her scalpel and sliced a Y incision into the victim's chest. The next couple of hours gleaned minimal facts about Dixie Simmons. She had not been sexually assaulted but she'd had an abortion within the last year. Her body didn't bear the needle marks of a drug user, nor did she have old fractures to suggest any kind of abuse. She had breast implants and she'd had her nose redone.

By the time Dr. Heller had finished her exam, Deke had more information on his victim but no real answers. After Dr. Heller closed the body she rotated her own head from side to side, working out the tension.

"I'll walk you outside," she said.

"Sure."

Deke and Dr. Heller stepped into the crisp morning air. He patted his jacket pocket and remembered he'd left his cigarette habit at the house he'd lost in the divorce.

She inhaled a deep breath and tipped her face to the sun. "I never take a pretty day for granted."

Deke pulled his own notebook from his pocket and stared at the number he'd scrawled off Dixie's napkin. "Let's see if finding a killer is as easy as dialing a number."

Dr. Heller pulled out a pack of cigarettes from the side pocket of her white lab coat. "That possible?"

"It would be about the easiest case I've ever solved." He watched her light up, the old cravings tugging at him. "That stuff will kill you, Doc."

She inhaled and then slowly exhaled. "Something's going to kill us all."

"Maybe." He unclipped the phone from his belt and dialed the number.

She offered the pack to him. "You look like you could use one."

"Thanks, Doc. I'll pass."

She tucked the pack back in her pocket. "How long has it been since you quit?"

"Six months and two days."

"I quit once for a year."

"As a doctor don't you worry about what it will do to you?"

She inhaled and grinned. "Nope."

"I'm not going back. I bought a one-way ticket, Doc." Deke studied the napkin and the dark number written in a heavy, masculine scrawl. It rang once. Twice. At the tenth ring, with no answer, Deke hung up.

"Looks like it's not your lucky day."

Deke shrugged. "I'll run the number back at the office. We'll have a name soon enough."

"I've no doubt." She studied him an extra beat, as if she wanted to say more but then turned and inhaled again.

"If you get a hit with the tox screens you'll let me know?"

"Always."

Deke left the doctor to finish her smoke. The drive across town and down Broadway to Rudy's honky-tonk took less than fifteen minutes. He managed parking on a side street within a half block.

He'd worked this area several times when he'd been undercover. In those days his hair had been long, his beard thick, his T-shirt and jeans dirty, and his leather jacket beat up.

At Rudy's he looked through a large glass window past the CLOSED sign toward the bar where he saw an older man polishing glasses. Standing over six feet, the man sported a gray beard that reached a barreled chest and salt-and-pepper hair slicked back into a ponytail. Rudy Creed.

Forty years owning a honky-tonk, Rudy had seen the area go from near slums filled with drug dealers and drunks to a bustling tourism center that brought a lot of money into the city. Rudy's was a legend in this town, known among the elite of country music for putting the best on fortune's road to fame.

Deke rapped on the window with his knuckle and held up his badge.

The old man raised his head, gray eyes narrowing. Slowly he set the glass down and moved from behind the bar. Rudy wore a blue western style shirt, and jeans and red cowboy boots.

He moved with the unhurried gait of a man who'd seen more than his share of cops. This wasn't the first time the police had visited his place and likely not the last. He unlatched the dead bolt and pushed open the door. He smelled faintly of soap and whiskey.

The morning light cast a harsh glare on the bar's scarred tables and scuffed floors. Pictures of singers covered every square inch of the wall. He recognized some images. Small cocktail tables clustered in front of the stage.

A chandelier hung from the center of the room, its crystal teardrops catching the morning light. An anomaly in the rough country interior, the fixture had been a gift from a country music star who'd promised Rudy a chandelier if she'd made it big.

"Mind if I come in? Got questions for you about one of your singers."

A frown deepened the lines around his eyes and mouth as if he'd bitten into a bitter apple. "Who did what to whom?"

Deke held up the victim's motor vehicle picture. "Dixie Simmons. What can you tell me about her?"

He shoved out a sigh, closed and locked the front door. "She sang last night until about two. She's good. Got a Patsy Cline sound that the folks like. She get herself into trouble?"

"Why would you say that?"

The question sparked amusement in his gray eyes. "Officer, you would not be here if there wasn't trouble."

"Dixie Simmons was murdered last night shortly after she left here."

Tension darkened his expression as he rubbed the back of his neck with a large calloused hand. "What happened?"

"We're still trying to figure it all out."

Rudy moved to the bar and reached for a bottle filled with a honey-gold liquid. He poured a glass, offered it to Deke and when he declined drank it in one shot. He winced slightly as it burned his throat. "Any ideas who did it?"

"No, sir. That's why I'm here. When's the last time you saw her?"

"Last night. Two thirty a.m. I always open and close the place. Fact I walked her out and locked the door behind her. There was another bartender, Jim, but he left an hour earlier. Jim's been with me a couple of years. I closed the joint right after she left."

"She have any issues with anyone last night?"

"No. I mean she had some of the boys riled up with her dancing and flirting on stage, but that's Dixie. Knows how to work a crowd."

"No one in the crowd gave you cause to worry?"

"Not last night. A lot of out-of-towners."

"I found a napkin in her purse and there's a number scrawled on it."

"You call it?"

"A couple of times on the drive over. No answer."

"Not the first wrong number given out here." He studied the bottom of his empty glass before carefully setting it on the bar. "Dixie wasn't the brightest girl in the world but she could sing and she was willing to work hard. And the crowds loved her. Don't see talent and drive in one package too often. But she had a weakness for men."

"What can you tell me about Dixie's personal life?"

"As long as my singers show up on time, give me their best and leave their issues at home, I don't ask questions."

"I'm willing to bet not much gets past you."

A half smile tipped the edge of Rudy's lips as if he agreed with Deke's assessment. "No, not much gets past me. Bad for business to let too much slip." He stood straighter, recapturing the energy Deke's news had stolen. "Dixie liked the men. Liked them a lot. Rarely did she go home alone. Last night was one of the rare exceptions."

"Why was that?"

"She said she had a man waiting for her. Said they'd been seeing each other on and off for months and she liked him."

"He have a name?"

"I didn't ask."

Deke cocked a brow. "No matter what your rules about not bringing the personal to work, words and conversations get overheard."

He peered back into the empty shot glass. "We had two other singers here last night. Chic Jones and Rennie Forest. You can ask those gals about Dixie. If she did any talking they'd have heard it."

"Contact numbers would be appreciated." Rudy reached under the bar and removed a black Rolodex stuffed full with cards. "If she was into this guy, why'd she take the number of another guy?"

Calloused fingers flipped through worn cards. "Hedging her bets, I reckon. Always good to have options." He plucked a card from the Rolodex and then fished for the second.

"Names of recent hookups?"

"Like I said, I don't ask a lot of questions as long as it don't spill into my place. Ask Rennie and Chic."

Deke scrawled the two women's names and their contact

information in his notebook. "Dixie have any confrontations that you remember recently?"

"No. Not a one. I had to give it to Dixie, when it came to work she was all business. She wanted stardom so bad she could taste it. Wanted to be on the top ten charts and land in the country music Hall of Fame. And she'd have done whatever it took."

"How'd she get along with the other singers?"

"From what I saw polite but not overly friendly. By her way of thinking they were her competition and after the recording contract she wanted."

"She get a contract?"

"Not yet. But it would have been a matter of time. Word was getting around about her. That's why I let her sing last night even though she wasn't on the lineup."

"What happened?"

"Said she received a text telling her to sing at midnight. She arrived early, dolled up and ready to work. I've had other singers pull that trick before but never Dixie. I cut the scheduled singer short and let her sing."

"Who lost stage time?"

"Dude by the name of Harrison Franklin. He wasn't happy but it's my way or the highway."

Deke asked for and received Harrison's contact information.

Rudy carefully replaced the cards on his Rolodex as he shook his head, his frown deepening with each moment. "Dixie was good with the customers. Could whip them up and bring them to their feet or have them crying in their drinks. She soaked up the attention like booze."

"She craved attention?"

"Just about."

A bucket rattled in the back of the bar. An older stoop-shouldered woman gripped a mop, a curtain of long gray hair covering her face.

"Cleaning lady," Rudy said. "Rattles around here in the daytime."

The woman vanished into the back. "Did she know Dixie?"

"No. She's day crew. They stop work at four in the afternoon, about the time the night crew comes in."

"And you work both shifts."

"As long as I'm behind the bar there ain't no trouble so I'm always behind the bar."

"Rough schedule."

"I don't notice anymore. And there's no better place than here as far as I'm concerned." He recapped the whiskey bottle like he must have done a million times. "Another gal who might help too is Tawny Richards. She and Dixie shared an apartment. They lived in east Nashville."

He wrote the name. "She a singer too?"

"Aren't they all?" He rubbed calloused hands over the scrubby beard on his chin. "Tawny did sing here. She's not as good as Dixie but she did all right. I used her as a last minute fill-in last August. She's better than an empty stage." He flipped through more cards and rattled off names and addresses.

Deke jotted down the information.

Rudy put the Rolodex back behind the bar. "You never said how she died."

"Beaten to death." He didn't mention Dr. Heller's theory of a tire iron, knowing some details he'd share after he had a killer in custody.

Rudy blanched. "Dear Lord. No girl deserves that."

The show of shock, Deke guessed, was rare for a man like Rudy who no doubt revealed as much as an iceberg's jagged tip. "Whoever killed her wasn't looking for money or sex. This was about rage." Recognizing a weakening in Rudy's tough exterior he added, "We confirmed her identity by her fingerprints."

Rudy unscrewed the whiskey bottle and again refilled his glass. He raised it to his bristled mustache with a trembling hand. "I liked Dixie. Liked her a lot. I should have told her she was dancing with trouble. Should have told her to ease up."

"Ease up on?"

"The men. Sooner or later you're bound to pick a crazy one."

The well-ordered row of booze bottles behind the bar and the freshly wiped countertop said this was a man who paid attention to details regardless of what he said. "How long had she been working here?"

"About a year. She started waitressing and then asked if she could sing. She surprised me. In a good way. Like I said, she built a following. She was in the nine o'clock hour a couple of Saturdays ago. I don't give that spot to just anyone."

Deke pulled a card from his pocket. "If you think of any helpful information, would you call me?"

He took the card. "Sure, I'll call."

Deke left the bar but glanced back to see Rudy drink the glass of whiskey. The old man shoved out a breath, as if expelling poison.

*October 22*

*Sugar!*

*I was surprised to see you waiting in the alley behind Rudy's tonight. When you stepped out of the shadows you gave me a start. I told you to stay away but I'm glad you don't listen so well.*

*The gift was really not necessary. In fact I can hear my mother's voice warning me against a man's unexpected kindness. She'd fear you'd lead me down the road of sin. But I'm not afraid of sin.*

*I smile when I look at the little diamonds that curve into a heart pendant and the genuine schoolboy kindness warming your eyes when you gave me the little black box. How can such a beautiful gift, given with such loving kindness, be wicked?*

*A.*

# Chapter Two

*You're poking the bear!*

Rachel Wainwright ignored her brother's unwelcome voice echoing in her head and resisted the urge to mutter back a rebuttal as she scanned the paltry collection of people gathering for her candlelight vigil at Riverfront Park near the banks of the Cumberland River.

The idea of a public gathering had come to her in a moment of desperation. To promote the event, she'd called local civic groups, churches, and media. She'd feared she'd have no takers from the media, but a last minute call from Channel Five offered real hope. The reporter had confirmed she and her crew would arrive momentarily to cover the vigil. She'd organized the event with the intent of drawing attention to her newest client who'd been referred to her by the Innocence Project, a nonprofit group dedicated to clearing wrongfully convicted people.

When she'd first read the summary of the Jeb Jones case, she'd quickly realized he'd been petitioning for the test for a decade. At the time of his arrest and trial, DNA had not been available and he believed DNA would once and for all prove he wasn't a murderer.

She wasn't naïve enough to take her client's word alone. But there was enough evidence to argue for DNA testing and once she had the DNA results she'd determine if she had a case. She'd sent her petition to the cops over six weeks ago and so far no word. She found out that the case had been assigned to a Deke Morgan and had gotten through to Morgan once. He'd barely said three words as she'd stated her case and demanded a time line for the test results. "When I know, you'll know," he had said before hanging up and cutting her off midsentence.

Subsequent calls to Morgan had landed her in voice mail where she'd left message after message. But no callbacks. When word came from the prison that Jeb's health had taken a turn for the worse, she'd decided to go public.

The vigil had looked great on paper but now as she looked out over her paltry collection of followers hovered around a table she'd stocked with donuts and coffee, she had serious doubts. Had any of these people come for justice or was it all about the food? At this point, she hoped the food lasted until the television crews arrived.

If the media took up her cause, as she hoped, they would videotape the crowd so that the event looked well attended. If they didn't sympathize with her point of view, they'd angle the cameras so that the group looked even sparser.

No telling with the media. They could be your best friend or your worst enemy.

"Are they coming?" Her law partner, Colleen Spencer, arranged white candles in a wicker basket, which she'd soon distribute to the crowd. Colleen was petite standing barely an inch over five feet. Her small stature belied a tenacity that was earning her a reputation as a successful criminal defense attorney. A royal blue Chanel suit amplified long auburn hair that framed an oval face sprinkled with freckles.

"Yes. Channel Five is sending a reporter and a camera. They should be here in about five minutes."

Rachel ran her fingers through her short dark hair. She shrugged tense shoulders under the pinstripe jacket, paired with a white blouse, dark pencil skirt, and heels she'd borrowed from Colleen. Successful lawyers, Colleen had often said, dressed the part, but dressing the part smacked of rules and Rachel hated rules. Rachel had conceded to the attire and to Colleen's pearls "to soften you up a bit."

"The sooner, the better." Colleen surveyed the collection of people who wouldn't linger long. "I think we've scrounged up every friend and friend of a friend we know. And thank God for the donuts." Colleen raised her hand to a group of guys she'd met at her local gym. "Here's hoping the candles catch more attention and more people gather."

Rachel skimmed her prepared statement, which she'd restricted to key talking points. No one wanted a long rambling speech. They wanted impassioned words easily caught and carried away. "Maybe one of the tour buses will drop off nearby. I'd take hungry tourists now."

Diamond studs winked from Colleen's ears. "One can hope."

"Go ahead and start handing out the candles. The sun will be setting soon and you can light the candles. It will look good for the media as well."

"Will do."

Rachel's hands trembled slightly when she shuffled through her papers wondering again if she'd made the right decision. This night had a greater potential for disaster than success.

Colleen nudged Rachel's arm with her elbow. "Relax. This is going to go well."

Being right didn't guarantee success. "Let's hope."

"Keep it simple. You are a good speaker, you have passion and your supporters will respond."

"My supporters." A survey of the crowd stoked her worry. "You mean the rag-tag bunch we've strong-armed or bribed?"

Colleen laughed. "That's right. They will make up for their numbers with passion."

"Do you really believe that?"

"No. But we can pretend." Colleen moved toward her friend, a smile on her face.

Rachel dropped her gaze to her talking points. Stick to the facts. Add emotion. Eye contact.

The facts were: thirty years ago a young mother, Annie Rivers Dawson, had been brutally murdered. Annie's younger sister had arrived for a visit and discovered the house covered in blood and Annie's newborn wailing in her crib. Police had been summoned. No body had been found but police concluded Annie could not have survived such blood loss. The case had gone unsolved for three months.

The public had been in a panic knowing a young woman and new mother from a good neighborhood had been brutally murdered. The press had put tremendous pressure on the cops. There'd been extensive searches for the body until finally a tip led cops to the remains of a woman wearing Annie's clothes and jewelry. The outcry for justice grew louder. Even the governor had weighed in on the case.

Rachel's client, Jeb Jones, had been a handyman in Nashville at the time of Annie's death. He'd had an eighth grade education, was considered a good, if not, an inconsistent worker who drank heavily at times, and had been married with a nine-year-old son. He'd never made much money but he got by. And then one night cops, acting on a tip from a paid informant, had searched the trunk of Jeb's '71 Cutlass sedan and found a bloody tire iron. Jeb had been arrested. Under interrogation, he'd confessed, though within twenty-four hours he had recanted. The blood testing available at the time, crude by today's standards, had indicated the two blood samples on the tire iron matched both Annie's and Jeb's types.

Further investigation revealed that Jeb had known the victim. He'd worked in her apartment building and witnesses had later said he had been caught staring at Annie once or twice.

His trial was set a month after his arrest and it lasted five days. Dozens testified that Jeb had a drinking problem and had cheated on his wife. Though Jeb had never denied he was a bad father and husband, he swore that he'd not killed Annie. He didn't know how the tire iron ended up in his car.

Rachel wouldn't discuss science tonight but would stick with her emotional plea to the public: we need to pressure the cops for a DNA test.

*Christ, Rachel, these people couldn't care less.*

Her brother's voice all but hissed as she stared at the uninspired crowd and her stomach knotted another twist. She might not muster passion in this group, but the right television airtime could turn up the heat on the cops.

The news van arrived and Rachel now coveted Colleen's smoothness. Rachel had no soft edges. Life had sharpened those edges into razors.

As the news crew unloaded a camera and the reporter checked her lipstick and hair, Rachel scanned the crowd one last time hoping for a flicker of excitement. Off to the left she spotted a man she'd missed the first time. He stood apart from the crowd, partly concealed by a shadow cast by the building protecting his back. Given his dark suit, white shirt, red tie, and black western boots she'd have cast him as a banker or another lawyer. His short dark hair and square jaw fit the possible scenarios. However, the hard angles of his face, frown lines that cut deep, and a battle-ready stance dashed her theories.

For a moment she wondered why a man like him would be here and then the pieces fell into place. He was Detective Deke Morgan.

She'd done some checking on the twice-divorced detective and knew about his undercover work before homicide. A decade of monitoring every spoken word, anticipating conditions to go sideways, and burying his true-self deep were habits not easily broken.

Her stomach clenched. She'd seen him once in court eight or nine months ago. He'd testified in a drug case and though his hair had been long and his beard thick, the eyes held the same intensity as the man edging the crowd. The Deke in her memory had a Tennessee drawl, adding a quiet authority the jury did not ignore. After he'd testified he'd returned to the gallery and remained in his chair, stoic and watching.

Now his gaze skimmed her meager crowd, studying them until he seemed satisfied that this group was not driven enough to pose a threat. His gaze settled on her.

Rachel drew in a breath, wishing she could cross now and ask him about her DNA results. But as the idea formed, the news crews turned on their spotlights and shone them in her direction. Now was the time to make her point. Now was not the time to argue with Detective Morgan. She smiled at him, nodded, and then dropped her gaze to her notes as if he did not matter.

At exactly six fifteen, as the sun set, she stood on the curb, lifted the microphone to her mouth, moistened her lips, and began to tell the story of Jeb Jones.

The crowd grew quiet and news cameras rolled. Several times she paused to gather her thoughts, which kept trying to skitter ahead. More people stopped to listen and the flicker of the candles in the crowd grew brighter.

She could see disinterested faces grow solemn as the impact of her words settled. Passersby stopped to listen. "He deserves to have the DNA test."

When she finished, the reporter, a woman with a tall lean build emphasized by a red body-slimming dress, moved to the front of the crowd and held out her microphone. A closer look revealed the woman was well into her fifties. "So do you blame the Nashville Police Department for a possible miscarriage of justice?"

"I can't speak to what happened thirty years ago. I can only talk about now. And today the Nashville Police Department has DNA evidence from the Dawson murder trial. They've yet to respond to my requests for retesting and my fear is that the test will be forgotten or worse, swept under the rug and my client will die in prison."

A murmur rumbled through the crowd. More hands shot up.

"What can we do?" Colleen shouted as if she too were part of the crowd.

"Call the police department. Call your councilman. Let them know that Jeb Jones deserves to be heard."

A rumble washed over the crowd and she had the sense she might be winning. She looked into the camera. "Jeb Jones has been in jail for thirty years. He's old and he's sick. His time for justice is running out and we have to act."

More rumbles. She was making headway. This might work.

"What about Annie Rivers Dawson? The *victim*!" The angry voice shot out from the edges of the crowd.

Rachel studied the cluster of people and settled on a woman dressed in a dark, loose-fitting dress who stepped forward. She wore her dark hair in a bun and no makeup adorned her pale angled face.

Rachel had thought someone might remember Annie

and had prepared comments. "My focus today is on Jeb Jones. He's been a victim of the system for thirty years."

"Annie Rivers Dawson is *dead*." The woman moved forward clutching a well-worn purse close, and moving to within feet of Rachel.

The reporter and her cameraman had also moved in closer. If Rachel dodged this woman or her question, it wouldn't play well. The eyes of Nashville were upon them.

"Annie deserves to have her real killer behind bars," Rachel said.

"Her real killer is behind bars." Despite a mousy demeanor, the woman's voice reverberated with fierce anger.

"Her death was tragic," Rachel said. "I've never denied that."

The woman fished an eight-by-ten picture out of her large purse. The image was a publicity shot of a young smiling woman and Rachel recognized Annie Rivers Dawson's face immediately. Annie had had long blond hair that billowed around a face with the perfect blend of porcelain skin, a high swipe of cheekbones, and smiling full lips that added a joyous spark to bright blue eyes. "She was a talented beautiful new mother and she was brutally beaten. Her house was covered in blood and her body was found in pieces because of *your* client!"

Anxiety singed Rachel's skin leaving her cheeks flushed. "Annie's death was a great loss. Tragic. But the police never adequately proved that my client was involved in her death."

"The murder weapon was found in his car!" Her voice had grown louder and her face flushed with anger. "How can you stand there and defend that human piece of garbage?"

Aware of the crowd's intense interest, she clung to her control with an iron grip as she lowered her microphone.

"This vigil is about Jeb and his right to have the DNA testing."

"His right!" The woman advanced a step. "What rights did Annie have? She had the right to live and raise her baby but those rights were stolen from her by Jeb Jones."

"The DNA—"

"The cops found lots of evidence against him, including witnesses who said he stalked her!" she shrieked.

"He concedes that."

"Of course." Her voice had grown louder and sharpened with a dramatic edge as she now played to the crowd. "Poor murderer. He's the victim." She spit on the ground. "The media loves to focus on the perpetrator. They always forget the victim silenced by death."

Rachel stepped off the curb and moved toward the woman. Her hope was to calm her and dial down the energy in their conversation. Later they could talk in private. "I haven't forgotten about Annie."

"You might remember her, but you don't *care* about her. All you care about is *him*." The woman's fingers fisted around the edge of the picture so tightly, her knuckles turned white.

"What if Jeb didn't kill Annie?" Rachel reasoned. "Have you ever considered that the real killer is still out there and perhaps killing other women?"

The woman shook her head, her gaze zeroed in on Rachel. "The real killer is *not* out there. He is rotting behind bars as he should be."

Rachel searched the woman's face trying to identify her. She'd read what files she could get a hold of but she couldn't place this woman. "You knew Annie."

Thin lips flattened. "I knew her."

"How?"

Unshed tears magnified the anger glittering from the woman's eyes. "She was my sister!"

The crowd hushed and Rachel was aware of the cameras rolling. "I'm sorry for your loss. What is your name?"

"Margaret Miller," she said, teeth clenched.

She'd known Annie's sister still lived in the area but she'd been unable to find her. She'd distributed hundreds of flyers about the vigil so it made sense that word would reach Margaret. "Ms. Miller, why don't we have this conversation in private."

"Why talk in private?" Angry laughter bubbled. "You picked this public place to make your plea so why shouldn't we have our discussion in public? You hate secrets, right, Ms. Wainwright? Let's have it out right here."

"I do hate secrets." This entire conversation was going sideways. "Ms. Miller, please know that I'm sorry for your loss."

"Don't tell me you are sorry when all you want to do is free her killer."

"All I want is for Jeb to have his DNA tested." And in a louder voice she said, "DNA testing did not exist thirty years ago."

"His blood matched the blood found on the murder weapon."

"All we know is that it was type O blood. We don't have any more specifics. Nothing. Testing then was not as precise as it is now."

"How much more evidence do you need?"

"I need to talk to the paid confidential informant that testified against him. I want to review the police interview tapes and make sure my client received counsel when he requested it."

"You are dishonoring Annie with all your legal wrangling. You are perverting justice." The woman all but screamed her frustration.

"I want the truth."

Dark eyes flared and she advanced, eliminating the final steps between them. "Liar!"

Rachel held her ground knowing this woman was primed to take a swing. "Please, we need to talk in private."

"You don't want the truth! You want publicity. You want the world to know how clever you are so you can grow your own business."

"That's not true. I want to know for certain that an innocent man didn't go to jail."

"Innocent! Have you read Jeb Jones's history? The man was a drunk and a cheater. He couldn't hold a job. He was trouble waiting to happen."

Murmurs washed over the crowd. Some folks laughed. "He's never denied that he had a troubled past."

"Oh, well that's good of him."

"Trouble doesn't mean he's a killer."

The Channel Five camera caught every word of the argument. Later the reporter would pluck chosen sound bites for the eleven o'clock news. "I want justice, Ms. Miller. DNA testing will prove once and for all if Jeb killed Annie."

"No test is going to change what I know in my heart! That bastard killed my sister!" More tears welled in her eyes.

Rachel, drawn by the tears, missed the woman's right hook, which rose up as quick as a viper. The bare-knuckled fist struck hard against her jaw sending pain reverberating through her head. Thoughts scrambled, she staggered, nearly caught herself, but teetered on her heels and dropped to her knees.

The sounds from the crowd grew distant as her head buzzed and popped. She was aware of Colleen calling for the police as she pushed through the crowd.

"Liar!" Margaret shouted. She raised her fist again, poised to strike.

Rachel braced for another hit as she pulled herself up.

Strong arms wrapped around Rachel's shoulders. "Can you stand?"

Colleen's perfume wafted. Someone else held a screaming Margaret back.

No. "Yes." Drawing a breath, she rose to her feet and wobbled. Colleen's surprising strength steadied her.

*You are such a wimp!* Her older brother Luke's voice rattled in her head, irritating her. Luke had treated her like one of the boys. He'd been a real bully when they were kids, but if Luke were here now he'd have come to her defense. *"Keep your fists up, Rachel. Shit. How could you let a woman like that hit you?"*

Rachel's head cleared and she planted high-heeled feet, wobbled, and pulled back her shoulders. She balled her fingers into a fist, focusing on Margaret Miller now being held back by a Nashville uniformed officer. The woman's screaming pounded inside her skull.

"Call an ambulance." Colleen's command snapped like a whip, prompting several to fish in their pockets for a cell.

Rachel blinked, worked her jaw. "That's not necessary."

"It is," Colleen said. "You could have a head injury."

Rachel readied to protest again when she saw Deke Morgan glaring down.

He looked amused. "She clocked you pretty good."

Rachel righted her twisted skirt and pulled away from Colleen's protective hold. She stumbled and caught herself.

"You really need to sit," Colleen protested.

Rachel met Morgan's smiling eyes. She'd eat dirt before she showed weakness. Margaret's screaming seared her nerves. "I'm fine."

Colleen held up two fingers. "How many fingers am I holding up?"

She glared at the manicured fingers. "Three."

Colleen's gaze narrowed as she studied Rachel.

"I'm fine," Rachel said. "Fine."

Colleen heard the extra emphasis on the last word and took it as a warning to back off.

If Morgan had heard it, he didn't care. In fact, his smile broadened. "You want to press charges?"

The cameras still rolled but now she wanted the press to go away. She'd meant what she'd said about talking to Margaret in private. She didn't want a war. "No charges."

A restrained Margaret shook her head. "You better arrest me! I'll hit her again given the chance. She is a menace."

The verbal threat earned the woman a set of handcuffs, which constrained her arms behind her back. She sneered at Rachel and spit. Spittle landed inches short of Rachel's feet.

Rachel worked her throbbing jaw and prayed it wasn't broken. "Ms. Miller, this isn't about disrespecting your sister," she said. "I want the truth."

"We have the truth!" Margaret said. "It's not convenient for you."

The cops led Margaret toward the squad car. She kicked and screamed of injustice.

"Sure about those charges?" Detective Morgan asked.

"Take her home," Rachel said above the woman's shouting.

Morgan nodded and without a word, cut through the crowd toward the marked police car. She'd have followed if not for the reporter who intersected her path. This press conference had gone wrong in more ways than she could count.

Rachel straightened her shoulders and smiled as the older brunette held out a microphone. A floral perfume floated out toward her.

"I'm Susan Martinez with Channel Five. Can I ask you a question, Ms. Wainwright?"

"Of course." Rachel remembered to smile and resisted the urge to rub her sore jaw. Colleen stepped back but hovered close.

Martinez's eyes sparked with excitement as if she'd stumbled on an unexpected gem. "You are counsel for Jeb Jones?"

Rachel imagined how Margaret's punch played on video. "That's correct."

"Have you met Margaret Miller before?"

"No, tonight was our first meeting. And let me say I'm sorry she's upset. It was not my intent to hurt her. My intent is to compel the Nashville Police Department to test the DNA found on the murder weapon."

"Do you really believe the test results will clear your client?"

Did she really believe? Good question. She had a strong suspicion that her client would be cleared but she didn't know for sure. As an up-and-coming defense attorney, she'd been given cases from the county. Those clients had not been innocent but that hadn't stopped her from mounting a defense. Everyone had a right to a fair trial. "He recanted as soon as he'd had a few good hours of sleep. Since then my client has professed his innocence for thirty years. As soon as DNA was available he started asking for it."

"Do you believe he's innocent?"

*Stick to the talking points. The world doesn't need to hear your worries.* "What's important is that the DNA is tested and the Nashville Police Department release it to the public."

Ms. Martinez edged the microphone closer to Rachel and dropped her voice a notch as if it were only the two of them. "Are you worried about Margaret Miller?"

The question didn't pertain to Jeb, but she'd roll with the punches. "No. She's upset. She'll cool off. She more than anyone deserves to know who really killed her sister."

"And you think the real killer is out there?"

She hesitated and then looked directly into the camera. "Yes, I do believe the killer remains free."

* * *

Deke stood on the street corner watching as the uniforms hauled Margaret Miller away. He'd been curious
about the vigil, had made a point to attend, but hadn't expected much. He had to give Rachel Wainwright credit.
She'd scrounged up more people than he thought would
care about a thirty-year-old murder case.

When he'd arrived she'd been arranging her note cards
as she'd cast disappointed looks at the crowd. She'd kicked
off her dog-and-pony show right on time and he'd settled
against the concrete wall behind him and watched her try to
galvanize a lifeless crowd. Then he'd spotted Margaret pull
away from the group. Her body twitched, tight and nervous,
as she'd gripped her purse strap in a brawler's bare-knuckled
grip and fixed her gaze on Rachel. He hadn't recognized the
woman but he could spot the body language of a disturbed
person. Immediately, he'd made his way through the crowd,
listening, as Margaret's voice grew louder and angrier. He'd
been a few feet away when Margaret had decked Rachel.

Rachel. Rachel Wainwright. She'd been calling him several times a day for at least six weeks. He'd taken her first
call and told her she'd have her results as soon as he did but
that hadn't satisfied her. She'd called back, leaving a long
message arguing that the whole testing process was taking
too long. She'd accused him of burying evidence to protect
his father.

That comment had pissed him off to the point that he'd
considered driving to her office and having it out. But he'd
worked undercover too long to let his temper or feelings get
the better of him. He'd zipped up his anger and put it aside.

A begrudging respect flickered for the woman who
didn't surrender. She had the tenacity of a pit bull. And
tonight, she'd held on to her composure after the blow.

With the media cameras rolling she could have demanded Margaret be jailed. She hadn't.

Rachel Wainwright wasn't his kind of woman. Her voice didn't sooth but snapped. High cheekbones and a keen chin were made sharper by short ink-black hair and milky pale skin. A long lean body didn't fill out her pencil skirt and white blouse but skimmed beneath the fabric like chiseled stone. What rescued her from severity were her eyes. They were the color of cut sapphires and looked upon the world as if it were filled with urchins and discarded puppies, all in need of her saving.

Deke believed Buddy had gotten it right thirty years ago when he arrested Jeb Jones. His father had often said fear had gripped Nashville after the violent attack and disappearance of the young beautiful mother. Women, Buddy had said, were afraid to go out. The police were flooded with tips or calls of suspicious-looking men. One man had been attacked by a group of young boys who'd believed they'd caught Annie's killer. Nearly beaten to death, the man had woken up in the hospital three days later with his name cleared after the cops had established his alibi.

And then there'd been the calls regarding Annie's body. The cops had received hundreds. Most had been ruled out but there were at least ten sites that the cops had dug up looking for her body. And then one of many anonymous tips had been followed and the fragmented bones of a woman had been found in the woods near the Cumberland River. Annie's necklace had been found among the remains. Diamonds shaped into a heart. The search had ended. But the terror and fear had not. And then the confidential informant, or CI, had given them Jeb. He'd been arrested. And the city had returned to normal.

Deke knew his father and the man's flawless integrity. He and his father, physical carbon copies, were also a match in temperament. Shouting matches and butting heads were more common than not. So Deke knew in his core Buddy might have been tough on Jeb during the interviews, but he'd gotten his confession fair and square. He wouldn't have steamrolled Jeb for the sake of closing a case. Justice was Buddy's life.

Deke had been about ten at the time of the trial and he'd remembered his dad coming home from work late, exhausted and paler than a ghost. He'd remembered his parents talking in the kitchen in hushed whispers and of his father's conviction that Jeb was the killer.

When Rachel's request for DNA testing had first crossed Deke's desk, he'd laughed. He'd heard Jeb had recanted but then Jeb wouldn't be the first killer who'd cried innocent when facing the rest of his life in prison.

Deke had wanted to dismiss Rachel's request, but he didn't. He'd trusted Buddy's work enough to believe it would stand up to science, so he'd sent the DNA to the state lab, knowing the backlog ran months and sometimes years.

Rachel wasn't so green an attorney that she didn't realize this. Every first-year law student understood the system could be slow—that current murder cases, rapes, and robberies took precedence.

The harder she pushed for an answer, the stronger his resolve not to rush the results. Let her prod all she wanted. She'd get her answers when he was damn good and ready.

*"Yes, I do believe the killer remains free."*

In the darkness, the small television framed Rachel Wainwright's face. Pretty expressive eyes announced worry and doubt as her unwavering tone added punch to her words. Whether she believed the statement or not didn't really matter. She'd spoken them out loud and into the lens of a camera that broadcast her face all over the Nashville metro area. Her words had planted seeds of doubt, not many, but one or two placed in the right place was all it took.

Rachel Wainwright was a do-gooder who didn't know how to keep her mouth shut. She stuck her nose where it didn't belong and stirred up trouble for trouble's sake.

Sitting back, Baby conceded taking care of Rachel would be easy. Ideas of hitting her with a car or striking her with a hammer elbowed their way to the front of Baby's mind. If Rachel died, Jeb's case died. No more problems. No more worries.

The ceiling above Baby's head creaked with the footsteps of another. The hum of the television had reached upstairs and aroused trouble. Baby took one last look at Rachel's face then clicked off the set.

The door at the top of the basement stairs creaked open. "Baby?"

"Down here."

"What are you doing? It's late."

"Watching television."

"It's late."

"I know." Baby rubbed tired eyes. "I'll be right up."

"Are you okay?"

"Yeah. Couldn't sleep. Go to bed. I'll be right there."

Rachel Wainwright was trouble but she could be an asset if pointed in the right direction. Killing would solve a lot, but sometimes the easy way wasn't the smart way. Smart people killed two birds with one stone.

And Baby was smarter than most gave credit.

*October 24*

*Sugar,*

*I've decided that diamonds suit me. When I hit it big, I'm gonna be dripping in diamonds. My roommates are jealous of the necklace and the dumb-luck grin always slathered on my face when I admire the way it catches the sunlight. They want to know who gave me such an expensive gift. Again and again they ask as if I will somehow slip. But I won't slip. Mum's the word. And yes, I will have dinner with you on Thursday.*

*Xoxo,*
*A.*

# Chapter Three

The alarm clock shrilled, jarring Rachel awake. She sat up and instantly her head throbbed and her neck cramped. When she breathed, her ribs flinched. She'd never been cold-cocked before and now realized the initial blow didn't hurt near as bad as the aftermath.

She swung her legs over the side of her bed to the chilled, roughly hewed wooden floor. Her toes curled. A draft wafted through large insulated windows that had appealed so much when she'd first looked at the former restaurant space on a warm spring morning.

Her bed butted against a tall brick wall. A salvaged wrought-iron door served as a headboard and pallets functioned as box springs. She'd covered the bed with a heavy indigo comforter and lots of pillows. A long dresser and a silver-streaked mirror, both scavenged at yard sales, hugged the long wall that stood opposite the bank of windows now covered with long strips of canvas. Some would have described her look as chic, in a scruffy kind of way.

She called it for what it was: cheap. She'd furnished the entire space for less than two hundred dollars.

She'd chosen the building because, like her furnishings, it was affordable. She'd found the place when it had gone into bankruptcy, had negotiated a great price and become a landowner. She lived in this space but also maintained her law offices on the first floor. Cursing the cold, she rose and hurried to the bathroom where she kept a small space heater. She clicked on the heater and turned on the shower. Soon the room warmed.

She wiped her hand over the steaming mirror, ignored spiked bed-head hair, and studied her jaw. Purples, blacks, and blues colored the pale skin stretching from her chin to her ear. She worked her mouth from side to side, touching her fingers gingerly against the skin. She flinched. A check of her teeth left her grateful that none had been broken or cracked. She didn't need a dentist's bill.

She threaded her fingers through her hair. Dark circles hovered under her eyes, a sign that she shouldn't have stayed up until two a.m. reviewing briefs in another upcoming case.

"Burning the candle at both ends," she grumbled as she stepped into the shower. The wet heat soothed the lingering chill, coaxed some of the aches from her bones and tempted her to loiter and disregard the time. But time was money and both were rare luxuries.

Her law practice was barely making ends meet and she'd scarcely made her mortgage payment and the light bill this month. She'd not drawn a paycheck in weeks but hoped enough billable receivables came through the door in the next day or two so she could draw a small wage.

Instead of choosing her regular work clothes—yoga pants, a loose top, and slip-on shoes—she opted for black slacks, a fitted black V-neck sweater, and black ankle boots.

Clients weren't on the docket today, which was all about cranking out the work. But after last night's media coverage she wouldn't be surprised if she'd ended up with a visitor.

Her memory flashed to the eleven p.m. newscast. It had lasted barely thirty seconds but the cameraman had caught Margaret's right hook connecting with her jaw. She considered herself physically strong and agile and yet a woman twenty years her senior had dropped her like a stone. She'd replayed the scene and then, irritated, had shut off the television.

The media. The vigil's coverage hadn't captured inspired sound bites but a street brawl. There'd been a quick mention of Jeb's DNA request, a flash of the crowd holding candles, but the lion's share of footage had been dedicated to Margaret's punch.

"At least they spelled my name right."

Rachel took extra time applying her makeup, using added layers of foundation and powder to cover the bruise on her chin. After several tries, she'd all but covered it and could admit in most lighting, it wasn't noticeable. She didn't need to be sporting a bruise for any media follow-ups.

Rachel worked stiffness from her jaw, remembering Detective Deke Morgan's amusement. She'd harassed the man nonstop and he clearly had enjoyed her public humiliation.

"Damn." She descended the iron spiral stairs to the first floor. A series of bookshelves created the feel of a smaller more intimate law office where she worked and saw clients. Beyond the shelves, she moved past dusty half-finished porcelain sculptures, bits of wires and gadgets, which she fashioned into chess pieces in her now rare spare moments. Through swinging doors, she moved into the former restaurant's industrial kitchen. Her growing practice had gobbled her days, nights, and weekends giving her little time for cooking, let alone art.

Behind the long stainless steel counter, she turned on her single-serve coffeepot. The kitchen equipment, designed to feed hundreds, now warmed pizzas and restaurant leftovers or witnessed the frying of an occasional egg. Most days she lived on peanut butter, which she doled out by the tablespoon. On the counter a collection of red and orange retro canisters added the lone pop of color to a sea of silver and black.

While the coffee perked, she tugged open the huge fridge, all but empty save for a bottle of milk, a tub of cream cheese, a half bottle of white wine, and what remained of a deli roasted chicken she'd grabbed at the grocery three nights ago.

She took the milk, smelled it to make sure it really was fresh and then splashed it in a mug. From the red cookie jar she dug out two teaspoons of sugar. From the cabinet she pulled an industrial-sized jar of peanut butter and scooped an extra large spoonful.

Peanut butter spoon and coffee in hand she moved to her L-shaped desk piled high with books and papers. She clicked on her computer and for the next ten minutes read emails as she ate peanut butter and sipped coffee.

There was an email from Channel Five. Susan Martinez requesting an interview. She quickly responded saying she'd be glad to meet. Several other messages weren't so positive. All had seen her on the eleven o'clock news. Some supported her efforts but most emails began with *bitch* and *whore* and ended with *white trash* and *prison scum*.

Her blood pressure rose as she read each message. Several times she typed a fiery response but each time hit delete. To argue with anonymous served little.

The hinges on her chair squeaked as she eased back. She tapped the side of her mug with her finger, more irritated as she reread the last email. MAKE THE WORLD A BETTER PLACE AND DIE!

"Think I enjoy this?"

Rachel sipped her coffee, which now tasted bitter despite the sugar and milk. She'd not grown up dreaming to be a savior of lost souls. She'd grown up dreaming of being an artist. She'd lived to fashion clay porcelain into beautiful pieces of art. She'd not chosen this life. It had chosen her the night cops had shown up at her mother's house and arrested her brother for murder.

*"She was alive when I left her!" Luke had shouted as cops dragged him away.*

This hadn't been Luke's first run-in with cops. There'd been a half-dozen drug- and alcohol-related arrests, but Rachel had sworn to help as she always had. She'd navigated the local jail channels to a private meeting with Luke, who had begged her for an alibi.

*"Tell them we were watching television," he'd whispered.*

*Rachel had been so sure that the truth would clear him. "Luke, we don't need to lie. The cops will find the real killer. They are on our side."*

Their mother had hired an attorney who favored cutting a deal with the district attorney rather than mounting a defense. The family had refused to bargain and subsequent legal defense fees had drained her mother's savings and Rachel's college fund. The night before trial, Luke had asked to see Rachel. He'd begged her again to lie. *Tell them you were with me.* But Rachel had still believed justice would prevail.

After a two-day trial, the jury convicted Luke of second-degree murder and sentenced him to twenty years in jail.

Luke's conviction had not only altered his life but hers and her mother's. Rachel had switched her major from art to political science and gotten a job as a bartender. She'd worked double time finishing college in a year and a half, and then entered law school where she'd learned how to request copies of her brother's police record and hire a private detective. One month after she'd graduated law school, Luke had been stabbed to death in a prison fight.

Rachel stared at the piles of paper on her desk, wishing she had time to sit with a fresh block of ceramic, sculpt and pour her emotion and frustrations into the figures. When she sculpted the outside world vanished. She wanted to disappear. But she'd learned ignoring trouble did not make it go away. As much as she wanted to forget, she couldn't.

Sighing, she boxed up the old longing and zeroed her focus on the mission. If she didn't stand up for people like Jeb and Luke, who would?

Yesterday's correspondence, which she'd not had time to read, topped today's to-do list. She'd opened the third bill when the front bell rang.

Annoyed by the interruption she crossed to the door. Through the glass strip on the side she saw a deliveryman holding a clipboard. She unlocked the door and greeted the man who had often delivered briefs and reports. "Morning," she said.

He offered a wan smile as he held out his clipboard for her. "Got a delivery. I need your signature."

She took the clipboard and pen, quickly scrawled her name as she'd done a thousand times before, wondering if the medical documents she'd subpoenaed in a workman's comp case had finally arrived. "So what's it today?"

He held up a small box. "Can't say. Doesn't look legal."

"Do you know who sent it?"

"It's not on my delivery slip. I can find out if you like."

Suspicion ran deep in her bones. "I'd appreciate that."

"I'll have the dispatcher forward the order."

"Thanks." She studied the shoe box wrapped in several layers of tape.

"Saw you on TV last night," the deliveryman said.

She offered a grin. "So how did it look?"

"That lady clocked you good." He studied her face searching for the bruise.

"Yes, she did." She held up the box. "Thanks for this."

"Sure." He hesitated. "You really think that guy didn't do it?"

"There're too many unanswered questions that deserve to be answered."

"He's been in for thirty years. He's an old man. Kind of a waste at this point."

She reminded herself to smile. "All the more reason to give him back what little life he has if he's innocent."

"My boss says people like you are gonna flood the streets with criminals given the chance."

"That's not the plan."

"He called you choice words."

"I doubt he'll be the last. Thanks." Without waiting, she slipped back behind the door and moved to her desk. She settled the package in the center, staring at it. The unconventional packaging worried her especially after last night's telecast. Clearly not everyone wanted the Jeb Jones case reopened. From her desk drawer she pulled out a letter opener.

As she pressed the tip to the tape, the front door opened to Colleen. Today she wore a bright sapphire silk top, a dark skirt, and black tights and a large reflective chunky necklace that brightened her green eyes. Colleen had a knack for looking the part of a lawyer while still bumping against the conservative edge of their profession.

"Morning," she said. "What a show on the eleven o'clock news."

Rachel worked her jaw, wincing. "Like I always say, negative attention is better than no attention."

Colleen laughed. "It wasn't that bad. You showed the

viewing audience that you keep your cool under fire. Most wouldn't have been as gracious after getting decked." She studied Rachel's face. "Was there a bruise?"

"Oh, yeah. It's a real beauty. But I'll survive." She nodded to the box. "This just came."

Colleen's gaze dropped to the package and her smile faded. "Doesn't look official."

"No. It doesn't."

"What do you think it is?"

Rachel opened her pocketknife. "I'll slice into it and see."

Colleen shrugged off her coat and hung it on a metal coatrack by the front door. "Does it make a sound when you shake it?"

Rachel picked up the package and shook. "No. And it's not super heavy. No rattling or hissing sounds."

Colleen straightened as if suddenly poised to run. "I hate snakes. Hate them."

Rachel grinned. "I think we're safe."

Colleen shook her head. "I don't have a great feeling about this."

"I don't either but better to open it and find out."

Colleen fished out her cell. "Just in case."

"In case of what?"

"Disaster." Colleen had grown up in a well-to-do family who'd been more amused than encouraging of her decision to attend law school. Her mother expected her to abandon the law and marry well. Colleen, with no eye toward a society life, had agreed to cast her lot with Rachel after a chance meeting in law school. Though Rachel admired her friend's drive, she still laughed at the sheltered upbringing.

"I think we'll be fine." Rachel sliced into the top layer of tape until the top flaps separated and opened. Despite brave words, Rachel held her breath as she peeled back the flaps. Both women studied the popcorn-filled box. Rachel flexed her fingers and then dug them into the popcorn. Colleen tensed.

"Snake!" Rachel screamed and jerked out her hand.

Colleen screamed and backed up a step. She had trembling fingers as she dialed. "I'm calling the cops! Are you bleeding?"

Rachel laughed and waggled all her fingers. "Sorry. Bad joke. Couldn't resist."

Colleen hugged out a breath. "Bitch."

"Guilty." She pulled out a stack of letters, bound by a faded red ribbon. The letters were in creamy envelopes yellowed and curled with age.

"Letters," Colleen said as she put her phone away. "At least it wasn't a snake or a bomb."

Rachel laughed. "You didn't really think it was a snake, did you?"

"Maybe not a snake but definitely a bomb."

Rachel undid the ribbon and carefully set it aside. She lifted the first letter and unfolded it. "It begins with, *Sugar, you make my heart sing.*"

"A love letter? Why would someone send you old love letters?"

Rachel studied the soft fluid handwriting, so precise and lovely. "I've no idea."

"Looks old."

"The paper feels brittle."

"Who wrote the letter?"

Rachel flipped over the first page. Her heart lurched. "It's from A."

"A. As in Annie? As in Annie Rivers Dawson?"

A chill oozed over Rachel's spine. "I don't know." She started reading the letter out loud.

*October 13*

*Sugar!*

*You made me laugh today. Not a snigger or a giggle but a belly-clutching laugh! And that was a complete shock. I'd expected you to be stuffy and humorless but you had me giggling all the way home.*

"Damn," Colleen said. "If A. is the Annie in question who is Sugar?"

"I don't know."

"Annie was married at the time of her death."

"I've not dug deeply into her past. I've read police reports but I couldn't tell you much about her as a person."

Colleen held the yellowed envelopes to her nose. "Lavender." She scanned the text. "The gal who wrote this sounds pretty fun-loving."

"Makes sense from what I did read about Annie. She was a singer who left her small Tennessee town to hit it big."

Colleen held up the envelope, letting the light shine through the thin paper. "Who gave up that career and settled into a routine life."

"She got pregnant. That changed a lot, I suppose."

"What happened to Annie's baby after she died?"

"Again, I need to find out. I've been focused on Jeb and getting the DNA and I've not had time to dig."

Carefully, Colleen refolded the letter. "There's no sense until you get the DNA back. Not like you've lots of Nancy Drew time in your docket."

"Right." Rachel dropped her gaze to the letter and reread it. "There's a month and day but no year. And A. doesn't necessarily stand for Annie."

"Yeah, but why send you old letters from another woman?"

"To throw me off. To mess with me. You'd be surprised what people do."

A frown wrinkled Colleen's forehead briefly. "But if your Annie wrote these letters, we know it's at least thirty years old. And I don't know about you, but I'd like to know Sugar's identity."

Rachel held the sheet of paper up and studied the faded pigment and the slightly yellowed edges. "That would be huge if the letters were written by Annie. A voice from the past."

"A peek into her private life."

Rachel wanted the letters to be real but feared to hope. "Why send them to me?"

"Why not you? You landed right in the center of the case last night on the news." Colleen cocked a brow. "Let's face it, no one stayed up all night, forging letters on thirty-year-old paper. Even for you, that's a bit of a conspiracy theory."

Rachel pulled her finger over the neat stack but didn't read another.

"Aren't you going to read them?"

"I need to put on rubber gloves before I photograph these. If these letters are real then I don't want my finger-prints smeared over them. How do you think it will look if I turn these in to the police? They'll be dismissed by virtue of the messenger."

"You don't know that."

"Cops distrust by nature. I've irritated more than a few with this case. These letters delivered by my hand would raise questions." Had she touched a nerve with someone yesterday? She feared to hope. "And these letters could be fake. Old doesn't mean Annie wrote them."

Colleen rolled her eyes and raised her hand. "Let's sup-pose they are real, for argument's sake."

"Fine."

"We've established you are the center of this brewing storm."

"Yeah."

"Whoever sent them to you must believe in what you are

doing," Colleen said. "Maybe they have information you don't and want to help."

"Or they sent fake letters to me hoping I'd take them to the cops and then be discredited."

Colleen winced. "Cynical."

"To the bone." Rachel rubbed her sore jaw knowing she'd be reaching for aspirin soon. "The question is why send the letters to me? And who sent them?"

"I don't see Margaret Miller sending the letters to you. She's not on your side."

"No."

"The letters are addressed to Sugar. Maybe someone out there knows Sugar's real name. Maybe Sugar killed Annie."

The idea had merit, but her mind jumped to the worst-case scenario. "Jeb could have been Sugar."

"I wouldn't bet on it. Annie was beautiful and her eyes were set on the big-time. What good would it do her to love a handyman with an eighth-grade education?"

Rachel laughed. "That's kind of a cold way of looking at love. What happened to the heart wants what it wants?"

"That's for saps," Colleen said. "What little I do know about Annie is that she was a woman with ambition. She wouldn't saddle herself with a man who barely had a hundred dollars to his name."

"So cold."

"Practical."

Rachel reached for her cell. "I need to photograph them and then I'll send them off to be authenticated. If Annie didn't write them, then Sugar doesn't matter. And if they are real I need to be able to prove it to the cops."

"Whom are you sending them to?"

"There's a private detective I know." She turned to her desk and flipped through the large Rolodex until she reached the name Lexis Hanover. "She helped me with my brother's case and I helped her with a legal case last summer. She's good at what she does and I trust her." She plucked the card free and reached for the phone. "She did all the work for Luke pro bono."

"Why?"

"Mumbling about paying it forward, but I sensed there was more. I never pressed." The ink of Rachel's law degree had barely been dry. She'd been trying to look and sound like a seasoned lawyer when she'd petitioned the court for her brother's retrial. Four years' distance from that day and she cringed at her naive bravado in the face of the judge's dismissive attitude and denial.

Lexis had been in the courtroom and approached her later. *"I can help."*

"Why?"

*"I like your spirit and despite a sloppy presentation you made good points. Let me ask around."*

*"I don't have money."*

*"Not asking for any. Someone did me a favor once and now I'll do one for you. Like paying it forward."*

Rachel had been suspicious, but also desperate and so she'd taken Lexis's card and soon sent her Luke's files. To her astonishment Lexis had helped, found key leads that had given Rachel the ammo she needed for a retrial. And then Luke had been murdered in prison. Now Rachel had a chance to pay Lexis back again. She dialed. "Lexis knows handwriting and if these are fake she'll tell me."

"You're going to need a baseline, won't you?"

"Lexis figures all that out."

Rachel neared the Vanderbilt University arches in her car when her cell rang. Distracted by her mission she picked up the phone without glancing at the number.

"Rachel Wainwright?"

"That is correct."

"This is Susan Martinez, Channel Five."

The light at 16th and Broadway turned red and Rachel gratefully accepted the delay. "Susan. We've been playing phone tag today."

"I know and I'm sorry about that. How's your jaw?"

Hurts like hell. "It's fine. Barely a mark."

"I called Miss Miller this morning. I'll be interviewing her and wondered if I might be able to follow up with you."

As much as Rachel wanted to keep her story in the spotlight, she hesitated before saying, "What kind of questions are we talking about?"

"Background on your client. What it's been like for him the past three decades."

Sounded good but she sensed bait on a lure. Still, the chance for more airtime could not be passed up lightly. "Sure. What time?"

"Say four. I'd like to make the six o'clock news."

"Sure."

"Your office?"

Her brain catalogued how much she'd have to clean before the news crew arrived. "Four it is."

"Great. See you then."

Rachel rang off as the light turned green and followed Broadway as it branched to the right. Five minutes later she'd parked on the street by Vanderbilt.

She walked down the brick sidewalk through the gates of the university and to a cluster of buildings called the Stevenson Center. The math department was in Building One where Lexis taught math. A short elevator ride found her approaching Lexis's basement office. She saw the name plaque that read DR. L. HANOVER and knocked.

"Enter."

The thick scent of cigarette smoke greeted her as she

entered the cramped office packed with shelves crammed tight with books and papers. Lexis sat behind a small desk teeming with stacks of books. An in-box overflowed with papers, an ashtray brimmed with ash and a half-dozen coffee cups lined the desk's edge. Judging by the stale smell, this place hadn't been cleaned in months.

Dark square glasses and a black turtleneck sharpened the lines on her angled face and whitened gray hair that flowed to broad shoulders. "Rachel. Loved the show on the news last night."

Rachel grimaced. "Not one of my finer moments."

Lexis stood. "Not at all. You'd not have made the news if that lady hadn't slugged you. Was she a plant? Did you stage that?"

Rachel rubbed her still-tender jaw. "No, it was not staged."

"Then count your lucky stars. Jeb Jones wouldn't have hit most radar screens if you'd not been slugged."

"Good to know it wasn't all in vain."

"Not at all. There a bruise?"

She tapped her chin gingerly with her fingertip. "Oh, yeah."

Lexis moved closer and inspected the spot. "Rub off some of that makeup and let the bruise show. Badge of honor."

"Feels like the mark of a fool. I should have seen it coming."

Lexis shrugged. "That reporter called you for a follow-up?"

"I spoke to Ms. Martinez minutes ago. We have another interview today."

"Good." She reached for a fresh cigarette and fumbled for a lighter. "How's Mr. Jones doing?"

Rachel frowned. "He's not well. And he fears he'll die in prison."

A frown furrowed her brow as she flicked the silver engraved lighter. It didn't ignite. "You'll make a difference."

"Let's hope a better job than I did for Luke."

"That wasn't your fault." Lexis shook the lighter, flicked again and a flame jumped. She lit the edge of her cigarette.

*No take-backs, Rachel!* "I could have kept him out of prison."

"He had no right to ask you to lie." She drew in smoke and then blew it out slowly. "You could have landed in jail yourself."

A wane smile curved the edges of her lips. "Woulda, shoulda, coulda."

"Remember you can't fix everyone, Rachel. You did a lot for Luke. How many times did you drag him out of bars or out of the gutter?"

More times than she could remember. "I'll always feel like I failed him."

"You changed your life for him. Not many go the distance like that, Rachel. I admire that in you."

An unexpected tear slid down her cheek and she swiped it away, embarrassed. "I didn't intend for this to be a therapy session."

Lexis smiled and inhaled. "I like to think I'm a jack of many trades."

Rachel laughed. "And does handwriting analysis still fall in your wheelhouse?"

"It does, as a matter of fact. Verifying signatures is a growing trend in the last year. No one trusts anyone."

"Makes good business for us both."

"I won't get rich on an adjunct's salary." She stabbed the cigarette into the ashtray.

Rachel looked around the room. "Kids treating you well?"

"I've a graduate class that is tolerable but the eight o'clock undergraduate class rarely is awake long enough to learn. Bit like talking to potted plants. Tell me about these letters."

Rachel recapped their early morning delivery and the content. "I wore gloves when I handled all but the first letter. I read them and photographed them."

"Thinking like a true conspiracy theorist." Lexis accepted the shoe box. "Who delivered them?"

"Standard courier. He's delivered to me before. And I called his dispatcher. The package was dropped at the courier's office early this morning. Paid in cash."

Lexis adjusted her glasses and studied the box of letters. "I did a little reading up on Annie Rivers Dawson after your television debut. She'd been married less than seven months at the time of her death. Her newborn was five days old. I don't know much about her husband."

"I've done a little digging too and have a list of people I need to talk to. Annie's husband, Bill Dawson, is top of the list."

"Do you really think someone out there is trying to help you?"

"I don't know. But I've touched a nerve."

Lexis removed the lid but did not touch the letters. "Be careful, Rachel. When secrets have been buried a long time there are people that don't want them dug up."

"I hear you," Rachel said. "And I'll be careful. When do you think you can get to the letters?"

"Later today. As soon as my office hours are over I'll head to my home office where I have all my equipment."

"What about a baseline for Annie's handwriting?"

"I'll find one."

Caution crept up her nerves like an early warning system. "I might need to defend the source in court."

"Won't be a problem." Lexis reached for another cigarette. "What do you think you'll find?"

"The real killer's name would be nice."

Lexis laughed. "You think you could be that lucky?"

"I'm due for some luck."

"Aren't we all?"

*October 28*

*Sugar,*

*My heart just about jumped out of my chest . . .*
<u>*Pow, Zap, Zing!*</u> *You said the L-word while you were*
*cuddled up to me last night. I pretended to be asleep,*
*but I heard that soft sweet voice in my ear. "I love*
*you, Annie."*

*Well, I love you too, Sugar. And no matter what,*
*you and I are gonna be stuck together like glue. You*
*never got to worry about me leaving you.*

*A.*

# Chapter Four

The heat of his boss's glare scraped against Deke's skin. When he worked the streets, survival often relied on a gut feeling, a glance, or a glare. Days on the streets were never predictable, always edgy, but there'd been a freedom he'd liked. He was back in a conventional unit, taking briefings, writing reports, but was still judging angry glowers not from snitches and drug dealers but bosses. Shoving aside annoyance, he looked up.

Captain Harry Saunders was a big man whose wide shoulders and tall stature all but ate up door frames. When he walked, the floor vibrated. When he smacked a fist against your desk, pictures rattled. A not too gentle giant, he was a real hard case who rarely minced words.

"Captain." Deke closed the file and studied the older man's deep frown lines. "That's not your happy face."

Gray eyes narrowed as he advanced a step into Deke's office. "It sure as shit is not my happy face. It's my irritated face."

Deke folded his arms, unaffected by his boss's ire, and

yet still respectful enough to keep his thoughts to himself. "Why are you irritated?"

"You didn't see the news last night? That damn woman is making us look like fools."

"Rachel Wainwright. No, didn't see the news but I was on hand to witness the live performance."

Saunders placed large hands on his thick waist. "Why didn't you stop her?"

Deke rose. "She's got the right to free speech."

"She's trouble." Captain Saunders all but spat the words.

"No doubt. But she's an attorney and she had an assembly permit that gave her the right to publicly say her peace."

"Doesn't mean anyone wants to hear her opinion. Shit, the way I see it she's pissing on your daddy's memory."

They'd gone round and round on this since Deke had put through the DNA request. "Buddy can stand up to a little heat."

"Yeah. Hell of a cop. Hell of a man." His ire cooled. "Did you see that Miller woman hit her?"

"I did."

Captain Saunders grinned. "Good for her. Where is Margaret Miller now?"

"At home, I assume. That's where the uniforms dropped her off. Ms. Wainwright didn't press charges."

Saunders rubbed a stiff hand over the back of his neck. "When Wainwright filed for the DNA testing in the Dawson case, I got a bad feeling in the pit of my gut."

"Really? All I've ever heard from Buddy and KC was that the case was airtight."

Captain Saunders grunted disbelief. "Attorneys can twist the truth."

"I've no doubt the verdict will be upheld."

Saunders shook his head as if memories rushed him. "That case drove every officer in this place damned near insane for months as we searched for the killer and Dawson's body."

"You never assumed she was alive?"

"Hopes were always slim. The inside of that house was painted red with her blood. We figured if she was alive she didn't have long. And then, no one said it but we knew we had a recovery not a rescue. You remember your old man talking about it?"

"I remember him talking to Mom but they clammed up when I came around. And as I got older, he shared stories about the case."

"That case aged Buddy a decade. Dark circles under his eyes. Worked around the clock."

"I remember him being gone. My brothers and I weren't easy and Georgia was an infant."

"Your momma was a damned saint."

"A point she mentioned often when I was growing up." His mother had endured thirty years of Buddy's demanding schedule, but Deke's wives had had little patience for his job, which required extended absences. Maybe if he'd had children, the story would have been different.

"I want this case closed. Once and for all. When will the DNA be back?"

"I called the state lab a half-hour ago. They're saying soon but aren't making any promises."

"I know you can lean on the best of them. Lean on the state."

The answers would come but he'd not push or prod. "They are swamped and working as fast as they can. Can't get blood from a stone."

"Bullshit. Squeeze 'em."

"Is there a reason I should be worried about the DNA test results?"

"Shit, no. Your daddy ran a clean investigation. Clean as

a whistle." A ragged breath suggested age had stolen some of his fire. "Time has a way of making people forget what we were up against when Annie Dawson vanished in a bloody mess. Those months we searched for her were a nightmare and I don't want to ever revisit them."

"Ms. Wainwright mentioned in one of her many phone messages that Jeb has been asking for DNA testing for years."

"What does that mean?"

"It means the request came across Buddy's desk. Why didn't he have the test done to vindicate his work?"

The lines of his face deepened. "I know Ms. Wainwright sees an old man who is sick and feeble. But Jeb Jones wasn't like that thirty years ago. He was a big strong man with a bad temper and a taste for gin. He put his wife in the hospital once and I saw bruises on his boy when we finally arrested Jeb."

"Rachel Wainwright hasn't argued that he was a choir boy."

"No one but the Devil himself, could argue the case on Jeb's character." Saunders wagged a finger as he always did when he lectured. "He might only have an eighth-grade education but he was street smart then and likely more so now. He's a pro at twisting the facts so that he looks like the victim. Jeb Jones is no damn victim. Buddy knew it better than anyone."

Buddy's world was black-and-white. You were a good guy or a bad guy and once you landed in either column, you stayed there forever. Deke knew firsthand what it felt like to be judged by Buddy Morgan and to come up short. "I did a search on Jeb Jones's wife. She's in a home. Suffered a stroke several years ago. The son still lives in the area."

"The boy was ten when his old man was locked up."

"No doubt he'd not be much help. But Annie's husband would remember a lot."

Saunders's frown deepened already-sagging jowls. "Don't stir up a hornet's nest, Deke. Leave the Dawson case alone and focus on the active murder cases on your desk."

Deke could have pointed out to Saunders that he wasn't a rookie. He could have said the weekly lectures grew thin. But like always, he held his cards close until a play mattered. "The Simmons case has my full attention."

"Any leads?"

"Still digging. I talked to the bar owner where she sang. I also ran her phone records and a credit check. I can tell you she'd maxed out her credit cards and her landlord was talking about eviction."

"If debt were a motive for murder more than half this town would be dead. Did she take drugs?"

"Clean according to Dr. Heller. She did like to date. A lot. I've spoken to several men in her phone address book. All said she was fun but no one had a reason to stick around. One-night stands."

"Could any one of those men get pissed enough to kill her?"

"Very possible. KC secured her computer and has taken it to forensics. Might be data on that as well."

"Keep on the Simmons case. I want it closed. What about the Ellen Roberts case?"

"We arrested a guy she dated. Oscar McMillian. He's in jail now trying to scrounge bail. I'll make that arrest stick."

"Good." Saunders didn't celebrate solved murders because he was too worried about the unsolved ones. "Put your boot on the backs of the lab rats. I want this Dawson shit cleared and out the door."

"Will do."

As Captain Saunders left, Deke sat and leaned back in his chair. He loosened his tie. The captain was a good cop and he worked hard. When the captain married, Buddy had been his best man and when Buddy died, the captain had been a pallbearer. He was protective of Buddy.

And it was hard for any cop to take down a criminal and then see him walk. He'd been through it during his under-cover days and it never failed to piss him off. Captain was no different.

And now one of Buddy's old cases was being questioned. This wasn't about a DNA test for the captain. It was a point of honor for a fallen comrade.


Deke and KC arrived at the music studio called Spinners Records. A small low-lying building, it could easily have been missed. But from what Deke knew about the company it had produced several successful artists in the last couple of years and was on the rise. In Nashville, simple jeans and unassuming buildings disguised fortunes.

"This was one of the last places Dixie Simmons called," KC said. He flipped through the pages of his notebook. "According to my notes she called here about ten times in the last few days. The extension she called was two-one-one and a little asking told me that the number belongs to Dusty Rehnquist, the owner and operator of Spinners Records."

Deke slammed his car door. "Anyone else she call other than Mr. Rehnquist?"

"Lots. But the other call that stands out is a burner phone. She called that number last, likely minutes before she died. No tracing that number."

"A burner." Burners and secrets went together like black and white.

"If I were a married man and a hot chick wanted to call me, I'd set up a separate number." KC held up a hand. "That's saying *if* I had a hot chick calling me. Which I don't, if Brenda is to ask."

A smile tweaked the edges of his mouth. "I'm sure she will be glad to hear that."

KC shook his head. "Got to say that woman rocks my old-ass world. After Sharon died I thought I was done. And then Brenda showed up. I love that woman but I suspect she'd cut off my balls and feed them to me if she caught me running around."

"She strikes me as well adjusted."

"Any sane woman loses it when she's been hurt. One hundred and thirty pounds of love turning into one hundred and thirty pounds of crazy and pissed off, just like . . ." He snapped his fingers.

Deke opened the glass front door to the studio. "Maybe that's what happened to Dixie. She found herself a man married to one hundred and thirty pounds of crazy."

"Could happen."

They walked the carpeted hallway decorated with hundreds of singers' photos. He didn't recognize most but that wasn't surprising. The world was full of wannabes and those dreaming of the big time, which chewed up people and spit them out by the hour. Buddy had warned Georgia over and over that Nashville was stocked with starving talent. He insisted she get an education.

"Dream all you want," Buddy used to say. "But pay the light bill."

Georgia had gotten a degree in forensics and now worked for the Nashville Police Department. She was one of the best in her field. Her eye for detail had solved many cases. And she liked her work. Deke could admit when she was on, a light switched on in her that added a glow no one missed. She spent all her spare time at the honky-tonks singing or writing songs. What she wouldn't give to have an interview at this place.

A receptionist with full, curly blond hair looked up at them. Her makeup was too heavy for his tastes and her rhinestone shirt over the top. Rachel Wainwright flashed in his mind. Her simple dark hair, stiff business attire that didn't fit her right, and little or no makeup had him wondering what she'd look like in a getup like this. No doubt the suggestion alone would irritate her.

The receptionist looked up, big blue eyes haloed with false eyelashes. "Can I help you?"

Deke removed his badge from his jacket pocket, tossing in a smile he hoped would soften his hard features. "Deke Morgan, Nashville Police Department. I'm here to see Dusty Rehnquist."

The request amused her. "Mr. Rehnquist is in meetings all day. If you want me to check with his secretary I'm sure she can find an appointment before Christmas."

Deke carefully tucked his badge back in the breast pocket of his jacket and adjusted his tie. "What's your name?"

"Nancy."

He restrained his voice's natural biting edge. "Nancy, I'm investigating a murder and I'm not waiting until Christmas to ask my questions. Murders aren't convenient."

"The schedule is the schedule."

Moments like this he missed his undercover days, simpler in many ways. Find a perp. Kick in door. Arrest bad guys. "Do me a favor and call the person you have to call and get me in to see Rehnquist. In case you forgot, the name is Deke Morgan."

"I didn't forget."

He leaned forward a fraction and in a lower voice said, "Good. Now call or I'm going to have ten squad cars parked out front in five minutes. Then I'm gonna have my officers search each and every person that comes in this building."

Her eyes narrowed. "You can't do that."

Deke's gaze remained fixed and hard as he smiled. "Oh, I sure can."

KC shook his head, smiling. "Never dare Deke Morgan."

Under the makeup her face paled. "You can't do that," she said.

He glanced at KC. "Do you doubt my word?"

"No, sir." KC's grin was about as friendly as a rattler. "I would not question you one bit."

The receptionist picked up her phone, dialed and then turned away from them to speak. She sounded calm at first but then grew more agitated as if she'd hit a roadblock. "I'm telling you, Delores, you need to let Mr. Rehnquist know the cops are here." Another hesitation. "Fine, I'll send them to your desk and you can tell them."

She hung up the phone. "Go on back through the double doors. I'll buzz you in. Last office on your right you'll see Delores. Dark brown hair, sour look on her face. Can't miss her. She's Mr. Rehnquist's secretary. Talk to her."

"Appreciate the help."

She rose and smoothed manicured hands down her skirt. "No one is going to jail?"

"Not yet, ma'am."

"If you have to arrest someone, start with Delores. She's a real bitch."

"Right."

She pressed a button, a satisfied smile on her lips. A buzzer buzzed and a lock clicked open. Deke and KC walked through the door and followed the carpeted hallway lined with gold and platinum records. At the end a tall brunette with a deep, annoyed frown rose from her desk.

"Officers," she said, stopping in their path. "Mr. Rehnquist cannot see you right now. He is busy. And I've half a mind to fire Nancy for sending you back here."

Deke grinned again but this time his patience had thinned. "Get your boss."

Her brows drew closer and she took a step back. "I'll see if he's here."

Deke watched as she moved briskly back to the corner office. A quick knock on the door and she vanished behind it.

"You're one scary son of a bitch," KC said. "Like Buddy in his prime."

Deke had not feared Buddy's long shadow when he'd joined homicide knowing it would fade in the light of his own work. But thanks to Rachel Wainwright's challenge, Buddy was back on center stage.

Deke and KC moved forward, knowing now that Mr. Rehnquist was indeed in his office or the gatekeeper would have said so.

Seconds later the woman reappeared, her angled face harder and more defined in a frown. "Mr. Rehnquist said that he'd see you."

Deke didn't thank her but moved toward the door with purpose and direction until he came face-to-face with a tall, reed-thin man dressed in head-to-toe designer denim gear that spoke of money. Rehnquist wore his blond hair long enough to brush the edges of a crisp collar. Buffed nails caught the light. Disregarding a Botox-smoothed forehead, Deke estimated his age to be early forties.

The light carpet was thick and plush, a contrast to the record producer's glass and metal desk. The walls sported pictures of Rehnquist with the top stars in country music.

Rehnquist grinned and extended his hand. "My secretary tells me you are investigating a murder. Sounds mighty exciting."

Deke's annoyance spiked but he kept it buried. Instead

he shrugged off his cop demeanor and slipped into the role of a fan. He'd learned working undercover that attitude and body language created as good a disguise as a costume. "Never a dull moment for us. Never a dull moment." He gawked at the gold and platinum records framed and hanging on the walls and whistled. "Looks like you've had some success."

Rehnquist's chest puffed. "We've done well. Hit the charts."

"I've got a tin ear but I appreciate a good song. You sign any singers I'd recognize?"

Rehnquist listed several singers. "Most don't realize how well we do."

"My goodness. That's impressive." He pulled his notebook from his breast pocket. "Wish I could talk to you more about the music. I know my baby sister would have a million questions. She's a singer." He shook his head, smiling as if he were more fan than cop. "But I got to take care of business. No rest for the weary."

A hint of annoyance flickered across Rehnquist's face. "I hear ya."

"We responded to a mighty bad scene last night. A young woman was brutally beaten to death."

The spark in Rehnquist's gaze dimmed. "That so?"

"Her name was Dixie Simmons."

What remained of the sparkle fizzled. "That name supposed to be important?"

"She called you several times in the last ten days."

"A lot of people call me." He reached for a pen and clicked the end several times.

Deke had played this cat-and-mouse game hundreds of times. What amazed him was that the mice always made the same moves. "Do they call your private line and talk?"

Tension rippled up Rehnquist's arm as he gripped the pen tighter. "I don't understand."

"What don't you understand? Dixie called your private line ten times in the last ten days and spoke to you at length one time."

Rehnquist clicked the button on the pen in and out. "There's no proof that I was on the other end of the line."

Deke stripped away his smile like a mask. "That won't be hard for me to prove. Won't be hard at all. So don't play games with me. What did you and Dixie talk about?"

"I've never heard that name." Rehnquist's lie bounced wild like a free throw hitting the rim.

Deke pulled his phone from his back pocket and scrolled to Dixie's driver's license picture. He held it up and watched as Rehnquist studied the picture, frowned and raised an eyebrow as if seeing the face for the first time. With the authority of a practiced liar said, "I do not know her."

"That so?" Deke didn't like games, but if Rehnquist wanted to play, he'd oblige. He casually scrolled to the brutally disfigured image taken in the medical examiner's office and held it close to his vest like a gambler with a winning card. "How did you know her?"

"I just said I didn't."

"Did you know this gal?" Deke turned his phone around.

Rehnquist looked at the picture, paled, and turned away. "Jesus."

"Not nice, is it? Someone wanted to erase Dixie's identity."

Rehnquist slid his hands into his pockets. "I didn't do that to her."

"Did you know her? And please do not lie to me again. I'm working on no sleep and as my partner will tell you, I'm difficult when I'm sleep-deprived."

He swallowed as if bile rose up his throat. "Okay, I did know her. We met at a party."

Reaching the truth one baby step at a time. "What can you tell me about her?"

"Not much. Other than she was pretty. I remember she wore red."

Another lie. Another giant step back. "Why was she calling you?"

"She was ambitious. She had talent and she had drive. I admired both. I see talent. I see drive. I don't always see both together."

"So your relationship was strictly professional?"

"Absolutely."

KC arched his shoulders as if he'd awoken from a long slumber. "You weren't sleeping with her? Because I can tell you, if she made an offer to me, I'd be hard-pressed to say no."

Color rose up in Rehnquist's face. "What's that supposed to mean?"

KC laughed as if chatting at the hunting lodge with an old friend. "You were sleeping with her. I hear it in your high and defensive voice." He looked at Deke. "But I'll give him credit; that hint of outrage and shock was a nice touch."

Deke folded his arms and studied Rehnquist. "Never sells me on a lie."

"Really?" KC shook his head. "There was a time I'd have fallen for it but not anymore."

Deke met the man's gaze. "You lying about sleeping with Dixie Simmons?"

"Maybe I better call my lawyer." Rehnquist moved toward his desk and reached for the sleek black phone. "I don't have any more to say."

"Shit," KC said. "I hate it when I ask a simple question and I get attitude. Hell, it's a simple yes or no question."

Rehnquist tapped an agitated finger on his desk. "You two are trying to trap me."

"So you didn't sleep with her or you didn't kill her?" Deke asked.

"Neither!"

Every bit of Deke demanded he haul the guy to jail, but he'd play one more round. "Frankly, I don't care who you sleep with, Mr. Rehnquist. I don't. I've no interest in telling your wife or your girlfriend or whomever that you and Dixie were sleeping together." That wasn't totally true. He'd do both if it meant solving the case. "But I need to have the basics of Dixie's life so I can find her killer."

"If you are hiding an affair, what else are you hiding?" KC asked.

Beads of sweat plastered wisps of blond hair to his tanned forehead. "I never said I was hiding an affair."

KC hooked his thumbs behind his thick brown belt. "One lie always makes me wonder what else they are hiding. I suppose now we'll be getting a search warrant for his office, house, and even his car."

Deke's gaze bore into Rehnquist. "Imagine what we will find when we search his residence."

Rehnquist fisted his fingers as his face flushed. "Is that a threat?"

"It's a promise," Deke said. "I'm willing to work with you on keeping your secrets as long as you work with me. But if you keep pushing, we'll take this all up to the next level. Won't be pretty or easy, and I'd just as soon not have to fuss. But I'll do it."

Rehnquist drummed his fingers on the phone's receiver and then curled them into a tight fist before drawing back. "I'd been sleeping with Dixie for about two months. We had no formal arrangement but we met for sex often. She was one of those gals who was fun to hook up with initially but she had a lot of emotional stuff that was tiring. She craved attention. It's what made her good on stage. She all but fed off the energy of the crowd and when she was jazzed she was hot in bed. But after a while her neediness had me avoiding her calls."

"Then in the last ten days?"

"I finally took her call a couple of days ago because she threatened to show up at the office and strip off all her clothes."

KC arched a brow as if the image flickered across his mind.

"I can't have that kind of bad publicity. We are like a lot of businesses these days. We're struggling and can't afford any trouble. I took her call and talked to her and told her what she wanted to hear."

"What did she want to hear?"

He sighed. "The usual. She was pretty. She was smart and I was hot for her. The same kind of crap chicks eat up."

KC scribbled notes. "When is the last time you saw her?"

"Two weeks ago. And that is the truth. We did talk on the phone but I haven't seen her since September."

Deke held up the mangled image of Dixie. "Who would do this to her?"

Rehnquist's gaze skirted away as if running to hide. "Holy shit. Don't show that to me again. I don't know who would do that to her. Shit!"

Torn flesh and blood quickly grew grotesque when the heart stopped pumping blood and life. "The person who did this was angry."

"Detective Morgan is right." KC pulled gum from his pocket and slowly unwrapped it. "Dixie's killer wasn't satisfied with killing her. He went out of his way to strip away all her beauty and humanity."

Rehnquist moistened his lips as if struggling to keep his stomach from upending. "I could never have done that to her."

He'd seen killers get sick at the sight of their work. In the heat of murder, the brain's morality values clicked off and urges turned primal and animalistic. After the fact, when the adrenaline cleared and conscious thought returned, regret and disgust reappeared. "You sure about that?"

Rehnquist's eyes widened as he shook his head. "I'm no saint, Detective. No saint at all, but I never would have done that to Dixie. For Christ's sake we were lovers."

And lovers killed lovers all the time. "Are you married?"

His spine stiffened. "Yes."

"Did your wife know about Dixie?" KC asked.

"No! I'm careful to leave the office behind me."

"Whoever killed Dixie was angry. Very angry. Could have been the work of a jealous woman."

"Judi is a gentle soft soul. She'd never hurt anyone." He hesitated. "Once she did find evidence of my playtime. She confronted me, but she was rational and calm."

"Maybe she ran out of calm," Deke said. "We all have violence in us, it's just a matter of dialing up the right combination."

"Not Judi. Not like that."

"You'd be surprised what people can do," KC said. "Saw a lil' bit of a woman kill her six-foot-seven husband with a baseball bat. Later folks kept saying over and over how nice she was. Even the nice ones snap."

"Judi wouldn't have the strength right now." Color rose in his face. "She's nine months pregnant and due any day. She can barely get out of a chair, let alone do that."

Deke suppressed an oath. "What do you know about Dixie?"

"Not much. I wasn't looking for love, just sex."

"You promise her a record deal?"

"I made no promises."

"You hint?" KC asked.

"Look, I'm no angel. We've established that. But I did not kill her."

"Where were you Thursday night?"

"New York. In meetings with attorneys and a singer until two in the morning. And I can give you names." He scrawled several names and numbers on a monogrammed sheet of linen paper. "I flew into Nashville early this morning."

Deke studied the list and then folded it in half with a crisp line. "Stay in touch until I've made these calls."

"Sure."

Outside Spinners Records, Deke slid behind the wheel of his car as KC climbed into the passenger side. For a moment the two sat, each soaking up the silence.

"My money says he's not the guy. Dixie talked with someone who was smart enough to use a burner phone. And clearly this guy had Dixie call his direct personal line."

Deke rubbed the back of his neck. "No, I don't think he's the one. But hell, I've been fooled before."

"So we head to Dixie's apartment." KC flipped through notes. "She has a roommate named Tawny."

"Rudy Creed mentioned Tawny. She's also a singer. Not as good as Dixie."

KC nodded. "Jealousy comes in all kinds of forms."

He fired up the engine. "So it does. Let's go find Tawny."

Fifteen minutes later they pulled up in front of the Wild Horse Saloon. The place was large, crammed full of tables hugging the edges of a stage that stretched across the width of the room.

Deke flashed his badge to the greeter. "Tawny here?"

The girl glanced wide-eyed at the badge. "She's on stage leading the line dance now. Should be finished in a minute or two."

Up front the young girl wore a mike and a rhinestone outfit. The dancers looked as if they were having fun though most missed steps or spun in the wrong direction. Tawny had long reddish brown hair and a full figure complete with round hips, a narrow waist, and a large bust. Her demeanor was relaxed and carefree as she joked with the guests, sang notes here and there and flirted with the oldest men.

Ten minutes later the audience was clapping and heading back to their seats as Tawny wished everyone a great day and promised to return at the seven o'clock show.

Deke and KC made their way across the restaurant. They showed their badges to a beefy man wearing a security shirt and moved down a long dark hallway toward the dressing rooms.

Deke knocked, waited. "Ms. Richards?"

The door snapped open. This close her makeup, which had looked natural from afar, appeared heavy and overdone. Large black eyelashes batted over brown eyes. "What can I do for you?"

Deke showed his badge. "We're with the Nashville Police Department. I have questions for you about Dixie Simmons."

Eyes narrowed. "What does she want? Is she complaining about what I said to her last week?"

"Refresh my memory. What did you say to her last week?"

She planted a hand on her hip, defiance sparking in her posture. "I told her I'd rip out that bleached blond weave of hers if she didn't keep away from my boyfriend. Bad enough to watch her take my spot on center stage, but it's another to see her wagging her butt in front of my boyfriend."

Her honesty nearly made him smile. "She flirted with your boyfriend?"

"If you can call it that. She all but stripped in front of him. She does that all the time. Any time she sees a man she starts wagging her butt in front of him."

Tawny used the present tense not past when she spoke about Dixie. "Dixie was murdered last night."

Tawny arched a brow. "Am I supposed to be upset about that? Am I supposed to cry or wring my hands?"

Deke tapped his index finger against the worn black leather of his holster. "Someone beat her up pretty bad."

She shoved out a breath. "Look, I get that it's tragic that someone young died. And murder is bad. I get that. But it's kinda hard for me to summon up tears for Dixie. She was a taker and she clearly took once too often from the wrong person."

"Where were you last night?"

She flicked a loose strand of hair out of her eyes. "Doing a show in Pigeon Forge. Stage manager will tell you I got off stage about midnight. It took four hours to get back because we hit fog. We arrived home about six a.m."

"Anyone ride with you?"

"As a matter of fact, yes. Two other girls. We all sing in the midweek show at Dollywood and then drive back to Nashville for day jobs."

"Rough schedule."

"Entertainment is a rough business. You want to get noticed you have to hustle."

Deke took the names of the stage manager and the girls sharing the ride. "Know anyone who would want to hurt Dixie?"

She arched a brow but swallowed a smart retort when she met Deke's gaze. "I don't have specific names."

"What did she do when she wasn't working?"

Tawny twirled an auburn strand around her finger. "Sometimes she went to church. Said a sinner like her needed saving."

"Which church?" KC asked.

"I don't know the name. But Pastor Gary runs it. She talked about him."

KC scribbled a note in his tattered notebook. "The big church north of town. New Community. Been there myself."

"I guess that's the one. Dixie had gone there and said she'd given confession. Maybe she shared information that would help."

"Thanks."

As they turned to leave, she asked, "So how did she die?"

Deke pulled out his phone, scrolled to the ME's picture of Dixie and held it out to Tawny. "Like I said. Beaten to death with a blunt metal object."

She stiffened, shook her head and closed her dressing room door.

"Doesn't look like Dixie had a lot of friends," KC said.

Deke replaced the phone. "No, it does not."


A knock at the door had Rachel rising from her desk and glancing around her office one last time to make sure it was reasonably clean. Susan Martinez at Channel Five had texted ten minutes ago announcing her arrival.

Rachel smoothed hands over black pants and checked her V-neck sweater to make sure it was straight. Boots clicked across the wood floor as she moved, not too quickly, to answer the door. *Don't look so damn nervous!*

Muttering, "Shut up," she opened the door. "Susan."

Red lips spread into a wide grin that deepened the feathery wrinkles around wide expressive eyes. "Ms. Wainwright. Thank you for seeing me."

"I'm happy to help. Please come in."

Susan glanced around the space. "I remember when this place used to be a restaurant. Some of the best barbecue in town. I could never understand why it went out of business."

"Owner wasn't good with finances." It had been on the tip of her tongue to explain he'd also had a gambling problem and there'd been an issue with drugs. But that fell under the category of TMI, too much information.

"That's a shame."

She'd not mustered much sympathy for the guy, who'd violated health code laws to cut expenses. It was a wonder no one got sick. But again, less information was more. "Can I get you a coffee?"

"No, I'm fine." They sat in the twin chairs angled in front of Rachel's desk. "As you can imagine we've had more hits on our station's website after your piece aired."

Rachel swallowed a quip about taking it on the chin. "I can imagine."

"I've had a chance to refresh my memory since yesterday. Jeb Jones had a troubled life before his conviction."

"We've never denied that. But that doesn't make him a killer."

"Why Jeb?"

Rachel crossed her legs and relaxed back against the hard chair. "Innocence Project sent me his case. They saw merit in his DNA request and so do I."

"I remember the Dawson murder case. I was in college and working as an intern at the station. It was horrendous. We did lots of stories on Annie. Tried to do a story on her husband and baby but Bill Dawson wouldn't speak to us. Her sister Margaret was a different matter. She was hard to get away from once she got talking. Talked several times to reporters in the months before Annie's body was found. I'd forgotten about the churches' candlelight vigils and the hundreds and hundreds of people who searched. Annie's death touched a lot of people."

Rachel was amazed by the emotion in Susan's voice. "Did you ever see Annie perform?"

"As a matter of fact I did. She was good. Had that star power. Gave you the sense she was going places."

Annie had been beloved whereas Jeb had been despised. Hers was an uphill battle. "What questions can I answer for you?"

Susan flipped through a spiral notebook. "So far the police have not commented on the case."

The police. Deke Morgan. Master of silence. "They are waiting on the DNA, no doubt."

"If you are right about Jeb Jones, this would be a huge upset. Biggest manhunt in Nashville history ends up arresting and convicting the most hated man in Tennessee who also happens to be the wrong guy. This request couldn't have won you a lot of friends in law enforcement."

"I'm after the truth. Not friends."

Martinez tapped her finger against her pad. "Good, because you are not a popular woman right now. Most of the emails that came into the station expressed joy that Margaret Miller hit you. I've not read so many insulting descriptions in years."

Rachel's pulse quickened. "I'm not afraid of being on the outside. That's basically been my life."

"Be careful. A lot of people do not like you now."

"Understood." Rachel didn't want to sound desperate. "So are you going to do a follow-up?"

"I talked to Margaret earlier and she's basically repeating what she said at the vigil."

Rachel swallowed a quip and let the silence between them linger.

"For now, I'm holding off for more stories. If the DNA goes your way call me and I'll cover every facet of your case. Until then, you aren't going to win any ratings for me." She rose.

Rachel stood. "If the DNA goes in my favor I might not need a reporter."

"Don't be so sure about that. DNA is the first step in a long road for you and your client."

Disappointment tempted her to beg for another interview. "Looks like we are all in a holding pattern."

Heels clicked as Susan walked toward the door. "Here's hoping we both end up with a story."

"Won't covering me make you unpopular?"

"Evidence will be on my side and I'll get a lot of attention. Negative attention gets ratings faster than positive and in the end it's all about ratings."

"Not justice?"

She arched a brow as if waiting for a punch line. When none came she said, "Sure. Justice is important, especially when it gets me noticed."

"You are popular enough."

"I'm fifty-two and I don't have a fresh face to dazzle my viewers. It's going to take a great story to get my airtime."


*Song notes. Flashes of light. Smiling faces.* The pictures flashed like lightning skittering and shattering across the night sky.

*Soft blue velvet. Red lipstick. A wordless melody.*

None of the sights and sounds made sense but the headache worsened and throbbed behind tired unfamiliar eyes staring back from the mirror. Frustration welled as understanding remained at arm's length.

"I want to understand. I want to know."

*Song notes. Flashes of light. Smiling faces.*

The pieces, tattered like fabric scraps, needed a master seamstress to take needle and thread and sew them together into a bright, big memory quilt. Perhaps this quilt would never be perfect or pretty, but it promised some kind of warmth and comfort. If the memories joined, calm was sure to follow. And perhaps the headaches would stop.

But even as she imagined a needle and thread basting fabric edges together, a slight jostle, a loud noise or a bad night's sleep undid the stitching in a blink and the scraps unraveled.

*Soft blue velvet. Red lipstick. A wordless melody.*

All that ever remained were worthless scraps.

And the headaches.

And the raw fury that burned like boiling water.

*November 1*

*Sugar,*

*You make me feel like a princess. Grace Kelly and Princess Diana ain't got nothing on me when I'm with you. The private dinner was so perfect. The twinkling lights. Music. Iced champagne. Fried chicken. And the kiss. The kiss so very sweet and so very . . . hot. I realize now why so many find you hard to resist. Your energy draws people. It certainly draws me.*

*I did not give you an answer last night but . . . yes! Yes! Yes! I would love to ride down to Memphis in your new candy apple red car. And stay at the fancy hotel you talked about. I look forward to silk sheets and breakfast served on silver trays.*

*Until next weekend . . .*

*A.*

# Chapter Five

Deke arrived home late last night, showered, and too jazzed to sleep, had grabbed a beer and sat in the worn recliner that had been Buddy's favorite. As ESPN played on the big screen, he'd sipped the beer and stared at football wondering how many hours Buddy sat in this chair, alone and chewing on a case? How many years would Deke sit here, doing the same before his heart gave out and he earned a big funeral filled with speeches, bagpipes, and a five-gun salute.

He'd fallen into bed at two and risen by six. He'd stopped for more coffee and an egg bagel and now found himself at his desk, the one place he belonged.

Deke sat at his desk, coffee in hand, and flipped on the desk lamp. Rolling his head from side to side he attempted to work kinks from tired muscles that needed a week's worth of rest, not more caffeine and paltry stretches.

He powered up his computer and waited as it came online. All the interviews he and KC had conducted yesterday had done little to get them closer to a killer. They'd heard an array of comments about Dixie. Most included her obsession with men and singing. And though some flat-out didn't like her, most liked her bubbly nature.

A check of his answering machine had him listening to Rachel Wainwright's voice. A familiar tension twisted his gut. "Detective Morgan, this is Rachel Wainwright. I'm calling about the DNA in the Jeb Jones case. Have you heard from the state lab? Call me."

He hit delete. She never made an effort to soften her requests. No *please* or *thank you*. She was all hard angles and edges. Not the kind of woman he pictured snuggling next to on a long winter night.

A knock at his door had him raising tired eyes to a uniformed officer sporting a dolly stacked high with dusty brown boxes. "Officer Morgan, you requested files on the Annie Rivers Dawson case?"

Deke rose, surveying the hefty stack of boxes. "I did. Tell me that's all you have."

The short, stocky officer grinned as he backed the dolly into the room. "Got one more pile as big as this one."

"Ten boxes."

"It was the case back in the day. Had every cop in Nashville working on it."

"Right." He jerked his head toward a corner. "Start piling them there."

The officer tipped the dolly back and moved it across the room. As he started to unload, he added, "You gonna go through all these?"

He lifted the lid of a dusty, yellowed box and glanced at the files packed so tight it would take a crowbar to wedge one free. "Not unless I have to."

"You think the DNA will go against you?"

"It pays to be prepared."

"So you do think there could be a problem?"

"No. I don't." He closed the lid. Better to cut rumors off at the knees. "I'm curious, that's all. Keep loading. I'll be back."

He headed to the forensics lab where he found Brad Holcombe. In his late thirties, Brad had a thick, stocky frame that built muscle as easily as it did fat. Lately, months away from the gym had softened the muscle and robbed the man of color. Red hair swept over freckled skin that burned with the slightest kiss of the sun.

"Brad," Deke said.

Brad looked up from a pair of overalls laid out flat on a large table. In one hand he had a magnifying glass and in the other a set of tweezers. "Deke. Come to ask about the DNA?"

He wanted free of this case and Buddy's shadow. "I have. Heard anything?"

"I called last night before I left the office. It should be here in a few days."

The door to the lab opened and his sister, Georgia Morgan, pushed into the lab, bursting with her customary gust of energy. Unlike her brother, Georgia had a fair complexion and blond hair that she kept twisted into a bun at the base of her skull while working. She had soft cheekbones, a heart-shaped face and full lips that easily split into a wide grin. A bundle of energy, she couldn't speak without using her hands or keeping her voice from rising or falling with emotion. "What will be here in a few days?"

Deke sipped his coffee. "Lab results."

Georgia scrunched up her face. "The Annie Rivers Dawson case?"

She'd been born with radar. "That's right."

"I saw the stacks of boxes in your office."

He'd hoped to avoid any drama with Georgia. "I must have missed you."

She dropped her backpack on her small corner desk and shrugged off her sweater. "Thought we could invite the clan over to the Big House in a couple of weeks."

"Why is everyone coming over?"

"It's brother Alex's birthday."

"Birthday." He'd forgotten.

She shook her head, an annoyed brow arched. "Yeah, I know. Not on your radar. That's my job to keep this rag-tag group of Morgans together. But I live in a one bedroom apartment and you're camped out in the Big House, so you're gonna have to host."

"Fine."

Since their mother's death, Georgia had tried to honor the birthday party tradition. The Morgan brothers had played along while Buddy was alive but now all had scurried away like rats on a sinking ship.

"I'm baking a cake like Mom always did," she said.

Deke grimaced as if he'd bitten into a lemon. "What if I pay you to buy one from a baker?"

Blue eyes flashed the first warning sign of Georgia's trademark temper. "Very funny. I can bake a cake."

Each time he stomached one of her cakes it weighed heavy in his gut for days. "Why don't you sing "Happy Birthday"? You're the one with a voice. I'll buy a cake."

"No, it has to be *made*. From scratch." Give her a murder scene and she was cool and collected. Mess with a family tradition, and then you better expect a meltdown. "It's what we've always done."

Deke rubbed the back of his neck. "Georgia, you damned near burned the house to the ground the last time you cooked."

"That was six years ago. And I have improved. Buddy said so."

"He was always a soft touch with you. You could serve him roadkill and he'd have grinned."

She scrunched up her face. "Funny."

"Not kidding."

She waved away his sour, if not begrudgingly playful

expression. Blue eyes narrowed. "I'll skip baking the cake if you let me help you with the Dawson case."

There was always an angle with Georgia. "No."

"I don't like that word."

"Tough."

She stepped closer and lowered her voice as if remembering Brad was in the room. "Why can't I help? I can handle the extra work."

He kept his expression neutral, knowing the more he fed this argument the hungrier she'd get. "No one's digging into the files until the DNA comes back. Right now it's a matter of *if* not *when* we reopen the case."

"I'd still like to read the files."

"No." Deke, his growing annoyance caught Brad's attention. "Brad, let *me* know when the DNA arrives."

Brad glanced quickly at Georgia before he straightened and met Deke's gaze. "Will do."

Georgia glared at Brad and mouthed the word "traitor" before following Deke out the door. "Why are you shutting me out?"

When he'd been fourteen and she'd been four they'd been riding in the car with their mom who'd been dropping him off at the movies to meet friends. Georgia had wanted to go to the movies with Deke. Mom had said no and Georgia had screamed during the entire drive to the theater. She'd never gotten her way but she'd taken hostages. "This is not your case, Georgia."

"But I'd like it to be."

A wry smile twisted the edges of his mouth. "I'd like to win the lottery but the chances are slim to none."

"It's not the same."

"Georgia, I don't have the time or patience to argue with you. Stick to your own caseload." He rarely pulled rank but didn't hesitate now. "Stay out of my case."

Eyes widened with shock and offense as if she hadn't

seen this answer coming from a mile away. "You aren't being fair."

"Life isn't fair."

"I'm baking that cake."

"Bring it."

A final glare and she turned and left. She didn't scream as she'd done when they were kids, but he sensed the idea tempted. A turn of the heel and she vanished around a corner.

Deke returned to his office and stared at the stack of boxes. He sipped his coffee as he flipped off the lid of the top box, which he discovered was as crammed full of files as the first box he'd inspected. His father had never left a stone unturned and he liked to document. If Deke had been under the gun on a high-profile case he'd have saved every scrap of paper.

Deke hadn't read any of his case files and could admit he was tempted. But there'd be no way Deke would have time to invest the one hundred and fifty man hours into a case reevaluation. He dialed his cell.

On the second ring he heard his brother Rick's garbled, "What?"

"Don't tell me you're sleeping."

"Sure why not? I was up late last night studying."

"I always figured you'd be the one to keep a routine."

"Not anymore."

The second Morgan son, Rick, had changed in more ways than Deke could count since he'd been shot six months ago. He'd taken medical leave and gone back to school. "Near death experiences," he'd said, "have a way of lining up all the stray ducks in your life."

"Want some freelance work?"

"Depends." He sighed into the phone.

"It's the Annie Rivers Dawson case files."

"DNA is back?" Interest sharpened the tone of his voice.

Deke slid his hand into his pocket and rattled the change. "Not yet. Any day now. But I've a gut feeling this case might go sideways. I want to be ready."

"For what?"

"If the DNA proves Jeb Jones didn't kill Annie Rivers Dawson. A shit storm."

In the background Rick's dog, Tracker, barked, his deep throaty voice still as menacing as it had been when he'd first been assigned to Rick seven years ago. Next came the sound of Rick moving through the house and opening the back door. "You think it will be that huge?"

"If Rachel Wainwright has a say. Yes."

Rick chuckled. "The fair Ms. Rachel. I saw her on campus yesterday."

Despite himself, his interest peaked. "Riding a broom?"

He chuckled. "Visiting the math department. There's a part-time teacher in that department who works as a private investigator from time to time. My guess is Wainwright paid her a visit."

"Why would she need a PI?"

"She's a defense attorney. They work with PIs all the time." Tracker barked. A door opened again. Paws scrambled back inside. "When do you want me to get started?"

"Whenever you can get here. And the sooner, the better. Georgia came by my office and saw the files. And Georgia being Georgia won't stay out of the boxes for long."

"I'll be by in an hour with my truck. Lend me a couple of uniforms and I'll have the files out of your office in ten minutes."

"Thanks. Oh and be warned, Georgia wants us to get together for Alex's birthday at the Big House."

A heavy silence crackled through the phone. "I'm not sure if I can make that one."

His terse tone hinted at another fault in the Clan Morgan's foundation. "You aren't still pissed with Alex, are you?"

"Like you once said, I can carry a grudge for years."

"Try and put this one aside. It's important to Georgia that we all stay close. She's baking a cake."

He groaned. "If you are trying to convince me, that's not doing the trick."

"We can all eat dry cake and manage to be civil with one another for a half-hour."

"As long as Alex keeps his comments to himself, I'll try."

"Great."

More silence. "Maybe we could use the time to make some decisions about the house."

Deke rubbed his hand over his short hair, missing the undercover days when he could hide behind long hair and grungy clothes. "The one time I suggested we sell and split the proceeds Georgia blew up."

"This conversation won't be fun for any of us. The house deserves to have someone living in it that wants to be there."

Deke wanted to argue. He wanted to say that he still loved the house and would find a way to make it family central again. But he couldn't promise that. He might sleep and eat quick meals at the house, but it wasn't home anymore. In fact, he spent as little awake-time there as possible because it felt as if the house, a monument to the unstoppable Morgan family, stood in silent judgment of his failed marriages and unsettled life.

Rick was right. The house deserved better. A decision had to be made.

"I'll let her sing "Happy Birthday" before I open the subject," Deke said.

"Do it before she cuts the cake."

"No way, bro. We eat her crappy cake and smile first. Then the house."

A whispered oath escaped through the phone line. "Agreed."

"See you in an hour."

"Will do."

Rachel slid the DVD into her computer and leaned back in her chair as the PC whirred and readied the disc. She sipped her morning coffee as the image of Jeb Jones appeared on the screen.

He had a long lean face, deeply lined but freshly shaven. An orange jumpsuit robbed what little color remained in his gaunt face and emphasized shoulder-length gray hair slicked back. A fading spiderweb tattoo clung to the side of his neck as a jagged scar meandered along his jawline. He'd gotten both in prison.

She'd made this tape six weeks ago when she'd driven three hours west toward Memphis to visit Jeb at the federal prison.

The camera shot over her right shoulder directly into Jeb's face. *"Jeb, I'm taping this so that I can show it in court if need be."*

*Silver handcuffs rattled around his wrists as he threaded his fingers together. His hands trembled slightly, not from fear but Parkinson's. "What do you mean if need be?"*

*"If the DNA proves you didn't kill Annie."*

*Jeb scratched his clean-shaven chin. "Unless the cops monkey with it, it will show I'm innocent."*

*"Jeb, I need for you to tell me in your own words what happened the night Annie Dawson vanished."*

*He looked at her and then at the floor before drawing in a deep breath. "I've told this story so many times. Can't you read my file?"*

*"I need to hear it from you in your own words. I need you to say it in the camera."*

He raised a manacled hand to his temple and scratched. *"Where do you want me to start?"*

*"Start from the moment you woke up. It would have been October sixteenth. A Tuesday."*

*"Oh, I know exactly what day it was. I've replayed it over the last thirty years and I don't imagine there is a detail I've forgotten."*

*"Tell me."*

He hesitated and then nodded. *"Like you said it was a Tuesday. And it was warm that day. Really warm. I had to get up early to work at the garage. There was a transmission job that needed to be done by lunch. A '71 Cutlass. Green. Anyway, I wasn't feeling so good that morning. Hungover. I'd won money in cards the night before and spent it on extra rounds at the bar."* His gaze grew distant.

*"What are you thinking?"* she prompted.

*"About my boy. He was nine at the time. I could have come home the night before and spent time with him, but I chose to go to the bar. At the time I thought I deserved a special night for myself. Thought I was owed a good time. So I left Kirk at home with his mom even though I'd been promising to spend time with him."*

Jeb's poor parenting had been a painful regret that he'd expressed to her often. He'd said several times that he didn't want to go to his grave branded a murderer in his boy's eyes.

*"What happened next?"* she prompted.

*"I grabbed a smoke and left the house about five. The transmission would take every bit of six hours and I didn't need to lose this job."* He sniffed, shaking his head. *"I spent the day at the garage working on the car. Took longer than I'd imagined and I didn't knock off until six. I could have gone home but I took a detour."*

*"Where did you go?"*

*His gaze dropped. "I drove by Annie's house."*

*"Why?" When he didn't answer, she added, "Jeb, there's no downside."*

*"'Cause I wanted to see her," he ground out. "I couldn't get her off my mind."*

*"Why?"*

*"Because back then I figured I was in love with her."*

*Rachel's off camera sigh cut through the silence. "When did you first meet her?"*

*"About a year before. I was doing work for her landlord. She was living with those two girls."*

*"Joanne and Beth."*

*"That's right. They were roommates." He shook his head. "Those girls was pretty enough, and that Beth girl had a boyfriend that lusted for Annie. I couldn't blame the guy. When I saw Annie . . . she made the other two look plain. She was a hard woman to forget."*

The office door opened and Colleen breezed into the building. Rachel hit pause. "Hey."

"What brings you in on a Saturday?"

"Work. A dismal personal life." Colleen's gaze skimmed Rachel's computer screen, which now paused on Jeb's craggy face. "Why are you watching the interview again? Haven't you seen it a dozen times?"

"At least. I've read my copies of the Annie letters this morning. I thought if I watched the interview again I might pick up a new tidbit. Annie was in love with someone she called Sugar. He gave her nice jewelry and took her on fancy vacations."

"I can't believe that was Jeb."

"No. Neither can I."

Colleen poured herself a cup of coffee and pulled up a chair beside Rachel. "What did the letters say?"

"I've emailed you copies. Basically, they're love letters. Annie is crazy about Sugar for most of the letters and then she turns bitter."

"Ah. So it goes with love. She use a name other than Sugar?"

"She never mentioned his real name. Always Sugar."

"That's sweet." No missing the hint of sarcasm. "What about the man she married? What was his name?"

"Bill Dawson. I've left him several phone messages but he's not returned my calls."

Colleen shrugged. "I can't imagine he'd want to revisit his wife's death."

"I don't want to hurt anyone but there are questions that need asking."

Colleen traced her finger along a strand of pearls. "So she could have been writing her husband-to-be?"

"It's possible." Rachel glanced at a legal pad full of her scrawled notes. "But Annie is careful about his identity and I get the vibe Sugar wanted their relationship kept secret. Bill wouldn't have had a reason for secrecy. He was an up and coming guy fresh out of college."

"Could his family have disapproved? College boy and honky-tonk singer. Like a Romeo and Juliet?"

"He wasn't from money. He worked his way through school. No family legacy. No wife or girlfriend from what I can find."

"What's he do for a living now?"

"He's a successful businessman. Owns a string of gas stations and convenience stores."

Colleen eyed the computer screen. "Is this really a valuable use of your time? You don't know if the DNA is going to help Jeb."

"You're right. I've paying work to tackle. But I can't let this go." Rachel held up her hand as Colleen opened her mouth to object. "And before you speak, this is not lingering guilt over Luke. Not today anyway. I've a gut feeling that there is much more to this case."

A raised brow broadcast Colleen's skepticism as she crossed for coffee. "So you're going to reinvestigate the case?"

"If it comes to it."

Colleen studied her. "When is the last time you slept a solid eight hours?"

A half grin tipped the edge of her mouth. "What month is it?"

Pearls jangled when she reached for more sugar, which she spooned into her coffee. "We both work hard but you work the hours of a crazy woman. You need to lighten up."

"I know."

"When will it stop?"

She glanced at Jeb's frozen face on the screen. "When DNA proves he didn't kill Annie and he's out of jail."

"Isn't that what you said when you were working on your brother's case? I mean you did what you set out to do. You cleared his name."

"I created reasonable doubt, but I never found the real killer. And Luke is dead."

Colleen's voice softened. "Killing yourself is not going to bring him back."

A rush of color flushed her cheeks. "I know that."

Colleen sipped her coffee. "How many days after Luke died did you contact Innocence Project?"

Rachel faced her computer. "I don't remember."

"I do. You told me it was twenty-four hours. You told me you rose early that morning, opened your laptop and sent them your résumé. What was the name of the first case you received?"

"Bobby Franklin." He'd been seventeen when arrested for rape. He'd been imprisoned twelve years when Rachel took the case.

"And you dug into his case for six months before police reopened it."

"DNA proved he wasn't involved in the attack. He was released."

"I know. You are an angel. And then there were a couple of other cases. All good endings. It wouldn't hurt to slow it up."

"I did take a break."

"Three months. And you worked the billable hours like a crazy woman. Innocence Project called you about Jeb and you were off again."

"Okay. What's your point?"

"Be careful, Rachel. You can't keep this pace up forever."

"It won't be forever."

Folding her arms, she leaned back in her chair and studied Rachel. "Are you sure about that? Because I see someone who now has a mission to save all the downtrodden."

"What's wrong with that?"

"If you don't slow up, you will self-destruct. You've got to live a little. It wasn't your fault that Luke died in prison."

Rachel traced the edges of her computer. If she'd been savvier about the system she'd never had blindly trusted justice. "When the cops came for my brother he looked calm but I could see he was terrified. It was awful. I kept telling him he had truth on his side." She swallowed. "When they filed charges I was sure we'd work it out. I thought the attorney Mom hired would fix it all right up until the jury read the guilty verdict." She closed her eyes. "Mom wailed and I had to take her out of the courthouse. And later when the judge was about to read his sentence, I thought *Don't worry, the judge will see. He will release my brother.* And then the judge sentenced Luke to twenty years in prison."

"It wasn't your fault he went to jail."

"I could have kept him out of jail."

Exasperation honed the pitch of her voice. "You would have lied for him?"

She released a breath. "One lie would have saved his life. He had so much in front of him. That experience scared him straight. I'm sure he'd have sobered and gone on to live a good life."

Colleen's glare conveyed her unspoken doubts. "Luke didn't deserve what he got but that doesn't mean you should be punished."

Rachel glanced at her cold coffee and rose, moving toward the microwave. She popped it inside and hit one minute. "Like Jeb."

"They are not one in the same."

Rachel shook her head. "Aren't they? I think they are exactly the same."

"So what happens if you do clear Jeb? What happens next?"

The pleas of countless men and women like Luke and Jeb rattled in her head. At times their cries could be deafening. Still, she managed a smile for Colleen. "One crusade at a time."

"Don't forget you."

The microwave dinged and she removed her steaming coffee as an uneasy laugh rumbled in her chest. "Let's listen to Jeb's story." Grateful to move the topic from herself she hit play.

*"I decided to drive by Annie's house. I know what it sounds like but it's not what you think. She was the prettiest woman I'd ever seen and seeing her always lifted my spirits. I was tired and dreading going home to a wife who was always angry with me. I thought I'd drive by. I know she'd had a baby. I didn't like thinking about the baby. I*

*liked thinking of her before the baby. That's why I'd stayed away while she was expecting." He leaned forward and studied interwoven hands wrinkled and calloused by a hard life.*

*"Did you see her?"*

*"I did. I saw her through the window. And she was as pretty as I remembered. Her long blond hair hung over her shoulders. She was wearing jeans and a T-shirt that showed off new curves. I stopped my car across the street, lit up a cigarette and sat there for a time."*

*"How long were you there?"*

*"Twenty minutes."*

*"Did you see anyone else at or around the house?" Rachel asked.*

*"No. There was no other car in the driveway and I didn't see anyone in the window. Finally, I caught an old neighbor lady watching me and I realized I had to leave before she called the cops. I left."*

*"What time was that?"*

*"About six thirty. I know that because it took me about fifteen minutes to get home. I always noticed the clock when I came in the front door because I was always figuring a lie to tell my wife."*

*Rachel shuffled through the pages of her legal pad. "And you never saw Annie again?"*

*"No. I never saw her again. I swear."*

*"Did you stay at home all night?"*

*"No. I was restless and left about eight. I spent the night drinking and going from bar to bar."*

*"Annie's sister came by her house at about eight thirty. She knocked on the door but realized it was open. She heard the baby crying and then saw the blood. She rushed to the nursery, picked up the baby, and called the cops."*

*"I know. I heard the story a million times. The house was doused in blood and there weren't no sign of Annie's body.*

*Cops said there was no way she could have survived that kind of blood loss. I felt sick. I'd lost the one person that made me happy. Broke my heart."*

*"Cops talk to you at all?"*

*"Yeah, a few times. That neighbor lady got my tag number. They couldn't pin the case on me but they kept asking over and over if I killed her. I must have shouted no a thousand times. But they couldn't pin anything and gave up."*

*"Did they search your car?"*

*"No. Not that time."*

*"What did you do when they found her bones in the woods?"*

*"Made me sick all over to think of someone dumping her in the woods like trash. She deserved better."*

*"When did the cops come for you?"*

*"After they found the body. They showed up at my work and arrested me. I was sure they'd figure out like before that I wasn't their man. But this time they kept hammering me. They kept asking me what I knew about Annie. Did I have a crush on her? Did I ever sleep with her? Did I kill her?" Jeb shook his head, his mouth flattening into a bitter line. "I kept saying no over and over but they didn't care. And then they told me about the bloody tire iron found in the trunk of my car."*

*"What did you think?"*

*"That it was all one terrible mistake. I knew I had a tire iron in my trunk, but I knew I'd never have hit Annie with it in a million years. Shit, I was in love with her!"*

*A long silence followed. "You were in love with her."*

*He dropped his head in shame. "I know what it sounds like. I know. But I did love her. Or at least I thought so at the time."*

*"If you loved her you'd hate the fact she was married to another man and was raising his baby. You'd have felt*

*left out and angry." Rachel's voice had sharpened to a
razor's edge.*

*Jeb's head raised and his eyes brightened with anger.
"That ain't true. That ain't true! I just wanted to see her. It
was enough to see her and know that she was happy."*

Rachel shut off the tape. "Annie didn't write those letters
to him."

Colleen folded her arms. "I agree."

Out of the file, Rachel tugged a picture of Jeb taken
thirty years ago. He possessed a rugged handsomeness but
there was no missing the rough edges. "She was pretty. New
baby. I see him loving her but not the other way around."

Rachel leaned back letting her gaze travel between the
decades-old images of the two. "So if her lover wasn't Jeb
or her husband, who was it?"

"That's the million-dollar question."

"Jealousy is a great motivator."

Rachel reached for her glasses. "The letters bother me."

"Why?"

"Read them and tell me what you think."

A smile tweaked the edges of Colleen's lips. "What am
I looking for?"

"Read them with a clear, unbiased eye and let me know
what you think."

The interest glittering in her gaze suggested she'd be late
getting to her own work today. "Now you've peaked my curiosity."

Rachel folded her arms over her chest. "Good."

The woman's scream shattered the silence, startling the
smug smile on the well-lined face. "You did what?"

Baby hated that tone of voice. What should have been a
simple announcement had soured into trouble. "I gave the
letters to Rachel Wainwright. She is the perfect person to

use them. Since that Margaret woman hit her on television everyone knows Rachel. She wants to reopen the case, so she is the perfect person to deliver the letters to the police."

"Assuming she does."

"She will. They will help her client. And when the cops announce they have the letters, he will get worried."

"I don't want him to worry." The woman cursed and pounded deeply lined fists. "Why would you betray me?"

Baby sighed, already weary of this discussion. "I haven't betrayed you. I'm on your side. I always will be."

"You took my letters."

"They tell the world that Annie had a lover. They might not ever be able to prove who the lover was but it will make *him* nervous. It will make him squirm."

"I don't want him to suffer."

"Of course you do. He's not been a faithful servant. I've heard you cry over him too many nights."

"That doesn't mean I want him punished." Silence made the air thick. "I want Jeb Jones to die in prison with the world believing he killed Annie."

"And likely that will happen. Jeb is running out of time. But in the interim, our faithless friend can suffer and wonder." Baby had lost patience with him when Dixie Simmons had wagged her pert ass through Nashville as if she were proud of the affair. Was there no depth to how low he'd stoop?

"I hate this." Wrinkled hands curled into fists. "I want my letters back."

This conversation was pointless. "You are not mentioned in the letters. I don't see the problem."

"No, of course not!"

"Then why are you worried?"

A weary face. "Stop talking so much. I don't want to hear any more of your chatter. Get the letters back."

Baby pouted, feeling as if the tribute laid at the feet of the master had been rejected. "If you really feel that way."

"I do! Get the letters back."

Baby's hackles rose. "It won't be easy getting them back."

"I don't care if you have to kill that attorney. Get those letters back, you stupid twit!"

Anger roiled. "Don't call me stupid."

"I call it like it is. You think taking care of Dixie makes you in charge, but don't forget I've been at this a lot longer than you."

Anger oozed in Baby like liquid iron.

"Now get those letters back."

*November 4*

*Sugar,*

*You still mad? You know I only have eyes for you. You are my man. Forget the bartender's attention. I get lots of men hanging around begging for what I'll never give 'em. I am yours, lock, stock, and barrel. Come by late tonight and I'll show you how good real love feels.*

*A.*

# Chapter Six

*Saturday, October 15, 3 PM*

With Bill Dawson still avoiding her calls, Rachel shifted focus to Annie's former roommates, Joanne Stevens and Beth Drexler. If anyone might have known about a secret lover, the roommates would know.

The two women had attended Vanderbilt University. Beth had been in the biology department while Joanne majored in music. Both women had graduated in the spring after Annie's death.

Rachel wasn't able to track Beth but was able to locate Joanne Stevens, who was now married to a doctor and living in Franklin, a small affluent town west of Nashville.

Rachel climbed in her ten-year-old Toyota and drove out I-40 to Franklin. Thirty minutes later she found the three-story brick house located at the end of a tree-lined cul-de-sac. Manicured lawns, flower beds full of blossoms, even a picket fence. The house had all the trappings of the ideal life. She'd dreamed of a house like this when she'd been a kid. She'd wondered what it would be like to have an address for more than six months, to have a yard, a bike, and lasting friends.

Rachel parked in front of the house, climbed out of her car and straightened her skirt. She ran fingers through her hair and wished she'd taken time to touch up her makeup as she glanced up at the brick house.

Feeling a bit intimidated and irritated that she was nervous, she walked to the large wooden front door, her heels clicking on the brick sidewalk.

She rang the bell, tightening her grip on her briefcase. Beyond the door there was silence and then the sound of steady, unhurried footsteps.

The door opened to a tall, slim woman in her early fifties. She wore simple dark pants and a silk blouse, which likely would have set Rachel back three months' pay. Dark hair swept over straight shoulders, a strand of pearls encircled a slim white neck, and a gold watch winked from her wrist. Understated money.

A quick sweep of the woman's assessing gaze had Rachel feeling as if she came up short. "Ms. Wainwright?"

"Mrs. Stevens. Thank you for seeing me." She extended a hand more aware of her calluses as she shook Mrs. Stevens's smooth manicured hand.

Keen eyes searched her face. "I saw you on the news the other night."

"I made a splash."

A slight smile tweaked the edges of her mouth. "A bit of drama always has a way of catching the media's eye. Why don't you come in?"

Rachel stepped into the marbled hallway, daring a glance up at a crystal chandelier that reflected a thousand points of light. Mrs. Stevens moved from the foyer into a room on the right decorated with whites and grays. Rachel wiped her feet before stepping onto the carpet and taking the seat that Mrs. Stevens indicated.

Rachel sunk into a plush couch as Mrs. Stevens took a seat at her diagonal. A large portrait hanging over the fireplace featured Mrs. Stevens wearing a lush full wedding dress. Time had been kind to Joanne Stevens who still looked remarkably as she had on her wedding day.

"I was surprised you called," she said as she crossed her legs at her ankles.

"I'm trying to learn as much about Annie Rivers Dawson as I can and you were one of her closest friends."

She shifted as she folded her hands and placed them in her lap. "We were roommates. I'm not sure if I'd say we were friends."

"How did you two meet?"

"Annie was singing at a party on campus. She really was wonderful and made the evening a hit. I came up to her after the show to tell her how much I loved her work and we got to talking. My friend Beth and I were looking for a third roommate and she needed a place to live. Seemed romantic to have an aspiring singer live with us. Within a couple of days, we'd signed an agreement and she moved into the house. Initially, it was great. She was always singing and the friends that came to see her were different. I felt a bit like a rebel, living with someone in show business." A slight grin hinted to the girl she'd been. "My dad was not thrilled, which made living with Annie all the more appealing."

Rachel had worked her way through college and had never had the luxury of rebelling because she'd been busy working. "Did she date anyone while she was living with you?"

"Men loved Annie. She had an energy and a vitality to go with those stunning blond looks. When she walked into the room men couldn't think. I was dating my husband at the time and I resisted bringing him by our house when I knew Annie would be there. I didn't want him falling under her spell until he knew me better."

"And did he meet Annie?"

"He did. In fact, I warned him that he'd fall for her the minute he saw her and he laughed. He said I was the girl for him. And then he met her. She was coming out of the house, her blond hair flowing and her skirt skimming her signature red cowboy boots. His mouth dropped open as if he'd been hit in the back of the head with a two-by-four. He saw me watching and recovered but he'd been caught in her net. She also had the same effect on our other roommate's boyfriend."

Rachel glanced at her notes. "Beth Drexler."

"Right. Beth's boyfriend was really taken by Annie and made a pass at Annie while Beth was in the shower. He claimed to be religious." She shook her head. "I happened to see it. Annie said no in such a way that didn't make him mad. Later she asked me not to tell Beth because she didn't want a fight."

"Did you tell Beth?"

"No. She had a temper and a jealous streak and I didn't want to stir that pot."

"And you are sure Annie and Beth's boyfriend didn't have a relationship?"

"No. I think he was terrified of Beth."

"I haven't been able to find Beth."

"She married that boyfriend but she was killed in a car accident about ten years ago. I saw the notice in the alumnae magazine that her younger sister had written."

"So Annie wasn't dating anyone?"

"She was private about her personal life. And though she never talked about it, I had the sense she was dating someone. I could hear her in her room late at night talking on the phone. She kept her voice low so I never made out what she was saying."

"This guy never came by the house? You never met him?"

"Never. Not once."

"But she got pregnant and then married." Rachel flipped through her notes. "She married Bill Dawson."

"That caught both Beth and me by surprise. We had never met the guy."

"But you said that you never met the guy she was dating."

Joanne hesitated and then leaned forward, a conspirator's glint in her eyes. "I never thought he was the guy who fathered her baby."

"Why would you say that?"

"I saw them together at their wedding. One day she's single and the next we are invited to a small wedding at the New Community Church. Beth and I were both blown away but we went. We saw Bill for the first time. He was tall, good-looking, the kind of guy you'd expect Annie to marry. And he was like all men. He had fallen under her spell."

Rachel was adept at reading between the lines. "But."

Joanne shook her head. "It was clear he loved her a whole lot more than she loved him. And she sounded stiff and formal around him whereas when she'd spoken to whomever on the phone at night it was clear she was excited and happy."

"She was unhappy at her wedding?"

"So much so that I asked her about it. She said she wasn't feeling well. That's when she told me about the baby. Not the first stressed-out shotgun marriage, I suppose." She shrugged. "She came by the house days later, paid the balance on her rent and moved out. That was the last I saw her."

"How did you hear about her death?"

"On the news. I was getting ready for my own wedding and was half listening to the television when the newscaster said she'd been murdered. I didn't know she'd had her baby." She shoved out a breath. "Beth and I did take time to go to the funeral. So sad. I think most of the music community in Nashville was there."

"Do you remember seeing her husband at the funeral?"

"I do. He was stoic and showed little or no emotion. Everyone, even the pastor overseeing the funeral was sad, but Bill looked resolute."

"What about her baby?"

"She wasn't there from what I could tell."

"What happened to the baby?"

"I honestly don't know. I didn't know Bill and it never occurred to me to check in with him after the funeral. My life was hectic then." Regret threaded through the words.

"What do you remember about Jeb Jones?"

Ice sharpened her gaze. "I saw him when he came by the house for maintenance. I didn't like him and told the landlord so. Very creepy man."

"What did he do to upset you?"

"He lingered a little too long. Asked too many personal questions. Always smelled of booze. He was particularly interested in Annie."

"You testified at his trial."

She sat a little straighter. "I did. I wanted the jury to know about the man who killed Annie."

"And you are certain he killed her?"

"He was the one that lurked around. A couple of times I caught him parked outside our house watching. I called the police on him."

Rachel glanced at her notes. "He wasn't arrested for loitering according to his record."

She fingered the pearls around her neck. "He should have been. And maybe if he had she'd still be alive."

"Did he ever threaten her, you, or Beth?"

She moistened her lips. "No. Never in words. But his presence was threat enough." She crossed her legs. "Why on earth would you defend someone like that?"

"He has maintained his innocence for thirty years and has been asking for DNA for five years. He deserves to have his DNA tested."

"As far as I'm concerned he doesn't deserve a second of anyone's time. He got what was coming to him and he's trying to worm his way out of jail." Her eyes narrowed. "You don't strike me as naïve, Ms. Wainwright. Why would you fall for a sob story like the one Jeb's spinning?"

*How many people said that about me!* Luke's anguished retort rattled in her head. "What if he's telling the truth?"

"He's not telling the truth. He's looking for an out. Men like him know how to play the system."

Rachel's irritation grated under her skin. "I'll leave it up to the DNA test."

"So what happens if the DNA test comes back and proves the blood on the murder weapon is not his?"

"Then he has grounds for a new trial."

She traced her fingertips over her collarbone as if breathing grew more difficult. "I'll have to testify again?"

"Perhaps."

Her fingers curled into a fist. "I won't change my story."

"No one is expecting you to. Tell the truth."

"The truth can be manipulated."

"Yes, it can."

Eyes narrowed. "What do you hope to gain from all this? Is this about getting publicity?"

"No. I was hired to do a job and that's what I'm going to do."

"But you are trying to set a convicted murderer free."

Rachel hesitated, sensing the tension in the room growing. "Have you considered that the real killer may still be out there? What if the person that really killed Annie is still walking the streets?"

That idea robbed a bit of color from Joanne's face. "Out there now?"

"If Jeb is proven innocent then there's a killer to find."

She glanced toward the window as if she expected to see someone out there lurking, waiting and watching.

Rachel closed her notebook. "You don't have to worry, Mrs. Stevens."

Her gaze shifted back to Rachel. Gone was the calm. "How can you be sure about that? What if you've stirred up a hornet's nest and innocent people like me get hurt?"

"Why would you be hurt?"

"Because I testified in the first case."

"But you testified for the prosecution."

"And if by some miracle you get Jeb off the hook what's to stop him from coming after me?" Worry and anger looped around the last words.

"Mr. Jones is ill. He has no desire to stir up trouble. He wants to reconnect with his son and live the remainder of his life in peace."

She brushed imaginary lint from her pant leg. "And you believe him?"

"Yes."

"Even if he was innocent, he's been in jail for thirty years. That changes a man. He could be angry with anyone who helped put him there."

"I assure you . . ."

Mrs. Stevens rose, raising her hand for silence. "I'm not interested in what you think. You strike me as an honest well-meaning woman, but I don't think you are as worldly as you might like to believe. In fact, I dare say you are naive."

Rachel rose, her back stiff with annoyance. "I'm not naive."

"You are too young to know that you aren't. You still believe that good wins over evil."

"I know that it doesn't."

She stretched out her hand toward the main entrance. "No, you are a dreamer. And as much as I admire dreamers they are a danger. Now, I really have to be getting on with my day."

The window that had briefly opened to the past slammed in her face. "Thank you for your time."

Joanne Stevens escorted her to the door, said a polite good-bye and closed the massive door behind her. As Rachel moved toward her car she acknowledged that time was her enemy. Thirty years had dulled memories and those involved in the original case were now entrenched in lives they guarded closely. A win on the DNA front would be the first of many battles.

She got into her car and for a moment sat in the silence. Colleen had warned she was overdoing it. Joanne called her naïve. Morgan thought she was a fool.

"Luke, there're so many uphill battles in the world." Weariness draped each word.

*Whiner.* Her brother's voice whispered out from the quietest part of her mind. *Whiner.*

Irritated, she opened her eyes and started the car. "F-you, bro."

*Get moving.*

"Ass." Energized, she drove. She dialed Bill Dawson's number and her call went straight to voice mail. "Mr. Dawson. This is Rachel Wainwright. I've left you messages before. Please call me."

She set the phone on her lap and at the interstate, opted to head west versus east. If she couldn't grab Bill Dawson today, she had another person on her interview list.

As Joanne watched Rachel drive off in her beat-up old car, she reached inside a ceramic box and pulled out a cigarette and a lighter. Standing at the screen door that opened off her kitchen into the backyard, she flicked the lighter and held the flame to the tip of her cigarette until she could inhale deeply. She waved the smoke's scent away from the kitchen.

She'd called Rachel Wainwright naïve but the truth was

she was the fool. If she'd been wise, she'd never have agreed to speak to the attorney.

But she'd been lulled by a need for excitement to break up the boredom of a daily life revolving around grown children and a busy husband.

She wondered if she'd somehow opened a can of worms.

Those days in the house with Annie and Beth had been great fun. Thanks to Annie the house had been full of odd and exciting characters.

Out on the deck she flicked the ash into a potted plant. She'd remembered how annoyed her father had been. Be careful with whom you associate. Lay down with dogs and you'll get fleas. She'd laughed. Called him stuffy.

When she'd been called to testify in Jeb's case her father had hired an attorney. He'd been worried about the family reputation. But in the end her "walk" on the wild side had been chalked up to youthful foolishness. She'd earned her way back in to his good graces with a stunning marriage and by producing three strapping grandsons.

Daddy would not be pleased if he heard about Rachel Wainwright's visit. At ninety-seven he still ruled the family and had a way of making her feel like a child.

She reached for her cell and dialed a number she'd not used in a couple of years. At the third ring, she received a curt, "Hello."

"This is Joanne Stevens."

"Joanne. It's been a while. Why the call?"

"I had an interesting visitor today. Rachel Wainwright."

"I saw her on the news."

"She's digging into the Jeb Jones case."

"So I gathered."

"What are you going to do?"

"I've nothing to worry about."

"You were at his trial."

"A lot of people were at his trial. Ms. Wainwright will

be a busy woman if she plans to talk to all the people that testified against Jeb Jones."

"So you aren't worried?" She took a long drag on her cigarette and exhaled it slowly.

"No. I'm not worried."

"Why are you so calm?"

"Because Jeb is guilty. And no amount of grandstanding by an upstart attorney is going to change that. Let Miss Wainwright have her little circus. It won't make a difference."

She inhaled and exhaled. "I don't see how you can be calm."

"You always were a nervous sort, Joanne."

She stared at the glowing tip of her cigarette. "Do you ever think about Annie?"

A long silence snaked over the lines. "Sure. From time to time."

"I dreamed about her last night."

"Really?"

"She was laughing and singing. Everyone in the room was happy to see her."

"Annie had a lot of talent. She could be amazing. But you and I both know she was not perfect. She had her faults."

"You never liked her."

"I saw her for what she was."

She flicked a long ash into the pot. "What are you going to do if Rachel Wainwright comes to see you?"

"I'm not worried. I'll deal with her. But then I don't have as much to lose as you do."


Rachel's next visit was one that she'd been avoiding. Kirk Jones, Jeb's son, was now thirty-nine and owned a garage thirty minutes outside Nashville. Jeb had spoken of his son many times and his desire to reunite, but Kirk had had no contact with his father since Jeb had been sentenced.

She parked in front of the custom auto repair shop. The low one-story building with three large garages was located to the east across the Cumberland River. The area was up and coming and had a mix of residential and small industry.

Out of her car, she tightened her hold on her purse strap and moved toward the large glass doors leading to an office. Inside she found an old man sitting behind a desk piled high with pink order slips, auto catalogues, and several empty coffee cups.

The gray-haired man sported half-glasses and a blue shirt with the name *Ronnie* over the right breast. He glanced up at her.

"My name is Rachel Wainwright."

He raised his hand and she noticed the phone receiver cradled under his chin.

She nodded and turned away, walking around the room to inspect the collection of automotive posters featuring trucks and bikini-clad women. There was a small table set up with a new coffeemaker and as tempted as she was to make herself a cup, she resisted.

A click of the receiver in the cradle had her turning as the older man rose. "I'm looking for Kirk Jones."

"Is he working on your car?"

"No, sir. I know his father."

The old man's eyes widened with shock. "His daddy's been in prison for more years than I can count."

The *whir-whir* sound of a pneumatic drill echoed out from the garage. "Yes, I know."

"They don't speak."

"I know. Is he here?"

A narrowing gaze sized her up. "Sure, I'll get him."

The man vanished into the bay and seconds later the drill silenced and a tall broad-shouldered man appeared in the office. He wore the same blue shirt as the old man but his was covered in grease, dirt, and sweat. Blond hair was cut short and he sported a goatee. Several tattoos covered well-muscled arms. Jeb had said his wife and son had really struggled after he'd left for prison. For the first year his wife, Dell, had visited him with the boy in tow but after the one-year anniversary of his incarceration she'd stopped visiting or answering his mail.

Kirk Jones reached for the rag tucked in his back pocket and slowly wiped his hands clean as he studied her. "You know my father?"

"That's right."

"You don't look like my father's type. From what I heard he liked the blondes."

"I'm his attorney."

He studied her a beat. "The one decked on the news?"

"I think everyone in Nashville saw that clip."

"Attention is what you wanted, right?"

She worked her jaw, still stiff after three days. "Your father is hoping the DNA tests will clear his name."

"He's been selling the same story for as long as I can remember."

"He's been writing you. Have you read any of his letters?"

"Sure, I read them. But my dad was always good at telling stories. There were times when I think he really believed them. He's been telling the innocent story for so long, he believes it."

"You don't believe him?"

"I did when I was nine. I wanted to believe it was a mistake. I also wanted to believe that he'd sober up and treat my mom right. But he never did either."

"You know he's sick."

"That's what he said in his last letter."

"He wants to see you."

Kirk shoved out a breath as he dropped his gaze to the grime under his fingernails. "I don't want to see him."

"I know your life wasn't easy after he left."

"You make it sound like he went on a business trip." Resentment dripped from the words.

"He feels terrible."

"Well, then that's all that matters. Look, if you want to chase a pipe dream and try to prove his innocence, have at it. But don't pull me into your world. I don't want none of it."

"I'm not here to mend fences or to fix your relationship with your father. I'm getting background information on Jeb and Annie."

Kirk shook his head. "Dad liked Annie. He said it often enough. And it upset my mother. They argued about it all the time toward the end."

"Do you remember any details that might help me figure out what happened?"

"My dad wanted Annie for himself and when she wouldn't run off with him he killed her."

"He told you that?"

"My mother told me that. And she still believes that."

"Where is your mother?"

"Old folks home. Her mind is all but gone. On a good day she remembers my name but there aren't many good days anymore."

"She was at the trial. She supported your father. And when the police first spoke to her she gave him an alibi."

"My mother loved my father and she'd have sacrificed her life for him no matter what he did to her. It took years before she realized he was no good."

"Did she ever speak about Annie?"

"The mention of Annie made her cry." He planted his hands on his hips and hesitated before saying, "I went to see Annie once. I took two buses so that I could get to the bar where she sang. I snuck in the back and hid long enough to see her on stage and to hear her sing. She was good. Great. She had all the looks and talent that my mother didn't."

"If your father loved her why would he kill her?"

"He hated the idea that she'd married. Hated it. I know he was biding time until the baby was born."

"What was he looking for?"

"He wanted her to run away with him." The man shook his head, a bitter smile twisting the edge of his lips. "He wasn't smart enough to realize that women like her didn't settle for men like him. And when he did figure it out, he killed her."

"He has a right to the DNA test."

"Sure, test all you want. But he'll disappoint you in the long run like he disappointed everyone in his life."

She half hoped to hear more words of encouragement from her brother. *Tell me I'm right. Remind me why I fight.* But he remained mutinously silent. In this, she was alone.

She dug an envelope from her purse. "He asked me to give this to you."

He eyed the envelope in her outstretched hand. "What is it?"

"A letter from your father. He wanted you to read it."

Kirk hesitated, took the envelope and shoved it in his back pocket. "That it?"

"You aren't going to read it?"

"No doubt it reads like all the other letters he's sent to me. I'm not interested in his sob story."

"He's not perfect, but he's not evil."

Dark eyes flashed. "Why are you doing this?"

"Delivering the letter?"

"Defending him."

She considered avoiding the subject but opted for a rare option for her: candid honesty. "My brother was convicted of murder. I thought he was innocent, and I did my best to get him out of jail. He died in prison before I could free him."

Kirk's head tilted and she sensed he was reassessing her. "So you think you can save men like your brother?"

"Yes."

He shook his head. "I didn't know your brother, but I knew my father. He's not a man worth saving."

"I don't agree."

"Then you are in a battle all by yourself."

Her gaze landed on a two-year-old calendar featuring a bikini-clad woman on a motorcycle. The woman looked fresh-faced and happy. What did that kind of happy feel like? "Tell me what I don't know."


KC took his regular seat at the bar and a sigh eased from his body as he scooped a handful of nuts. For thirty-two years he'd been coming here, enjoying a beer or two and sorting his thoughts about the job before going home. Rudy's allowed him to transition from the job to home.

Hard to believe that soon he'd not need the transition. The job would be gone and there would only be home. Jesus. As much as he'd bitched about the job over the years he really didn't know what the hell he'd do without it.

A cold beer settled in front of him and KC glanced up at Rudy. "Thanks."

"Countdown is coming. Two days or three."

"Two. Fast and furious."

Rudy had listened to KC a lot over the last three and a half decades. He listened when KC had a case that would not let him go. He listened when he was hyped about an arrest. And lately he'd listened as KC hinted at the worries nagging him about the future.

"So are they giving you a party?"

KC took a healthy gulp of beer. "I told them I didn't want one and then my gal Brenda said I had to go out in style. That's part of the reason I'm here."

"How's that?"

"She thought it might be fun to hold the party here."

Rudy wiped his hands on a white rag. "Why here?"

"It's not the office and it's not home. The bridge in between." KC took a gulp of beer. "Rudy's has been my home away from home over the years and it's a fitting place to end a career and start a new life."

Rudy sniffed. "Yeah sure, if you want to have a party here, go ahead. A weeknight is best. Not so crazed."

"That will work. How about Monday?"

"Sure."

KC sipped more beer and glanced up at the television playing behind Rudy. It was on mute but when the picture of Annie Rivers Dawson flashed he didn't need sound to know what was being said. He tipped his beer toward the screen. "Been following that story?"

Rudy glanced back and frowned. "Ain't that some shit."

A bitter taste soured the beer. "Thirty years since a righteous conviction and some attorney wants to unravel it all."

"She's making a name for herself. In a week people won't care about her request."

KC shook his head. "If the last thirty years have taught me anything, it's that any good case can be undone. Any case. The right attorney can knot up the truth and twist it in all sorts of ways."

Rudy took KC's mug and refilled it. "That was a bitch of a case. I remember you talking about it and the brutal hours you all worked. All you cops looked like the walking dead."

"Had us tied in knots. Shit. I had nightmares about that crime scene for years."

The lines in Rudy's face deepened with a frown. "I can't imagine."

"We were all afraid he'd get off. Without a body we knew a conviction would be tough."

"But you found her. Gave her a proper burial and sent the bad guy to jail."

KC raised his mug in salute. "Yeah. God bless, anonymous tipster."

Rudy glanced back at the television. "You think the DNA is gonna go against you?"

"Hell no. I don't."

"There was a cop here on Thursday. Deke Morgan."

"My partner."

"Looks a hell of a lot like his old man."

"Buddy could've spit him right out. But don't tell Deke unless you want to piss him off."

"He was asking about Dixie."

KC shook his head. "Hell of a murder."

Rudy filled a glass with water and took a long swallow. "Nice kid. Had her issues. But then who doesn't?"

"Kinda reminded me of Annie."

"Maybe."

KC gulped the beer and set the mug carefully on the bar. "Hey, I need another favor?"

Dark eyes grew darker. "What's that?"

"There's a gal in the office. She sings. I'd like her to sing at my party."

Rudy shook his head. "Hey man, I got a reputation to uphold. Only the best here."

"I know. But Georgia is top notch. Really. You won't be sorry. Even Brenda thinks she's great."

Rudy hesitated as if he'd never offered a fast *yes* in his entire life. "One song."

"Three."

A smile quipped the edges of his lips. "Two."

Rudy shrugged. "Deal. This Monday?"

"Sure."

"So what the hell are you gonna do with yourself after the Force."

As tempted as KC was to have another beer and cling onto his old life, he rose from the bar, refusing to second guess today. "Hell, if I know."

Deke parked in front of Rick's small one-level house and grabbed the cold six-pack of beer. He crossed the cracked sidewalk and up to the well-lit front stoop. He rang the bell. The baritone bark of the wolf dog reverberated through the house and the bay window's thick curtain flickered.

After the scrape of two dislodging chains, the door opened to Rick wearing a battered Vanderbilt T-shirt, jeans, and no shoes. His hair stuck up on end as if he dug his fingers through it a thousand times.

The dog appeared, big, black, and menacing as he stayed close to Rick's side. Rick gently rubbed the dog between the ears. "It's big brother, Tracker. We're safe for now."

Deke held up the six-pack. "You texted. Said you were digging through the case files."

Rick pushed open the door. "Come on in."

Deke held out his hand. Tracker sniffed until he was satisfied he posed no threat and then retreated to a large dog bed. Beside it, an electric space heater blew out warm air onto his thick fur. Tracker closed his eyes but his body clung to a tension signaling he remained on duty.

Deke glanced toward the old dining room table that had come from his family's house. When Buddy had died, Deke had offered any furnishings to his siblings. Rick had put dibs on the table that had hosted so many gatherings. Alex had taken a guest bedroom set and Georgia had taken all the family pictures. "Looks like you jumped right to it. How long have you been at this?"

"Since I got home."

"Nonstop."

He shrugged. "Love a puzzle."

Deke twisted off a beer top and handed it to Rick. "I always thought all the puzzle pieces had been put into place."

Rick grinned as he raised the bottle to his lips. "No such thing in life."

"True." Deke set the six-pack next to an open file box and grabbed himself a beer. A twist and the top opened. "So what pieces are bothering you?"

"I've only scanned the records at this point. Buddy was as meticulous then as he was the day he died." He reached in a box. "Found a picture of Buddy and KC. Amazing how much you look like our old man."

Deke took the thirty-year-old image of Buddy and KC standing by the 1971 gold Cutlass that had belonged to Jeb Jones. Buddy stared stone-faced directly into the camera while a mustached KC grinned. The caption read, *Annie Dawson's Body Found.*

"Annie Dawson's bones were found in the woods by a hunter who called it in."

"Scattered bones were found. Along with the necklace and blood remnants of soaked clothes identified as Annie's. The bones found were badly mauled by animals."

"Dental records?"

"No head found. Only arms and torso. Severed with a hacksaw."

Deke set the article aside and let his thumb click over the dusty, faded file tabs. "Any evidence found on the remains?"

"None. Not after months in unseasonably warm weather. And given what science they had available, they couldn't have done much with it."

Today if those bones had been found they'd have extracted DNA from the marrow and been able to positively identify her. "Anything else jump out at you?"

"You do know that Jeb recanted his confession."

"Ms. Wainwright pointed that out to me in one of her many phone messages. That doesn't mean much."

"No. But I'll keep digging."

Deke tipped the lip of the bottle to his mouth and took a liberal sip.

"Think that attorney is digging into the case?"

Deke imagined Rachel Wainwright tracking all the people connected with the case. If he'd been in her shoes, he'd have done the same. "I would not be surprised. Not at all."

"So what is her gig?"

"What do you mean?"

"What drives her? Most crusaders have some incident that set them on the path." Rick studied Deke. "And if I know you, you've asked around about her."

He'd asked when she'd first crossed his path. He knew about the family's endless moves, her brother's substance abuse and her devotion to family. "Maybe."

Rick laughed. "So?"

"Her brother was convicted of murder. She went to law school because of his conviction. Her hope was to get him a retrial. He was killed in prison."

Rick arched a brow. "That will do it."

Deke scraped his fingernail against the beer label. "Luke Wainwright had been partying with the victim. Both were using. Next morning, he's passed out at his mother's home and the victim is found strangled in a ditch. Long story short the victim was well-connected and Luke had a bad attorney. The DA went for second-degree murder. That shouldn't have held up in court but his attorney caved."

"So Rachel was right about her brother?"

"At least partly. I'm not convinced he killed the woman but he was a train wreck waiting to happen."

"She could be right about Jeb."

Tension slithered up his spine but he kept it from his voice. "We'll know soon."

Rick took a sip of beer. "Wainwright's hot."

Deke glanced up, his gaze sharp.

Rick laughed. "So you've noticed, too?"

"I noticed."

"After this is all over, maybe you two could hook up."

Deke shook his head. "I'm two for two as far as marriage and divorce go. No thanks."

His gaze danced with laughter. "Why not? You don't have to be alone forever. Maybe third time's the charm."

"Shit. I've more than proven I'm a lousy partner in romance."

"Doesn't have to be a forever."

"Rachel Wainwright takes life seriously. Relationships would be no different. And I don't do serious anymore."

*November 10*

*Sugar—*

*You are so cute when you are mad! I love the way
your lip curls up and the lines crease your forehead.
So sexy. So hot! Like I said last night, you don't have
to worry about those men hanging around. You are
my number one.*

*A.*

# Chapter Seven

The passage of thirty years made the task of authenticating the Annie letters difficult but not impossible for Lexis. To accomplish the job, she needed a sample of handwriting that was undeniably Annie's. She knew Annie had attended a small high school north of Nashville, but likely her records wouldn't contain a sample. Annie had worked an odd collection of jobs after graduating high school but the chances of an employment application still existing were nil. A signature on the lease she'd shared with Joanne and Beth or the marriage license wouldn't be enough.

Bill Dawson would be a hard case so she figured her best bet was Margaret Miller, Annie's devoted sister who must have saved letters or the handwritten songs Annie was rumored to have written.

Lexis parked in front of the little, one-story clapboard house. As a female private investigator, she had an advantage. Women could blend better. A maid's uniform allowed her to go unnoticed in a hotel. A white collar shirt, jeans, and a clipboard enabled her to pass as a meter reader, cable employee, and a car rental agent. Lexis had learned an outfit could sell her story better than words.

Out of the car, she hiked up the waistband of her designer jeans. She wore a *Nashville Rocks* T-Shirt and her best cowboy boots. The shirt was too small and the jeans too tight, a reminder she needed to cut back on the bagels and sodas. Still, despite the tight fit, she'd achieved the look she was after.

She moved up the cracked sidewalk to the front door adorned with a fall wreath decked with a yellow bow embossed with the words *Happy Birthday*. From what she'd learned, Margaret Miller had kept a yellow ribbon on her lawn for the last thirty years. Yellow had been Annie's favorite color and Margaret had dedicated her life to the memory of her sister.

Moistening lips heavy with lip gloss, she knocked on the door. Inside she could hear the television and then steady footsteps. The door on the other side of the screen opened to Margaret and the smell of fried chicken. She wore her white waitress outfit complete with name tag and hamburger and ketchup stains.

Margaret studied Lexis through the screened door. "What can I do for you?"

"Ms. Margaret Miller?"

"That's right."

"I'm with Lane Producers. Sorry for the late night visit but my flight just arrived from LA."

Margaret folded her arms. "Why are you here?"

"We do documentaries on country music stars of the past. Your sister Annie Rivers Dawson's short-lived career came to our attention the other night when my boss was watching the news."

Margaret's gaze narrowed. "Everyone saw that. I've been hearing about it day and night since."

"I saw the show of you and Ms. Wainwright."

Margaret frowned. "It wasn't a show for me. I was damned mad at her."

Lexis had guessed Margaret would be sensitive on the subject and knew she had to handle this with extra-soft kid gloves. "I could see you were upset. Must be painful."

Margaret twisted a brass button on her sweater. "You've no idea."

"Maybe I do. I lost my sister." Bits of the truth enhanced credibility as the right outfit did. "It's been fifteen years, but there're days when it feels like yesterday."

Margaret's chin raised a fraction. "Yeah. It hurts. Especially when all you had were bones to bury. But no one cares about that."

"I care. In fact, I did a little digging on your sister's short-lived career and I must say I was impressed. She was a star on the rise."

The hard lines burrowing into Margaret's forehead softened a fraction. "That she was. Ask anyone and they'd tell you she was an angel."

"No doubt."

"Why are you here?"

"We, the other producers and I, were talking about Annie over coffee last night. We were all thinking she could be the subject of a documentary. She was talented, beautiful and now she's gone."

Her eyes widened with delight. "You want to make a movie about Annie?"

"This is all preliminary, but I thought it would be worth it to talk to you."

"What do you want to know about Annie?"

"I want to know about her as a woman. Her hopes and dreams. What she loved about music and singing. You knew her better than anyone."

"That's true." Margaret frowned. "This ain't gonna be one of those tell-alls, is it? I don't want you bashing Annie."

"I'd never dream of bashing her. I want to tell her story."

Margaret hesitated and then pushed open the screened door. "Come on in. I got mementos I can show you." Inside, the sweet scents of a baking cake greeted her. "Can I get you a lemonade? I was about to have one."

"I'd love one."

The hallway sported dozens of framed pictures featuring two young girls and their parents. Beyond the living room furnishings were older, threadbare on the arms, and looked as if they'd been purchased in the seventies. The carpet was gold shag and the chair rail trim on the walls an avocado green.

Margaret appeared with two glasses of glistening lemonade. "I'd offer you cake but it isn't cool yet. Today's my momma's birthday and I always bake her a cake."

"How old is your mom?"

"She'd have been eighty-two. She passed this time last year. She left me her house. I've lived here my whole life."

Lexis sat with Margaret on the couch, accepted the lemonade, sipped, and smiled when the cold bitter wetness hit her tongue. "Are those pictures of you and Annie?"

Margaret beamed. "They are. That one is of Annie and me. She was nine and I was three."

Lexis studied the picture of two little girls dressed in matching sailor suits. Annie's blond hair shimmered in contrast to Margaret's dull brown hair and whereas Annie's smile was radiant, Margaret's was goofy and awkward. Annie's arm was wrapped around Margaret's shoulders but it wasn't a casual easy touch. Annie looked a bit stiff and strained as if she wasn't crazy about her little sister.

"She was good to me," Margaret said. "So sweet. She was always thinking about me."

"You two grew up in this house?"

"Yes. We had the same momma but different daddies. That's why we look different."

Lexis didn't miss the threads of apology and shame. "I think you look a great deal alike. Especially around the eyes."

"Really? You think so?"

"I do." Lexis shifted her gaze to another picture. Again two girls. Annie had bloomed into a stunning young woman whereas Margaret still sported that goofy grin as well as thick glasses. "Must have been hard when she moved out to live on her own."

"I cried for days. But she kept promising that she'd come back and see me and I could come see her. We were less than thirty miles apart but it felt like a million miles."

"I heard she did well in Nashville."

"She did. She started singing in a local church but quickly found work in the honky-tonks. She sang and looked like an angel."

"I also heard she was a songwriter."

Pride had Margaret standing straighter. "She was. I kept all her songs in a scrapbook."

"Could I see them?"

"Sure!" She set down her lemonade and hurried to the back of the house. Seconds later she emerged with a large and well-stuffed yellow scrapbook. Margaret indicated they sit on a couch of shabby crushed velvet.

Margaret laid her hands on top of the book, drawing in a deep breath as if she were touching a Ouija board and summoning Annie's spirit. "I can imagine her sitting right here when I read her songs."

Lexis peered over Margaret's arm as she opened the book. The pages were jammed with publicity shots, handbills for gig nights, and bits of ribbon and flattened flowers. Margaret had a story about every picture as she turned each page. In Margaret's stories, Annie played the role of angel and heroine. However, the letters sent to Rachel painted a woman who wasn't afraid to get involved with an unavailable man.

In the center was a stack of handwritten songs written on napkins, scraps of paper, and a diner menu.

Lexis studied the samples and knew if she had one she could authenticate the letters.

"When did she start dating Bill Dawson?"

Margaret frowned. "They didn't date long. Fact, Momma and I were surprised when she called saying she'd gotten married. Right out of the blue. We were stunned. But he was a nice enough fellow and Momma wanted her to have security. Being a singer is a tough life, even if you got talent."

"A pretty woman like Annie would have dated more than one man."

Margaret giggled. "The boys loved Annie. Loved her."

"She never confided in you?"

"Not about boys she dated. I asked, of course, but she said I was too young. When I pushed she did say she had a special Sugar she liked."

"Sugar?" Lexis slowly turned a scrapbook page as if the name had no meaning.

"She blushed when she spoke about him but she never did tell me his name. Even wrote a song about him. She said one day I would meet him."

"That must have been Bill Dawson," Lexis suggested.

"Must have been." She frowned. "But I never could picture the two of them together. He was stiff. But she said she loved him. Momma and I didn't get invited to the wedding. Of course, when Momma and I finally saw her after the wedding, Momma guessed right off about the baby."

"Was Annie excited about the baby?"

Margaret's face glowed with appreciation. "She was. Said she'd find a way to be a big star and a great momma."

"What was Bill Dawson like? You said he was stiff."

"Nice enough. Kept saying she didn't need to sing no more because he was gonna make them rich. I could tell he loved her more than she loved him. But that was the way it always was. Boys was always falling for Annie and she kept moving along like none of them mattered."

Lexis thought about the letters. She'd read the first few and based on them alone Annie had loved one man.

The phone rang and Margaret frowned.

"Feel free to get that. I'll sit here and look at the book if that's all right?"

Margaret hesitated. "Sure. It's the best way to get to know Annie."

Margaret vanished around the corner to a kitchen phone mounted on the wall.

Lexis turned the pages of the book searching for a loose scrap of paper with Annie's handwriting on it. She soothed her guilt with the promise that she'd return the sample as soon as she'd authenticated the letters. In her mind she was doing Margaret a favor. If Rachel was fighting for Jeb there was a good chance he was innocent and the real killer remained free.

She turned the scrapbook page to find a crumpled sheet of notebook paper filled with lyrics written in thick dark ink that reminded her of the letters. She carefully tugged the paper free, cringing when it crinkled and then tucked the sheet of paper in her purse.

From the kitchen Margaret's voice was low and nervous. Carefully Lexis turned the page hoping for a picture with Annie and her Sugar. There were plenty more pictures but most were of Annie on stage. Margaret's voice grew more animated. The receiver slammed into a cradle.

Margaret came around the corner, flushed face and angry. Lexis cocked a brow. "Everything okay?"

"No, it is not."

Lexis kept her hand steady, already wondering how she'd explain the stolen song notes if Margaret pressed. "What is it?"

A deepening frown added to her plainness. "That reporter. She wants to talk to me again."

"Is that bad?"

"We met the other day and she told me she'd not cover the story until the DNA came back. Now she wants me to guess who might have killed Annie, if it wasn't Jeb." She curled fingers into fists. "It was Jeb. I know it was."

"Did you ever see Annie and Jeb together?"

"I saw him once. It was the time I went to see her at her apartment, before the baby and before her marriage. He was there cutting the grass but he had a creepy way of staring at her. Made my skin crawl."

"Did you ask Annie about him?"

"I did. And she said not to worry, that he was harmless." Margaret's lips flattened. "She was the sweetest girl in the world and it was her sweetness that got her killed. She didn't see his evil, but I saw it then and I saw it at the trial. He killed her."

Time had erased all Annie's faults and magnified all Jeb's sins. "Why?"

"He wanted her. Plain and simple."

"Were there other men that gave her the creeps?"

"I heard her telling Momma that the bars were full of sloppy drunks. She longed for the day when she could sing on a big stage."

Lexis turned a brittle scrapbook page to a picture of a very pregnant Annie who gently cradled her belly. "Whatever happened to Annie's baby?"

"You'd have to ask her husband. He never would tell Momma or me. We begged him over and over to tell us. Momma was willing to raise the baby as her own. But he wouldn't tell. Said it was none of our business. Momma was fixing to sue but then she had her stroke. She had to go to the home and I was too young. No judge would have given me that baby."

"I'm sorry."

Margaret slid the scrapbook back to her lap, smoothing her hand over it as if she'd done it a thousand times to calm frayed nerves. "If you don't mind would you see yourself to the door? I'm getting one of my headaches."

"Can I get you an aspirin or a water?"

She closed her eyes, smoothing her hands over the pink fabric covering. "No. Just leave. I do appreciate you coming." Her voice had an otherworldly quality that sounded broken. "We'll talk soon."

"Okay."

Slowly Lexis rose, feeling sorry for the woman. Annie's death may have destroyed Jeb's life but it had also destroyed Margaret's as well.


Margaret moved to the window and watched the music film lady drive off. She glanced at her business card as she turned from the window. Despite the headache she was buoyed by the thought about somebody making a movie out of Annie's life. "Sure would be special, Momma, if they made a movie."

A movie made sense. Annie had been a star ready to take the world by storm. No telling where she'd be now if she'd lived. No telling. But safe to say she'd have been rich and living in a fancy house right here in Nashville. And she'd have taken care of her baby sister. No doubt about that.

Margaret moved back into the living room and sat on the sofa. Too bad Momma hadn't lived to see this day. Too bad. She sipped her lemonade, squinting at the bitter sweetness. She opened the scrapbook she'd made of Annie and slowly turned the pages. The first image was of Annie and Margaret. They were both smiling for the picture but Margaret remembered enough to know they'd not been happy. Nine-year-old Annie had not wanted to wear an outfit that matched her three-year-old sister's. She'd wanted to look older, like a grown-up girl she'd seen in a magazine.

But Momma had ruled the house then with an iron fist. She'd ignored Annie's carrying on and crying during the whole drive from their home to the photographer's studio. When they all pulled up, Momma had looked in the rearview mirror and threatened to beat Annie within an inch of her life if she didn't smile like a damn angel. In the backseat, Margaret had grinned. As much as she loved and wanted to be Annie, she couldn't help but enjoy it when she suffered.

And so Annie, who'd tasted Momma's anger once too often, had stopped her wailing and had smiled. She'd charmed the photographer who had all but ignored Margaret.

Every moment Annie had been alive, she'd cast a long shadow that had trapped Margaret.

Margaret set her glass down and glanced at her palms, slick with the condensation from her lemonade glass. Carefully she closed her eyes and felt the droplets against her skin, remembering the feel of Annie's blood on her hands.

"Momma, you'd think after thirty years I'd forget, but I can't," she whispered.

On that long ago day, Annie's blood had wiped away all her thoughts. It had mesmerized her. Taunted her. She'd never told her mother how Annie's blood had pooled on the floor and splashed the walls. Never told.

At first she'd been shocked and broken and then she'd found herself thrust into the limelight. Annie's death had turned Margaret into the story's heroine. Poor girl, she discovered her sister's bloodied house and found her infant niece howling. Bless her heart.

For a time, Margaret had been center stage. She'd been the one reporters had hounded and clamored to see. She'd been the star. For a time.

And then time distanced the world from the murder leaving Annie and Margaret forgotten.

She dried her hands on her skirt and turned the page of the scrapbook, smiling, imagining the warmth of the limelight that would beam on her soon. This time around, she'd see that no one forgot her. No one.


Deke parked on the corner, shut off the engine and sat in his car taking in the area where Dixie had been killed three nights ago. The yellow crime-scene tape strung by the techs was now gone. He'd wanted to secure the scene longer, but budget and manpower wouldn't allow it.

Out of the car, he loosened his tie as he moved up the side street toward the stained stretch of sidewalk. Keys jangling in his hands, he studied the area trying to imagine the killer's approach. Tall shrubs to the right could easily have hidden someone and in the dark the area would have been bathed in shadows. Crime in this area was low and there'd been no reported problems suggesting a predator stalked the area.

He moved up the sidewalk stopping short of the exact murder spot and squatted. Clean-up crews had removed most of the debris, but fading dark stains hinted to the blood that had stained the concrete.

The blood had drawn him back to the scene. There'd been so much. The splatter would have sprayed the killer and his clothes. In daylight, he'd not have gone far unnoticed but the darkness would have given him enough time to get away.

The blood. Dixie's mangled face.

Both would join the ghosts of the other atrocities he'd seen on the job and haunt him for the rest of his life.

The blood.

It characterized Dixie's death but also Annie Rivers Dawson's as well. The dominant image in Dawson's crime scene photos had been the blood painting the floor and walls.

There were similarities between Dixie and Annie. Both singers. Blond. Beautiful. It was conceivable that the same person could have killed them but a search of the last thirty years had revealed no other crimes that fit this precise victim profile.

A killer could lay dormant for thirty years. It had happened before. But what would have been the trigger this time? Rachel had been publicizing her vigil for a good week. Had her flyer triggered the killer? Or had the killer never heard of Annie and simply been angry or jealous? The latter was the likely scenario.

Headlights shone behind Deke's vehicle. He rose and turned in time to see a female officer get out of an SUV and open the back door to her vehicle. She unclipped a leash from her waist and reached in and clicked it onto the collar of a hound dog.

A cap covered the officer's blond hair twisted and pinned into a tight bun. She stood about five eight, had a trim, lean body and moved with confidence as her hound dropped his nose to the ground and sniffed. Fresh-faced, her clear green eyes surveyed the scene before meeting Deke's gaze. "Detective Morgan?"

Deke extended his hand. "Officer Phillips?"

"Yes, sir. And this is my canine Bo. I hear from your brother you'd like us to follow a trail?"

Police canines were a specialized unit. Whereas Rick's dog had been trained in protection and apprehension techniques, others were trained to sniff drugs, explosives, or cadavers. Rick had told Deke to call Jessica Phillips. She and her dog Bo were two of the best trackers in central Tennessee.

"That's right. A blood trail."

"Do you know where the trail begins?"

"Ten feet down the sidewalk. Rain the night of the murder washed almost all of it away."

"Let's give it a try." She rubbed Bo on the head and then guided him to the spot. Bo instantly dropped his nose to the ground and began sniffing. Seconds passed as Bo sniffed the entire area and then cut right toward the woods.

Officer Phillips followed and soon the two threaded into the stand of trees toward the park. Deke waited until they were several feet ahead before he followed. He stepped over brush, cursed briars grabbing his clothing as Phillips and her hound moved as if they'd been born to hike the woods.

They punched through the thicket to the edges of the park close to a parking lot. Bo sniffed up to the curb of the parking lot, stopped his advance and barked.

As Deke moved closer, Officer Phillips commanded Bo to heel and from a side pants pocket pulled a treat. She fed it to Bo and praised him. "Whatever blood trail started on the other side of the woods, ends here."

Deke surveyed the area. "Easy enough to park a car here and wait behind the trees."

Officer Phillips searched the woods. "Killing doesn't seem random, does it?"

He imagined the killer parking here, cutting through the strip of brush and waiting for Dixie. After killing her, it would be easy enough to retrace steps and leave without being noticed. "No, it does not."


It was ten o'clock when Rachel finally found the time to put aside her work and go for a run. Lexis had said she might come by but Rachel had been too antsy to wait. She'd left a note on her front door and headed out.

Outside, the night was cool, but not so cold as to inhibit the itch to move and sweat. Long hours behind the desk were part of a lawyer's life and though her mind accepted the sacrifice, her body did not.

She stretched her muscles and then satisfied they were warm enough, she began a light jog. It didn't take long before she'd picked up her pace and now raced through the night. A sense of freedom washed over her.

She ran most days, going as far as ten miles. The exertion kept her muscles loose and her stress low.

*What are you running from?* Her brother's tone had been light, joking, when he'd first asked the question years ago. She'd been surprised by it. Years had passed since that exchange and she still didn't have an answer for Luke.

As she approached her building, she slowed her pace, letting the strain of her muscles ease. Sweat dripped from her forehead as she slowed to a walk, her hands on her hips. Her breathing still fast and her heart beating hard, she glanced up at the quarter moon savoring its crisp angles.

She reached in the pocket tucked inside her running pants and fished out her front door key and cell phone. As she approached the door she noticed the note she'd left for Lexis was gone. Deciding to call Lexis ASAP, she unlocked the door.

*Be careful, Rachel!*

Unease rippled up her spine as she quickly glanced from side to side as if expecting to see someone there. Had

Colleen returned to tell Rachel about yet another date that had gone wrong? When she saw no one, she jiggled the door handle. Locked. Again, she had the sense of dread. She turned and gripped the key between her fingers ready to jab. "Who's there?"

No reply. Her heart beat loudly, drowning out the distant sound of cars on the street. The fear did not ease but logic took over and ticked off reasons why she was overreacting. Tired. Worried. Hungry.

Shrugging aside her qualms, she unlocked the door, opened it and disarmed her alarm. A heavy silence greeted her as she glanced inside her darkened house. Again nothing. And still fear outmaneuvered logic.

Rachel opened her cell. Just in case.

She flipped on the lights and found her office in disarray . . . as she'd left it. Every item was as it should be.

*Jesus, Rachel, be careful. Think before you act.*

As she turned to glance back toward the open door, she heard the *swoosh* of a thin object slicing through the air. She pivoted seconds before a stinging pain ripped through her shoulder.

Rachel screamed and backed into her office, trying to get a look at her attacker as she braced for a second blow. She fumbled with her phone and hit the 911 buttons as a figure wearing a mask and loose-fitting clothes moved from the shadows. A low-hanging hoodie obscured all facial features, but there was no missing the gloved hand gripping what looked like a tire iron.

Rachel hollered so loud her vocal cords strained to the point of snapping. From her cell she heard the 911 operator say, "What's your emergency?"

"Get the hell away from me!" She cradled the phone to her ear. "Rachel Wainwright. I'm on First Street. I'm being attacked!" She screamed louder and backed up until she bumped into her desk. Her heart raced. Pain bolted through her body. She could barely process clear thoughts as a primal need to survive kicked up her adrenaline.

The attacker hesitated and then lunged wielding a long metal rod. She dodged, grabbed blindly at a bookshelf, snatched a book and tossed it at the attacker. The book hit the rod, deflecting the next blow.

Pain in her shoulder throbbed and her vision blurred. "Help!!! I'm at . . ." She rattled off her address again.

The attacker stopped, breathing hard, and gripping the rod in a black-gloved hand. And then without warning, turned, and ran.

Rachel held her breath, her fingers of her left hand balled into a fist as her other hand gripped her phone. She stood, weak-kneed, heart pounding as she collected her thoughts. As the seconds ticked in silence, the shock ebbed and the pain rolled over her in full force. It robbed her breath away and nearly buckled her knees.

In the distance, she heard sirens. "Lady, are you okay?" a woman shouted.

Gentle hands reached out to Rachel but she screamed and struck back. "Get away!"

"Lady, it's okay," the woman said. "The cops are on the way."

Rachel hugged her injured arm and lowered herself to the floor as pain sliced her.

*November 16*

*Sugar,*
  *Saw you in the back of the bar while I was singing*
*tonight. I miss you.*

                    *A.*

# Chapter Eight

*Saturday, October 15, 11 PM*

Deke Morgan arrived at the hospital emergency room, minutes past eleven to the sound of stretchers rattling, machines beeping, and conversations humming. Fluorescent lights highlighted a pallid uneasy feel that agitated his nerves with memories of the night Rick had been shot. He moved to the nurses' station where a young woman with long dark hair swept into a ponytail frowned over a chart. She glanced up, her gaze sharp and direct. "Can I help you?"

He pushed back his coat so that she could see his badge. "I'm looking for Rachel Wainwright."

She glanced at her computer and punched buttons. "Room six."

He let the coat drop over his badge. "Can you tell me how she's doing?"

"She's back from X-ray and we're waiting on the results. You can go see her if you like."

"Thanks. I'll do that." He found his way to the curtained door. On the other side he heard a woman's irritated voice cursing. He knocked on the door frame and pushed through to find Rachel standing by the bed, dressed in a hospital gown. She leaned heavily on the bed as she stared at an overhead television screen featuring Margaret Miller.

*The real killer has been caught. Rachel Wainwright is perverting justice. Lord, it's my momma's birthday and that attorney is tearing into old wounds that never healed.*

The camera angled back to the reporter, Susan Martinez. Rachel cut her off midsentence with the click of a remote.

Her muscles contracted as if guarding against any movement that would trigger pain. In the full billowy gown, she looked small and petite. Her left arm was in a sling and already he could see black-and-blue marks marring the pale skin of her shoulder. And with no makeup, Margaret Miller's bruise shadowed her jawline.

Vulnerable came to mind. Afraid. Despite his best efforts, his pity flickered.

A glance at him and her eyes darkened with embarrassment, anger, and frustration. She straightened but the move cost her some pain. "Detective."

He lingered by the door saddened to see her so rattled. He'd gotten the call forty-five minutes ago from the dispatcher who had reported her 911 call. She'd barely been conscious, her back pressed to a wall, the phone gripped in her hand. Several onlookers had gathered around her house but there'd been no sign of the attacker. "Not one of your better nights."

She clutched the folds of her gown. "I've had better."

He admired the spunk. "From what the responding officer said, three inches to the right and the attacker would have struck you in the head. Do you know who hit you?"

She shook her head, lifting her chin a fraction. "No. I saw loose dark jeans and a mask and hoodie covering his head. But I didn't see a face."

"Did he speak to you? Maybe the sound of his voice."

"No. He didn't. He came out of nowhere and struck. I

twisted out of the way, for the most part, at the last second. And then I started screaming like a madwoman."

"That's likely what saved your life. Too many victims don't stand up to their attacker and die without uttering a sound."

She pushed fingers that trembled slightly through her short hair. "Half of Nashville heard me."

"That's what the witnesses said. They heard you scream and several called nine-one-one."

She nodded as if the weight of what happened settled deeper onto her shoulders. "I was lucky."

"Have you received any menacing letters, emails or texts? Has anyone threatened you?"

She pressed her fingertips to her forehead. "Yeah, there have been emails. There are several that don't appreciate what I'm doing. And the news station received angry responses to the piece aired about the vigil."

"Who told you that?"

"Susan Martinez. I saw her yesterday." She snorted. "She told me she'd not cover this case again until the DNA came back. That was a load of BS."

"What about Margaret Miller? Looks like she's still pretty angry with you. Could she have done this?"

She glanced toward the dark television screen. "I don't know. The woman lost her sister. She's clearly still hurting. My intent is not to hurt her. I just want the DNA test."

He eased into the room still careful to give her space. "Old wounds can generate a lot of hate."

"Jeb deserves to have that test run. Which by the way, I've not seen results on yet." Fire sparked in her eyes.

Good. He didn't like seeing fear reflecting back. "I checked with the state lab. They haven't finished the testing yet."

She latched onto this bit of normalcy with a drowning woman's zeal. "When do you think they will be finished?"

"A week. Give or take. They've a hell of a backlog."

"Jeb's case should be moved to the front of the line. He's been asking for this test for a decade."

Her irritated bark drew him closer. "If he'd had you in his corner ten years ago then he would have gotten his results."

"That a compliment?"

"Let's say I know a pit bull when I see one."

She wiggled the finger of the hand in the sling. She winced. "I'm not feeling much like a pit bull now."

"You put on a good show."

A smile tugged the edges of her mouth. "That's good to know." A silence settled between them before she dropped her gaze to her phone's keypad. "I better try Colleen again. They won't let me out of here without an escort."

"Have you heard about the X-rays?"

"Not yet. But I don't want to wait anymore. I hate hospitals."

"I'll find the doc."

"That's not necessary."

Her thready voice suggested mustering energy bordered on Herculean. Shit. One thing to go head-to-head with a pit bull, but it was another to kick a dog when it was down. No need to let her struggle. He had enough pit bull for them both right now. "Be right back. Do not move."

"Look, you don't need to—"

Her protests were swallowed up by the sounds of the hospital. It didn't take him long to find the doctor and insist that he be informed of Rachel's results. Fifteen minutes later Deke and the doctor returned to discover Rachel had wrangled on her jogging pants up under her gown and slipped on her running shoes. Her shoelaces dangled free and the tight jogging top lay on the unmade gurney, clearly discarded in frustration, leaving her stuck with the billowing mint green gown as a top. He pictured her walking out of the hospital half dressed, her head held high.

"You're leaving like that?" Deke asked.

She gathered the gown and balled it at her waist so that her pants showed. "If I have to."

Admiring her, or liking her, was not supposed to be in the cards. He chalked up this unexpected tenderness to fatigue. "Before Ms. Wainwright heads out of here half dressed, Doc, can you tell us about her injuries?"

The doctor, slim, young, and tired, peered through thick glasses at the report. "Ms. Wainwright did not sustain any fractures or breaks. And there is no damage to the shoulder, which had been my initial worry. There is deep bruising and she's going to be sore for days but with rest and lots of ice packs she'll be fine." He pulled a pen from his pocket and clicked the end. "I'll write you a prescription for a painkiller."

"I don't need drugs," she said. "I'll make do with aspirin."

The doctor eyed her. "We gave you a mild sedative before your X-ray and that's deadening some of the pain. It will wear off soon."

"I have aspirin at home."

Deke nailed his gaze on Rachel. "Write the script, Doc. And ask the hospital pharmacy to fill it."

Rachel glanced at her jogging top as if considering how she'd get it over her wounded shoulder. "I don't do drugs. I'm fine."

When the doctor hesitated, Deke glared. "Get the meds."

The doctor pulled the script pad from his coat pocket. "I'll be right back with them."

She tossed the jogging top aside again and this time sat in a chair. She leaned forward to tie her shoes but pain halted her halfway.

"You're stubborn," he said.

"Tell me what I don't know."

He tapped his belt with his forefinger. "Did you try Colleen again?"

"Yes." She glared at her phone as if willing it to ring. "She's not picking up. Likely on a date."

He knelt in front of her and grabbed the laces. With a hard jerk he tied and double knotted the first shoe. "She'll ignore a call from her partner?"

Rachel shrugged and winced. "Especially from her partner who calls her far too often late at night with work-related issues."

He tied and double knotted the second shoe. "Anyone else you can call?"

She clutched her phone tighter. "No worries, Detective. I'll catch a cab."

Translation: she had no one to call. "I'll drive you home."

She shook her head as if this indignity was the straw that broke the camel's back. "Not necessary. Really. Not necessary."

"But it's what's going to happen." He rose and unfastened his button-down shirt.

"What are you doing, Detective?"

"Giving you the shirt off my back, Ms. Wainwright. I'm wearing a T-shirt underneath so you are safe."

That made her laugh. "That's a relief."

He shrugged off the shirt and held it open for her. "Turn around and I'll help you put it on."

She stood slowly and let the gown fall to the floor. The sight of the darkening bruise slashing across her back stoked his temper. Shit. She'd taken a hell of a hit.

Rachel slipped her good arm into the sleeve and he draped the other side over her other shoulder.

She fumbled with the shirt's buttons. "I won't be getting any dates in this getup."

He'd never thought about her in the context of a love life but now found himself curious about the kind of man she dated. Whoever the poor bastard was he'd have to be one tough customer. When she turned he brushed her hands away and buttoned the shirt. As his knuckles grazed the shirt the muscles in her body tensed. She smelled of clean air and the faintest scent of basic, practical soap.

At that moment a nurse arrived with a wheelchair. She glanced at Rachel's attire and nodded. "That will work."

Rachel moved slowly toward the wheelchair as the nurse pushed it toward her. Gently, she lowered into the seat, flinching when her shoulder bumped the edge slightly.

The nurse, a tall fit woman with dark brown hair, held up the bottle of pain meds as she leveled her gaze on Deke. "I know you."

He looked at the nurse and flipped through his memory. For a moment her name escaped him and then he remembered. "Brenda."

"That's right. We met a month ago."

"Right." She dated his partner KC. He only knew about her what KC had shared. She seemed to be good for the guy so he took her on face value.

Brenda smiled. "I guess we'll see you on Monday at his retirement party."

"Right. Wouldn't miss it."

Brenda held up the bottle of pills. "Ms. Wainwright should have one of these, with food, as soon as she gets home."

"I don't do drugs. I don't want to be loopy," Rachel focused on the woman's name tag. "Nurse Tilden."

Brenda smiled as if a naïve child had spoken. "Oh, you sure will want to be loopy when that shoulder starts hurting. Take the meds."

Deke took the pills and pocketed them. "She'll take her pills."

Brenda raised her eyebrow. "And you are her husband, boyfriend?"

"Doing my job."

"Good enough." Brenda patted Rachel on her good

shoulder. "Take your meds and the night will go better and you'll heal faster."

Rachel fingered a button on the shirt. "Right."

Deke stepped aside. "Lead the way."

The nurse pushed Rachel through the double doors and out next to the curb as Deke followed. Outside, she moved in front of them. "Hold while I get my car."

"I can take a cab," Rachel protested.

"Shut up."

"Don't tell me to shut up." She collapsed back in the chair.

Without a backward glance, he moved through the lot toward his car wondering why he was bothering.


Rachel watched Deke Morgan stride across the parking lot, his shoulders back and his gait purposeful. He reminded her of so many cops she'd met over the years. Self-assured and confident. There might have been a time when she'd have believed or followed that confidence but no more. She knew better than anyone that cops weren't right all the time and the ego that allowed them to charge into darkened alleys after a criminal was the same ego that blinded them when they were wrong.

A self-assured cop had arrested her brother. No amount of talking or reasoning would sway his mind. He'd been sure.

As Deke pulled up in front of the circle in an SUV, he moved around the side of the car opening the passenger door. Without asking, he reached for her good arm to steady her as she rose. His touch was as gentle as it was un-yielding. As much as she wanted to deny his help, she needed it. Rachel had her share of quirks, but above it all she was practical.

She'd allowed him to guide her to the car and hover as she eased into the car. He pulled the seat belt out and leaned over her as he clicked it in place. The faint scent of soap and leather wafted around her as he moved with clinical precision away from her and closed her door. Seconds later, he slid behind the wheel and they were driving away from the hospital.

She released a sigh as they drove off. "I do not like hospitals."

He relaxed back in his seat, his hands resting easily on the steering wheel. "Can't say they are a favorite of mine."

She resisted the urge to tip her head back against the seat and close her eyes. In the cocoon of his car she felt safe, protected, a feeling that came rarely. The effects of the meds had softened her mind, lowered her guard and she heard herself saying, "My mom died three years ago and I was on the cancer ward more often than not. Never got over the smell of the place or the glow of those damn lights."

He sat in the dark, his face in shadows, his hand resting on the steering wheel.

"She'd said over and over she didn't mind dying. She minded leaving me."

He tightened his grip on the steering wheel. "Where do you want me to take you?"

"Home. There's no other place."

He frowned. "What about Colleen's place?"

"No."

"Whoever hit you knows where you live."

She watched as the lights of the city rushed past her. "They didn't get far. And I have good security. I'll set my alarm, lock all my doors."

Irritation darkened his expression. "You should be worried they'll return."

Her eyes closed halfway. "You are trying to scare me."

"Stating the facts."

A ripple of fear passed through her. If she'd had the choice perhaps she'd have stayed somewhere else tonight.

But there was nowhere else. She was on her own. "I'll be fine," she said with more emphasis.

He took the exit and wound through the city streets until they'd reached the warehouse district. As he slowed and they grew closer to her place, panic elbowed its way past the calm. She sat a little straighter, grimacing when pain shot through her shoulder.

Deke parked on the street in front of her building. The momentary calm evaporated. When the cops had come, they'd done a complete search and locked the place up. She glanced toward the spot where a stranger had lunged from nowhere and hit with such force her entire body felt as if it would fracture.

"How about I get you inside?" he asked.

"I'd like to play this tough but I'm scared. Stupid. But, there it is."

"It's not stupid. It's smart. Stay put while I come around." He was out and around the car in seconds. He opened her door and extended his hand to her.

When a family friend had offered her brother a job when they'd first moved to Nashville, he'd refused because he'd been hungover and irritated. But Rachel had doubled back and accepted for him. When her mom had been sick and the church offered to bring meals, she'd pushed pride aside and accepted. She knew when to cut her losses.

She took his hand and gave him a good bit of her weight as he eased her out of the car and helped her to the locked front door where she held up her jogging top. "The officer said he put the key in a pocket."

He fished through the fabric and dug out the key. Opening the door, the alarm started to beep. "Code?"

"1995. The number of days my brother spent in prison."

Without comment, he punched in the number and the *beep-beep* silenced. She flipped on the main light, which flickered on. Her office looked as she left it but the place had a different feel. Before, this had been her haven, her safe place. Now, well it was another place to keep up her guard.

"The nurse said you have to eat," he said.

She touched the buttons of his shirt. "I'll grab a bagel in the morning."

"That's not what the nurse said."

She managed a dismissive shake of her head. "She didn't mean it."

Laughter rumbled in his chest. "She doesn't strike me as the type to say what she doesn't mean. My partner has said so often enough. Where's your kitchen?"

"Beyond the barrier and through the double doors."

He glanced around, studying the tall ceilings and the large brick walls. "What's upstairs?"

"Bedroom."

He guided her beyond the screen and paused when he saw the collection of porcelain figurines, miniature wheels, gears and wire she fashioned into art.

He picked up a white porcelain elephant. "You are an artist?"

Watching him examine her sculpture felt more personal than stripping off her hospital gown earlier. "In name only for most of the last year. I've been too busy to do much more than work."

"What are these to be?"

"Chess pieces. I used to sell them in college and law school for extra money."

"They did well?"

"Yes." She might not like or trust the guy, but he'd keep her safe and for now safe was good enough.

She moved through the swinging doors and flipped on the kitchen lights, which blinked and brightened to reveal a long industrial counter, a stove designed to cook hundreds of meals daily, and a double refrigerator.

"How did you find a place like this?"

"It went into bankruptcy. A fire sale price and a low interest loan made me a landowner."

He studied the rooms with blatant curiosity. He snapped his fingers as a memory fell into place. "Used to be a barbecue place?"

"It did. Bad management."

"When I worked undercover, we busted drug dealers working in the alley behind the place."

"Its checkered past is part of the reason I bought it. We fit."

As she moved to the refrigerator, he blocked her path and pointed toward a chair. "Sit."

Without a word, she took the chair nestled close to the bar. "I'll be back on my game tomorrow and I won't be easy to boss around."

"Good." He opened the refrigerator and studied the paltry contents. "You live on this?"

"I'm due a trip to the grocery store."

"I'd say so. How old is the Chinese food?"

"Yesterday."

"You're sure?"

"For the most part."

He left the container in the refrigerator and opened the freezer. "Frozen pizza. A step in the right direction. This been here a year, or two?"

"It might have been in there when I moved in," she joked.

Shaking his head, he turned on the oven and unwrapped the pizza. "And they say cops are bad about eating well."

"My mom was never much of a cook and I never picked up the habit. I eat enough to keep going."

"Explains why you are skin and bones."

"I like to think of myself as gristle. Tough and hard to

chew." She shifted, grimaced. "So how long did you work undercover in Nashville?"

"Ten years."

"I'll bet you've got war stories."

"A few." The oven beeped signaling it was preheated. "Shitty eating is going to catch up with you one day."

"So my law partner keeps telling me."

He put the pizza in the oven and filled two glasses with water. He put a glass in front of her and sipped his as if a thought stirred.

"So who am I keeping you from tonight, Morgan? I can't believe you don't have plans on a Saturday night."

"You saved me from unpacking."

"Saved? Don't like the domestic chores."

"Not a fan."

"So where'd you move?"

"Back into the family home."

She winced. "Ouch."

"Exactly." He rested his hands on his hips and let his gaze settle on her.

She arched a brow. "You trying to read my mind? I can promise it's a dark and scary place."

A shake of his head confirmed his agreement. "Wainwright, the idea of rambling around in your head scares me."

"Good." She cocked her head. "So if you're not trying to read my mind why are you still looking at me?"

"We had a case a couple of nights ago. A homicide."

She sipped her water. She'd seen enough crime scene photos to know that he'd witnessed the most grisly. She waited for him to decide what he wanted to share.

"The victim was a young singer. She'd been walking to her car."

"I saw a mention of that in the paper, but didn't have time to get past the headline."

He hesitated as if measuring each word. "She was

beaten to death. The medical examiner thinks with a long metal object."

She straightened, making the pain in her shoulder throb all the harder. "Do you think there's a connection to my case?"

He met her gaze. "I don't know. Her killer's first swing didn't miss but landed on the side of her head. She wasn't recognizable by the time the killer was finished."

She set her water down and traced the rim of the glass. "Who was she?"

"A singer. Dixie Simmons. Popular at the honky-tonks and well-liked."

"I don't know her. Or the name. I don't have much time for the honky-tonks these days."

"I don't know if there is a connection but you need to be extra careful."

"Most women are killed by people they know. A spouse. Lover. Exes."

"That's what I thought. But all the men I've talked to have alibis. You have any exes that could be a threat to you?"

That made her smile. "I barely have time for a run in the evening. No time for men. No exes. Unless we go back to eighth grade and Jonny Danvers. He had a crush on me." She frowned. "That sounded flip and I didn't mean for it to. I know this Dixie woman wouldn't be laughing."

"Cops rely on dark humor to survive. We'd go insane if we didn't joke."

"Right."

"When I received the call that you'd been attacked with a blunt object my first thought was Dixie. The similarities were too close for comfort."

His assessment didn't sit well.

"What about clients? Could one of your clients have done this to you?"

"It's always possible. I do a lot of public defender work. See all kinds in that business, but I've not had much trouble."

"You were visible on TV the other night."

She grimaced. "The punch seen around Nashville. The station received unflattering emails about me."

"That put you on a lot of radars."

"Not my intent at all. I was trying to push you on the DNA testing."

A smile quirked the edges of his lips. He wasn't a handsome man. Too hard and too many rough edges. But when he smiled he had an appeal. "Really? That never occurred to me."

"Sarcasm is the lowest form of humor."

"I never said I was smart."

He'd give a fox a run for its money. "Well, if you'd answered one of my calls, I'd not have been driven to organize the vigil."

"I answered your first call."

"And left me a voicemail message that you'd get back."

"I meant that."

"That was six weeks ago."

"I don't have an answer from the lab." The slow deliberate clip of his words suggested she was being childish. "What do you want me to do, call each day and chat about the weather so we can connect?"

"No. That's ridiculous. I want an answer for Jeb."

He cocked a brow. "Do you really believe the guy is innocent? Really?"

"My gut tells me he is."

"Your gut?"

"What, you've never relied on your gut?"

An exasperated sigh seeped over his lips.

Rachel traced the rim of her glass. "And there are a lot of unanswered questions."

"Such as?"

The letters came to mind but she wasn't ready to tell him or anyone else about them. Definitely, TMI. "The arresting officers didn't allow him counsel."

"You mean my father?"

"He was the arresting officer."

"Jeb refused counsel at first and later when he asked for it, he got it."

"After three days."

"If he'd waived his rights no cop was going to beg him to call an attorney. All they cared about was closing their case." No hint of apology softened dark eyes. "That was their job."

"Their job was to serve justice."

His gaze cut like shards of glass. "My father was a great cop. And from what I've read about Jeb he was an accident waiting to happen."

Another cop had said the exact words about her brother once. Anger ripped at her good humor and she smacked her hand on the counter, regretting it the instant it triggered jolts of pain up her arm. For a moment, she struggled to catch her breath. "See it's that kind of attitude I'm worried about. That kind of attitude will get my DNA tests delayed or lost."

"You calling me a liar?" He was as calm as a hurricane's eye.

"You are loyal to the job and your family. I think you'd protect them at all costs."

"I don't lie. Can you say the same?"

She ignored the barb. "When my brother was arrested he asked me to lie for him. I didn't lie for him, and I've regretted it every day since."

"You were right not to lie."

Rachel traced her eyebrow. "Really? You make it sound black-and-white. Easy. One lie would have solved so much."

"If you'd lied you'd not be here now. You'd have been arrested and you'd never have gotten that law degree."

The oven dinged and he pulled out the cooked pizza, which he cut into four slices. He removed a white plate from the open shelving above the counter and served up her food.

She lifted her slice, pausing as it neared her lips. "You're not eating."

"No. Already ate supper. But you need to eat so I can give you your pill. I'll lock up on my way out."

Pill. She didn't want to take meds or have her mind in a fog. Luke had lived that way for the last decade of his life. But the night would be long and she'd sleep little without help. And she needed to be sharp tomorrow.

She bit into the pizza, quickly realizing she was far hungrier than she first thought. He sipped his water as she ate the first slice and then half of the second. When she pushed her plate away, he pulled the meds from his pocket and doled out two pink pills into her palm.

"You are taking them."

She curled her fingers over the pills. "Is it always an order with you?"

"Is it always a major discussion with you?"

She shook her head. "Not this time. I can admit when I'm wrong. The nurse was right. Whatever she gave me at the hospital is wearing off fast." She swallowed the pills and chased them with water. "Let me give you back your shirt before I pass out."

"Keep it for now," he said.

"No, that's not right." She eased off the stool and reached for the shirt buttons. Her good hand shook as she fumbled with the buttons.

He moved around the counter and brushed her hand away. "Send it along later."

Pain throbbed and she glanced at the clock wondering when the meds would take effect. "Fine."

In the main room he glanced toward the staircase that stretched to a darkened second floor. "Can you make it that far?"

Yeah. Sure. Maybe. "I'm a champ. I'll be fine." She moved toward the front door. "I'll walk you out and set the alarm."

He moved to the front door, opened it, and stopped. "You sure you'll be all right here tonight?"

The space behind her felt vast and empty and suddenly filled with dark shadows. But it wasn't her nature to borrow trouble when it filled her plate. "I'll be fine. Really."

"I'm going to have patrols stepped up in your area for a while. And I'm calling your partner."

"Thanks."

He stepped outside. "Glad to help."

Feelings of gratitude triggered a vulnerability that left her brittle and wishing he'd stay. Sentiment wasn't her style. Must be the drugs. "Don't forget my DNA tests. I'll be calling you soon."

Detective Morgan laughed. "Be surprised if you didn't."


Lexis shrugged her shoulders working the kinked muscles free as she rose and moved to the coffeepot filled with black dregs.

She poured the sludge into the cup, sniffed it, and grimaced. As much as she liked to drink coffee and flaunted a cast-iron stomach, even she had standards. She took the glass carafe, rinsed it out at the sink, and refilled it with fresh water. After dumping and refilling coffee grounds, she clicked the machine on and moved to a small fridge. Inside, she found two slices of yesterday's pizza.

Working her neck from side to side again she glanced back at the letters Rachel had left with her. Beside them were Annie's lyrics.

She'd gone over the letters again and again and her first instinct had been that the letters were authentic. The shapes of the letters were consistent: a deeply grooved looping O. A flourish and tail on the A's. Spacing between the letters, words, and lines were consistent.

Initially she'd thought this job was a slam dunk, but as she moved through the letters doubts bothered her. She couldn't voice the niggling worries that kept her from calling Rachel with a confirmation.

She paced back and forth staring at the letters. "What is it about you, Annie, that is such a puzzle? Who were you?"

Picking up her phone, she called Rachel. The call went to voice mail and she left a quick promise to call tomorrow.

As she closed the phone, a loud bang outside had Lexis turning toward her door. She wasn't expecting clients or guests this late at night. Naturally suspicious, she reached for the loaded thirty-eight she kept in the top drawer of her desk.

She moved to the door and looked through the peephole. No one was outside. She shoved out a breath and wondered if the raccoons had gotten into her garbage again. She'd just bought those new cans that were supposed to be critter-proof and it annoyed her that the same lingering pest problem had returned.

Gun at her side, she moved out the front door around the side of the house toward the cans. She was tempted to shoot the damn animal, which last week had ripped through her trash bags and spread debris around her land. But as she moved toward the cans, she realized that they were undisturbed. She hesitated, raising her gun again. If it wasn't the raccoons, then what the hell had made that noise?

As she turned to retreat back toward the house she heard the rustle of leaves and then a *swish* through the air. Milliseconds later a blunt hard object smashed into her gun hand. The pain paralyzed her arm and her fingers twitched. The gun fell to the ground. Grabbing her hand, she tensed, ready to fight when a second blow caught her on the side of her head. Stunned, her cry sounded distant, more animal than human. She'd never felt such pain.

Lexis staggered and dropped to her knees.

Another blow caught Lexis in the shoulder.

Vision blurring, she glanced up at her attacker's face and found it covered with a hockey mask and dark hoodie. She ticked through the people that might want her dead. The list wasn't long but one was all it took. "Why are you doing this? I've got money. I'll get it for you. Or you can take my car."

A heavy silence lingered in the air and then her answer came in the form of another blow, which crashed against her knee. Her body crumpled within itself. Vision blurred to near black and her thoughts scrambled toward oblivion.

"You should have stayed out of my business," a now-distant voice rasped. "Too nosy."

Pain garbled and short-circuited basic thought. Lexis could not find the words for another question.

Another blow struck her across the shoulder. Pain fired. In the past, she'd always been able to see herself clear of any problem, but this one wouldn't get fixed. She was gonna die.

Baby stood over the woman, savoring the frenzied panic in her eyes. Rational thought vanished, prompting another blow and then another. It was hard to stop. Energy zinged up through the rod into Baby's arm with each blow.

Breathless and arms aching, Baby swiped a trembling bloodstained hand over the mask. "You should have kept your damn nose out of my business."

Baby savored the rush of power. Such a thin line separated life and death.

Remembering the purpose for the visit, Baby turned from the body and entered the house, moving straight toward the lit desk where the letters lay strewn on the table.

Annie's neat handwriting glowed under the examiner's light. Lexis had written in the margins of her copies. *Authentic. Match. Correct.* And then a series of question marks on subsequent letters as if a puzzle plagued her.

What was the puzzle? What about the Annie letters had bothered Lexis? Mother would know. She always knew a lot more than she'd ever told. Mother's lack of faith in Baby had been a constant source of anger and resentment.

A quick swipe of the hand and the papers were scooped up and crammed in the oversized jacket pockets.

"So much trouble for a bunch of damn letters. So much trouble."

Out the door, Baby glanced at the crumpled, bloody body. Thoughts of Rachel swirled. She'd been quick, lucky tonight. Baby had underestimated her, thinking she'd be as easy as the other one. But Rachel had moved fast, pivoting out of the way and then screaming all to bloody hell. But failures were lessons not to be wasted but absorbed. Regret was for fools. And that was why Lexis Hanover's first blows had been quick and crushing. Not enough to kill, but enough to send crippling pain through her body. The fun rested with the screams, the struggles and the *knowing* that blinked in the victim's eyes as death approached.

Mother would be glad to have the letters back but would be angry that Baby had tried and failed to kill Rachel.

Baby didn't want to tell Mother about Rachel and see the disappointment in her eyes.

Baby moved away from the cabin. The idea of keeping Rachel's attack a secret initially weighed heavily. But as the seconds and minutes passed, Baby grew accustomed to the burden. The secret grew lighter and became more treasure than worry.

Mother kept secrets. And now so did Baby.

Rachel had gotten away. She'd been clever. But Baby would be smarter and faster the next time.

*December 1*

*Sugar,*

   *Or should I say Dirty Boy. You have dark, dark demons driving you. They scare me. They thrill me. And I have to say your darling Annie understands you better than anyone. And you are smart never to forget that.*

                *A.*

# Chapter Nine

No doubt Rachel Wainwright had a list of folks who'd like to do her harm, Deke thought as he parked the car in front of the diner. But the list of people who would actually try to kill her had to be much smaller.

He stared at the diner where Margaret Miller worked. She'd been so angry with Rachel at the vigil she'd thrown a punch. But had she been mad enough to return and attempt murder?

Out of the car, he moved up the brick sidewalk and through the front door of the Blue Note diner. It wasn't an upscale place but the parking lot remained full around the clock. Bells jingled overhead and he found himself about sixth in line for a table. He moved past the line to the greeter, a tall redhead with pale skin and eyes lined with dark makeup. He showed her his badge. "I'm looking for Margaret Miller."

"She's working right now."

"I'd like her to take a break, if you don't mind."

"Is this super important? Sunday breakfast is our busiest time."

He summoned a smile he suspected did not look that friendly. "It's important."

She scrunched up her mouth in disapproval. "Give me a minute." She left her station and vanished into the crowded restaurant.

Minutes later a harried Margaret Miller pushed through the restaurant. "What's this about?"

Aware that the line of patrons now watched his every move he showed Margaret his badge. "My name is Detective Morgan and I'm with Nashville homicide. Can we talk?"

She smoothed a stray strand of hair flat and shrugged. "Sure. There's a room in the back."

"Lead the way."

He followed her through the restaurant and kitchen into a back room equipped with a small table and four chairs. An overflowing ashtray set on the edge of the table.

From her apron pocket she pulled out a rumpled pack of cigarettes and a green plastic lighter. She quickly knocked a cigarette free and lit it. "What's this about, Detective Morgan?"

"Rachel Wainwright."

"I thought as much. This about the punch I landed on her smartass jaw the other night?" She arched a brow. "I thought she wasn't going to press charges."

"She's not."

She inhaled deeply and slowly released the smoke. "Then what's this about? If I ain't in trouble I got to get back to work. I'm losing money standing here."

He stepped to the side, blocking her exit. "Where were you last night?"

A thin trail of smoke drifted past narrowed eyes. "What's it to you?"

Margaret Miller wasn't the befuddled, damaged creature

he'd first imagined. "You can answer me now and I can be polite or you can answer my less polite questions at the station. Doesn't make the least bit of difference to me."

She frowned, determination festering. "You can't arrest me. I ain't broken a law."

"Tell me where you were last night."

"I didn't get off work until eight p.m. and then I went home, watched a movie, and ate cake. It was my mother's birthday on Friday and I had leftovers with cake."

"That so?"

She nodded, her gaze not as resolute. "She always loved her birthdays. We always celebrated by going to the movies and eating cake. So that's what I did."

"Must have been an emotional day for you. All those memories."

"Sure. It's never easy. She was my best friend, the last one I could trust. She and I understood the pain of losing Annie."

"Did anyone see you at home?"

"Last night, no." She took another puff and then snuffed out the cigarette. "A lady came by the house on Friday. She's with a movie company. Asked me about Annie. Said she wanted to make a movie of her life."

"What was her name?"

"Don't remember. Her card is back at the house. Lexis something."

He scribbled the name. "What time did she come by?"

"About nine. Why all the questions?"

He closed his notebook. On the streets he could smell a lie a mile off. He watched and waited for Margaret's tell. "Rachel Wainwright was attacked last night."

Margaret arched a brow. "And you think I did it?"

"That's why I'm here."

She fiddled with her name tag and then adjusted her collar. "I didn't hurt nobody."

"But you don't have an alibi."

"I shouldn't have to prove it. I think I already proved that if I've a beef with ol' Ms. Wainwright, I'll have it out right in public like I did for the television cameras. I've been up-front with her."

"Got a stick in your gut that she's trying to free Jeb. And seeing as it was your mother's birthday yesterday it could make the perfect storm. You might have had a few drinks. You got madder and madder and then like that—" He snapped his fingers. "You got up, drove across town, and waited for her outside her building."

Gray eyes narrowed. "It wasn't like that. I didn't hurt her."

"It would solve a lot of your problems. Without Rachel, few people would champion Jeb's cause."

"I don't need to hurt her to see that justice remains served. That man killed my sister and he left her body in the woods where animals scavenged her flesh until she was nothing but bones. Those tests are gonna prove that he's the killer and that cops like your daddy were right all along."

"You sound pretty sure."

"I am sure. You should be sure too. Your daddy was one of the best policemen in this state. No one tougher or smarter than Buddy Morgan. You'll have to go a long way to fill his shoes."

Deke's stony expression shrouded traces of doubt. "There are several surveillance cameras around Ms. Wainwright's building. I'll be checking them today."

Disgust deepened the lines on Margaret's face. "Why would you want to help someone like her? She's out to ruin your daddy's good name."

"She's not going to do that."

"She's saying he screwed up. The case that made his career is a lie. She's saying your daddy was a liar."

Irritation snapped at his insides. "That's not what she's saying."

"Really? What do you think the media will do to his memory if they find out he screwed up the case that made his career?"

He slid his hand into his pocket and rattled his change. "I'm leaving to check those surveillance cameras now, Ms. Miller. Let's hope I don't see you on them."

Deke strode out of the diner annoyed and irritated with himself. He'd seen a different side to Rachel last night and her gumption didn't annoy him like it had. He'd also seen a different side of Margaret today. Her devotion to her late sister bordered on fanatical.

Deke was halfway to his car when his phone rang. It was his partner KC. "We've another victim that was beaten to death like Dixie Simmons."

Tension crawled up his back as he glanced back at the diner. "Give me the address."

KC rattled off street numbers. It took Deke twenty minutes to cut through the city and to find the log cabin–style house located at the end of a dirt road. A collection of cop cars, blue lights flashing, crowded the top of the circular driveway.

KC stood outside the yellow crime-scene tape, his badge hanging from the breast pocket of his blue blazer. His white shirt looked rumpled and his khakis a size too small. When he spotted Deke he motioned him over.

Deke observed the home's open front door and the collection of forensic techs on the right side of the house. "The victim is on the side of the house?"

"She is. A client came by this morning for a scheduled meeting and found the door open. Looked around the side of the house and found her."

Deke pulled plastic gloves from his pocket. "Where is the client?"

"In the squad car. She's a mess."

Deke glanced toward the car and saw the woman in the front seat, face buried in her hands. The female officer beside her leaned in as she spoke. Judging by the witness's tears, the officer's words had little effect.

He'd give the witness time and let the storm of hysteria pass. "What did the victim do for a living?"

KC glanced at his notebook. "Ms. Lexis Hanover, aged forty-seven, was an adjunct math professor at Vanderbilt University and she owned her own private detective agency. According to her website she did insurance fraud, small claims cases, and surveillance. She's had her license for ten years."

"Did you say Lexis?"

"I did."

Lexis. A memory elbowed its way forward. Lexis, like the movie person who'd visited Margaret. Could be chance.

Annie. Dixie. Rachel. Lexis. Names that did not fully connect. "My brother Rick saw Rachel Wainwright on the campus of Vanderbilt recently. She was visiting a woman who is a private investigator and a math teacher."

"This gal's got math degree diplomas hanging on her walls." KC shook his head. "What are the chances of that being a coincidence?"

"None." Annoyed, he loosened his tie. "Let me have a look at the body."

"Around the side of the house near the trash cans."

Deke ducked under the crime-scene tape, the crisp fall leaves crunching under his feet as he moved toward the body, which lay facedown. Even from ten feet away he could see the blood and destruction.

Brad Holcombe looked up from a sketchpad. "Detective Morgan."

Deke kept his gaze on the body. "Is Georgia here?"

"She's working the inside of the house."

Good. Deke didn't like the idea of Georgia around this body. He never would have said it out loud because Georgia hated coddling and babying. But he and his brothers rarely apologized for protecting her. All the boys could still remember the day their parents had brought their screaming pink baby sister home. She'd been so tiny. Protecting her had been as natural as breathing.

However, their wishes meant squat to Georgia. She wanted a forensics career and never once shied from a difficult crime scene. And she was damn good at what she did. Detailed. Thorough. Tenacious. They'd wanted a desk job for her, but she'd jumped knee deep into the family business.

"What can you tell me about the murder?" Deke asked.

"She was struck at least seven times. Each blow did maximum damage and was excruciating. Her kneecaps are broken, her elbow is shattered and the killing blows struck the right side of her head."

Deke studied the mangled bloody mess that had been Lexis.

"We also found a thirty-eight." Brad pointed to a tented yellow number that sat beside the handgun. "It hasn't been fired so I think the first blow was to her hand. That would have sent shock waves up her arm and she'd have dropped the gun."

"So when she came outside she was expecting trouble or was she the kind of gal who always figured trouble was around the corner?"

"Hard to say."

"Do we have any idea what she was investigating?"

"Haven't dug that far yet."

Deke squatted by the body. Lexis had been in fair shape. She'd brought her gun with her, so how had the killer gotten the upper hand? "Were there any signs of struggle?"

"The medical examiner will know better."

He studied the surrounding woods. "The killer would not have happened by out here. He would have come with a single purpose."

"Yeah."

"I'm gonna have a look inside." Deke rounded the side of the house and climbed the three steps to the rustic porch. Inside the smell of burned coffee hovered. He found Georgia standing next to a simple plank desk with a state-of-the-art laptop. On a side table there was a high-tech scanner as well as several cameras. They'd all have to be searched for images that might explain how Lexis Hanover had caught the eye of the killer.

Georgia glanced up, blowing her bangs out of her eyes. "Deke. Looks like your victim was a fairly successful PI."

"I never crossed paths with her."

"Neither did I. She must have been good at keeping a low profile."

He glanced toward the desk and the bright magnifying glass. "Do you know what she was analyzing?"

She glanced toward the light. "I don't. I've searched all around the room but there's nothing."

"Might have been what the killer was after."

"The techs downtown can have a look at her computer and they might be able to figure it out." She pointed to blood drops marked with tented yellow numbers. "But the killer was in here. Blood all around. Brad says the victim never fired a shot so I'm guessing we'll find that blood belonged to the victim. There would have been blood spray judging by her injuries."

Of course, she'd seen the body, but logic didn't temper the sadness as he moved closer to the desk and noticed a ruler, a small magnifying glass and tracing paper. "She was authenticating handwriting?"

"Looks like it. It's more common today with contracts and wills. When money is at stake, people fight."

A smile quirked the edges of his mouth. "That gonna be in one of your songs?"

"As a matter of fact it might be. I've been working on new tunes." Her eyes brightened. "And did I tell you I'm singing at KC's party and it's gonna be held at Rudy Creed's?"

"Really?"

"KC set it up. Said he and Rudy go way back."

"Didn't know that." KC had been a friend of his father's, which had made it hard for Deke to warm up to the guy. He knew the basics about KC but little below the surface.

"Do you remember where Rudy's is located?"

"I was just there the other day."

A frown wrinkled her brow. "Why?"

"Linked to a case."

"Thank God. I had visions of you, Alex, and Rick demanding a spot for me."

"The thought had crossed our minds, but we're too afraid of our baby sister's temper to pull a stunt like this."

She blew out a relieved sigh. "You bet your ass."

Smiling, Deke glanced around the desk searching again for evidence that would connect Lexis to Dixie, Annie, Rachel, or Margaret. There were invoices yet to be mailed, a handful of checks attached to a deposit slip and several sets of maps of the Nashville area. He moved away from the desk toward the large fireplace, now dark and cold. Clustered together on the mantel was a collection of pictures. Lexis had a close-knit group of friends. His gaze skimmed the images and halted immediately on the third from the right. It featured Lexis, a man, and Rachel Wainwright. Deke picked up the picture, his gaze instantly drawn to Rachel's face. She appeared younger. Her hair was slightly longer and she had a wide, happy grin. He'd seen her mad, angry, slightly amused but never out-and-out happy. Her beaming face and sparkling eyes drew him before jacking up his suspicion. How the hell did she know Lexis?

His gaze shifted to the man beside Rachel. He wore a prison jumpsuit and casually slung his arms around Rachel and Lexis's shoulders. Thin, gaunt, and pale, he sported several tattoos on his forearms and shared Rachel's square jaw. He was her brother.

"Georgia, have a look at this picture." He turned to show it to her as she closed the gap between them.

"The attorney clocked on television the other night."

"Rachel Wainwright."

"Wasn't she attacked last night? I'm sure I heard that in the shift report."

"You did. Someone took a swing at her and hit her hard but didn't break any bones. She's lucky." Damn. How the hell was Rachel tied into all this? "Any guess on the guy's identity?"

"Definitely family. Can't miss the genetic link between the two."

"Like ours," he joked as he tugged a lock of her blond hair.

"I got all the pretty genes."

"No argument here. The Morgan boys landed on the short end of the stick in the looks department."

She nodded her agreement. "This guy's not too bad-looking. He's what? Early thirties?"

"About."

"So he's her older brother." She shook her head. "It looks like he's leaning on these gals, as if he's a little desperate and he needs them."

Deke realized she was right. "You have a knack for body language."

"All those years of singing in front of rough audiences.

Good to watch the body language in case a patron is tempted to throw a beer bottle."

"You've never had one tossed your way."

"Always a first." She tapped the picture. "So what does the curious Ms. Wainwright have in common with the victim?"

"That's the first question I intend to ask."


Deke arrived at Rachel's building an hour later. By the time he'd crossed town and fought traffic he'd built up a full head of steam. She had a habit of keeping secrets and he figured this one was gonna be a whopper.

He parked and rang her bell. He glanced up into the security camera and glared as if to say "let me in" and waited for the buzz of the lock as it opened. He found Rachel rising from her desk.

She wasn't dressed in her customary suit and white starched shirt but a loose pair of coveralls and a T-shirt. In these clothes she moved with more ease as if she'd shed a skin that was too tight. She wasn't wearing a sling but there was no missing the black-purple bruise darkening her right arm.

"Detective. Come for your shirt? I have it. Cleaned and ready to go."

"Not here for the shirt." He jabbed his finger at the camera. "That tape?"

"I wish."

"Too bad."

She nodded. "Here to give me those DNA test results?" She might be dressed differently but she remained a hard-edged smart-ass.

"How's the arm?"

She didn't bother to glance at the bruise. "Hurt's like hell. But aspirin is keeping it in check."

"You working today?"

"Hard to get away from the job when you live feet from it. I'm guessing by the look on your face that you don't have DNA on your mind."

"Do you know a Lexis Hanover?"

Her face stilled and a wall shuttered over her gaze. "Who?"

She hid it fairly well, but she knew Hanover. Slick. But not slick enough. "How do you know her?"

She moved to fold her arms, winced, and dropped them back at her sides. "I didn't say I did."

"Don't bullshit me." The words all but growled in his chest.

Her brow arched. "Why the tough words and harsh tone, Detective?"

He glanced around her office, noting that since last night she'd dusted and straightened up. He'd imagined she'd been either too rattled to work or too restless to sit still. In the corner, the partition was gone and the sculptures had been moved and outfitted with some of the many pieces of junk she collected. Made sense Rachel would collect the broken to rehabilitate into art.

He studied the piece gently wedged in a vise and noted carving tools covered with porcelain dust as if she'd been working when he arrived. He picked up the sculpting knife and studied the pointed edge. "I just came from a crime scene. A murder scene. The woman was beaten to death."

Grimacing, she slid her good hand up over her bruised arm. "I'm sorry to hear that. What was her name?"

He touched the sharp edge of a jutting slice of metal. "Lexis Hanover. Private Detective."

A heavy silence settled in the room.

He glanced back at Rachel. The color had melted from her face and for a moment she swayed. If she'd not lied to him seconds ago he'd have summoned pity or even reached out. Instead he relished a twist of the knife. "Name familiar now?"

"You said she was beaten to death?"

"That's right. Hit with a blunt object seven or eight times."

Rachel moved to an old metal chair and dropped into it. She leaned back and closed her eyes. "You aren't playing a game with me, are you, Detective?"

"That would be sick and twisted, don't you think?"

Wordless, she shook her head as she clung to composure.

Despite the lies between them, his voice was softer than he'd intended. "How did you know her?"

A ragged breath wobbled pale lips. Watery eyes looked up at him. "We met on a case years ago. She stepped in and helped."

"Would the case have involved your brother?"

The educated guess had her widening her eyes, but the consummate attorney weighed and measured each word before speaking. "Why do you ask?"

He rested his hands on his hips, his knuckles brushing the butt of his gun. "I don't have time for games, Rachel. No time. For. Games. Tell me about Lexis." When she didn't speak he reached for his cell phone. "I'd be glad to show you pictures from the crime scene. It was a hell of a mess."

She held up her hand as she rose. "That's not necessary." She sighed. "My brother was convicted of murder."

"I've read up on his case."

She wasn't surprised. "He swore over and over he didn't do it but that didn't stop the cops from arresting him. He had a crap attorney and he landed in jail. I was in college when it happened."

He waited, sensing she'd struggled with this family truth for years.

"Fast forward five years and I'm fresh out of law school, hell bent on proving he didn't kill anyone. I met Lexis in court. We hit it off and she agreed to do some digging for me. I told her right off I couldn't pay, but she didn't seem worried. Said the day would come when I'd be in a spot to help someone else."

A sigh shuddered from her. "It's a long and complicated story. Luke died in prison before we could get him a retrial."

"Luke being your brother?"

"Yes."

No happy endings for the Wainwrights. But then they were few and far between. "Lexis did a good deed for you. What were you two working on now?"

"That's confidential." She tugged at a loose thread at the corner of her pocket.

Rachel shook her head. "I left a note on my front door." *Lexis, I'm running. Back in a half-hour. If you've got the letters, I'd love to talk.* "The note was gone when I got home."

"I'm betting the someone who attacked you used it to find Lexis."

A tear trickled down her cheek but he couldn't summon pity. "Someone killed her. Brutally. And this nut also beat another woman to death. Tell me what the hell was going on between you two." His voice rose to a shout that reverberated off the walls.

She twisted the thread around her finger until it cut into the skin. "After my media sensation the other night, someone must have been paying attention to what I was saying about Jeb Jones and the DNA."

He folded arms over his chest, waiting to see how much of the truth she'd spit out this time.

"I also mentioned Annie Rivers Dawson, as you remember. It was the mention of her name that caught her sister's attention."

He wondered if the woman could answer a question outright without weighing each word. Natural suspicion combined with a law degree equaled passive sentences conveying little. He waited.

"I received a hand-delivered package the day after the vigil. Courier sent it. I later checked and found out the sender had paid in cash and the company had no record of who paid for the delivery."

"What was in the package?"

"Letters."

He leaned toward her a fraction, frustration reverberating from every muscle. "Jesus, would you stop being an attorney for a second and tell me. It's like pulling teeth, Rachel."

"I don't trust cops."

"Figured that much out. Talk."

The words hitched in her throat. "The letters appeared to have been written by Annie Rivers Dawson."

"What?"

"I know. It sounds crazy that thirty-year-old letters would be delivered to my doorstep. I read them and wasn't sure what to make of them. They were compelling."

"Why didn't you bring them to me?"

A half smile tugged the edge of her mouth. "Right, give the potentially winning hand to you, the guy who stonewalls at every turn."

"I don't stonewall. I have no answers to give."

"So you say."

He held up his hand, annoyance shooting through his body. "You are the definition of trust issues." When she arched an unapologetic brow, he asked, "What did you do with the letters?"

"I gave them to Lexis to authenticate. One of her talents is handwriting analysis. I hoped she could tell me if they were real or not."

"When did you give her the letters?"

"Tuesday. She was supposed to call me last night. She

sent me an email, which I didn't see until today." Before he could prompt her to finish she said, "It said she wanted to read and study the letters a little longer. Her first impression was that they were real but something bothered her. And before you ask, she did not say what that was. She said to stay tuned. I'd planned to call her today."

This explained the visit to Margaret. "Did you have a sample of Annie's handwriting?"

"She'd said she'd find one." Suddenly, her shoulders slumped as the weight of Lexis's death settled deeper. "I can't believe she's dead. She was the smartest woman I knew. No one fooled her."

"She had her thirty-eight in her hand. But the killer knocked it out before she could fire."

More tears streaked down her cheeks and she quickly swiped them away as if ashamed. He gave her a moment to collect herself.

"Did you keep copies of the letters?"

A conspirator's look darkened her watery gaze. "What do you think?"

"I think you are a paranoid control freak who wouldn't have let the letters out of your sight without keeping copies."

"I not only kept copies but I didn't give her all the originals. Didn't want to toss all my apples into one basket."

"Always thinking, aren't you?"

"I try." She moved toward her desk and opened the third drawer. She removed a file folder. "These are copies of the letters."

"And the other originals?" He took the file, opened it and scanned the neatly written handwriting. The first line of the first letter caught his attention. "Sugar! . . ."

"Locked in my safe."

He waited for her to retrieve the letters but when she didn't move he scratched his head as if plagued by a puzzle. "Do I have to get a warrant? Do we have to make this ugly?"

She shook her head. "Normally, I'd say, hell yes. Take your best shot. But not this time. This time I want you to find the guy who killed Lexis." She moved to a wall. She pressed several boards and a door popped open to a safe with a combination lock. Several turns of the dial and the lock opened. She removed a yellowed stack of letters.

Rachel held them close. "There were twenty letters in the original packet. I gave them to Lexis. You have ten originals here, plus copies of the missing ones. You now know all that I know."

As he studied her pale, direct eyes, he sensed the truth.

She held out the letters.

He took them, watching as she shoved a shaking hand through her hair. "Thanks."

"You said she was beaten."

"It was rough, Rachel. No way to get around that. I don't know what's driving this nut but there's a hell of a lot of pent-up rage."

As she spoke her voice broke, forcing her to hesitate until she could speak without emotion. "You told me about the other woman last night. Dixie?"

"Dixie Simmons. A singer in a honky-tonk."

"Could she have hired Lexis?"

"I don't know. I don't know how the two women are connected. I'm hoping these letters will give me an idea."

"The letters are Annie's. I don't understand."

"I can't explain it now. But Annie is in the mix."

Moistening her lips, she shifted her stance as if holding steady was more than she could handle. "Where are they taking Lexis? To the state medical examiner's office?"

"Yes."

Her lips flattened and fresh tears welled. "I hate the idea of them cutting into her. There's no dignity in that."

"No. But it's necessary if we're going to figure this out."

She tipped her head back as if ordering her tears to stop.

"Lexis better than anyone would want you to chase all the leads. She liked puzzles." She shook her head. "She didn't deserve this."

"No, I don't imagine she did." He thought about the pain Lexis would have endured in her final minutes but couldn't bring himself to share any of the details with Rachel. He'd been bluffing about showing the crime scene photos to her.

"When the medical examiner is finished with her body, then what?"

"We'll contact next of kin. They'll arrange for a funeral home to pick her up."

"She didn't have family. There was a sister but she died about fifteen years ago. It had been the two of them for most of their lives." Her gaze sharpened. "I'll take custody of the body and see that she's buried properly."

"That's a legal question for the courts."

Challenge sparked in her gaze. "I like legal questions. And I'm angling for a fight right now."

Deke wondered what a full-on mad Rachel Wainwright looked like. That was a show he'd have paid to see. "I'll smooth the waters on my end with the medical examiner's office."

A sigh shuddered through her. "And if you don't, I'll do what I do best."

Deke didn't crack a smile. "Bitch?"

She pointed her index finger at him as if he'd hit the nail on the head. "Exactly."

*December 29*

*Sugar,*
   *Don't you worry, now you hear me? No one saw us. We are safe. We weren't spotted the other night. Close. But we are in the clear. Come on around this evening after work. The girls will be gone and we can snuggle in my bed without anyone watching us.*

*A.*

# Chapter Ten

Restless energy churned in Rachel hours after Deke had left. She worked on her sculpture but found the work frustrating and futile. She paced. Attempted to write a brief but the more she corralled her thoughts, the tighter and tighter her skin grew. As much as she wanted to go for a run and sweat away her grief her injury wouldn't allow it. She was trapped in these four walls with her thoughts.

Last night when her attacker had struck her shoulder, the pain had been blinding. It had robbed her of breath and thought. And that had been a glancing blow. Not the full-on blows that Lexis had endured.

She closed her eyes, trying to shut out the image of her friend dying so brutally. Rachel finally gave up any stab at work or art. She changed into jeans and a long-sleeved button-down shirt that she eased into slowly. Bending her arm was painful but she managed it and fumbled with her buttons until they were fastened. She slipped her feet into loafers, grabbed her purse, and she left the office.

The walk to her parking spot was a half block but her

nerves snapped as she passed parked cars able to mask an attacker. Her heart raced as she neared a familiar alley, glanced down and searched for a hooded attacker. Seeing no one, she hurried to her car. A click of the button, the doors unlocked and she slid behind the wheel, breathless. For a moment she let the warmth of the seat seep into her bruised shoulder. Getting around wasn't as easy as she'd imagined.

She started the car and pulled onto the side street. Less than thirty minutes later, she arrived at the rustic address that Lexis had loved so much. She stopped one hundred yards from the cabin studying the crime-scene tape and the police car positioned by the forensics van.

She studied the cop car, knowing he'd be the gatekeeper she'd have to get past if she wanted a look at the crime scene. When she realized he wasn't in the patrol car, she grabbed her purse and hurried the last one hundred yards. Her shoulder throbbed and begged her to stop but she kept moving, hesitating at the yellow crime-scene tape. Everyone entering the crime scene changed it in some way, whether they picked up critical fibers, tracked foreign dirt or smudged a fingerprint.

Rachel wanted to go into the house and stand where her friend had lived. She wanted to tell Lexis that she was sorry. How had all this spiraled so badly out of control?

As much as she wanted to do all this, she didn't cross the line. Her grief did not trump the cops' job of catching this killer.

"Tell me you aren't thinking about entering my crime scene."

Rachel turned to see a petite woman dressed in a blue Nashville PD jumpsuit. Behind her stood the uniformed officer. He was tall, lean, and annoyed.

"Who are you?" the officer asked.

Rachel's attention went to the woman. She wore heavy

boots and had wound long strawberry blond hair into a bun at the nape of her neck. She wasn't tall, in fact delicate described her better but her gaze possessed a fierceness that told anyone with half a brain that she didn't mess around. Her name tag read, *Officer Morgan*.

Morgan. This woman might not look like Deke Morgan but she shared his demeanor. And with the way Rachel's luck had been going, they were kin.

Rachel stepped back from the tape. "I wasn't going to mess with the crime scene."

"What are you doing here?" Officer Morgan approached, her booted feet thudding into the dirt.

She tightened her fingers around her purse strap. "I was a friend of Lexis Hanover's."

A delicate brow arched. "I know you."

Rachel stifled a grimace, knowing her name would now end up in some report that would land on Deke Morgan's desk. Crap. "I'm Rachel Wainwright."

Officer Morgan tilted her head as if her interest-meter spiked. "You look different without your business suit."

Another TV fan. "And I covered the bruise on my cheek with makeup. I will forever be known as the woman decked on the eleven o'clock news."

A smile twisted the edges of her lips. She turned to the officer. "I got this."

He hesitated and then returned to his vehicle.

"There're worse legacies." Officer Morgan held her sketchpad close. "So you're trying to get Jeb Jones freed?"

"I'm trying to get the DNA testing back. That will tell me whether I should keep listening to him or walk away."

"Do you think he did it?"

"It's not for me to judge."

Eyes as brittle as glass studied her. "But you have an

opinion. I've never met an attorney that didn't have an opinion."

"I have thoughts."

"Which are?"

Rachel could verbally fence with the best and she was up against the best. Time to thrust and parry. "You must be related to Deke Morgan."

That tipped her off guard. "Why would you say that?"

"You have his way of asking questions. Not satisfied until you get the answer you really want."

Blue eyes narrowed. "Maybe that's a cop thing."

"The name tag aside, I'd say it's also a Morgan thing. Family gatherings must be interesting."

"I never said we were related."

Rachel shook her head slowly. "You could be a cousin, but my vote goes to sister. Kid sister."

Tight-lipped but curious, she shrugged. "Bingo. I'm the kid sister."

Rachel inventoried the milky skin and the splash of freckles partly hidden by powder. "You don't look much like him. But you act and sound just like him."

"Guilty as charged. I've been hearing that since I was five."

"Is police business the family business?"

"I joined eight years ago after I graduated from college. I loved forensics so it was a natural. Another brother is retired police. Another is with TBI."

"A police family dynasty."

Weight shifted from foot to foot as she readied a battle stance. "A dynasty founded on the conviction you are trying to overturn."

"I'm looking for the truth, Officer Morgan. If Jeb is guilty then the matter is closed. Have you considered that he might be innocent?"

"He's not."

She clung to her position. "If he is innocent, then the real killer got away with killing Annie Rivers Dawson."

"I don't believe the killer did get away. My father arrested the right man."

And so they'd reached the impasse that would not be crossed until the final test results. "Look, I didn't come here to fight. I came to see . . . to see the home Lexis loved. I'll let you get back to your work."

As Rachel turned, she saw the tented yellow numbers that indicated evidence. Deke had said Lexis had been drawn outside and attacked. An anguished breath shuddered through her and her own shoulder throbbed, a reminder she'd forgotten to take her aspirin. Her fingers massaged her shoulder.

From behind her Officer Morgan said, "You were attacked last night."

The tented yellow numbers wound around the house like Oz's yellow brick road. Would they lead the police to the killer? "Yes."

"Did you find evidence to help catch this guy?"

"I wish I had." Rachel faced Officer Morgan, surprised to find concern had wiped away the anger. "I wish that I'd been able to ID him. If I had, Lexis might still be alive. But I didn't see him. If I can help with this case, Officer Morgan, please let me know."

"Sure."

Rachel turned from the crime scene and the officer's questioning gaze. She walked seven feet before the tears welled.


Rebecca Saunders loved sin.

Perhaps because she'd been raised to believe that all forms of pleasure were evil. Liquor, loud music, short skirts . . . they were all one-way tickets to hell, according to her daddy and momma.

By age twelve she'd learned to hide her devils behind an angel's guise to avoid the beatings. She'd learned to keep her skirts long, her diet modest, and her music classical. But the devils never left her and as she grew older they coaxed her truest self to life.

By day she worked hard, made the best grades, and landed a prime job. But at night, when the sun dipped low and darkness masked sins, she'd changed into her short skirts and high heels and hit the honky-tonks. She liked meeting men. She was intoxicated by her feminine power over them. She liked to watch their eyes light up as she slowly peeled off her clothes and then teased them and told them that perhaps she'd changed her mind. She liked to hear them whimper and beg.

It was well past eight when Rebecca stepped off the hotel elevator and walked the carpeted hallway toward her room. She smiled. Tonight she had an old customer and a new fantasy to fulfill.

She opened the door and dropped the key on the mahogany side table by the door. She kicked off her shoes and savored the way her bare feet sunk into the plush carpet.

A long time ago, she'd learned to set her standards high. If a man wanted her, they'd not be meeting in a dumpy motel. No, sir. She wanted the best. She wanted to hold her head high when she crossed a lobby decorated with marble and fine carpets. She wanted to know she could call room service on a whim and order strawberries and champagne if it suited her or step into a marble shower bigger than her old bedroom.

She set her purse on the end of a bed made with a lush white comforter, shrugged off her jacket, and shimmied out of her slim skirt. She'd been looking forward to tonight. It

had been nearly impossible to concentrate as she thought
about slipping out for this meeting.

She turned on the television and switched to an all music
station. The music was a soft, seductive jazz that made her
sway as she glanced toward an ice bucket with an open
bottle of chilling Chardonnay. She smiled. He'd followed
her instructions well.

"Good boy," she purred as she poured herself a glass.
"I'll reward you for that."

In the bathroom, she sipped her wine and filled the tub
with hot water. She pinned her hair up loosely, letting key
strands drape over her breasts. He would like seeing her
this way. Warm. Wet. Seductive.

Rebecca sipped her wine and leaned her head back against
the tile. A sigh shuddered through her. She closed her eyes,
letting the warm water waft over her skin. When she'd finished her wine, she rose out of the tub, pulled a plush towel
from the rack and dried. She picked up her empty wineglass and moved toward the bottle for a refill.

As she filled her glass she had the sudden sense that
someone was behind her. Her skin tingled. Stiffening, she
slowly replaced the bottle into the ice bucket. Her fingers
clutched her wineglass as unexpected anxiety sliced through
her body.

As she slowly turned, her peripheral caught the form of
a tall, thick man. A black mask covered his face and dark
gloves covered fisted fingers. Gripping the glass tighter,
she hurled the wine toward him hoping for an extra second
to race to her purse still sitting on the bed.

The stranger dodged the paltry attack and returned with
his own. A hard open hand slapped her face.

Pain rocketed through her jaw and head as she stumbled
toward the bed. She caught herself from falling into the
plush comforter and scrambled off the side of the bed

toward the back of the room. Her attacker laughed, clearly enjoying the chase. She reached toward the wine bottle and picked it up by the neck.

As she raised it over her head and wielded it like a club, cold expensive wine sloshed her arm and over her naked breasts. "Get the fuck away from me."

"You try to hit me and I'll make this worse."

"Fuck you."

He laughed. The hunt excited him. He moved toward her and she swung, a glancing blow striking his shoulder.

"Bitch," he growled. He closed the gap between them, grabbed her by the throat and backed her up to the curtained windows. As he squeezed her windpipe, he pressed her into the silk fabric and the cold glass behind it. She choked for air but didn't release the bottle. He squeezed harder, banging her hand none too gently against the thick hard glass. "Keep fighting. Please. I'd love to snap your neck."

She stared into the masked face, dark gray eyes staring at her with feverish intensity. She screwed up her face and spit.

He grabbed her naked breast and dug his fingers into the soft flesh around her nipple. Pain mingled with a lack of oxygen and soon her vision blurred. The fight drained from her body. She dropped the bottle. Seconds before she would slip into unconsciousness, he yanked her away from the window and threw her on the bed.

She choked in air, the skin around her nipple burning, as she scrambled to gather her wits. The tip of a knife pressed to her jugular tracked the blue-green line along the column of her throat past the hollow of her neck. "Make a sound and I'll skin you alive."

Her gaze narrowed and he must have read the defiance because with the knife tip he nicked her breast. Pain shot. Blood trickled down the side of her breast.

"Be a good girl?"

She nodded.

He reached in his jacket pocket and pulled out handcuffs. Cold metal clinked around her right and left hands. In seconds both were secured to the bedpost.

The man ran his hands over her naked mound, squeezing hard before clamping metal around both her ankles.

"Spread your legs," he ordered.

When she hesitated he traced the knife the length of her thigh. She spread her legs.

"Wider."

She complied.

He fastened the cuffs to the end of the bed. She lay spread-eagle on the bed, gasping for air, hurting, and bleeding.

He moved back a step to admire her form. He reached in a jacket pocket and pulled out several metal objects and tossed them beside her on the bed.

"Have a good look," he said.

She shook her head.

Laughing, he stripped off his jacket and then ripped off his mask, giving her a good look at his face. The makings of an evening shadow darkened his face. He wasn't much to look at and if she'd passed him on the street she might not have thought twice about him if not for his expensive haircut and hand-tailored suit. He unfastened his shirt, slowly, one button at a time.

"I've been watching you for days," he rasped. "I've dreamed about this."

She glanced at the bulge in his pants. Instead of fear, desire pricked her skin. She moistened her lips. "You're a dirty man, lover."

"Sugar," he said. "Call me Sugar." His was a baritone's voice, deep and seductive. He tugged off his gloves and ran his hand roughly over her body.

"Sugar," she whispered against his ear.

"You drive me crazy."

"Stop talking." Her voice held an air of command now. "I don't want any more talk."

Hesitation flickered in his gaze.

She was chained to the bed.

But she was in charge.

"Are you ready?" she asked.

"I'm always ready." Shoes kicked off and tailor-made pants whooshed to the floor.

He climbed on top of her, straddling her body. His erection pressed against her flat belly.

He could have penetrated her in a second and she'd have been powerless to stop him but he waited for her next order. His breathing was fast with his desire.

She liked it when he was on the knife-edge of desire, his wanting so acute that it hurt more than the nick in her breast. To make him suffer more, she wriggled under him, pressing her sex into him.

She had designed the entire scene. She'd picked the hotel, she'd told him when to arrive and how to act.

"Now," she said. "You can fuck me now."


Baby watched him slip out of the hotel side door, cross the parking lot and get into an older car that would blend into traffic unnoticed. Most days, he liked to be noticed. Liked the limelight. Liked the center stage. His red car. He ducked into the shadows when he wanted sin. And judging by the flush in his cheeks and the spring in his step, he'd been a bad, bad boy.

This bad boy had gone unpunished for a long time and clearly Dixie's lesson had not been enough to reform his ways or redirect him back to what was important.

Another lesson would have to be taught.

Settling back, Baby waited for the woman he'd no doubt

come to see. Baby didn't have a name for the woman and didn't know what she looked like but it wasn't hard to spot his type. Blond. Buxom. Pretty. So pretty. He was predictable when it came to women.

Fifteen minutes later a woman emerged from the side door. Blond hair flowed over narrow shoulders clad in a tailored suit. Her blouse was made of silk and her jewelry gold. Demure kitten heels kept her from being overly obvious. No fuck-me-pumps for this gal.

But this little lady possessed a swagger, a confidence that fit his perfect woman profile. He spent his days telling the world what to do, how to live, but alone, behind closed doors, he liked to be told what to do. He liked the strong ones.

The woman fished keys from a large leather purse, clicked open a car door lock and slid behind the wheel of a black Cadillac. She checked her makeup in the mirror and then carefully pulled into traffic. Baby fired up the engine and followed.

Wouldn't take much digging and poking around to find out if lady-in-the-suit would be his next lesson.

*January 5*

*Sugar,*

    *I know you are disappointed you couldn't help. I understand that you got a lot to lose. And really who would have seen that guy coming? He was on stage and hitting me before Rudy could grab his bat and knock him flat. And don't worry about the bruise. The doctor said it will heal fast. No broken bones.*

            *Xoxo,*
            *A.*

# Chapter Eleven

Hoots and high-fives had Deke glancing up from a forensics report through the glass walls of his office into the office center. Many of the officers had risen from their desks and were gathered around someone. Deke pinched the bridge of his nose and leaned back in his chair as he waited to see who had caused the commotion.

When the crowd cleared, he saw his brother Rick and Rick's canine, Tracker, moving from the circle of officers. Both Rick and Tracker paused and allowed back-slaps as if both understood returning to the station and being surrounded by the sights and sounds of cops was good.

Deke knew Rick had not wanted to take leave from the department, but he and his dog had been deemed unfit for street duty after the shooting. There'd been talk of wanting a desk job but Rick had resisted, opting to keep his options open while on unpaid leave. "Better to retrench and return," he'd said last year. "If we're not working the streets we'll go insane."

Rick had returned to school where he now was finishing up his undergraduate degree. Tracker spent his days always close at Rick's side. He'd become an honored mascot at school, no one ever questioning the right of a retired police dog to sit in class.

With Tracker on his heel, Rick entered Deke's office. Tracker jumped up on a worn leather couch and closed his eyes, though his ears remained perked.

Deke rose. "Welcome."

Rick shook Deke's hand. "I hear you have another victim."

"That's right." Deke settled in his chair as Rick carefully eased into the seat across from him.

Rick had taken a bullet to the hip. Even after six months, he struggled with discomfort and pain.

"What can you tell me about Lexis Hanover?"

"I didn't know her all that well. She was in the math department and I'm in the history department. But the school is like a big small town. Everyone knows everyone else's business. She was liked and respected. Some of the students have already started putting flowers at her office door."

"Anyone have a beef with her?"

Rick crossed his legs, resting his ankle on his knee. He laid a manila file on his thigh. "None that I heard of, but I can ask around if you like."

"I would. I want to know anyone who might have had a grudge. She died hard."

"Has the medical examiner looked at her yet?"

Deke checked his watch. "She will soon. You're welcome to sit in if you like."

"What about your partner?"

"Busy with personnel, getting the last of his retirement papers squared away. Tonight is his retirement party."

"You and KC have been partners six months?"

"Give or take."

He shifted his weight as if moving away from the pain. "Must be odd working with a guy who worked with Buddy."

"It's been an experience." All the Morgan kids had

worked under Buddy's shadow. He'd been a damned legend in Homicide. But Deke had born the brunt of most of the comparisons.

"So what do you have for me?"

Rick flipped open the file. "I've been digging nonstop. Interesting case."

Deke leaned back in his chair. "I can tell by that twinkle in your eye that you found something."

"Buddy had two big breaks on this case. The first came eight weeks after Annie vanished. Her bones were found in the woods. Not much of her left. Head and hands were missing. But a silver heart-shaped necklace was found with the bones and later identified as Annie's."

"Not much forensic evidence."

"The arm bones did show severe unhealed fractures. Best guess was that she'd been beaten to death."

"Like my current victims."

Rick raised a brow. "Similar, as a matter of fact. Without the skull it is impossible to tell about facial injuries but her extremities were shattered with a hard object."

Deke leaned back in his chair. "What are the chances it's the same killer?"

"Killers do go dark for any number of reasons, and then for equally unknown reasons they reactivate."

"What was Buddy's second break?"

"Four days after Annie Dawson's body was found a confidential informant named Max Quincy who was in county jail on theft charges told his guards that he had information on the Annie Dawson case. Said he'd trade his information if charges were dropped."

"And Buddy went for that? The story was all over the news and radio. How many CIs or false witnesses did they have to sift through?"

"A few. But Buddy didn't pass up any leads. He talked to every nut that called in with a tip, including Max."

"And what did Max tell Buddy?"

Rick pulled out a piece of paper and handed it to Deke. It was Max's rap sheet with a photo of the blurry-eyed informant staring toward the ground. He sported a day's growth of beard and his hair stuck up as if he'd run his fingers through it a hundred times.

"Max is the man that broke the case. He's the one that refocused the cops onto Jeb who had been questioned after Annie had vanished but never arrested for lack of evidence."

"I know they'd gotten a lucky break but a paid CI?" Paid CIs could be valuable, but cops always weighed the CI's greed versus the truth.

"In exchange for his testimony, Max had the charges dropped and he received a small cash sum."

"How did he know Jeb?"

"They were drinking buddies. Saw each other in the bars all the time. Max remembers Jeb talking about Annie a few weeks before she vanished."

"I came across some letters." He gave Rick a rundown on the letters' backstory along with copies.

Eyes bright with interest, Rick studied the letters. "Are you going to have them authenticated?"

"That's what Lexis Hanover was doing when she was killed. The letters she had were taken. But our Ms. Wainwright kept copies and some originals. I've given those to Brad Holcombe in Forensics."

Rick shuffled through the pages. "It pays to be suspicious."

"Brad should have an analysis within days."

Rick frowned. "Have you told Georgia about the letters? She's good with handwriting."

"Let's have Brad take a crack at them first." He reached for a mug and took a sip. Cold coffee tasted bitter. "Has she asked you about the case files?"

"She's called and offered to bring me dinner."

"She's slick."

"Don't I know it."

"So why tell me about Max?"

"Because he's alive and well and after a little checking I found out that he's in lockup once again. Thirty years has not done much to mend his ways."

Deke took the piece of paper with Rick's handwritten notes. "So Max says he saw Jeb before Annie vanished and Jeb was talking about Annie."

"He wouldn't be the first killer who couldn't keep his mouth shut."

"After a chat with Max the cops searched Jeb's car trunk and found the bloodied tire iron."

"A blood test reveals the type is O, a match to Annie, and B+, a match to Jeb. The cops believe they have found their man. When he's arrested, he's drunk. Buddy talks to him but gets nowhere fast. Tosses him in the drunk tank until he sobers up."

"Buddy's under pressure to get a confession."

"Sure. But you know Buddy didn't bow to pressure. Fact, he welcomed a good fight. No, he was gonna get a righteous confession or none at all. I watched the interview tapes. A lean, mean Buddy is on his game. Jeb is confused. At first he says he didn't hurt Annie. And then he cries. Jeb is hungover and sick but at this point he has enough sense to demand an attorney. Buddy gets him a public defender. The PD has alone time with Jeb and then Buddy reenters the room. Jeb is really not well now. Buddy promises he'll feel better if he tells the truth. The attorney warns silence but Jeb takes "better" to mean booze and confesses to killing Annie. After that he found himself on a runaway train that could not be stopped."

"Exactly."

"DNA is not back yet, is it?"

"I just checked. A day or two more." Deke opened his

desk drawer and pulled out his gun and slid it into his holster. "Why don't we go have a chat with Max."

Rick grinned. "Tracker. Want to go ride in a car?"

Tracker's eyes opened and he barked. Rick rose and helped the dog off the couch. Tracker wagged his tail and barked again. "You want me to drive?"

Deke rattled the keys in his hand. "I'll drive."

Fifteen minutes later, Deke, Rick, and Tracker arrived at the city jail. The three were taken to an interview room while the guard located Max.

"You can't miss this part of the job," Deke said, staring at the gray walls.

"I miss it all."

"Ever thought about requalifying?"

"Sure. I've thought about it. And I think if I hit it hard I could make it happen. But Tracker's done. And if he can't work, I'm out. We're a team."

"How's his hip?"

"Giving him trouble. The supplements help a lot but he'll never run again like he did." Loyalty ran deep in Rick. He'd stayed in Nashville for the family. Given up a job he'd loved for a dog he loved. Lost a woman because of his brother Alex. Deke had allowed Rick to step into Buddy's shoes but now realized that hadn't been fair. It was his job to hold the Morgans together.

Before Deke could comment, the doors swung open and a handcuffed older man wearing an orange jumpsuit entered the room. The man's body bordered on withered and the long gray hair tied at the nape of his neck had thinned to stringy strands. Fading tattoos covered his arms.

A uniformed guard held him by the arm and guided him to the bench by the table.

"Max Quincy?" Deke asked.

The old man studied him with squinted, leery eyes before grinning. "You got to be Buddy Morgan's boy."

"That's right."

"That man had an unforgettable mug. And when he was pissed he could scare Satan himself."

Legends cast long shadows. "You were a CI for Buddy."

"That's right. Gave him good information. Helped him crack all kinds of cases." Max sniffed and sat back in his chair with the confidence of a man holding all the cards.

"You gave him the big tip on the Annie Rivers Dawson case." He smiled. "Launched his career."

Max puffed out his chest. "Buddy knew it too. He always looked out for me after that. Fact, if he were still alive today, I'd be out of jail by now."

Deke leaned forward. "I'm getting some heat on the Annie Rivers Dawson case. See it on the news?"

"That lawyer." His lips flattened into a grim line. "She don't know what she's talking about. She wasn't born when it happened. But I was there. I know."

"You still remember the case?"

"As if it were yesterday."

Deke doubted the old man recalled the details as they'd happened. The ego might cling to memories, but the truth was, time faded details into half-truths and tall tales.

"Tell me. Buddy and I never talked about his old cases. And I'd like to know what you remember."

Max rolled his head from side to side, exposing a fading skull and crossbones tattoo on the side of his neck. "I can tell you for sure that Jeb Jones is a damn liar. He killed her."

"Tell me what you remember."

"It was days after she vanished. We was sitting in a bar and drinking. I was a heavy drinker, fact, few men could drink me under the table, but Jeb could. Anyway, he'd gotten paid so he had extra money. Meaning extra drinks."

"He was drunk."

"As a skunk. Anyway, he started talking about Annie.

Said she was pretty. Said she'd had the baby but you couldn't tell by looking at her that she'd ever been pregnant. She was still perfect. And even though she was married, he'd never stopped dreaming that they'd be together."

"You think Jeb and Annie had a thing going? Did they ever sleep together?"

"The way Jeb talked about her, you'd think they was knocking boots, if you know what I mean. He was always talking about how pretty she was and he described her body as if he'd seen it naked enough times."

"Did he say they were lovers?"

"He said it enough times but none of us at the bar believed him. I mean how could a loser like him land a beauty like her?"

"It's happened."

"Maybe. Whether he slept with her or not he wanted to real bad and he thought he kind of had a right to her. In his mind she was his."

Jeb, guilty or not of murder, had been stalking Annie. There'd been enough evidence at his trial to prove that beyond a shadow of a doubt. And stalkers did turn on their victims when watching no longer was enough. Murder was the ultimate control over an individual. "Did he say anything after news of her murder hit the papers?"

"Oh, he was all tore up. Balled like a baby. Odd to see a tough guy like him crumble." Max cocked his head. "Funny he should blubber when he killed her."

Not funny or odd at all. Killers often felt remorse for a victim they'd killed in a moment of anger. "How'd you figure the tire iron was in his trunk?"

"He told me he'd done something bad. Wouldn't say what it was but he said it was bad. From there I put two and two together."

"You called Buddy and told him you had a tip on the case."

"That's right."

"Why'd it take you four days to talk to Buddy?"

"'Cause it didn't make sense for me to talk until I was in trouble. A good card player keeps his hand close to his vest until the time is right."

"So you were in trouble and needed a way out. And you happened to have information on the most publicized case in the city."

"Better to be lucky than smart, I always say."

"Oh, no, you hit the jackpot that go-around. Did Jeb ever tell you why he cut up the body or where he dumped the head and arms?"

Max sat back. "I've been giving you a lot of good information and I'm now wondering what am I getting in return?"

"So far you've given me what's in the public record. I could have gone to the courthouse and pulled the transcripts and gotten the same information."

Rick shifted behind him, his impatience palatable. "He doesn't know anything."

Max glared at him with the eyes of a seasoned player. "I told you what I remembered."

"Bullshit," Rick said.

Max wagged a long pale finger bent and turned with arthritis. "Maybe I do. Plus I've info on a drug deal that will be going down on Broadway."

"I'm not here for the drugs, Max. I'm here about Annie Dawson. Jeb swore he never killed her. If he felt as bad about her death as you say then he'd have said more."

"He gave me a few clues."

"Such as?"

"I'm not telling until I get some kind of promise."

Deke rose from his chair and glanced at Rick. "We're done here."

Rick nodded. "He's full of shit."

The two brothers moved to the door. The sound of Max's chains clinked as he pounded the table. Fury blazed in his eyes. "You can't leave me like this! I can help you!"

Deke reached for the door. "I bet if I leave you in a cell for a few more days and you can't get a fix, you'll be one hurting guy."

"That's not right. That's torture!"

"I'm hearing noise now, Max."

Rick chuckled. "I hear withdrawal is a bitch."

Deke shook his head. "I sure as hell would hate to go through it. Throw up, shakes, and sometimes they see spiders and bugs that ain't there."

Max swallowed and rubbed a shaking hand over his forehead as if he'd travelled this road before. "Okay, okay."

With his hand on the door, Deke hesitated. "Okay what?"

"I might remember where he dumped Annie's head."

"You might?" Rick snorted. "Not good enough."

"Okay, I'll tell you exactly where."

Rick shook his head. "It's been thirty years. I don't think he remembers. He wants out of that cell so bad he'll make up any story."

Bloodshot eyes seized onto Deke. "No. That ain't true! I know stuff."

Deke yawned and checked his watch. "Then why didn't you play the card sooner, Max? Why wait until now?"

"'Cause it's been thirty years and I didn't think anybody cared about yesterday's news."

Deke folded his arms over his chest and leaned against the wall. "Where's the skull?"

"If I tell you, will you let me out of here?"

"If I find what I'm looking for, I surely will let you out of here. But if I don't then you'll stay put for a real long time."

"That's not fair! I can't help if the terrain has changed over the years. Nashville has grown a lot."

Deke smelled lies on Max. Stinking lies. And he wondered if the con man had ever had information. Maybe Max had played Buddy thirty years ago. Buddy wasn't the kind of cop to let a drunkard lead him by the nose, but he'd been desperate and under a lot of pressure. And desperate men made bad decisions. "Where's the head?"

"It's off I-40. Near exit 201."

"That's not very precise."

Max's hands trembled. "The skull is there, I tell you. I remember. Near a tree."

Rick's gaze sharpened as it had when he was a cop. "A tree off Exit 201. That's bull. Those directions are worthless."

"Take me there. I'll show you. I know if I see it I will find the spot."

This all smelled wrong. "Why didn't you ever tell Buddy?"

Max sniffed. "Like I said, I figured the day would come and I'd have to play the card."

"There's a lot of houses in that area," Deke said.

"Not when Jeb buried it."

This stunk. "I'll be back."

Max's cuffs rattled as he sat straighter. "What's that mean?"

"It means if I find what I'm looking for, I'll let you out."

"Aren't you gonna let me out of jail so I can show you?"

"Nope. And if you're lying to me you're gonna be here as long as I can keep you here."

Max fisted his hand, clenching until his knuckles whitened. "If you'll get me out of here, I'll lead you to your skull. Go on and see. Off Dabney Road, near a gas station."

Deke moved toward Max. "You're lying."

Max's gaunt face turned ashen. "I ain't."

Rick laughed as if Max's words reminded him of a child's statement.

Deke grinned. "I can smell it. Rot and stench. Lies."

Max chewed on his thumbnail. "I heard there was a skull there."

Heard. Didn't see. "When did you hear?"

"Back in the day. Jeb must have mentioned it."

The waters grew murkier and murkier. "Tell me now, Max. Did you lie about Jeb and the tire iron all those years ago?"

"No! They found it in his car, didn't they?"

Deke crossed to the table, planted his hands on it and leaned toward Max. "Did you put it there?"

"No!"

Rick hung back but his gaze burned into Max. "Fingering Annie Rivers Dawson's killer would have been a hell of a coup."

"I didn't put it there. But I heard around town it was there."

"Where'd you hear?"

"I don't remember, but it's good information."

"This is crap," Rick said. "None of this is right."

Chains rattled as Max lifted his hands. "I was right about the tire iron and I'm right about that skull. Let me show you!"

Deke backed away from the table. "We'll let you sit and think. When you got more details we'll talk again."

Deke called for the guard and he and Rick watched the guard lead a screaming Max away. As they walked outside, both remained silent.

Inside the car, Deke hesitated before he started the engine. "You're right. This all smells like shit."

Rick glanced back at Tracker and rubbed him on the head. "Buddy was too sharp to be played."

"Under normal circumstances."

Deke started the engine as Rick adjusted his seat until he was comfortable. Two murder victims had him questioning every fact. "What if it was someone else? What if someone else set up Jeb?"

Rick shook his head. "Like space aliens or Big Foot?"

Deke ignored Rick as if he were a pesky seven-year-old wanting to tag along. "Say whoever killed Annie is killing again. All the victims have a link to her."

Rick tipped his head back against the headrest. "Okay, I'll play. What would set him off after thirty years?"

"Birthdays, deaths, med changes, job changes, a spouse dies. Hell, if I know."

"Buddy could sniff out lies like no one else. He had to have believed Max was legit. Max is lying to us now but back in the day he had real information."

Deke drummed his fingers on the steering wheel. "Who else wanted Annie dead?"

Rick shook his head. "She was a beautiful woman. Talented. Buddy did question other suspects during the investigation."

"What about the husband?"

"Cleared. Was in Knoxville at the time of the murder."

"What if he hired someone?"

"Possible. But that doesn't explain why he'd kill again. I checked into his life. He's done well. Remarried. Has kids. He doesn't make sense."

"Then who?"

"And we are back to the question that drove Buddy to near exhaustion."

Deke imagined his father weeks before his death. "I never saw Buddy tired. The man had the energy of six men."

"We were kids. Parents hide information from their

children. He lowered his guard around Mom. She'd have been the one he'd have told about his heart."

"He sure as shit never allowed any of his kids to keep information secret."

A half smile tugged the edges of Rick's lips. "Like that time you hid that bottle of bourbon under the bench in the backyard. What were you, fourteen?"

"Fifteen."

"Buddy took one look at you and started asking questions."

"'Don't you lie to me, boy,' he kept saying." Deke had always had a knack for secrets and hiding. Made him a great undercover officer and a lousy husband. "To this day I don't know how he figured it out."

"I always thought it was Georgia who ratted you out. She was about five."

"She swore she never told."

Rick laughed. "And you believed her? Hell, she was the only one who could fool Buddy with a fib. She had his number from day one."

"Yeah."

Deke pulled into traffic. "Shit. We're all wrapped around her finger."

"Lot's going on in that head of hers. We hear a tenth of what she's thinking."

"Like always."

A silence settled between them. "She wants in on this case."

"Tough."

"She's a grown woman, Deke, not a knob-kneed kid. She's proven time and again she can handle herself."

"Don't care."

"My best advice is to not go all Buddy on her."

"What's that mean?"

"You're her brother, not her father. Buddy could get

away with treating her like a kid, but you can't. She'll come out swinging."

Deke shoved out a breath. "Easier said than done."

"You don't have to fill his shoes."

Deke shook his head. "What do you mean?"

"Buddy is gone. We all miss him like hell but he's gone. You can't fill his shoes. Shit. I couldn't do it."

Unease had him shifting in his seat. "I'm not trying to fill Buddy's shoes."

"Bullshit. You're trying to hold us together. It's why you moved back into the Big House."

"I moved back into the Big House because it's cheap living."

"You hate the Big House."

Deke glanced up in time to see Rachel Wainwright striding across the parking lot. He frowned. "It's growing on me."

Rick followed his gaze. "The very attractive Ms. Wainwright."

He leaned forward in his seat. "Yeah."

"So do you love her or hate her?"

"What?"

Rick leaned back in his seat, grinning like a cat. "Dude, with an expression like yours, it's either love or hate. No in between with that gal."

Deke shifted, but his gaze lingered a beat before turning away from Rachel. "I don't know what you're talking about."

"Don't shit me, bro. Love or hate?"

He didn't answer. Instead he fired up the car. "I'll take you to your car, then double back to court."

Rick grinned. "If you're saying it's hate then that's good because I'd take her out in a heartbeat. She rocks those pants."

Deke growled. "Don't even go there."

"I can date whomever I want." Laughter brightened his gaze. "So it's not hate?"

"I don't know what the hell it is." Deke tightened his hand on the steering wheel. "But she's off-limits."

Little brother had found a sensitive spot and couldn't resist grinding into it. "For how long?"

"Not her. Not ever."

*February 1*

*Sugar,*

    *A record producer gave me his card after my second set tonight. He said I got it. I don't know exactly what that means but I like the sound of it. IT!!*

          *Xoxo,*
          *A.*

# Chapter Twelve

*Monday, October 17, 1:15 PM*

The news of Lexis's death clung to Rachel like a shroud. Thinking was difficult, even putting one foot in front of the other was a struggle.

It had been like this after Luke's arrest. He'd been hauled away and their mother had been devastated. Rachel had been overwhelmed and paralyzed with indecision. But life had refused to allow her time to wallow. It had forced her to get moving, to prop up her mother, and to keep Luke's hopes alive.

And now as much as she wanted to call it quits on Jeb and the countless other lost causes that found her, she didn't. Lexis, more than anyone, would have expected her to keep fighting.

*So you gonna quit?*

"No," she muttered.

Her gut told her to dig deeper into Annie's case because she sensed the killer had murdered Dixie and Lexis. Thirty years may have separated the three deaths but a connection existed.

As tempted as Rachel was to put her paying work aside

longer, life didn't care what she wanted. It demanded she work and pay bills. If her practice went bankrupt, she'd be no good to anyone. And so here she was at the jail ready to talk to the client assigned to her by the public defender's office. The cases didn't pay the big bucks, but any case was better than no work.

She arrived ready to argue for her new client, Mr. Oscar McMillian, a forty-six-year-old waiter who worked at a trendy restaurant in the tony area of Franklin. According to the police report, written by Detective Deke Morgan, Oscar had dated Ellen Roberts several times before police had found her strangled to death in her apartment. Oscar had been the first suspect Deke had interviewed.

Deke Morgan.

He'd come through for her the other night. In fact, she wasn't sure what she'd have done if not for his help. But professionally, he was a menace. And now they had another case to argue over.

After showing her identification to the officer on duty, and having her purse checked, she was escorted to the interview room. She had a little time to open her file and review the McMillian case one more time.

The door opened to a tall attractive man. He had a slim build, a thick shock of black hair and a pleasant face. Not overly handsome, but he would gain a second look from many a female. He sported a bandage on the side of his neck.

When their gazes met he grinned. His smile was electric and added a devilish quality that ratcheted up his attractive factor tenfold.

She rose. "Mr. McMillian. I'm Rachel Wainwright. I'm your public defender."

He nodded, moved to offer her his hand but stopped when the guard shook his head. "Thank you for coming. I've felt pretty lost here until I heard about you."

"From who?"

"You've a solid reputation here."

They sat across from each other at the table. She glanced at her notes, aware that he was staring at her. "What happened to your neck?"

"Got into a scuffle." A smile tweaked the edges of his lips. "The jail infirmary patched me up."

"Were you mistreated by the police?"

He shook his head. "No. Just a scuffle."

Her gaze lingered as she imagined the scuffle. When he didn't offer any more information, she asked, "Mr. McMillian, do you understand the charges against you?"

He shook his head. "Murder. I'm accused of killing Ellen Roberts."

She met his gaze. "The cops say you strangled her."

Threading his fingers together he shook his head. "That's not true. I liked Ellen. We'd dated and had laughs, but I never hurt her."

She glanced at the case file she'd received from the police. "They found your DNA in her apartment."

"That makes sense. Like I said, we dated. I spent the night at her place a couple of times. All that fits."

"Police said you also used her credit card."

"She asked me to go to the liquor store and buy fixings for a party. She was working and didn't have time. I didn't think about it. I thought I was doing her a favor."

His gaze remained unwavering but desperation hummed under the words.

"Witnesses said you two fought the night before she died."

Dark circles hung under his eyes. "Couples fight. If every fighting couple were arrested the jails would be overflowing."

"Why did you fight?"

"She was mad at me. I was late and she hates it when

anyone is late. I told her I had to close at the restaurant, but she didn't care. Said I should have called. I told her I didn't think to call. I said I was sorry and we made up. End of story. No drama."

He sounded convincing but the best liars pass a lie detector test. "Witness said the argument sounded heated."

"She has . . . had a temper." He dropped his face into his manacled hands and paused as if trying to gather himself. "I still can't believe she's gone. She didn't deserve this."

She studied her notes. "She worked in a restaurant located across the street from your place."

"The Yellow Bird. She was the store manager."

"How'd you two meet?"

"We all know each other on that block. Our places close about the same time and we all see each other. It's natural to want to grab a drink and unwind before going home."

"At the time of her death were you two dating?"

"I wouldn't say dating. Laughs and sleeping together."

"Sounds like dating."

He shook his head. "Dating sounds more intimate to me. When you date someone you have to have a level of trust, I think."

"So you didn't trust Ellen."

"I didn't know her that well. She was attractive and fun and that was enough." He nodded toward the police report. "Don't believe all that cop said about me. I could see from the get-go that he had a chip on his shoulder. Thought he was a real badass."

She looked at her notes. "You are referring to Detective Deke Morgan."

"That's right, Detective Morgan."

"He do anything inappropriate?"

"He was being a cop. Pushy. Abrupt. Not nice to be around."

Deke Morgan's notes had been precise and clear. He'd

sketched out crime scene notes and had talked to several people that had worked with both Oscar and Ellen. Most had said the couple appeared happy. One witness had reported the fight. "He was investigating a murder."

"He looked at me like I was guilty from the moment he laid eyes on me."

"Again, anything inappropriate?"

"Technically, he followed the book. But like I said, he had it all figured out minutes after meeting me."

Funny that McMillian received such a strong vibe off Deke when she couldn't figure him out. He was a hard-ass but then when she'd needed someone he'd been there.

"Look," McMillian said. "I'm fighting for my life here. I didn't kill Ellen and I feel like the cops are railroading me. It's like I'm caught in a bad dream and I don't know how to get out of it."

Rachel drew in a breath. She wasn't blind to the fact that he could be guilty. "You've a bail hearing in less than an hour. I'll tackle the issue of bail and in the next few days I'll go over your case."

His look softened and he swallowed as if tears tightened his throat. "Thank you, Ms. Wainwright. I'm counting on you."

"I'll be in touch."

Rachel left the jail behind and walked the block to the courthouse. She paused at a sidewalk vendor and bought a large cup of coffee, which she flavored with two sugars and cream. Purse slung over her shoulder, she sipped the bitter coffee. It was her third cup and had done little to ease her fatigue.

She arrived in the courtroom as the bailiff was calling the case that she knew was several before McMillian's. When she'd first started practicing she'd arrived early for her cases but as the weeks and months and now years had passed, she'd learned to time her arrival so she spent as little time in court as possible.

She dug the McMillian file out of her briefcase and reviewed the statistics. She could argue that there was enough reasonable doubt to at least get McMillian's bond dropped or reduced.

The noises of the courtroom buzzed around as she burrowed deeper into the file. Suddenly, she had an odd sense of unease. She looked up and across the aisle sat Deke Morgan. He was staring right at her. When their gazes locked he nodded and then turned back toward the judge.

She swallowed, wondering if he was here for McMillian's bail hearing.

Her answer came swiftly when the bailiff called McMillian's name and armed deputies led her client into the courtroom. She rose and moved to stand beside him.

"Council for the defense is?" The judge was in her early fifties and wore dark graying hair in a short bob. Dark-rimmed glasses magnifying her eyes had earned her the nickname of Owl. Owl, or rather Judge Osborne, was a stickler for the rule of law.

"Rachel Wainwright for the defense."

Large brown eyes peered over the brief. "Ms. Wainwright, we are here today to discuss Mr. McMillian's bail, is that correct?"

"Yes, Your Honor."

Judge Osborne rifled through a collection of papers on her bench. "And do you have a comment about bail?"

"It's far too high. My client has no prior arrests for violent behavior."

The judge pulled off her glasses. "There is a first time for everyone, Ms. Wainwright."

"He is a solid citizen, who has lived in the same apartment for two years. He's held his job for over two years. He is not a flight risk."

The judge glanced past Rachel. "Detective Morgan, you are now standing. Do you have a statement?"

Rachel's spine straightened as she imagined Detective Morgan pulling back his broad shoulders.

"Yes, Your Honor." The deep timbre of his voice carried the weight of authority.

"You are the arresting officer?"

"Correct." His voice reverberated through the court-house.

The judge sat back in her chair and folded her arms over her chest. "And what say you about the defendant?"

Rachel faced Deke, who kept his gaze on the judge as if she didn't exist.

"There is clear evidence against him in this case, Your Honor. We have eyewitness testimony that suggests he should be held until trial."

"This is not a trial, Detective," Rachel said. "It's a bail hearing."

His gaze flickered to Rachel and then back to the judge. "I understand that. But I would argue that Mr. McMillian is a danger to society and should remain behind bars until his trial. There're details of his past I'm investigating. He is a time bomb. Not a matter of if he goes, it's a matter of *when*."

"Do you have facts or merely opinions?" Rachel asked.

Deke shot her a glance. "He should not be let out of jail before his trial."

The judge sighed and glanced at her notes. "And he has no priors?"

"Correct," Rachel said.

The judge shook her head.

"I would also add," Rachel said. "That Ellen was dating two other men at the time of her death and it is possible that either could have killed her. I know we aren't trying the case now but there is enough today to lower the bail from one million dollars to ten thousand dollars."

The judge smiled. "Nice try, Ms. Wainwright. Bail is set at one hundred thousand dollars and the defendant is ordered to stay in the Nashville area until trial unless he has permission from the court." She banged her gavel.

Deke shook his head and then left the courthouse as McMillian turned to thank Rachel. "Thanks, Ms. Wainwright."

She gripped the handle of her briefcase. "You have a bail bondsman?"

"Yes."

She handed him her card. "As soon as we have a court date, I'll contact you. Don't leave Nashville."

"No, no, I won't." Tears welled in his eyes. "Thank you again, Ms. Wainwright."

She left the courthouse knowing if she hustled she could beat the evening traffic. As much as she needed a run, her shoulder still ached and she wasn't ready to jog alone at dusk.

Outside she fumbled with her briefcase, keys, and coffee when a shadow cast over her. Tensing and heart racing, she gripped the handle of her briefcase, ready to swing. She looked up to see Detective Morgan glowering at her. His menace didn't dampen her relief. "How is your afternoon been going, Detective?"

"Not great." He shoved his hand in his pocket and leaned toward her. "A cold-blooded murderer scored bail."

"If you are referring to Mr. McMillian, you must use alleged in your sentences when you talk about him."

"Nothing alleged about it, Ms. Wainwright. The guy killed Ellen. He picked her out of a crowd, stalked her, finally convinced her to go on a couple of dates and when she didn't want to see him again, he killed her."

Her skin prickled, singed by his fiery intensity. "Nice theory but no proof."

"I'll prove it. Make no mistake. Let's hope he doesn't kill anyone in the interim."

She dropped her keys, cursed, and then crouched to pick them up. "You are being dramatic. The guy has no criminal record."

"Dig a little deeper. No formal charges have been filed but talk to the women who work with him. He's made several of them nervous."

"He makes them nervous. Please. That doesn't mean he killed Ellen."

He studied her, his frustration reminded her of an adult talking to a child. "Be careful around him. He's clever and he could easily turn on you."

She unlocked her car door. "I'll keep that in mind. By the way, how is my DNA coming along?"

"You've a one-track mind."

She tossed her briefcase and purse in the backseat, grateful to have the weight off her shoulder. "So I've been told."

"How's the shoulder?"

"Hurts like hell. Have they done Lexis's autopsy yet?"

"Today. The medical examiner will release her body soon."

Suddenly the fire and vinegar seeped from her bones. "Good. You'll let me know when I can take custody of her?" She couldn't bring herself to say *body*. A simple word but it reduced Lexis to a thing and she couldn't do that.

"Sure." His own heat and fire still radiated, but it had cooled. In the courtroom he'd been all business and now she saw the face of the man who'd come to the hospital for her. That man she could almost like.

"Thanks."

"Had any trouble?"

"No. But I'm as nervous as a cat."

"Good. Stay that way and be careful."

"Always."


Deke was still irritated with Rachel when he arrived at the medical examiner's office. Despite her know-it-all attitude, she was wrong about McMillian. On a hunch, he'd called dispatch and requested all uniforms to keep an eye out for McMillian, especially if he made a move on Rachel who would be an easy unsuspecting target.

KC spotted Deke and pushed away from the wall as he studied his notebook. "I won't miss these dates of ours, Deke."

Deke crossed the lobby. "I can't see you retiring. Hard to believe today is it."

Weariness weighed KC's shoulders. "It's time. I'm a dinosaur. You're the new guard."

"So what do you plan to do with yourself?"

"Heading east to see my son."

"What about Brenda?"

"She's working and her mother is sick. And it doesn't seem right to take her to meet my boy. She's younger and well, I'm not ready to take her to prime time, if you know what I mean."

"Sure." Deke pressed the elevator button. "I hear there's a party for you tonight."

He grinned. "A hell of a blow-out. Cannot wait. Georgia said she'd sing."

"So I hear. You going to spend more time with Brenda after you get back into town?"

He laughed. "Sure. But the trick will be not to piss her off. She's already annoyed when I'm underfoot on my days off."

"Trading one danger for another."

"Murders I get. Premenopausal women not so much."

Laughter rumbled. "Christ, KC, that's a big word. I didn't realize you knew it."

"It's another disadvantage of getting old, my boy. Your day will come."

"I'm not getting married again. I'm no good at it."

"Maybe you never met the right woman."

"My wives were good women. I was the wrong guy and that's never going to change."

"That's a bit dramatic."

"Nope. Just practical."

Deke pushed into the exam room. As soon as he saw the exposed body of Lexis Hanover, all good humor vanished.

Dr. Heller appeared dressed in scrubs, her dark hair pulled in a tight ponytail. "Gentlemen."

In this room Deke never felt in his element. Crime scenes he understood because they told a story that he could figure out. But in the autopsy room he was an outsider.

"I finished the autopsy." She moved to the pale, still, brutalized body now marred by a large Y incision on her chest. "The blow to her head killed her." She pointed to the crushed right side of Lexis's skull. "This blow killed her quickly. But judging by the wounds on her knees and elbow, I'd say this was not the first strike. I'd say your killer tortured her before killing her."

Deke studied the shattered knees and the elbow. "The majority of Dixie Simmons's blows were to her face. Lexis Hanover sustained injuries all over her body."

"Her face was all but obliterated. But not in the case of Ms. Hanover. Her features are still recognizable."

KC rubbed the back of his neck. "Dixie was pretty. Sexy. Lexis was smart. Had more the librarian look. Two very different victims."

"And then there is Rachel Wainwright," Deke said.

KC frowned. "I heard about her attack. Happened outside her office."

Deke nodded. "Struck with a blunt object. But she heard her attacker coming and dodged at the last second. Hit hard but avoided the killing blow."

Dr. Heller reached for a sheet and pulled it over Lexis Hanover's body. "Ms. Wainwright called earlier to see when we'd release Hanover's body. Professional, but she sounded upset."

"They were friends," Deke said.

"So we got an Annie lookalike that's killed," KC said. "A woman stirring up Annie's case attacked. And Hanover had the letters."

"What letters?" Dr. Heller asked.

"Letters apparently written by Annie Dawson were sent to Rachel. She'd sent them to Hanover for authentication."

"It all goes back to Annie," KC said.

Deke nodded. "Was there anyone else you and Buddy suspected before Max gave you the big tip?"

KC rubbed his chin. "We vetted the husband, cleared him soon enough. Checked out the bars where she sang but no hits. Talked to her roommates, pastor, and her boyfriend from high school. They all checked out."

"You suspect any women?"

KC shrugged. "Her roommates were Beth and Joanne. I remember Beth didn't like Annie at all. Not at all. But she died about a decade ago."

"How'd she die?"

"Believe it was a car accident."

"Was it in Nashville?"

"Believe it was."

"Do me a favor and pull any reports on her."

"Why?"

"Can't say, exactly. But I want more details."

* * *

"You didn't get all the letters."

"I got all the letters at that woman's house. All of them. I was careful."

"They aren't all here. There are ten. There should be twenty."

"There are more than ten letters there."

"Half are originals and half are copies."

"I searched and that's all I found," Baby said. "Even got you that song Annie wrote."

"You've created such a mess."

"Why is it such a mess? I read the letters," Baby challenged. "No names are mentioned."

"You don't understand."

Baby frowned. "I understand. I understand that whatever I do for you is never going to be good enough. Never."

Instead of a rebuttal, the woman shifted through the papers again. "I know there were twenty letters in all. Twenty." She shook her head. "Rachel Wainwright is smarter than she looks. I'll bet she didn't give that woman all the letters."

"Why wouldn't she give them all for testing?"

"She's smart. She's always planning for the worst."

"I can go back to her building and search." Mother still didn't know about the attack on Rachel. "I'm smarter than both of them together."

"Don't be so sure of yourself. If you were real smart you'd never have given the letters to her and we'd be in the clear."

"We are in the clear. He's the one that has to worry."

"This is our problem, not his."

"Why do you always protect him?"

"Be quiet. Let me think."

A clock ticked on the wall. The old woman shifted in her wheelchair, as if hating the immobility. "Dixie Simmons was selfish and self-absorbed. Trouble waiting to happen."

Baby smiled. "Killing her was like shooting fish in a barrel. Lexis was easy to fool." But Rachel. She was a cagey woman. A survivor.

"Rachel will have to die. And soon."

A teapot whistled in the kitchen. Baby rose. "I was thinking about Rachel. I was thinking . . ."

"Stop thinking about Rachel. There's someone else we need to consider visiting first."

"Who?"

"Serve the tea and we will talk."


The evening television newscaster gave a recap of the construction on I-40 and the traffic delays as Rudy Creed settled in front of the television with a cup of tea. It was busy tonight at the bar and he could spare only five or ten minutes before he had to run back downstairs and get behind the bar.

He settled on the couch next to Nikki whose attention was held by the cup of tea in her hands. She slurped from the edge of the cup.

"Did you have a good day?" Rudy asked.

"I cleaned." *Slurp.* "The bar was dirty."

"You do a good job." He glanced at Nikki's vacant lost stare.

"I know. I'm a good cleaner." She brushed back a strand of graying hair with the back of her hand.

She'd been cleaning for him for more years than he could remember and in the beginning when she'd taken the job she'd been terrible, barely knowing what end of the mop to use. But she'd wanted to please, wanted to work so he'd been patient until she'd learned the bar's less glamorous routine.

Rudy smiled and turned his attention to the television. The newscaster had switched from traffic and turned the show over to Susan Martinez who wore a blood red suit jacket that sharply contrasted with her hair's inky blackness. "Sources close to the Nashville Police Department say that there are no suspects in the murder of Dixie Simmons, a local singer beaten to death last week. Police are also investigating the death of Lexis Hanover, a private detective and teacher who was also beaten to death. Currently police are saying there is no connection between the killings."

Rudy shook his head, deep worry spreading through his body. He'd not been too surprised when the cops had come to talk to him about Dixie's death. The way that girl lived and the men she ran with, it was a matter of time before someone did her harm. Even when that detective had asked questions of her, he'd not worried. Dixie wasn't the first young singer to end up brutalized or dead.

But the death of Lexis Hanover had him thinking that maybe . . . no, no, no. He halted his train of thought, refusing to give credibility to his worries. He focused on his tea, knowing it would be several more hours before he could take a break. Nikki continued to stare into her teacup, seemingly unmindful of the news or much else around her.

Nikki was like that. Simple. She didn't ask much and if directed to work she did her chores without hesitation. She wasn't much of a talker and she never could survive in this world alone.

Rudy's life had been on such a different path before Nikki. And when she'd first come to live with him it had been a burden to look after her. Now, he never thought twice about seeing that she ate well, dressed herself right, or did her chores. He'd been taking care of her for so long, he couldn't imagine what it would be like to live alone, without Nikki lumbering around the house.

Rudy finished up the tea. "I've got to get back to the bar, Nikki. I'll be back."

Nikki slurped. "Okay."

"Do you want me to take your teacup?"

Nikki glanced into her cup. "No. I still have more."

"Put it in the sink when you're finished. Like I showed you."

"Okay."

"See you soon."

"Rudy?"

"Yeah?"

"Be careful."

"Be careful of what?"

She nodded toward the television. "Bad guys."

Rudy glanced toward the television, never realizing that Nikki had been paying attention. "I'll be careful."

"Good."

*February 5*

*Sugar,*
    *Not this weekend. I'm not feeling so well. I'll see*
*you soon.*

                    *Xoxo,*
                    *A.*

# Chapter Thirteen

*Monday, October 17, 9 PM*

"You've got to get out of the office," Colleen said. "All you do is work."

Rachel glanced up from her stack of papers. "I gave too much time away to the Annie Dawson case and now I'm way behind. It's a busy time. It will let up soon."

"That's what you said last month and the month before." Her thick hair brushed, a sparkly silver dress, and long dangle earrings winked in the lights. "Rachel, you really have to give it a rest. You can't keep going like this."

Her shoulder had stiffened, the pain now radiating down her back. "The light looms at the end of the tunnel."

"The light is always out of your reach. You will never catch it." She moved to the desk and closed Rachel's file. "Now you have five minutes to change into fun clothes and get in the car with me. We are going to have drinks, listen to great music, and maybe dance a little."

She rubbed the back of her neck. She needed to keep working but fatigue had slowed her thoughts, which weren't connecting as easily. "Fine, I'll take off."

Colleen raised her hands to the air. "It's a miracle."

Rachel rose, her body stiff. "I'm not that OCD."

Colleen rolled her eyes. "Five minutes."

Changing was an easy proposition for Rachel because she had few clothes. She had her two suits for the office and clothes for her art but the in-between outfits weren't many. She settled on a black pair of jeans and a funky leopard print shirt, large gold hoop earrings, and her favorite cowboy boots.

When she emerged, Colleen shook her head. "I like the look. I always forget you are really a funky artist in disguise."

"Lawyer by day, and well, these days, lawyer by night."

"Not tonight!" Colleen hustled Rachel out of the office and into her car. She drove to the club cutting and winding through the streets at a dizzying speed.

Rachel laughed. "You should drive for NASCAR."

"If the law doesn't work for me, I might." She beeped her horn and cut through an intersection seconds before the light turned red.

"Stick with the law. Really."

They arrived at Rudy's on Broadway after ten. Colleen found street parking a block away. As they moved closer to the honky-tonk the sounds of music drifted out. The tension in Rachel's shoulders melted and she realized she needed this break.

The place was packed with bodies bumping against bodies. Some danced, others talked and many watched the singer on stage. Rachel paid their cover charge and the two headed to the bar. Colleen ordered white wine. Rachel ordered a soda. She took a long sip, savoring the cool liquid.

She glanced up toward the stage, curious about the woman whose voice added a throaty feminine edge to a Willie Nelson song. Faded jeans and a black silk top showed off the woman's petite figure as an explosion of curls framed her face. Eyes closed as she held the microphone, the singer was lost in emotion.

Rachel studied the singer. "I've seen her before."

"Really?" As Colleen sipped her wine she waved to a tall broad-shouldered man.

Rachel watched the singer. "How did you hear about her?"

"A friend of a friend."

Memories that didn't jive with this setting pushed to the front of her mind. "I've met her. She's a cop. She works forensics for Nashville PD."

Colleen grinned. "I know. Her name is Georgia."

Rachel lowered her soda. "Georgia Morgan. She'd worked Lexis Hanover's crime scene."

Colleen paled. "Oh, Rachel, I didn't know that. I heard from some of my buddies that she's a great singer."

Rachel glanced around the room at the patrons. They were all in plain clothes but it wasn't hard to guess that most were cops. Short hair, a bearing that radiated power and confidence. Shit. "We are in cop central."

"Look, if this feels weird, we can leave."

"No." She would not run or hide. "That's fine. And she's good." Rachel was drawn in by the sound of Georgia's voice. "How does a singer that good end up working as a cop?"

"My guess is she likes to eat and pay her rent. Let's face it, this town is full of talented starving artists." Colleen caught sight of a man who raised his glass to her. "Hey, do you mind if I go visit with a friend?"

"Have at it. I've my soda and the music is great."

"Mix and mingle."

Rachel grinned. "Don't push your luck."

As a laughing Colleen threaded through the crowd, Rachel leaned back against the bar and watched as Georgia sang to the crowd. People close to the stage had eyes only for her. She had them wrapped around her finger as she moved across the stage with a seductive familiarity.

"She's not half bad." The deep baritone voice had her turning to find Deke Morgan standing beside her with a beer. He wore a casual dark shirt, jeans, and simple cowboy boots. He smelled faintly of soap and his hair was damp. She imagined him dashing from his desk to shower before hurrying here.

"I never would figure you two as siblings. She definitely received the talent genes."

"How'd you finger us for sibs?"

"I went to Lexis's house. She was working the scene."

He nodded. "Still don't see how you connected the dots."

"Name tag helped. The in-your-face attitude sealed the deal."

A hint of a smile lit his eyes. "No argument here. She can run circles around the Morgan men."

Energy radiated from him. "Has she been singing long?"

"Since she could talk."

Nervous energy thrummed in her veins. "Looks like you've collected most of Nashville's finest out here tonight."

His gaze remained on her as if the crowd held no interest. "It's a retirement party for my partner, KC. He asked if Georgia would sing for him."

"KC Kelly. He worked with your dad."

"He did."

When he didn't elaborate, she asked, "How many cops are here tonight?"

He sipped his beer, staring at her. "A lot."

Rachel watched Georgia move across the stage as if she were right at home. "I almost didn't recognize her."

"I could say the same for you. I did a double take."

"The real me emerges." In her pencil skirts and tailored jackets she felt as if she had on her armor. Now dressed as herself she felt more exposed.

"I'm guessing the real you doesn't get out much."

He didn't say whether he liked the real her or not and she found herself wondering. And her caring one way or the other wasn't good. His opinion shouldn't grace her radar. "No. Not these days."

"So what dragged you out among the living tonight?"

"Colleen. My law partner. She's been threatening to get me out for weeks."

"Good for her."

She shifted her weight, trying to keep the muscles in her shoulder from stiffening.

"How's the shoulder?"

"I'll survive."

"Any trouble since that night?"

She was kind of enjoying herself and didn't want to talk about trouble. "All is clear. I did call the ME. She won't release Lexis yet but said she'd do it as soon as she could. Thank you."

"You are welcome." He held her gaze.

Somewhere in her, ice melted. As much as she wanted to lean into the feeling, she recognized it was not a good idea. The twice-divorced Morgan was as intense as she, and she likened their personalities to fire and gasoline.

He glanced toward the stage as Georgia hit a high note at the end of her song. When she finished the crowd clapped, wild and excited.

Rachel clapped. "Does she sing here often?"

Deke held a thumbs-up to his baby sister. "No. This is her first time. She's been after the owner for some time and then KC asked to have her sing."

"I hear it's hard to get a gig here."

"It is."

She sipped her soda. "Annie Rivers Dawson sang here. She mentioned it in one of her letters."

He cocked a brow, as if she'd told him something he already knew. "Did she?"

She leaned a fraction closer. "Have you had a chance to look at her letters?"

"A guy in Forensics is looking at them. We're set to meet Wednesday."

"I would like to be in on that meeting."

"No."

"Why not?"

Slowly he shook his head. "Have you always been this pushy?"

"Since the day I was born."

"Anybody ever tell you to be patient?"

That made her laugh. "Plenty of times but as you can see I haven't listened."

The crowd around them swelled with congratulations as Georgia cut her way through, talking and laughing. When she reached Deke she blew out a breath. "So what are you two huddled up here talking about?" She opened a bottle of water and drank heavily. "Looks serious."

Deke straightened and she sensed the veil dropping once again. "Talking shop."

Rachel nearly mentioned Annie's letters but Deke's demeanor kept her silent. "Boring."

Georgia's eyes danced. "Didn't look boring. Looked intense."

"Not so dramatic." Rachel noted some of the tension in Deke's body ebbed. "I didn't recognize you when I first arrived."

"Georgia sans the uniform. The real me. Or at least the other half of me."

"Your brother says you've been singing since you were little."

"About drove the clan crazy." She studied Rachel. "You do not have a Tennessee accent."

"Guilty as charged. I grew up all over the country and three foreign countries. Army brat."

"So how many places did you live?"

"Fourteen. We moved to Nashville after my parents

divorced. Mom got work here as a teacher. I was sick of moving so I stayed."

"I used to dream about being the kid that moved. But I was the kid that grew up in the same house, who knows the same friends from elementary school and who didn't go away to college."

"I dreamed of being the kid that didn't move. Grass is always greener, I suppose."

"I guess." Georgia glanced at the clock. "Time for my next set."

Deke raised a brow. "You're getting a second set?"

"Yeah. Rudy liked what he heard, believe it or not. Said I could sing more songs. I owe KC a big thank-you for setting this all up."

Deke smiled. "Good for you."

"Yeah, I know. Right?" She drank more water. "See you two lovebirds later."

Rachel and Deke both stiffened at the comment.

After a moment's pause, Deke raised his bottle and when KC approached with a woman in tow, smiled his relief. "The man of the hour."

KC had his beefy arm slung around the woman's shoulders. The hints of makeup on her eyes and cheeks suggested she didn't use it often.

Rachel cocked her head and studied the woman. "I know you."

The woman returned Rachel's gaze. "Shoulder injury."

"Yeah. You were my nurse the other night, right?"

"That's right."

Rachel shook her head. "My memory was a bit fuzzy."

KC sipped his beer. "This is my gal, Brenda. And I guess you know she's a nurse."

Deke kept a sliver of light between his body and Rachel's. Close but not touching. "Brenda did a great job."

Brenda's gaze sparked with curiosity. "You take those meds?"

"The first night. And thank you."

KC studied Rachel. "You are that attorney."

"Guilty."

KC picked at the label on his beer bottle. "You are a pain in the ass."

"So I've been told."

He leaned toward her, the scent of beer thick on his breath. "If I hadn't had a few beers I'd have a word or two to share with you."

She'd faced her share of angry cops. Still wasn't fun but it got easier. "You can find me most days in my office."

Brenda tugged on KC's arm. "This is a night to have fun. No work."

Georgia moved up on stage and joked with a couple of the band players. "KC, where are you? Come on up here?"

KC's annoyance ebbed as he glanced toward the stage. "Looks like the boss is calling."

"Don't let us stop you," Deke said.

Without a glance back to Rachel, KC, with Brenda in tow, headed to the stage.

Deke remained at Rachel's side until Georgia called him up on stage. "Duty calls."

"Have fun."

"Always."

Deke moved through the crowd, which naturally parted as he nudged his way forward. On stage he kissed Georgia's cheek. She laughed, clearly enjoying the night.

Rachel felt a twinge of jealousy for the woman so in her element. It had been a long time since she'd not felt like the perpetual fish out of water.

To her surprise, a smiling Oscar McMillian approached her. He had a mixed drink in his hands and was dressed in dark jeans and a gray V-neck sweater. His dark hair was slicked back. His grin was wide and welcoming. "Attorney Wainwright. You are about the last person I'd expect to see here."

She hugged her soda closer. "What are you doing here?"

"What do you mean?"

"You are on trial for murder. Do you really think partying is wise?"

"I didn't kill anyone. And I'm innocent until proven guilty."

The cavalier attitude surprised her. It took more stones than brains to crash a cop party. "Perception is important. You should live low-key until the trial."

"That could be months. And I'm not going to change my life because the cops screwed up." He sipped his drink and seemed to will his anger to calm. "Like I said, I'd never have expected to see you here."

"Why is that?"

He flashed a devil's seductive smile. "You don't strike me as the type who has a lot of fun. All work, no play kind."

No matter how charming he was, he was not her friend, nor would he ever be. "Nice seeing you, Mr. McMillian. But I've a friend to meet."

He reached out and touched her arm. She froze.

"Thank you," he said. "I'd still be in jail if it wasn't for you. If I hadn't gotten out and had a chance to talk to my boss, I'd have lost my job. And my apartment. You literally saved my life."

Carefully, she pulled her arm free. "We've a long way to go, Mr. McMillian."

"Oscar. Please call me Oscar."

She shook her head. "No. We'll keep it formal."

"Sure. Sure. Whatever you want. I want you to know how much I appreciate you."

"Sure." A small smile teased the edges of her lips. "Have a good night, Mr. McMillian."

He said his good nights and as she turned toward the bar she caught Deke's gaze. He was frowning. Very unhappy. She faced the bar and raised her hand toward the bartender. He came her way. "Beer."

"Sure."

He pulled a long neck from the cooler and handed it to her as Georgia started to sing. The bartender raised his gaze and stared past Rachel toward the stage. Craggy features softened with a bewildering wistfulness.

"Wow," Rachel said. "She's a real talent."

The man jerked his gaze from Georgia as if embarrassed by the unguarded moment. "All kinds come through the door and think they can sing. Most aren't as good as they think they are, but she's a rare one."

"You been here long?"

"Forty years. I'm Rudy. I own the place."

"Forty years ago this area of town was pretty rough from what I hear."

"We didn't get the tourists and nice folks then. It was drug dealers, bikers, and working girls. Never knew when there'd be a fight in the back alley and someone would get themselves killed."

"Why'd you stay?"

He regarded the packed house of cops, tourists, and locals. "This is my home. And I'm a tough bird. No one takes what's mine."

Rachel had said similar words to Deke the other night when he'd questioned leaving her home the night of the attack. She raised her drink. "I hear ya."

Rudy served several more customers as Georgia's voice washed over a crowd now rapt in each note and melody. When he returned she said, "I don't suppose you remember Annie Rivers Dawson? She'd have sung here thirty years ago."

Rudy picked up a glass and wiped it with a clean towel. "Folks have asked about her."

Since her appearance on the news. "You remember her?"

"Sure. I remember Annie. She was a big hit here. And she was nice. Beautiful. The whole package."

"I've gotten real curious about her. I guess dying young immortalizes her like Marilyn Monroe or James Dean."

"I suppose."

"What kind of songs did she like to sing?"

"The classics with a rock edge. She was ahead of her time." He listened as Georgia sang the last notes of her song. "I pulled tapes of her the other night and was watching them."

Keen curiosity grabbed hold of Rachel. "You have tapes of Annie?"

"Have several, as a matter of fact."

"Could I see them?"

He studied her, curious. "Why would you care?"

A lie would smooth out so much, but she heard herself saying, "I'm the attorney that's representing Jeb Jones."

His eyes narrowed. "The man convicted of killing her?"

"Yes."

Old eyes studied her. "You're the attorney that was punched. You look different."

"The suit makes me look more respectable."

He leaned forward. "Thirty years ago everyone in Nashville thought that guy deserved hard time. Black-and-white to me."

"Might have looked that way then."

"Time has a way of making us all second guess old decisions." He picked up a rag and wiped the counter as if trying to rub out a spot. "Do you really think that Jones guy is innocent?"

She sensed genuine curiosity, not anger. "There're a lot

of unanswered questions. And I like to have all my questions answered."

"A lot of people don't agree with you."

The hate emails were her first clue. "I know."

As Georgia's voice eased into her last song, Rudy studied her. "Come on in the back."

No hint of welcome or asking in his voice. An order. "Why?"

"You'll be glad." He motioned for another bartender to cover his spot and then gestured for her to follow. When he vanished behind a swinging door without looking back she glanced around hoping someone had seen their exchange. Finding no one, she shoved out a breath, took a swig of her beer, and followed. Behind the door stretched a hallway leading to a light streaming from a single door. The music from the bar faded as she walked down the hallway. She was wondering if she'd lost her mind. Rubbing damp palms on her jeans, she peered inside the door and found a cubbyhole-sized office.

Rudy hovered over a small desk buried in papers. Boxes of liquor stacked high against a wall covered in dozens of black-and-white photos of singers over the decades. The windowless room smelled of cigarettes and age.

From the desk drawer Rudy pulled out an unwieldy VHS videotape. "I was watching it this morning."

In here, he looked larger, more imposing. "I haven't seen one of those in years."

He turned the tape over in his hand as if realizing it was a relic. "My video machine is upstairs so I can't show it to you."

"It's a tape of Annie?"

"A recording of her last performance here." *Annie* was scrawled in dark black ink along the white-labeled spine. There was no date.

She accepted the bulky cassette. "When was this taped?"

"I never was good at dating items. But I'd say about eight months before she died."

Annie's letters came to mind. *February 5, I'm not feeling so well.* "I have a friend that can convert it if you'll let me borrow it."

His gaze lingered on the tape. "Sure. Take it."

The cartridge rested heavy in her hand. "Why are you doing this?"

"Why?" He shrugged. "Maybe I've questions about who killed Annie. Not all the pieces added up for me. And I don't like it when facts don't add up."

A musty scent clung to the tape. "You dug this out because you saw me on the television?"

As if she'd not spoken, he nodded toward the door. "In part for you. In part for Dixie. I liked her."

"What do the two women have in common?"

"Talent. Beauty. A bad death. And maybe nothing."

"Could the same person have killed both women?"

"Not likely, I suppose." He shifted and nodded toward the door. "I've got to get back."

"Sure." She tucked the tape into her satchel. "I'll bring it back."

He waved away her offer. "Keep it. I don't need it back."

"Are you sure?"

Sadness lingered around him. "No amount of watching a tape is gonna bring her back. She's dead and gone."

"You miss her?"

He was silent for a moment. "Yeah. I miss her."

Tenderness crept into his voice. Rudy, like so many men, had fallen under Annie's spell. "Ever hear of a guy named Sugar?"

"Who?"

"Sugar. A friend of Annie's."

His face registered blank. "No. How'd you come up with that name?"

"Research."

"What kind of research?"

"This and that."

He frowned but sensed he'd not get any more from her. "No. Ain't heard of Sugar."

She patted her purse. "Okay. Thanks for the tape."

Without another word, he brushed past her knocking her sore shoulder. She cringed, hesitated as the pain rolled over her. She drew in a deep breath. Anxious to watch the tape, she sent a text to Colleen telling her she was leaving and headed out the front door to catch a cab.

"Looking for a ride?" Oscar McMillian stood feet away jangling his keys.

"No, thanks."

The keys clinked as he tossed them up and caught them. "So this formal relationship we have means that I can't give you a ride?"

"I'm afraid it does." She gripped the handle of her satchel tighter.

He offered a smile designed to charm and influence. "I'm not a bad guy, Ms. Wainwright. I'm offering a ride."

"Thanks. But, no. I'll call you as soon as I have details of your case."

"You're being sensitive. Fussy. Like an old lady."

Rachel glanced toward a yellow cab parked across the street, raised her hand and held it up. "Why are you pushing this?"

The slow shake of his head added to his amused look. "I'm not. You are a prude."

"Don't pretend to know me, Mr. McMillian."

The smile faded. "You ashamed to be seen with me?"

The shift in his tone had her wishing they weren't alone. "Good night, Mr. McMillian."

McMillian advanced a step and then stopped.

Deke Morgan stepped out of the shadows. "There a problem?"

The cab stopped short of her by a block, nabbed by a pretty girl with auburn hair and a short skirt. Rachel cursed. "No. I was catching a cab."

McMillian eyed Morgan. "I offered her a ride."

"Which I've refused," Rachel added quickly. "I'm fine as soon as I can get a cab."

Deke whistled to a cab on the other corner, held up his badge and motioned him forward. The cab did a U-turn and in seconds was parked in front of her. "There you go."

McMillian grinned and saluted. "Problem solved. See you in court, Ms. Wainwright." He grinned at Deke. "Detective."

Deke remained silent as McMillian strolled around a corner. "That guy is trouble."

Whispered warnings agreed. "He's a client. We shouldn't be talking about him."

"Don't be fooled by his smile."

Oddly shaken, she hid behind legal reasoning. "It takes more than a fake smile to convict a man of murder."

"There's plenty of evidence. And when you dig through his files you'll see."

"I will dig through the files and then find a way to discount it all. That's my job."

His smile was feral. "I've no doubt. Lawyers have a talent for twisting facts. You have a knack for it."

Anger jabbed. The cab driver honked his horn. She opened the door. "Nice shot, Detective. We'll see who manipulated the facts."

When she reached for the door handle, he brushed her hand aside and took hold of the door. He hesitated, his body inches from hers. "Why did you go in the back room with Rudy?"

The question threw her off balance. She didn't think anyone had noticed. "You were watching me?"

"Happened to glance over."

He didn't *happen* to do anything. "I didn't realize I was accountable to you."

He worked his jaw. "So you won't answer me?"

"Nope."

"Do you lie or hold back the truth with everyone?"

Bitter laughter rumbled in her chest. "The truth does not set you free, Detective. I learned that lesson the hard way."

He leaned toward her. "We all have to trust someone."

She remained steady, resisting the urge to plaster her back to the cab. "Do we? I'm not so sure."

He pressed his finger against the hollow of her throat. "You are on a lonely path."

Her heart rattled. "Is that experience talking? That the reason for the two divorces?"

A slight narrowing of his eyelids sharpened icy eyes, warning she'd hit a nerve. "Have a nice night, Rachel."

The emphasis on her name roughened it in ways she didn't like. "Thanks for the cab."

"Any time. Be safe."

She slid into the cab and he slammed the door closed. As the cab pulled away she felt his gaze on her. Her cheeks flushed. "Take me across town." She gave her address.

She pulled the tape from her purse, wondering what Deke would have said if he'd known she had the tape of Annie.

At her house, she scrounged twenty bucks from her purse and paid the cab driver. She considered returning to work but the videotape weighed heavily in her purse. She fished her keys from a side pocket and got into her car. Thirty minutes later she'd bought a dozen glazed chocolate donuts, driven across the Cumberland River and stood in front of a small one-story house. The windows were barred and the front door well lit by a halogen and monitored with a camera. She dialed a number on her cell.

It rang once. "Better be good."

"Chocolate glazed donuts." She held the box up toward a security camera.

"How many?"

"A dozen."

"You may enter."

The door lock clicked open and she entered the dark house. Sid Danvers was in his early twenties and though he'd never graduated from any school he was brilliant with all electronics. She and Sid had met a year ago when she'd helped with a legal matter regarding an alleged hacking incident. She'd gotten him acquitted and he'd promised his future help in exchange for donuts.

Out of the shadows stepped a tall, thin man with long hair tied at the nape of his neck. He wore grungy jeans and a shirt embossed with Bogart's image. He studied her. "Attorney Wainwright."

She nodded. "Sid. Keeping your nose out of other people's operating systems?"

"Of course."

She knew enough not to push. She held up the box, "I need a favor."

He took the donuts. "I did promise you one favor in exchange for donuts."

She reached in her satchel and pulled out the VHS tape. "I want to watch this tape but don't have the equipment."

"That's it?"

"Not much of a challenge, I will agree."

"No. I'd have figured you wanted me to hack into Nashville PD computers and see what they are saying about your case. Or that reporter's computer. That would no doubt be amusing."

"No. This is totally legal." Her grip on the satchel tightened. "Tell me you haven't done that."

A smile twitched the edge of his lips. "I have not."

Again, better not to press. "Just the tape."

"Do you want it transferred to a CD?"

"That would be great." She scanned the piles of dusty, haphazardly arranged electronics. "Could we watch the tape now?"

He opened the box of donuts. "They're still warm."

"Out of the oven fifteen minutes ago."

He held a donut up to his nose and closed his eyes. "We'll watch the tape now."

"Thanks." Dragging in a breath, she entered the house. The main room, originally designated as a living room, was now his office and crammed full of hundreds of electronic devices. There were old projectors, computers, copiers, and a bellows camera. The stack of electronics left little floor space to maneuver, so she followed him along a narrow path to a long desk sporting four computer screens. One played a movie, the other news, the other a series of numbers, and the last satellite images.

He bit into the donut and chewed slowly. "So what do you have for me?"

She pulled the cassette from her purse. "It's a recording of a singer performing at Rudy Creed's thirty years ago. The singer is supposed to be Annie Rivers."

Nodding, he gobbled the donut in two bites and then turned to his pile of electronics. He studied the collection, as a surgeon would his tools. He set several aside so he could reach an older dusty model. Chunky and thick, the machine looked awkward and clumsy.

"State of the art in 1981. Should do the trick if your tape is intact." He settled the player on a lonely bare spot on his desk and using a mismatch of cords attached it to a power source.

She handed it over. "Here's hoping."

He took the tape, inspected it, and then pushed it into the machine. The image on the right computer screen turned grainy. Sid grabbed another donut and sat on a swivel chair in front of the computer. "Not looking good."

She pulled up a small stool and watched, tapping her foot. "Could it be your machine?"

A thick brow arched at the imagined insult. "My machines work. It's your tape."

"I was told the tape worked."

He shot her a glance. "If these donuts weren't awesome I'd toss you out for questioning me."

She grinned. "I actually waited until the donuts came out of the oven. The clerk tried to sell me donuts made an hour ago but I refused."

He plucked another from the box. As he bit into the soft dough the screen's static cleared to a faded color image of Rudy's stage. It hadn't changed in three decades and could have been filmed today. Same scarred floor covered with a small red rug. Same stool. Same collection of images in the background. The telltale giveaways were the large and unwieldy microphone and the curly or winged hairstyles of the women in the audience.

The crowds to the side and front of the stage cheered as two guitar players and a fiddler assembled on stage. Young guys dressed in jeans, they all sported long hair and thick beards. The musicians were laughing, finishing off the last of their cigarettes, as they started to play a lively tune.

A guitar player, which she realized was a younger leaner Rudy, leaned forward and stroked his beard as he smiled. "I guess ya'll heard that Annie is here tonight."

The crowd whooped and hollered with enthusiasm. Several started to chant, "Annie."

Rachel scooted to the front of her seat. Seeing stills of the woman didn't compare to seeing and hearing her on tape. Though age had yellowed the image and diminished some of its original color, her anticipation didn't wane.

Finally a woman emerged, her head turned toward the band, the thick blond curtain of her hair hiding her features. She wore a blue cowgirl outfit cinched at a narrow waist, a silver concho belt, and blue boots.

She spoke to the band, tapping her foot as the crowd shouted her name. With a showman's panache, she slowly lowered her head and grabbed the microphone. The crowd cheered. She waited a beat, raised her hand in the air, and then looked directly into the camera. A wide grin accentuated full red lips, enhanced a high slash of cheekbones and brightened blue eyes. She possessed a charisma, a glow that drew Rachel into the screen.

"Damn," Sid said. "Hot as hell."

"Her photos don't do her justice."

*"I'm glad you all could come out here tonight," Annie said. "Always does my heart proud to see so many happy faces." She tapped a long index finger on the mike as she looked into the camera, a sly seductive grin warming her face. "Sugar, this one is for you."*

Rachel drew in a breath. Sugar. Annie's Sugar. The man Rudy didn't recognize.

The camera picked up the sounds of the hollering crowd and Rachel hoped the cameraman might pan to the crowd for a second. But he kept his lens on Annie who turned to the band and after exchanging words they started playing. Annie nestled the microphone closer to her mouth, offered a sly secretive smile and led with a fast-paced song that immediately had the crowd cheering. Her smile widened and she sang louder.

Both Rachel and Sid sat in silence watching the thirty-minute tape. Both remained mesmerized.

Sid ate a third donut. "I'm a little hot for her."

"She died thirty years ago."

"You're talking to the big head when the little one doesn't care."

She shot Sid a quick glance as she leaned closer to watch Annie who had a familiarity Rachel could not define. Was it her showman's allure? Did Annie have a way of making everyone feel as if she was friend to all?

Annie began to sing and Rachel and Sid fell under her spell, sitting in silence listening and absorbing. The aging audio did not diminish the clarity of her voice nor stop the chills from prickling Rachel's skin.

By the time Annie had finished the crowd cheered. *"God bless," she said as she hurried off the stage.*

Rachel now understood Jeb's obsession with Annie, her roommate's jealousy and the city's demand for justice when she'd died.

Sid stopped the tape and rewound it. The machine hesitated and then whirred as the tape rewound. "And you are defending the guy that killed her?"

"Yes."

Sid puffed his cheeks and blew out a breath. "It's a wonder the town didn't lynch him."

It was a wonder. "He swears he didn't do it."

Sid folded his arms. "Don't they all?"

She clung to her beliefs with an ever-tightening grip. "He deserves to have his DNA tested."

Sid shook his head. "If you say so."

As tempted as she was to argue, she didn't. "How soon can you convert this to a CD?"

"I can have it ready for you in the morning."

She scooted to the edge of her seat and laid her hand on his arm.

He stilled, looked at her as if he didn't know how to handle the contact.

"Sid, there is someone out there that doesn't like my

poking around in Annie's life. I left letters with a friend and she was killed."

He laid his hand over hers. "I heard about that. Lexis, right?"

"Yeah."

He gave her hand a quick squeeze, pulled it free and reached under his desk to remove a .45. "I'll be fine."

His confidence reminded her of Lexis the last time they'd spoken. "Sid, I don't want anyone else hurt. Lexis was nobody's fool."

"There are less trusting souls than me. Fact, you are the first person I've let in here in six months."

"But you go out."

"Nope. An assistant brings me what I need and leaves the goods in a utility room off the back. When he's gone, I retrieve my stuff."

"I know you are careful, but—"

"No worries, Rachel. This is a fortress. I should be finished by morning."

"I'll come by and pick the CD up early."

"My assistant will deliver it."

"Thanks."

She rose, absently replaying the tape in her head. It struck a chord in her subconscious, but this single viewing couldn't solidify a peculiar feeling.

Rebecca Saunders arrived at the hotel room to find everything as she liked it. Wine chilling in a bucket, white coverlet on the bed, and rose soap waiting for her in the bath. She shimmied out of her slim skirt, slipped off her silk shirt, bra, and panties and left them in a trail that led from the bedroom to the bath.

A glass of wine in hand she drew a bath and slipped into

the hot water. The warm water soothed her skin. It had been a long exhausting day at the office and though she'd not expected to see him tonight, his text, all but begging her to come to their hotel room, was welcome. She liked it when he begged.

When she heard the room door open she hesitated. He had gotten adept at entering the room without being heard. That's what she'd told him to do and clearly he'd gotten sloppy. He must have been looking for reasons to be punished. Eyes narrowing, she sipped her wine.

She listed as he moved into the room. Sloppy. Terrible. She thought about all the ways she'd make him suffer for being foolish.

Knowing he'd be impatient, she lingered in the bath. That would make him anxious. He had precious little time to give her.

Finally, she rose from the tub, set her glass down and then slowly toweled off. She donned the fluffy white robe hanging on the back of the door and tied it at her waist. She checked her makeup in the mirror and then, wineglass in hand, sauntered into the room.

She found him facing the window, wearing a hoodie, hands clasped in front. This was different. Not their usual scenario. But she was adaptable and would play along because it suited her. "What's this about? Who the hell are you?"

He didn't turn, lunge, or grab her. Another break with their routine. She could be a little adaptable but she set the script for their encounters. Not him.

Annoyed, she advanced a step. "I asked you a question."

Slowly, he shifted his weight and then he turned. When she looked up she blinked, her shock fast and acute. He was wearing a white hockey mask. The eyes that stared back at her though had a startling, intense quality she'd never seen before. "Is this some kind of game? I don't get passed around."

He shifted and she realized that this man gripped a tire iron. The first flicker of fear ignited inside her.

She took a step back. "I don't like this game."

Eyes sparkled with amusement. "I do."

Before she could react, he closed the gap between them and swung the tire iron high. It cut through the air and struck her on the side of her head. The blow sent her wineglass spilling to the carpeted floor and her eyes rolling back in her head. She dropped to her knees and fell face first on the carpet. Warm blood rushed from the gash in her temple to pool on the carpet by her head.

Agony cut through Rebecca's head as she struggled to gather her shattered thoughts. She clawed at the carpet, hoping to crawl to safety. The simplest movement stoked fire in her skull.

"You won't get away."

A strong arm grabbed Rebecca's shoulder and shoved her on her back. Through blurred vision, she stared up at her attacker. Words scrambled in her head but they wouldn't form into sentences.

As blood seeped down her cheeks, she whispered, "Why?"

Bright, dark eyes blazed from the mask. "You should have stayed away from him. He's not yours."

The voice held a menace that terrified her as much as the pain. "Who are you?"

Her attacker loomed and raised the tire iron. "Say goodbye, Rebecca."

The blow struck with blinding speed and struck her on the side of the face. Like a light switch clicking off, her world went black.

\* \* \*

The force of the strike rattled up Baby's arm. Over and over Baby smashed the tire iron against bone until the woman's body stilled.

One heartbeat stopped and another ratcheted up. This was thrilling. Exciting beyond words. A drug that could easily become addictive.

Baby raised the tire iron again. More strikes sent bolts of energy radiating up through the metal. Hot blood splashed against flushed skin and splattered the white coverlet as blow after blow obliterated Rebecca's once lovely face.

Finally, the fever of the kill eased. Breathless, Baby stepped back and stripped off bloodied hoodie and coveralls and shoved them in a plastic bag. In the bathroom, blood rinsed away easily under the tap. Baby grabbed a white towel and dried hands and face.

A heavy, satisfied smile curled thin lips. This was a good day. A very good day.

*February 9*

*Sugar,*
    *I love you, Sugar, but I won't beg.*

                    *A.*

# Chapter Fourteen

*Tuesday, October 18, 12 NOON*

With KC officially retired Deke, for the moment, was without a partner. The other members of the squad were consumed by their own cases so he arrived alone at the West Hotel to a flash of lights and uniformed cops surrounding the main entrance. Nodding to the uniforms, he made his way inside and up the elevator to the fifth floor. On the right, yellow tape and a half-dozen uniforms marked the entrance to the crime scene.

Pulling on rubber gloves he watched as Brad snapped pictures of the victim who lay on the other side of the bed. From the door he could see the spray of blood on the white comforter and on the walls. Pale white feet peeked out from behind the bed. "Brad, can I enter?"

His camera dangling from his neck, Brad reached for a logbook in his pocket and made a note. He was careful about documenting who entered and who left his crime scenes, a trait that had come in handy during trial.

When Deke received the thumbs-up, he slipped on paper booties and ducked under the tape. He moved into the room slowly, absorbing details. To his left he saw the drawn bath, rose petals floating on the surface. On the bath mat by the tub he spotted the impression of one set of small feet. The victim. Across from the tub, the blood splashed the sink, mirror, and the white countertop. A bloodied white towel lay discarded on the floor. Also by the sink the faint impression of a larger set of footprints. The killer.

In the room, he directed his attention to the bed where expensive lingerie draped over a black designer dress. Judging by the way the garments had been casually discarded, she had not been worried when she'd arrived and undressed. The attacker had come after she'd stepped out of the tub.

Brad's camera flashed as he took more pictures of the body.

Another step and Deke saw the crumpled body of the woman, now curled on her side. The side of her head was an unrecognizable mess. The white hotel robe was soaked with blood.

Whereas Lexis's blows had landed on her extremities, this victim, like Dixie, had been beaten primarily around the face.

"How long has she been dead?" Deke asked.

"I'm guessing twelve to eighteen hours. She was supposed to have checked out by eleven today. The maid found her when she came into the room. Blunt force trauma killed her." He nodded toward the bed and an expensive handbag. "Her driver's license identifies her as Rebecca Saunders, age thirty-one. She also came armed today with a box of condoms in her purse."

"Expecting someone."

An open wine bottle tilted in an ice bucket now filled with room temperature water. One glass sat untouched by the bucket and the other, stained with red lipstick, lay on the floor.

"No doubt." Brad shoved out a breath and looked away

from the body. Horrific scenes like this stayed with the responding team for a long, long time. "If the first blow didn't kill her then surely the second did. The other blows were overkill."

Deke studied the position of the body. "The first blow on the side of her head brought her to her knees."

"That's exactly what I think. The killing blow landed on top of her head. She'd never have felt the remaining blows."

"Dixie and this victim had died almost instantly whereas Lexis Hanover suffered before she died."

"This murder definitely matches the first. Lexis is the anomaly."

"Maybe the killer wanted something from Lexis. That explains why her first blow didn't kill her outright." Rebecca and Dixie looked like Annie. Rachel and Lexis had been working on Annie's murder case. All roads led back to Annie. "Have you had a chance to look at the Dawson letters?"

He craned his neck working tension from the tense muscles. "It'll have to be tomorrow or the next day. I'm tied up here all day."

"Sure. Are they real?"

He stretched the tightness from his lower back. "I think so."

"Think?"

He lifted the camera back to his eyes. "I'll explain later. I'm not sure it's black-and-white."

Deke brushed aside the urge to press for more questions knowing Brad needed to process the scene. "Sure. I'll let you work, Brad. We'll talk later."

"I'll be here the better part of the day. Make it later."

"Done."

He headed into the hallway and to the registration desk. He found the manager, a short pale man with thinning black hair sitting in his office. In shaking hands he held a cup of coffee.

Deke shoved on the door. "Are you the hotel manager?"

The man started, making coffee slosh on his hand and his burgundy shirt. He set the cup down and rose. "Yes. I'm Jimmy Winters."

Deke held up his badge. "Detective Morgan. I've questions about the woman on the fifth floor."

The reference was enough to send him back into his seat. His face paled another shade. "Worst I've ever seen in my life. I'll never be right."

The scene had been awful, but not the worst he'd seen. Fifteen years on the force had hardened him to the worst life had to offer.

"What can you tell me about the woman?" Deke asked. He settled in the seat across from the manager. "Has she ever been here before?"

The man pursed his lips and drew in a deep breath through his nostrils. "The officer told me you'd be asking questions like that so I searched our records." He turned toward a computer screen and punched a few keys. "She's been coming here every Sunday for the last eight weeks. She always pays cash and she doesn't stay the night."

"She's a hooker?"

The manager frowned. "We don't have hookers at our hotel. This is a good place."

"So what do you think she was doing here once a week?"

He sat a little straighter and adjusted his tie. "She was dressed well, polite to the staff and we never had an issue with noise or payment. I didn't ask too many questions."

"She must have had clients?"

"If she did, I never saw them."

"I assume you have security cameras on the entrances?"

"Yes."

"Which require a key to get in."

"Yes." He frowned. "She always requested two keys."

"So she was expecting someone?"

He closed his eyes and shook his head as if willing the carnage away. "I don't know."

Deke pressed. "And you do have cameras on the side doors?"

"Yes. But the one on the back entrance is not working."

"Where does that entrance lead?"

"Parking lot."

A good entrance for someone who didn't want to be seen. It would be a simple matter for Rebecca to slip out the back door and leave a key for her intended. "What name did she use when she registered?"

"Rebecca Saunders."

That matched the name in her wallet. "Did she ever say anything to you or your front desk person to make you think twice?"

"No. She was always polite and always nice." He frowned. "She was pretty and the men liked it when she came. Looked forward to her weekly visits."

"She always came on Sundays?"

"Yesterday was Monday."

"She's never stayed here on a Monday."

Her pattern had changed. And she'd been murdered. Dixie's routine had changed the night she died. She had been a last-minute show at Rudy's. She'd received a text telling her she had a spot if she wanted it. Rudy had not been expecting her but he'd let her sing.

"Can you print out a list of all the days she was here?"

The manager picked up a printout. "I thought you might ask that question. I already did it."

Deke took the page and scanned the dates. "Pull all of

the security footage from the side doors the nights she was here. Might get lucky and see who was visiting her."

"Sure. Sure."

Three dead women and one who narrowly escaped an attack. Time to talk to Rachel Wainwright again.


Rachel had been on the phone with the medical examiner's office again trying to get the release date of Lexis Hanover's body. The medical examiner had spoken to her directly and explained patiently that she still needed to keep the body longer as the investigation was still open, but promised to call as soon as it was released. Rachel had wanted to argue, pester, generally be herself, but held her tongue.

Rachel rose, and stretched out her shoulder, still stiff and discolored. Days after the attack the bruise had deepened to a dark purple and stretched over the back of her shoulder across her arm.

The front bell rang. She rose and crossed to the front door, taking time to look through the peephole. The man on the other side of the door faced away but she recognized him instantly. The dark hair and the broad shoulders gave him away. Deke Morgan.

Tension melted. She opened the door. "Detective."

He turned and when his gaze landed on her he studied her as if peeling back the layers. He frowned when he saw the dark purple bruise. "Counselor."

"Don't tell me the DNA has come in?" The question travelled as easily as her.

"You only know how to play one note, don't you?"

"I never said that I was far thinking or original." She cocked her head. "I take it that the answer is no."

"It's a not yet. May I come in?"

"Sure." She stepped aside and allowed him to cross the threshold. As he passed, an unyielding, focused, and forceful energy radiated around him. When his sights zeroed in on a target he couldn't be stopped. She closed the door. "What can I do for you?"

He glanced around her office, studying the disarray of papers and files on and around her desk. "You had any trouble in the last couple of days? Any other strange people?" His tone might be conversational but he wasn't a man who stopped to chat.

"All is quiet."

"And McMillian?"

"He's keeping his distance." She ran her fingers through her hair. "Did you come all this way to check up on me?" And then unable to resist a sarcastic twist, she added, "Because if you did, I'm really touched."

Lips curled into a little used smile. "Don't be."

She folded her arms over her chest. "No DNA. Could it be about the letters?"

"I'll know more on those tomorrow."

All hints of teasing evaporated. "You've had them analyzed."

"I have."

"And?"

"As I said, I will know more tomorrow."

"No information on DNA or the letters." She raised her hands in surrender. "I give up. Give me a clue. Why are you here?"

For a beat a heavy silence stood between them. "We have another body."

Darkness rose up from the earth and wrapped around her like a shroud. "Who?"

"A woman named Rebecca Saunders. She was beaten to death at the West Hotel."

"Beaten like Lexis?"

"Not like Lexis. Like Dixie Simmons."

"That singer."

"Yes."

"What does this have to do with me?"

"You survived an attack."

"We aren't certain it's the same person. It could have been a mugger."

"I don't think so."

"What do you think?"

"I don't know. The first and third victims were beaten strictly on the head and the face. Lexis, well she wasn't killed right away."

The shroud tightened. She was grateful to have received the tape and CDs this morning. "This all ties into the letters. I had them. Lexis had them. And now they are gone."

"That's what I'm thinking."

"Why would anyone care about the letters? If they are real they are over thirty years old and from what I could tell they were written by a talented, if not volatile, woman who didn't identify her lover."

"You've pried open a can of worms and someone is not happy."

"Dixie Simmons was killed before my press conference."

"But whoever attacked her, came after you and killed Lexis. You all are connected to Annie, either in appearance or association."

"Annie's cause of death was never determined."

"The skull was never found. The bones found did have unhealed fractures, but none of those injuries were deemed fatal. And a tire iron similar to the one found in Jeb's truck was used in the recent killings."

Frowning, she saw his logic. "So what do you want me to do?"

"It's time we compared notes."

She thought about the Annie tapes. *Don't open your mouth, Rachel. He's a cop. The enemy!* "Really?"

"You held back the letters. Anything else you've held back?"

"If you haven't noticed, we are on the opposite side of the Jeb Jones case."

"There is a killer out there now." A steady tone did not dull the meaning's razor sharpness. "I'd like to think we are on the same side in that case."

"And if the two cases are connected?" She shook her head. "I owe it to Jeb not to play all my cards." *Lexis understands.*

A vein in his neck pulsed with frustration under the tight hold of his collar and tie. "If you get in my way or I find out you held back again, I'll file obstruction charges against you." The words rumbled in his chest like a growl.

She'd been in enough legal brawls over the years to know she could hold her own. "Take your best shot."

"I will."


Deke arrived at the public relations firm before five. The glass and chrome front doors opened into a lobby tiled with marble. The interior decorating incorporated sleek chrome and leather and told clients they'd found their ticket to success. A guard sat behind a shiny console.

Pulling out his badge, he approached. "I'm here to see the president of TNK Public Relations."

"Suite 301."

"Great." Seconds later he rode the elevator to the third floor where doors opened to the TNK Public Relations agency. More sleek glass, cool metals, and soft grays wrapped around the reception area. He moved directly to the receptionist, a cool redhead, and explained himself again.

Within minutes a tall, well-dressed woman in a burgundy suit stood in the doorway.

She extended a neatly manicured hand. "Detective Morgan. I'm Taylor Knight. I own the company."

"I'd like to talk to you about Rebecca Saunders."

A slight frown wrinkled her face. "Come into my office."

He followed her into the corner office. As she closed the door behind her, she indicated a sitting area. He took a seat in one of the plush chairs while she took the couch opposite him. "Rebecca is one of our best client servicers. She's been with us three years and is on track for a big promotion." She checked her watch. "She did not come in today, which has raised some concern. What's happened?"

"She was murdered."

Taylor sat back against the couch, the energy deflating from her like a popping balloon. "What?"

"She was found this morning by the maid at the West Hotel."

"The West Hotel? That certainly would have been her style. She had expensive tastes."

"She was a regular visitor there. Every Sunday for the last eight weeks. Have any idea who she might have been meeting?"

She hooked a finger in a slim chain encircling her neck and moved it back and forth. "No. She broke up with her boyfriend a couple of months ago but it was all friendly. They remain friends."

"What's his name?"

"Jake Wheeler. He works for the association of churches."

"Churches?"

"That's how Rebecca and Jake met. They went to the same church."

"What is the church?"

"New Community. She was active in her church. Had a

real love for it all. I always thought that's why she did so well with our nonprofit clients."

Annie had been involved in her church. Dixie had sung in church. Was it New Community? "Do you have names of anyone she might have dated after Jake Wheeler?"

"No. From what I gathered she was single. She seemed happy and her work was top form. I could supply you with a list of the clients she serviced. She might have met someone through work I wasn't aware of."

"That would be helpful. What about friends in the office?"

"No female friends. Liked the company of men more." Taylor typed a message into her phone. "I've asked my secretary to print a list for you."

Ms. Taylor's image of Rebecca did not line up with what he'd found in the hotel room. "No exes? No threats? No trouble?"

"None." She leaned forward.

The door opened and a neatly dressed woman handed a list to Taylor. She glanced at it before giving it to Deke.

When the secretary closed the door behind her, he said, "Looks like you work for a lot of nonprofits."

"Not all our clients are nonprofits. Rebecca had a knack for taking what could have been a small account and growing the book of business. A nonprofit might want press releases sent out and in no time she'd have revamped their website and had them making a promotional video. She knew how to stretch a dollar and get them to dig a little deeper into their pockets. Though I'd dare say all her clients were pleased and reported that their sales or outreach increased significantly as a result of her efforts."

The list contained the names of churches, animal outreach centers, and food banks. "Places she liked to frequent such as bars or restaurants?"

"I can't picture that. She was class. She liked to live well and liked the nicer restaurants and clubs. I don't know where she went but I can show you her office and you can have a look."

"That would be great."

She rose and led him to an office. It wasn't overly large but it had long plate glass windows that overlooked the city. In the distance he could see the capitol. She flipped on the light. "Take whatever you need."

"Thanks." He sat behind her desk.

The woman folded her arms over her chest. "I still can't believe she's dead. So, so sad."

"Yes, ma'am." On the credenza behind him were several pictures framed in silver. They all featured Rebecca. One was at the Animal Rights gala. Another at New Community Church's groundbreaking. And another at a breast cancer awareness fund-raiser. She had a bright vivid smile and looked directly into the camera as if she owned it. Her blond hair swept over slim shoulders and full breasts. She looked like Dixie. And they both looked like Annie.

A sigh shuddered through Ms. Knight. "Can you tell me how she died?"

"No, ma'am. Not now."

"I understand." She drummed manicured fingers against her thigh. "People here will be devastated. Just devastated."

As he studied the images, his mind drifted to the stills he'd seen of Annie Rivers Dawson. The three women could have been sisters. There'd been instances of killers going dormant for long stretches and he wondered now if Jeb had not killed Annie, then perhaps Annie's real killer was active again.

He opened the drawer to his left and found neatly arranged files. The names on the folders matched the client's names on the list he'd been given. To the right, there were three drawers. The top two were filled with note cards, several tubes of lipstick, perfume, and aspirin. The third was locked.

"Do you have a key to the drawer?"

"No. But I can get a letter opener if you think that will help."

"Not necessary." He pulled a penknife from his pocket and opened it. It didn't take much to pry open the lock. He folded the knife and tucked it back in his pocket.

Inside this drawer were condoms, a set of handcuffs, a black mask, and what looked like gags.

Deke dangled a handcuff from his index finger. "I don't suppose Ms. Saunders mentioned bondage."

Ms. Knight's mouth dropped agape and then snapped shut. "No. I'd never have pictured her doing that."

"There're a couple of clubs in town that cater to people who like bondage. Maybe Rebecca was a member or at least a frequent visitor."

Taylor shook her head as she stared at the items. "Looks like she had more secrets than I'd imagined."


Deke drove straight to the New Community Church and following the signs found himself standing before a receptionist outside the pastor's office. A flash of his badge and a brief explanation earned him an escort into the pastor's office.

A thick man with near white hair rose from behind a massive hand-carved desk. He wore an expensive light gray suit, a silk tie, and gold cuff links. As he came out from behind the desk Deke noticed well-polished shoes and manicured hands.

"Officer Morgan, I'm Pastor Gary."

"Thank you for seeing me."

"My receptionist said this was about a murder."

"Yes, sir. Rebecca Saunders."

Pastor Gary's face paled three shades. "Rebecca?"

"Yes, sir."

"I saw her a couple of days ago."

"Where?"

"At her offices." He moved to one of two cushioned chairs in front of his desk and sat.

Deke took the other chair beside it. "How long have you known Rebecca?"

Pastor Gary's gaze looked vacant as if still processing the information. "About six months."

"Did you know a woman named Dixie Simmons?"

Pastor Gary rose, his eyes sharpening and then fading. "No."

"The two women looked much alike."

"I didn't know her."

"I did some checking. Dixie sang in your church about a year ago."

"We seat upwards of a thousand people here on Sundays. And we have dozens of singers. I shake hands with them all but I don't know them all."

"Who books the singers?"

"The music director."

Pastor Gary sat back in his chair and drummed his fingers. "I'm stunned by this news."

Deke studied the man and didn't doubt for a moment his shock was genuine. "You don't happen to remember an Annie Rivers Dawson, do you?"

"I heard about her in the news. I checked church records and she did attend New Community when we were just starting. I also married her. But beyond that I'm sorry, I don't remember her well. Poor soul."

All three women had connections to Pastor Gary. New Community was a big church and coincidences did happen, but not too often in his book.

Deke handed Pastor Gary his card. "You'll call me if you think of anything that might help me solve this case."

Pastor Gary took the card, absently flicking the edge with his index finger. "Sure. Of course."

Deke didn't press, knowing he'd dig deeper and likely return to see the pastor. He said his good-byes and left. In his car he called Rick.

His brother picked up on the first ring. "Yeah."

"See if there are notes in the files about Pastor Gary Wright. He married Annie. And he's loosely connected to Dixie and my latest victim."

"Think he could be your guy?"

"He's connected to all three women."

"Consider it done."



Georgia Morgan was good at manipulation. The youngest of four and the only girl, she'd learned early on that she couldn't win with strength. She'd tried to strong-arm her brother Alex once when she was ten and he'd gently pushed her aside as if she were a feather. She'd been mad, and she'd screamed until he'd given her what she'd wanted.

She'd attempted screaming again with Rick but the noise had gotten her mother's attention. When her mother realized what she was up to, she'd sent Georgia to her room. *Too much noise!* As she'd stomped up the stairs of her parents' house she'd glanced back and spied Rick grinning. She'd learned to keep her voice low, to wheedle and to cajole until she got exactly what she wanted.

She hoisted the box of chocolate glazed cupcakes up as she rang the bell of Rick's house. Inside she heard Tracker's deep *woof* and then Rick's uneven gait.

The sound of his footsteps gave her pause. They'd nearly lost Rick six months ago. The family had huddled in the hospital waiting for the surgeon's report. Though they were siblings with a reputation for verbal sparring no one had argued once that night. And when the doctor had announced Rick would live, she'd wept.

As much as guilt nudged her now, she wouldn't spare Rick any of her manipulative ways. He'd been saying for months he didn't want to be treated differently. As far as he was concerned the shooting had never happened. She'd give him exactly what he'd requested.

Her grin widening, she held up the cupcakes seconds before the door snapped open. Rick's black hair stood on end as if he'd run his fingers through it once too often. He wore a threadbare UT T-shirt and faded jeans. Tracker nudged next to Rick's thigh and sniffed.

Rick arched a brow. "What are you doing here?"

She held up the cupcakes. "Thought we could bond."

Suspicion darkened his eyes. "Why?"

"Do we need an excuse?" She pouted, one of her signature moves. "We never see each other."

A sigh hissed over his lips as he pushed open the door. "Fine. Come in."

"Is that coffee I smell?"

"Just made a pot."

"I have great timing."

"Right."

He padded barefoot through a sparsely decorated living room furnished with a couple of easy chairs and a wide-screen television. On the Big House dining table, he'd stacked boxes that smelled of must and dust. She wanted to ask if they were the Annie files? But she kept quiet, letting the smell of Colombian coffee pull her into the kitchen. She set the cupcakes on the table and opened the flap.

He pulled two Titans mugs from the cabinet and filled both with coffee. He dumped two teaspoons of sugar in his and added a splash of milk in hers.

"So how's it going?" she asked, grinning.

He tossed her a wary glare as if nice from her was as unexpected as snow in July. "Good."

She pushed the box of cupcakes toward him. "I've your favorite."

He glanced in the box at the bright confections and then her as if he was expecting a punch line. "Really."

"Yeah, sure, why not?"

"Or better, why?"

"Why what?"

"Why did you bring treats?"

She reached for her mug and took a sip. "Can't I be nice to you once in a while?"

He laughed, hard. "Yeah, I guess you could but you never do. You aren't the warm and fuzzy type."

She considered his assessment and didn't disagree. "Rick, I brought cupcakes. I'm not making a political statement." She plucked a pink cake from the box and took a bite.

He eyed her an extra beat before selecting a vanilla with extra chocolate icing. He bit into it and his eyes closed, as he clearly savored the taste. "I don't know why you decided to be nice but I'm glad you did."

She arched a brow, growing slightly annoyed with him now. "You make me sound heartless."

Silent, he popped the last of the cake in his mouth and grabbed another one. "Not heartless. Strategic."

She glanced toward the boxes in the living room. Of all her three brothers Rick was the hardest to manipulate. "How's it going with the Dawson files?"

He stared at her over the rim of his coffee cup and for a moment didn't speak. She thought he'd stonewall her like Deke but finally he said, "Slow. Lots of details."

She sensed a tiny opening. "Buddy liked to document."

"That he did."

Surrendering to feelings was hard for her. Most days she kept a wisecracking façade that made her feel safe. But now she couldn't summon one tart remark. "You think Jeb killed her?"

He leaned back in his chair. "There's a mountain of evidence against the guy. I would have arrested him."

She glanced into the milky white coffee, grateful and frightened of his honesty. "I can help. I'm pretty good with sifting through data." Her grin was automatic but not heartfelt. "Deke is not a man to cross."

"He tries to do what's best for us all."

"He's not Buddy. He isn't in charge of this family. Hell, he all but ignored us the last decade." He'd been working. Her mind understood, but her heart cringed at the abandonment.

"You know he couldn't hang out with us while doing the undercover work. Hell, the job cost him two marriages."

"His wives were cool. But neither could stand up to the allure of his work."

He studied her. "That's why you brought the cupcakes— to talk about Deke?"

If she thought she could play Rick for the fool, she was wrong. She opted for directness. "No, they are a bribe. I want to look at those files."

"You aren't here for my winning personality?"

The dry humor in his tone had her swallowing a small smile. "Tell me a tidbit about the case. I know so little since Deke is being Deke. Silent."

With his thumb, he absently traced the embossed T on his mug. And then slowly and carefully told her the standard details of the case that she'd already found on the Internet.

"Did you hear about the letters?" she asked.

He tossed her another glance as if wondering if he'd been played. "Yeah."

"You got copies?"

He rose slowly and moved into the living room. He glanced at the pile of papers and plucked out a file. He returned and laid it on the table.

She opened the file and saw the copies of the letters. This time her smile was genuine. "Thanks."

"Sure."

Georgia skimmed her hands over the letters, wanting to devour them.

"You're going to read those now?" he asked.

"I might have a thought or two to add."

"You might."

Doubt lingered behind the word, but she ignored it. Her attention shifted solely to the letters, which she was certain held the key to the secret.

Max Quincy slumped over a shot glass, half-full with an amber liquid. He raised the glass with a trembling hand and slurped the remainder of the liquid before pounding the tumbler hard against the wood bar. "I want another."

The bartender, a tall burly man with biceps covered in tattoos, glanced up from the register before slamming the till closed. "No more for you, Quincy. You haven't paid for the last three."

Frowning, Max struggled to focus his gaze. "I'm good for it. I am. I've been out of commission for a couple of weeks. Cut me some slack."

"Out of commission." He snorted. "You been in jail selling your latest story to the cops."

"Maybe, but the money I make I spend here." Indignation hummed under the slurring words.

The bartender shook his head. "Well, you've run through whatever money you had."

"I'm good for it!"

"No more credit."

Max stared into the empty depths of his glass and seeing the smallest pool of amber liquid upended it over his mouth. A single drop dripped on his tongue and he greedily lapped it up.

He barely noticed the person sliding onto the bar stool beside him, but he noticed the twenty slid so easily toward the bartender. If only he had that kind of money.

"Two more."

Licking his lips, Max watched the bartender reach for a bottle and serve up the drinks as he swiped the twenty off the counter. The dim light of the bar danced in the whiskey's liquid depths.

When a tumbler full of whiskey made it Max's way he didn't look up or ask questions. He drank, savoring the exquisite burn against the back of his throat. "Been a long time since I've had as good as that. Tastes like spun gold."

A second glass moved his way. "You looked like you could use a drink."

"Yeah," he breathed as he reached for the glass. He held it up to his lips and this time sipped a bit slower. "I've lived long enough to know nothing is for free. Nothing. What's this drink gonna cost me, pal?"

"Call me Baby."

He glanced sideways catching the edge of a gray hoodie pulled forward. "Sure. What's the cost, Baby?"

"Not much really. Just a half-hour of your time."

"Thirty minutes for two drinks." Max gulped the last of it. "Do I know you?"

"You might."

He grunted. "You'll have to do better than that."

"I'll pay you a thousand dollars for your time."

"A grand." His nerves hummed with interest. "What kind of job are we talking about?"

"Simple. Quick."

A chuckle rumbled in his chest. He might be a drunk but he wasn't stupid. "If it's simple and quick then why don't you do it yourself?"

"If you don't want the work, I'll find someone else. There're lots of guys like you who'd be grateful."

Max held up his hand realizing the buying power of a thousand dollars was too much to pass up. "I didn't say I wouldn't do it. I was just asking a question."

"It's not the kind of job that comes with questions. You do the job, you get paid and we go our separate ways."

"So what's the work?"

"Outside."

Max drew small circles on the bar with his empty glass. "It's warm in here."

"I've a full bottle of what you had in my car. It's yours to drink while we talk."

Max set the glass aside. "A full bottle?"

"All for you."

Max staggered behind Baby out of the bar toward the dimly lit side street to a four-door car parked by the curb. The license plates said Tennessee but it was a rental.

A click of the lock and the car door opened. Max slid inside as Baby moved behind the wheel. A twist of a key and the car engine fired and the heater was blowing out warm air. "Your bottle is in the glove box."

Max snapped the glove box open and all but laughed like a kid on Christmas morning when he saw aged bourbon. He cracked open the top lid and took a long swallow. When he'd finished, he sighed, content as an old alley cat playing with a fat mouse. "So what is the job?"

"It's easier to show you than to say. I'll drive us. It's close by."

Max eased back against the seat, relaxed. He took another gulp. "How close?"

"Minutes."

"Sure." He replaced the cap and cradled his bottle close as the car pulled out of the spot. He watched the night's lights blend and swirl past him. "I've not felt this good in a long time." His eyes drooped heavy. A snore rumbled in his chest.

When the car stopped Max jostled awake. His head felt heavy and his arms the size of tree trunks. He could barely move.

Baby opened his car door. "Looks like you had a bit of a nap."

Max opened his mouth to speak but found he couldn't get the words out.

"A nap is good. I'll bet you were exhausted. Prison can take it out of a man."

"How?" How did you know about prison? The question couldn't push past the brain sludge.

Teeth flashed. "I know a lot." Baby grabbed his hand and with surprising strength pulled a staggering Max to his feet.

Out of the car the scents of the Cumberland River greeted. In the distance, the river lapped against the shore.

"That job I need for you to do is steps away."

"Job?"

"That's right, the job. Remember, you'll earn your thousand dollars and that bottle of bourbon?"

One step. Two. Steps. Each foot moved as if it weighed a couple of hundred pounds. The bottle slipped from Max's embrace and fell to the ground hitting a rock and shattering. He paused and stared at the glass shards glittering among rocks in the moonlight.

"My bottle."

"I'll get you another." Strong hands pushed him forward three more stumbling steps.

With the next step his foot sloshed in water. "Where am I?"

"At the job site."

He raised his gaze to the cool waters of the river that caught the moonlight in its watery reflection. "What the hell?"

The firm hand in the small of his back shoved him forward hard. He stumbled and fell face-first into the cold waters. Immediately, he fought to lift his face and breathe. But those same hands that had shoved him threaded through his hair and held his face in the water.

Panicking, he jerked his face out of the water, but a knee in his back forced it back. His arms flailed, but the weight pressing against him coupled with the heaviness of the booze was too much to fight. Soon his oxygen-starved body forced him to inhale. And when he did, water flooded his mouth, nose, and his lungs.

Above the water Max heard, "Say good-bye to the last link."

He fought harder but strong hands held him down. Finally, his mind drifted, and drifted away from the panic and then in a blink went black.

"Yeah, I'm watching her right now," Oscar McMillian said as he cradled the cup of coffee in his hand. He stared up at the dark window. "She is my type."

"Be careful. Be subtle. You don't want trouble from the cops."

Annoyance flared. "I can control myself."

A heavy silence crackled through the line. "I know you can." The line went dead.

He closed his phone and sipped his coffee. He'd been sitting out here for a couple of hours watching Rachel Wainwright's building. Though his back ached and he longed to stretch out, he couldn't bring himself to leave. What if he took a break and missed something important? He didn't know what important meant, but when he saw it he'd know it.

He couldn't stop thinking about Rachel Wainwright. If he were smart he'd stay far, far away from her. That cop had spotted him at the honky-tonk and had chased him away. He could have really enjoyed himself because given time he'd have gotten Rachel to lighten up. But the cop had interfered.

But there was no cop in sight tonight. Just him, the night, and Rachel alone in her house.

She was like a drug to him. From the moment he'd first seen her, she'd infected his blood. And like an addict, he couldn't give her up. He sat in his car staring up at her warehouse apartment. Learning every little detail he could about her.

The lights in her office remained on. She'd had Chinese food delivered at seven. She'd risen from her desk at nine to stretch and make more coffee. She worked long hours. Slept little.

He'd dozed in his car at one point and dreamed of peeling her clothes off as she moaned pleasure. Of her screaming his name as he drove into her.

Rachel had infected his blood as Ellen had all those months ago. He'd gotten carried away with Ellen. He'd acted too quickly. Foolish. Reckless. And now he was in a hell of a mess.

But he'd figure his way out of this mess, as he had gotten out of the trouble in Kansas City and years ago in Portland. Rachel would see him clear of his troubles. All he had to do was play the game. Be the man she needed him to be so she could believe in him.

And then when he was a free man, he'd find Rachel and turn some of those dreams of his into realities.

*February 19*

    *I dreamed about you last night. You were sleeping
like a baby, like you did in my arms so many times. I
leaned over to kiss you as you opened your eyes. A
smile teased the edges of your lips. You raised up
your head to kiss me. I smiled. And moments before
our lips touched, I jabbed my carving knife between
your ribs. Funny. Why would I dream that?*

              *A.*

# Chapter Fifteen

*Wednesday, October 19, 11 AM*

Rachel double-checked the address on the sticky note clutched in her hand and glanced again at the black mailbox. 2317. "Finally," she muttered as she parked in front of the white rancher.

She'd been up last night watching Annie's taped performance. The woman had been vibrant, alive, and not like the woman in the last letters to Sugar. She'd dug through her notes and reread her interviews. She'd spotted the name Kate Tilden, whose sister, Beth, had been Annie's roommate. Joanne had said Beth had died ten years ago in a car accident but her sister Kate had been a frequent visitor to the house.

Rachel had called Kate this morning but had gotten her voice mail. She'd left a message and then, taking a chance, had driven to her house.

Now she wondered how well she'd be welcomed. Stirring up the past had earned her a good bit of resentment and anger and she braced for Kate's reaction.

Out of her car, she hurried up the front sidewalk neatly

lined with winter pansies in a well-mulched bed. She rang the bell and waited.

Seconds later footsteps sounded behind the door and it opened in a quick rush. Standing on the other side of the screened door stood a tall woman with dark hair and striking brown eyes. Her face was wide, her jaw lantern. "Can I help you?"

"Brenda?"

She grinned. "Rachel Wainwright. What brings you here?"

"I left a message earlier today for Kate Robertson Tilden."

Brenda nodded. "My mom mentioned a call. Did she get back to you?"

"No."

"Sorry. Our pastor visited Momma this morning and she was real tired after he left."

Rachel resisted asking the impatient questions firing in her head and took time to build rapport. "KC is officially retired then?"

"He is. He's driving east to see his son. He should be back soon."

"Thanks again for your help at the hospital and for seeing me now."

"How's the shoulder?"

Rachel tightened her grip on her purse strap. "Sore but better." The unexpected connection was a nice bonus. "Do you think your mother would be open to talking to me about Annie Rivers Dawson? I'm trying to talk to everyone who knew her."

"Momma is in the sunroom now. And she's rested up. I don't see why it would hurt to visit. She doesn't get many visitors." Brenda pushed open the screened door. As Rachel stepped inside, Brenda glanced past her and frowned. "Did you notice that car parked a half block behind yours?"

Rachel followed her gaze to a dark sedan parked across

the street. She recognized the driver instantly. Oscar McMillian.

"You know that man?" Brenda asked.

"I do. He's a client. But he shouldn't be here." Tension rippled through her body.

"Should I call the police?"

The police translated into Deke. His words of warning about Oscar rambled in her head and she pictured him staring at her as if she were a child. Oscar was more of a problem than she'd realized, but to admit that to Deke . . . well, she'd rather eat dirt. "No. Thanks. I'll deal with him later."

Brenda stared past Rachel to Oscar. "I don't like the looks of him. He can't be up to any good."

"If he bothers me I'll call the cops."

Brenda glared at the man. "Trouble."

Tension slipped up her spine. "I'm sorry, I didn't mean for this to be about me."

Brenda's smile warmed. Clearly conflict didn't rattle her. "I've worked in the prison ministry for years. I've seen my fair share of scary men and I can handle myself. Don't worry. Come on in then and you can have a talk with Momma."

Rachel followed Brenda through the house, walls cluttered with dozens of pictures of children, old folks, and wedding couples. Rachel imagined the entire family history had been mapped out on this wall. She thought about her own home and her lone family picture. It had been taken at her high school graduation. She'd been dressed in her white cap and gown. To her left stood her mother and to her right her brother. Her father had passed by then but it had been one of the happiest days she could remember. For mere moments there'd been no conflict, no arguments and life had been good and filled with promises of art school.

Even then she'd realized happiness could be fragile, but

then she'd still believed that destiny was in her control. If only she'd realized happy endings weren't really possible.

Brenda showed her into a brightly lit sunroom filled with green plants. Soft music played in the background. Sitting in the corner was a woman nestled in a wingback chair. Her body had been ravaged by disease and though she couldn't have been more than sixty, she looked eighty.

Eyes closed, the woman tilted her face back, savoring the heat of the sun on her face. When her mother had been ill, it had been the simplest pleasures she'd enjoyed most toward the end. The sun's heat. A child's laugh. A trip to the market. A kind word.

Brenda moved toward the woman and with a loving hand touched her cheek. "Momma, you've a visitor."

The woman opened her eyes and looked at her daughter and then at Rachel. Blue eyes possessed a keen, alert edge that defied the illness decimating her body.

"I saw you on television the other night."

Unable to begrudge this woman a laugh at her expense, Rachel smiled. "I made a real impression."

A grin softened the woman's hollow lines. "You can take a hit, that's for sure. Didn't cry or bellyache. Got up and stood your ground. That's good for something."

Rachel's tension melted. "Thanks."

"I guess you know I'm Kate Tilden."

"Yes."

Brenda said, "Momma, Ms. Wainwright is here to talk to you about Annie Rivers Dawson."

She shifted in her chair and winced as if the slightest movement triggered pain. "I didn't think she'd come to talk about the weather."

Rachel and Brenda's gazes met and for a moment she saw in Brenda's strained smile the apologetic look of a daughter not sure how to handle her dying mother's candor. "Do you mind if I ask you a few questions?"

"Not at all. I'd enjoy the conversation. Sit."

Rachel perched on the edge of a cushioned chair.

Kate looked at Brenda. "Would you get us some tea? Might be nice to make an occasion of a rare visitor."

Brenda hesitated, as if she didn't want to leave her mother alone, and then smiled. "Sure, Momma. I've also made cookies."

Kate waved her veined thin hand. "That's a good girl."

Rachel shifted on the chair wanting to sit back but feeling as if she didn't have the right to be informal.

"Go on, sit back and make yourself comfortable. I might be sick with the cancer but I don't bite."

"I'm not afraid of the cancer. I lived with it daily when my mother was ill."

"She died."

"Three years ago." Rachel understood the disease; it sapped energy fast and she didn't want to give the impression she'd stay past her welcome. She settled back in her seat. "Let me know if you get tired or you need for me to leave."

"I'm always tired and I'm always alone. If you can manage a yawn or two then I'd like to have your company."

"Deal."

"So what do you want to know about Annie? I'm not surprised you found me. I don't think there're many people left that knew her personally."

"Your sister roomed with her."

"That's right. I met Annie when I stopped by the apartment to drop off papers for Beth."

"What were your impressions of her?"

"Bright, bubbly, ambitious. Could sing like an angel. She worked hard and wasn't afraid to ask for what she wanted."

"She also sang at your church."

Watery eyes brightened with admiration. "You've done your homework."

"I try."

"Yes, Beth introduced Annie to our pastor. She sang "Amazing Grace" on Easter Sunday and there was not a dry eye in the house."

"She sang there often?"

"Pretty regular for several months. That's where she met her husband, Bill Dawson. You talked to him yet?"

"He's a hard man to catch. He won't return my calls and I can't get past his receptionist."

"He wasn't the easiest man from what I remember. But he sure did love Annie." She winked. "I hear he likes to run early in the morning about seven. Centennial Park."

"How do you know that?"

"I was church secretary for thirty years. I heard it all."

Rachel thought about Annie's letters. If Bill had been her great love, why not mention him by name? She'd noticed Annie had been careful to include no identifying information on her lover. "Was she seeing anyone else?"

"Like that Jeb Jones fellow, the one that murdered her?"

"Him or anyone else."

"She flirted with every man she saw. Beth's boyfriend had a real thing for her. Turned to mush every time she came in the room and it made Beth powerful mad. The ladies at church loved to listen to her sing but didn't like it when she lingered after service at the socials and talked to the married men."

"I keep hearing that." She hesitated. "Did she show an interest in any man?"

"If she did, I didn't notice." Her gaze warmed with a memory from the past. Gently she touched the headscarf that covered her thinning hair. "I used to try and style my hair like hers. I wanted it to be long and blond. Once I went to the drugstore and bought a bottle of blond hair dye. My husband found it. He made me pray with him for hours."

Rachel's heart reached out for the young girl.

Kate curled thin, deeply veined fingers into fists. "That story makes my husband sound like a bad man. He wasn't. He wanted the best for me, and the idea of me copying a barroom singer was terrifying. He saw the troubles behind Annie's smile."

"What did he see?"

Kate hesitated a moment. "I never like to speak ill of the dead. And I never spoke against Annie."

Rachel heard the hesitation in her voice. She didn't have to say a word because Kate had the look of a woman ready to talk.

"She was real sweet and nice when I first met her at the church. But over time, when I'd see her at the house she was moody and angry. She got into a heck of a fight with Beth one night. Beth was sure Annie was sleeping with her boyfriend."

"Was she?"

"It wouldn't have taken more than a wink to encourage him. He all but drooled over Annie."

"So no?"

"I don't know. Annie was messing around with someone." A sigh lifted and released fragile shoulders. "Since I saw you on the TV I've done a lot of thinking. Not much else I can do these days. I don't have a future, only a past. Behind Annie's bright smile and sweet voice were lots of dark secrets."

"Her sister Margaret says that she was perfect."

"I remember Margaret. She was about sixteen when Annie died. And she adored her sister. But she was sixteen and Annie was one person for her baby sister and another when she went out at night."

"What about Jeb?"

"Another admirer. Another man who fell under her spell." A hint of bitterness coated the words and then a quick smile to soften it. "That sounded judgmental. I'm sorry."

"How old was Brenda?"

"Twelve years old. I was married to the assistant pastor of the church. When Ray died, Pastor Gary gave me a job in the church office and I've been there ever since."

Brenda gave off the vibe of an energetic woman. She couldn't see this woman dating KC. "You have any idea who Annie might have been seeing?"

Rattling teacups signaled the return of Brenda who carried in a large serving tray with a teapot, china cups, and a plate of cookies. She smiled as she set the tray in front of Rachel.

"It's nice to have the company," Brenda said. "These days it's me and Momma. We don't get many visitors from the church these days."

Kate frowned. "That's not true, Brenda. Pastor Gary was just here."

Brenda smiled at Rachel as she poured her tea. "We understand he's a busy man and has a lot of duties with the new church expansion and all. He's a good man."

"He was like a second father to Brenda after Ray died. We'd not have made it without him."

Rachel accepted the cup, declining the sugar and milk. "I hear it is one of the biggest churches in the region."

Kate sat a bit straighter, her pride clear. "He built it from near nothing to a real palace for the Lord." She waved away a cup heavy with milk and sugar. "We were meeting in a community center when we first started that church. There must not have been more than one hundred people attending in those days. But he had a fire in his belly and God in his soul. It didn't take long before the congregation outgrew the community center. We had our own building in two years. Not fancy like today but it was big and we were all proud to call it our church home."

Her love and respect for the man energized her. "Would he remember Annie?"

Kate reached for a cookie and broke off a piece. "I'm sure that he would. He loved her singing and he was the one that married Bill and her. She was such a pretty bride."

"You were there?"

"I played the organ."

"I understand many local churches helped search for her when she went missing."

"Our church was one of many that sent volunteers. We searched all the woods, abandoned buildings, and along the river. Never found one sign of her."

"Did Bill Dawson search for her?"

"No. He was too torn up, or so he said. Many thought he might have been the one that killed her."

"Why?"

"The husband is the first suspect, isn't he? And they fought a good bit right before the baby was born."

"What did they fight about?"

"I never could tell. But I saw them arguing after church one day."

"You are still involved in the church?"

"Until six months ago when the cancer made me too sick to work."

Brenda shook her head. "That was a sad day when we boxed up Momma's desk. She was the heart and soul of that church. Pastor wouldn't be the man he is today without Momma."

Kate nibbled the cookie. "That's not true. He would have done fine without me."

"He would have done well enough, but you were the one that helped him stay focused."

"I'm glad to know I had a part in the success." She

rolled her head from side to side, closing her eyes. "Ms. Wainwright, I know I said I wouldn't mind the fatigue, but I think I overspoke. My energy dropped as if someone opened a trap door."

Rachel set her cup down. "Of course. Thank you for your time, Kate."

Brenda rose. "I'll show you to the door."

They wove through the house and a framed image sitting on a half-moon table caught her attention. It was Kate in younger, healthier days standing next to a vibrant, laughing man in front of a red car. "That's a nice picture of your mother. Is that your father?"

"I wish." Sadness passed over her gaze like a spectator before she picked up the picture and wiped a piece of dust from the glass with her sleeve. "That's Pastor Gary. That picture was taken about the time Momma started working at the church."

"She clearly thinks a lot of the man."

"He and the church were her entire life," Brenda said. "She's devoted her life to them."

"A rich full life, judging by all the pictures."

Brenda replaced the image. "Yes."

Rachel reached for the front door. "Do you go to church there, Brenda?"

"I did until three months ago. Between work at the hospital and taking care of Momma I don't have much time. And I want to take what time I have with her."

"You're a good daughter."

She raised her chin. "I've always tried to be the best I could be for her. She sacrificed so much for me."

Brenda watched as Rachel stepped out onto the front porch and scanned the street for signs of Oscar. "He seems to be gone."

Rachel tensed. "I think you're right."

"What did he want with you?"

"He's a bit overzealous."

Brenda shook her head. "I didn't like his look. You need to be careful of him."

She fished her keys out of her purse. "I will. Thanks for the tea, Brenda."

"Any time, Ms. Wainwright. Any time."

Rachel slid behind the wheel of her car and locked the doors before firing up the engine. She glanced back at the house and saw the faintest flutter of lace curtains in the front window as if Brenda lingered to watch over her.


"Keep tailing him," Deke said. "He'll make a move sooner than later." He listened to protest on the other end of the call. "Don't care what the captain says. I'm right about this. Stay on him."

Deke ended the call as he arrived at the Forensics lab. Brad had arranged the ten original letters on the light table in chronological order as well as the copies Rachel had made of the missing letters.

Deke shrugged off his coat and set it aside. He moved to the table and studied the arrangement. "So what do you have?"

"An interesting story."

"Entertain me."

Before he could answer Georgia breezed in the room. She shrugged off her jacket and laid it on top of Deke's. She didn't bother a glance at the men as she scanned the letters. "Hope I'm not late for the party."

"Georgia," Deke warned. "This doesn't concern you."

Georgia glared at her brother. "Since when? I don't see why I can't be a part of this. Fact I was helping Rick review the case files the other night."

Shit. As much as he wanted to bark at Rick, how could he? Rick was no match for Georgia, who since she was a small kid, had hated being left out. She'd nosed her way into more private conversations. How many times had she hammered on a closed door, demanding it be opened? If Georgia wanted in, there was no stopping her.

He shifted attention to Brad. "Go ahead."

Brad glanced at Georgia who folded her arms. She remained in battle stance as if expecting Deke to change his mind and toss her out. She'd not leave without one hell of a fight.

Brad cleared his throat. "The first letter is fairly straightforward. The victim . . ."

Georgia shook her head. "Call her Annie. She had a name and deserves to be remembered as a person."

Brad scratched his neck. "Sure. I'm assuming this is Annie's handwriting based on a sample Deke obtained from her sister."

Georgia glanced at Deke. "How did that meeting go?"

Deke kept his expression neutral, giving no hint to the tense exchange he'd shared with Margaret. "Fine."

"She gave you a sample just like that?"

"For the most part."

A frown wrinkled her brow. "Okay."

Brad watched the interchange and, certain that it had ended, continued. "Note the large looping style? Also note the way she adds an upward flourish to her letters. It suggests a woman wrote the letters but of course that is not a given. It suggests an emotional immaturity."

"She was in her early twenties," Georgia added.

"Understood. But I've seen folks in their late forties write in a similar manner. Handwriting can't confirm age but it suggests emotional maturity."

"Young and reckless fits her profile, Georgia," Deke said.

She ignored the comment and waved a hand toward the letters. "What else do you see?"

"Note the size of the letters. That suggests a confidence. Maybe vanity. Arrogance."

Deke rubbed the tensing muscles in the back of his neck. "Anything else?"

"Note how small her A is at the end of each letter. Suggests perhaps isolation, loneliness."

"How can we be sure Annie wrote these letters?" Georgia asked.

Brad glanced toward a frowning Georgia and then back at Deke before pulling out the song sheet. "This is the sheet from her sister. It's our control. We know she wrote this. And I can say for sure that she wrote the first sixteen letters. The handwriting is consistent."

"And all the remaining letters?"

"I see small changes that I missed on the first pass. I noticed them on the second pass and they make me question the validity of the latter letters."

"Why?" Deke asked.

"Note the way she crosses a *t* on the song sheet and in the initial letters. A clear loop at the front of the *t*. But in the last letters the loop is much smaller and tighter. And note the signature A is larger."

"Maybe she was under stress," Georgia said.

"Maybe," Brad said. "All the handwriting looks like hers in the last five letters but closer inspection reveals a tighter command of the lettering. It's as if she's not writing naturally but thinking about each letter."

Deke straightened. "The last five letters are fakes?"

"That would be my professional opinion." Brad pointed to the last letters, which he'd grouped together. "The word choices are different, courser, and angrier. It's as if two different authors wrote the letters."

Georgia picked up the last letter. Frown lines deepened. "Are you sure Rachel Wainwright hasn't had some hand in this? She's been trying to tear into Buddy's case. Maybe she faked them all to cast reasonable doubt."

"I don't see her doing that," Deke said without much thought.

"She's trying to make a name for herself," Georgia challenged. "Attack the victim is a common technique for defense attorneys."

"The paper stock is thirty years old and from the same lot," Brad said. "The ink is as old."

Deke said to Georgia, "This would not be Rachel's style."

Georgia arched a brow. "How do you know what her style is?"

Shit. He did not need to open a nonexistent can of worms with his sister. "Georgia, stop talking."

Her eyes narrowed. "You stop."

Brad cleared his throat, fatigue making him edgy. The Saunders crime scene had taken twenty hours to process. "Intelligent."

Georgia glared at Brad.

Brad looked at Deke. "Bottom line: two different people wrote these letters thirty years ago. Annie and someone else."

Georgia shook her head. "And that someone sends them to Rachel and attacks her and kills another woman to get them back. Why? Change of mind?"

"Or one person went against the wishes of another," Deke said.

"You've three murder victims who were all beaten to death," Georgia said.

He nodded. "Your point?"

"Those crime scenes," she said. "The blood spray and

the pools of blood. Annie Rivers Dawson's crime scene looked similar."

The lines in Deke's face deepened as he imagined Georgia scanning the Dawson files. "Remind me to kill Rick."

She rolled her eyes. "My point is that if not for the thirty-year gap I'd have concluded the same person killed all four women."

Deke arched a brow. "Jeb's in jail."

"Perhaps he didn't work alone all those years ago. Maybe he was working for someone. Perhaps when Rachel stirred the pot she made someone nervous."

"Dixie was killed before the press conference."

"Rachel requested DNA a month before that press conference. Someone might have heard about the retest."

"Damn." He reached for his phone.

"Whom are you calling?"

"The state lab. I want those DNA tests on my desk tomorrow."

"The blood could still come back as Jeb's."

"I wouldn't bet on it now."

Rachel arrived at the address that once had been shared by Annie and her husband Bill. It was a tiny house, made of brick with cracked and peeling shutters. The front lawn had long ago turned to seed and the gravel driveway was washed out from rain and erosion. She parked in front of the house spying a public notice sheet on the front door. She moved past a mailbox crammed with flyers and papers down the uneven rutted driveway toward the house.

She glanced around the empty street, trying to imagine where Jeb might have parked his car that last day of Annie's life. She stared at the large picture window, now covered with yellowing, torn curtains. Had he stood here

**and** watched her through the window? And if he had, had there been someone else that had watched Jeb and set him up for the murder? Perhaps Annie's lover?

Gravel crunched under her feet as she moved closer to the door. Walking up cracked front steps, she read the eviction notice on the front door before opening the screened door and trying the front door. It was unlocked.

She twisted the rusted brass knob and pushed it open. Immediately, the smells of mold and dust leapt from the dimly lit living room, now stripped of furniture. A flip of a light switch up and down confirmed the electricity had been cut off. She pulled open the front curtains, coughing as dust escaped into the musty air. Light streamed into the darkened room, shining on the piles of trash in the corner and dust coating the floor. In another room little feet scurried into the shadows.

Rachel turned to her right and searched the darkened corridor that cut into the deep shadows. She knew from the police report that Annie had been killed in the front hallway off the living room. The white walls were sprayed red with blood and on the hardwood floor puddles of blood. There'd also been signs that her body had been dragged out the back door.

Rachel reached for her phone, turned on the flashlight app and cut into the darkness. The first door on the right had been the baby's room. A girl. She'd been named Sara. And just five days old when her mother had died.

Rachel peered into the dark room that smelled more of mold and decay. She didn't venture toward the room Annie shared with her husband, a man who'd refused all interviews with the press and had been immediately cleared by the cops.

Bill Dawson had moved out of the house the day Annie had died and never returned. He'd tried to sell it but the foul history had tainted new buyers for a year before a man from out of town had bought the house. And then it had passed from owner to owner, slowly falling into disrepair as the neighborhood had crumbled under hard times.

There had been rumors of ghosts and strange noises in the house and some had theorized that Annie had come back searching for her baby. A cold shiver passed down Rachel's spine and she rubbed her arms. Turning to leave she came face-to-face with a shadowed man. She started, took a step back and gripped her phone, tension and fear making her heart throb.

"Who's there?" she demanded.

For a beat, silence and then a soft chuckle as Oscar McMillian stepped out of the shadows. His cheeks looked flushed, his hair wild as if he'd been drinking. "Rachel, you are a hard woman to catch."

She gripped her phone. "What are you doing here?"

He glanced around the house and she sensed he liked the creepy seclusion. "I'm here for you."

"Is this about your case?"

He shook his head. "It's about you."

Fear moved up her spine like an electric shock. She had held no illusions about Oscar McMillian when she'd taken his case but she realized now she'd underestimated him. "You need to leave."

"Why would I want to leave?" He moved a fraction closer, reminding her of a cat that played with a mouse.

"I'm leaving." She grit her teeth and heart beating fast, moved forward, praying she could get out of this house and away from him.

His arm shot out and he grabbed her. "You are like her."

Breath stinking of whiskey-pumped fear. "What do you mean?"

"Ellen. She thought she was better than me."

His long fingers bit into her arm. "I don't think that."

"Liar."

"Oscar. Let me go. I'm your attorney. I'm on your side." Who would hear her if she screamed?

A sneer curled the edge of his lips. "No you are not. You pity me. Like Ellen." His second hand settled at the base of her neck.

"Did you attack me the other night?"

"I wish I had." He pushed his weight forward, backing her up into the shadows and against a dark, dusty wall. "After tonight, you won't pity me, but you will fear me."

Rachel drew in a breath as his hold tightened and she screamed. The sound reverberated off the small house's walls and felt as if they bounced and slammed right back into her.

Oscar's white teeth flashed in the near darkness. "I like screams."

She dropped her phone and reached for his hands, hoping to pry them free. They didn't budge. They tightened. Oscar's dark eyes glistened in the shadows.

Rachel coughed and kicked her foot into his shin, which earned her a grunt but no relief from the pressure on her neck. She kicked again. Scratched at his face.

*Jesus, Rachel, why did you come here alone?*

Footsteps thudded from the front of the house. She kicked and whimpered but couldn't catch enough breath to scream. Please find me.

And then the pressure around her neck released and Oscar cursed as rough hands pulled him away from her. She blinked, his cries of frustration reverberating on the walls, as two uniformed police officers handcuffed him. One of the uniforms radioed for an ambulance as a third man strode into the house.

"What are you doing here?" The voice, a rough blend of sandpaper and nails, struck a familiar chord. Deke Morgan.

Relief flooded Rachel and if not for pride she'd have cried. "I could ask you the same."

"You're trespassing," he said.

"I didn't see any posted signs." A galloping heartbeat left her voice a bit breathless.

One of the uniforms returned and informed Deke that Oscar was screaming for a lawyer from the back of the squad car.

Deke looked at Rachel. "Ms. Wainwright?"

*Cut your losses.* "No. Not me."

"Tell him to call the public defender's office," Deke said.

When they were alone, she cleared her throat and gulped down pride. "Thanks. You were right about him."

A dark brow arched as if he'd not expected that admission, and after a small grunt, he turned from the hallway and moved back to the living room. She picked up her phone and quickly followed. In the main room the sunshine and flash of lights from three cop cars was a welcome sight.

His back to the window and the lights, Deke surveyed the room. "Anything of use?"

She shook her head. "I wanted to see what the cops might have seen thirty years ago. I wanted to walk in their footsteps."

"And?"

"Thirty years changes a lot. What are you doing here?"

"Dispatch called ten minutes ago when the uniforms saw McMillian follow you into the house. I figured it was a matter of time before he made a move on you."

"You figured?"

"I told you he was dangerous. This isn't my first rodeo, Rachel."

"How could you know?" The sting of Oscar's fingers around her neck lingered.

"A hunch."

"So was I some kind of bait?"

"More or less."

"That's cold."

"It worked."

"Just barely."

Calloused fingers that had held her steady as she'd left the hospital days ago flexed. "Does seeing this house give you any insight?"

The door to Oscar and her outrage closed. She teetered between anger and relief. "Jeb said he was parked in front of the house. Watching Annie. No one ever saw him at the front door or walk around the side of the house. All reports had him in his car. With thirty years of tree and shrub growth there is no way he could have made it to the door without being seen."

"Assuming the neighbors were still watching." In this confined space he looked taller. He absorbed the energy around him.

"No one heard her scream. No one saw him take her from the house."

"The tire iron was found in the trunk of his car."

"That means squat until I have the DNA test results. Any word on those, by the way?"

"By tomorrow, I'm told."

"Really?" Better to argue with Deke than to dwell on what could have happened here.

"I don't run the lab."

"Really."

"You overestimate my influence."

The false modesty did not sway her. "Did your father ever consider other suspects?"

"You know he did. He interviewed dozens."

"And then the paid informant gave him the break he needed."

"My father was an honest man. He wouldn't frame a guy to close a case."

"How do you know that?"

Large hands fisted at his sides. "I knew my father."

"Do we ever really know our parents?" Her own came to mind. As an adult, she could see now her parents' marriage had been riddled with problems. "The face they show us is not necessarily their true-self. They want us to see the best in them, not the worst."

His jaw tensed. "Much like your client."

The zing hit the mark. "Yes."

He shoved hands in his pockets and paced. "I gave my brother the Dawson case files to review."

"Another Morgan in the mix. Outnumbering the competition?"

He muttered an oath. "I was about to suggest that we work together."

That surprised her. "Why?"

"Do you always look for a dark motive?"

"Yes. Always."

Amusement relaxed his stance a fraction. "We both want this case resolved. I want to prove Buddy did his job. You want Jeb cleared. One of us is right and the other is wrong. But we are on the same path."

"Why would you want my help?"

"The sooner this is resolved, the sooner it can be closed." A smile quirked his lips. "Many hands make light work."

"Maybe." She folded her arms over her chest. "What about the letters?"

"Brad thinks the first fifteen are real. He's not sure about the last five."

Her hackles rose. "What's that mean? If you think I did the forgeries . . ."

"No, I don't think you tampered with the letters. Brad dated the letters back thirty years. They were all written about the same time but perhaps they were not all written by Annie."

"Then who?"

"I don't know."

"Certainly not Jeb."

"No. He'd not have had the talent to pull off that kind of forgery. The man wrote at a third-grade level."

"Then who?"

"That's what I want to find out."

"If it wasn't Jeb, someone got away with murder."

The shadows behind his eyes darkened. "I know."

"It would explain why I was attacked," she said. "Someone has a secret to keep." She tapped her finger on her phone. "You believe whoever killed Lexis killed those other women and maybe Annie?"

His nod was sure and slow. "I think the cases are connected."

"So the man who killed Annie is killing again."

"Maybe."

She shoved out a breath. "Could there be others before Dixie and after Annie?"

"We're looking into it but so far haven't found any."

Rachel rubbed her neck with her hand. "I'll help."

Outside, an ambulance pulled up behind the remaining marked car and Deke's vehicle. Deke nodded toward the door. "As soon as the paramedics check you out."

"I'm fine."

He didn't speak but his manner suggested that No was not on the option list.

*Cut your losses.* "Fine."


As each moment passed, Baby's hatred for Rachel Wainwright grew. The woman meddled. Didn't know how to leave sleeping dogs alone. Baby watched Rachel get out of her car, punch the security code on her office and vanish inside. Gripping the tire iron, Baby imagined what it would feel like to beat Rachel to death. How sweet it would sound when her bones cracked and crunched under the blows of the tire iron. If Baby had another chance at Rachel, there'd be no missing. Rachel might be quick and gotten away the first time but Baby had learned and would be faster the next time.

The next time.

Baby had been told to leave Rachel alone, but Baby wasn't as good a listener as before. The stakes rose each day Rachel kept stirring the pot. Kept digging deeper. And now she'd peeked the interest of that cop. Before Morgan had thought she was a kook. But not now. Now, he'd saved her from Baby's perfect trap.

Not good. Not good at all.

*March 1*

*Sugar.*
*I hear you've been asking after me. You are curious. Worried. Don't be curious, worried and don't come near the baby or me. We are done.*

*A.*

# Chapter Sixteen

*Thursday, October 20, 7 AM*

The first steps of Rachel's run had started stiff and awkward. Each initial foot strike on the pavement jarred her bruised shoulder enough to make her grit her teeth. But she kept running, hoping for the best. To her relief, after a half mile her body warmed a little and she fell into a rhythm.

As she jogged the path at the park, her breathing soon calmed. In the morning light surrounded with a park full of runners she hoped she'd be safe, but still she kept her gaze swiveling from side to side half expecting to duck an attacker's blow. She glanced behind her and checked her watch.

She would have loved to say this was a moment of rest and relaxation for her. But she had an important mission. Bill Dawson, Annie's husband and the man who'd refused all her calls, jogged every morning at seven through the park. She figured if he wouldn't see her, she'd find him. She sucked in a breath and slowed her pace, hoping he'd shown while her shoulder cooperated.

When she heard the steady clip of footsteps, she glanced

back to see a tall, lean, olive-skinned man with hair more gray than black. He was fit, held his head up as he moved and looked as if he'd barely broken a sweat. Earbuds peaked out from his cap. He was attractive and she imagined thirty years ago he would have been stunning. A perfect match to Annie's beauty.

As he passed, she quickened her pace and called out to him. "Mr. Dawson."

He kept running.

"Damn," she muttered, hustling faster until her fingertips brushed his sleeve. "Mr. Dawson!"

At her touch, he slowed and flashed her a look of pure annoyance.

She puffed a stray hair, which had drifted over her eyes. "Mr. Dawson, can I have a word?"

He jerked the earbuds out. "Who are you?"

"My name is Rachel Wainwright. I wanted to ask you some questions about Annie Dawson."

His breath hitched seconds before his frown deepened with a menace that could make most flinch. "I don't talk about her, especially to the press."

"I'm not press, Mr. Dawson." Her breathless tone forced her to pause. She'd underestimated the toll of her injury. "I'm an attorney and I'm representing Jeb Jones."

Annoyance didn't turn to anger as expected but curiosity. "Why the hell would you represent that monster?"

She didn't rise to the bait that many had dangled in front of her the last couple of weeks. "I'm not sure that he killed your wife."

"What the hell are you talking about?" The loud barking tone matched his reputation as confrontational and hard. "The cops sent him away thirty years ago."

In a calm, I've-got-to-win-this-jury-over tone, she said, "I think they made a mistake."

He shook his head. "I don't have time for this."

As he turned she said, "The cops cleared you immediately after Annie went missing because you were out of town at a trade show."

Deeply etched crow's feet deepened. "Look, if you are trying to pin this on me . . ."

"I'm not. I'm trying to find out what happened to Annie. Your alibi was solid."

He released a breath as if he'd been holding it for thirty years. "That piece of crap client you are representing was obsessed with her and then while I was gone he came into my home and beat her to death. He beat my wife to death and took her body and dumped it in the woods."

"While your daughter Sara slept in her crib."

*Your daughter* triggered the tiniest of flinches. "Get to the point, Wainwright, or I'm calling the cops."

She pressed the point she'd been mulling for days. "Were you the biological father of Annie's baby?"

"What the hell?"

"I was given letters written by Annie from an unknown source. The letters were written to a lover. The way Annie talked I assumed this affair was a secret and yet you two dated openly, meeting in church from what I understand. And then the day after her body was found you signed papers relinquishing parental rights."

"None of that is your business."

The raw anger on his face divulged more than words. The nerve she'd struck might be thirty years old but it remained sensitive. "Please," she prompted. "We need to find this man. I think he could have been involved in her murder." His angry silence sliced the air between them. "Did she have a lover?"

"What if she did?" The loud question blasted like a

double-barreled shotgun. "What the hell difference does it make now?"

"It could make a lot of difference to my client. This secret lover of hers could have been the one that killed her."

He shook his head, aggravated. "You are chasing a pipe dream. Jeb killed her."

The door that had cracked might burst open if she pushed a little harder. "Did she identify him?"

He glanced down the path as if common sense told him to leave now, but he lingered, no doubt weighed by an old secret pain. "This is none of your business."

"If that guy was linked to Annie's death then it sure is my business. Did you ever get a name?"

Under the anger simmered temptation. He wanted to talk. Wanted to vent.

"You carried the secret all these years. Was it to protect the baby?"

He clenched his fingers. "She didn't deserve the mess she was born into."

"No, she didn't."

"I couldn't love her. Not like she deserved. I gave her away to parents who wanted her."

"That was kind."

"Or selfish. Depends." He studied her. "The media has been all over me for another interview. You are the reason the past got stirred up. I missed your news broadcast."

"My television debut was a hit." When curiosity darkened his gaze she said, "I'll give you the shorthand version. Annie's sister decked me on live television."

"Margaret." The word came out like a growl.

"She's not too thrilled with you either. She demanded contact with her niece."

His eyes narrowed. "Annie looked out for her sister but she did not want her to have the baby." His jaw tensed and released. "The last month before the baby was born Annie worried a lot about dying. She begged me never to give the baby to Margaret or her mother. I thought it was hormones, but I promised Annie that they would never raise the baby."

"You loved Annie."

Pain deepened the lines on his face. "Go away."

"Who was Annie's lover?"

"Christ, you are a bitch."

Rachel shrugged. "Tell me what I don't know."

He flexed his fingers. "I don't know who the hell he was! She was pregnant with his child when we married. I didn't know that at the time. I thought I was one lucky bastard who'd landed a hell of a catch."

"She told you?"

"Hell, no. When the baby was born, two months early by my count, healthy and whole, I knew it wasn't mine." White teeth flashed and contrasted with his tanned olive skin. "And do you really think I could make a pink baby with blond hair?"

Rachel had barely pulled a C in biology but she understood that his dark traits would likely have overshadowed Annie's fairer ones.

"Annie tried to convince me otherwise but I knew. I'm not that stupid. That's why I wasn't in town when she was killed. I'd left to think and figure out what to do next."

She doubled back to the critical question hoping for an answer this time. "She never told you who he was?"

"I demanded she tell me but she refused. Said it would do no good to ruin another life." He shook his head, his disgust clear. "Okay for her to lie to me and mess with my life but she didn't want to hurt her boyfriend. If I found out who he was today, I think I'd shoot the bastard. He did a royal job of fucking up my life."

One week Dawson had been a man in love with a baby on the way and the next he'd lost both. "I see why you were mad."

"Yeah, I was pissed. Real pissed. But not so pissed that

I forgot Annie's warning about Margaret." He shoved out a breath. "That's all you are getting from me."

She followed. "Who adopted the baby?"

"I don't know."

"How could you not know?"

"The cops took her away and I never saw her again. I signed the papers but didn't read them. End of story."

"Just like that."

"I had enough trouble on my hands in those days with the media hounding me." He cursed. "What a nightmare. Annie was pretty but she was a lying bitch." He grabbed his earbud. "If I see you again, I'm calling the cops."

She watched him jog away, no desire to follow. The letters had not been to Bill. Who had been Annie's lover? And what had the cops done with the baby?

Pastor Gary had arranged the marriage. Perhaps he remembered Annie.

Rachel showered and dressed in dark dress pants and a dark V-necked sweater. She chose simple jewelry and enough makeup to cover her bruise. She arrived at the large white church minutes after three. The parking lot was full, but she'd heard the church ran an aggressive outreach program. She pushed through large double doors and followed signs marked PASTOR'S OFFICE. In the distance she could hear a choir practicing. According to the church's website they were known for their music. She'd watched video clips on the church's site. The Saturday night and Sunday morning services rivaled many Broadway productions. Pastor Gary knew how to draw people in to fill his one thousand seat auditorium.

She made her way to the office and found the reception area empty. She glanced around, looking for a receptionist, and when she found none she peeked down the hallway to a door marked PASTOR'S OFFICE. After one last look and seeing no one she made her way toward the door that was slightly ajar. She glanced through the opening and found a richly carpeted office furnished with deep mahogany furniture. A man's baritone voice echoed out. She looked in and saw a tall, gray-haired man staring out a large window, a cell phone pressed to his ear.

Rachel knocked once. The man turned, he muttered into the phone before closing it. "I'm looking for Pastor Gary."

He smiled, as if that were his go-to response for everyone. "I'm Pastor Gary. How did you get in here?"

"Just walked in."

"No one was at the receptionist desk?"

"No."

He shook his head. "I've had a series of temps since my secretary had to take medical leave."

"Kate. I met her." She tightened her grip on her purse strap. "My name is Rachel Wainwright. I'm . . ."

"I know who you are." His lips curled easily into a soft smile that made her feel at ease. "You made quite a showing on the TV."

She adjusted her purse strap, which weighed heavily on her bruised shoulder that still ached from her run. "One of my more memorable moments."

"You are representing Jeb Jones."

Relieved by his lack of censor, she inched into the office. "I am."

"He was a poor lost soul. What he did was horrible but he was a sick man and I know God has forgiven him."

"How well did you know Annie?"

His gaze turned wistful and sad. "Cops asked the same question."

"Deke Morgan visited you?"

"That's right." He adjusted his cuff. "Like I told him, she sang in the church choir. She had the voice of an angel and we always loved having her sing. Good music has a way of freeing the soul." His soft even tones resonated like a lullaby.

"You introduced her to her husband, Bill Dawson."

"They met at my church. He was a good kind soul as was Annie. A natural fit. I married them."

"And her baby was born seven months later."

He frowned as if she'd struck a sour note. "It is not my place to judge, Ms. Wainwright."

"Bill Dawson was not the baby's father."

He raised a brow. "Who told you that?"

"He did."

"When?"

"This morning."

He glanced toward a cross on the wall and then back at her. "I think he has allowed time to rewrite his story."

"Why would he do that?"

"I don't know. Guilt. He all but threw that baby away after Annie went missing. As soon as her body was found he signed the adoption papers."

"He said he figured out the baby wasn't his after she was born. He confronted Annie and she confessed. He was furious. Felt as if he'd been played for a fool."

His head tilted as if she'd struck a sour note. "Did she tell him this mystery man's name?"

"No. She refused to tell. I was hoping as her pastor, you might have known his identity."

"She never confided in me. I didn't realize Bill wasn't the father until about thirty seconds ago when you told me."

"You don't remember her hanging around with anyone at the church? No one showed her any special interest?"

"A lot of men showed her interest. She was beautiful."

"But no one special?"

"No." He frowned. "And I'm not comfortable having this conversation with you. Annie is with the Lord now and she does not deserve to be maligned. She may not have been perfect but those who are without sin can cast the first stone." The minister stood silent as he might have done at the end of a sermon.

Instead of an amen, she asked, "Who took Annie's baby?"

"Even if I knew I wouldn't tell you. She was a total innocent in that terrible mess and she deserves to be left out of it."

"She has a right to know what happened to her mother and the identity of her biological father."

"We all wanted that child to have a happy life. And it is my fondest hope that she received one. Don't dig it up."

Rachel shifted tactics. "Kate misses this place."

A ghost of a strained smile played on his lips. "Kate is a beautiful soul. She helped build this church and we won't be the same without her. I saw her yesterday." He let the words trail. "How is she doing?"

"The cancer is taking a toll."

"Yes. It's tragic." His voice dipped, like the low note in an opera. "I need to get by and pay her another visit."

"I'm sure she would appreciate that."

His tone hinted of deep annoyance rarely seen. "Why did you go see Kate?"

She studied his face closely. "I was sent letters written by Annie. I thought she might know who sent them."

"Letters?" The lines in his face deepened. "Who did she write them to?"

"I don't know. She was careful not to name the man she called Sugar."

He tugged at his white, crisp cuff. "All evidence pointed to Jones."

"Maybe, but I want to find this lover and see where he was when she died."

Cuff links winked in the light as he smoothed hair back from his temple. "That doesn't mean your client is innocent."

A woman appeared at the door. In her midfifties, she was tall, slim, blond, and dressed in a neat red pants suit that matched her lipstick. "Gary?"

Gary stepped away from Rachel and moved toward the woman. He kissed her on the cheek. "Jennifer, I'd like to introduce you two. Ms. Wainwright, this is my wife Jennifer."

The woman's bright smile fell short of warming her eyes. "You are representing that man in prison."

Rachel nodded. "That's right."

"Gary has an active prison ministry. He tries to save as many lost souls behind bars as he can. Several have since been released and are working in the church. Good men, bad starts, but happy endings."

Jeb could have been one of those men thirty years ago.

"Ms. Wainwright was asking me about Annie Dawson. She is playing detective and trying to find more suspects for the police to consider."

"That was thirty years ago. That can't be easy." Jennifer's Southern drawl coiled around the words.

"No, not easy."

"I was a member of the church then and had begun dating my first husband." She smiled as if sensing Rachel's next question. "Gary and I married about ten years ago after my husband died and his first wife died."

Curiosity poked Rachel. "Did you ever meet Annie?"

Jennifer adjusted the diamond watch on her slim wrist. "Saw her sing in the church once. Lovely, lovely voice. But we never formally met. I remember I helped search for that poor woman. Those first days we had hope and then, well, we all realized this story wasn't going to have a happy ending."

Gary laid his hand on Jennifer's shoulder, causing her to smile up at him. "Ms. Wainwright, if you don't have any other questions, I promised I'd take my wife to an early lunch."

Jennifer preened. "He's been working many long hours and I told him he had to make time for me." She arched a playful eyebrow. "I won't be ignored."

Gary kissed her on the cheek. "No, I know you can be bossy."

Rachel studied the two, wondering if the emotion was a brilliant stage performance or genuine. "Thank you for your time."

"Would you keep me posted on what you find out?" Gary asked. He followed her toward the main door and reached for the large door handle. "It may have been thirty years ago but Annie was a good soul and I don't want to forget her."

"Sure. I'll keep you informed."

"I will pray for her. And for you."

She nearly told him to hold the prayers on her behalf. She'd spoken to God often enough when Luke had been in jail but she'd been ignored. "Thanks."

She left the office, the choir hitting a high note, their notes chasing her out into the sun.

*March 30*

*Sugar,*

 *I hear you were asking after me. I always said bees can't stay away from honey. Remember, bees sting.*

*A.*

# Chapter Seventeen

*Thursday, October 20, 4:45 PM*

Deke waved Brad into his office. "Tell me you have the DNA."

Brad closed the door behind him, a breath easing from his lungs. "I do."

Deke rose, all but ready to bolt across the room, even as he held steady, too conditioned to let emotion run the show. He'd never questioned his father, but now as he waited for the test results and stared at Brad's solemn face he feared Buddy had made a terrible mistake thirty years ago. "Spit it out."

Brad opened the file. "Two blood samples were found on the tire iron. The first is Annie's. The second is not Jeb's."

The news hit Deke like a fist to the gut. For a moment, he didn't speak as his mind tripped through the scenarios. "Are you sure?"

Brad held out the report to Deke. "That's why the results were late in coming. They ran it multiple times. Results came back the same each time."

Deke took the file but didn't bother to study the numbers and charts. "What can you tell me about the second sample?"

"It's female."

"Female?"

"Correct."

"Did you run the DNA through CODIS?" CODIS was the Federal DNA database.

"I plugged it in, but no hit yet."

Deke released a breath and imagined Ms. Wainwright unleashing a firestorm over the news. Knowing her, she'd have a release petition before nightfall. She might not get her client right out of prison but it was a matter of time now. Buddy's case would be publicly picked apart.

He rubbed the tense muscles banding the back of his neck. "Thanks, Brad."

Seconds after Brad left, Georgia burst into the room. "What were the results?"

Deke rested his hands on his hips and gave her the rundown.

Georgia's pale face flushed with color. "That attorney is going to bust this case wide open when she hears."

"I know."

She shook her head. "The press could eat Buddy up."

"We won't let that happen." He and his old man had locked horns often enough but he'd go to the mat for Buddy and his legacy.


The sun had long set when Rachel clicked off the CD and placed the disc in a case. She realized if she analyzed what she was about to do, she'd stop.

*Jesus, Rachel, don't be a blabbermouth.*

"Shut up," she whispered.

A short drive later, she found Georgia as she'd finished her run. Sweat dampened her forehead and the collar of her shirt. She jerked her earbuds free. "Ms. Wainwright. What brings you here?"

She hesitated, unable to scrounge up any small talk. "You know I was at Rudy's bar the other night."

Georgia lifted her chin. "Yeah."

"Is there somewhere we can talk? I'd like to show you something."

Blue eyes flashed with suspicion. "Like what?"

"Better I show you than explain out here."

Georgia hesitated and then fished keys out of a jogging top pocket. "Yeah, sure why not. Come inside the house." They climbed the stairs and she unlocked 3B. She shoved open the door to a small apartment furnished with over-stuffed furniture covered in pale shades. "What's on the mystery CD?"

"Might be better to play it."

She frowned. "Sure."

Rachel handed the CD to Georgia who inserted it in a player under a flat-screen television. She reached for the remote but hesitated. "What am I about to see?"

"It's Annie Rivers Dawson singing. At Rudy's."

Georgia glanced at the blank screen and then at the remote. For a moment she didn't move as if the next step might carry her over into the abyss. Then drawing in a deep breath she hit *play*.

The grainy color image of the stage flickered on screen and in the background the crowd roared for Annie, whose smile was electric and bright. Blond hair framed a delicate face with full red lips and high cheekbones.

The band struck up a lively tune and Annie immediately started to sway with the music. She grabbed the mike, began to sing and the crowd cheered. Soon lost in the tune, her body and soul wrapped around the words and added a richness and depth not conveyed by mere words. At the end of the set she held up her hand and closed it into a small fist. "This was for you, Sugar!"

"Sugar," Georgia said.

"Yeah."

Both women sat in silence and watched the fourteen-minute tape. When it ended and the screen went to gray, Georgia shut off the machine. She glanced at the remote and then slowly released a breath. "Why did you bring this to me?"

Rachel had put most of the puzzle pieces together but still wasn't one hundred percent sure that she'd figured out the image. "I thought you might like to have it."

"Why?" The whisper sounded childlike, vulnerable.

Rachel glanced toward a framed picture of Georgia with her brothers. A riot of blond hair and backed up by three tall olive-skinned boys. "Because I thought you'd like to have a positive memory of Annie."

Georgia rose and faced her. "Have you been talking to Deke?"

That almost made her laugh. "No, why would I?"

A frown wrinkled her brow. "How did you find out?"

"I figured it out. Deke never said a word."

Georgia replied, "How?"

Rachel moistened her lips. "Buddy Morgan was the chief detective and Bill Dawson said the cops took the baby and a cop brought him the adoption papers to sign. You don't look like your brothers and when you sang on stage, you sounded exactly like her."

Tears pooled in her eyes and one escaped. "It's not a huge secret. I've always known I was adopted and that Annie was my birth mother."

"Deke is protective of you."

She tipped her head back, corralling her tears. "I know. He always has been."

"That's part of the reason he's been angry with me. I'm raising old questions."

"He never doubted Buddy's work. We all know Buddy

was a great cop. But he worried that people would start to ask about Annie's child and then I'd be thrust in the spotlight."

"You don't strike me as a wilting violet."

A ghost of a smile reached her gaze. "Everyone knows it but Deke."

"It's good to have a brother looking out for you. Mine did when I was a kid."

"It's a bit overwhelming at times but it can be nice."

Her heart pinched. "Yes."

She nodded to the screen. "Where did you get the CD?"

"From Rudy. I talked to him the night you sang. He mentioned the tape, and I had it converted from VHS to CD. That's for you."

Watery eyes widened. "Thanks. That means a lot."

"It was taped eight months before she died."

"She would have been pregnant."

"Yes. I thought you'd like to have something of her."

"I have a couple of pictures but that's about it. It's nice to hear her voice and see her happy."

Rachel tapped her finger on her thigh. "You've heard about the letters."

"I've read them. Not a flattering picture. And I was worried at first."

"I spoke to Bill. He knows he's not your biological father."

"I know. I insisted on testing when I turned twenty-one. He wasn't happy to oblige but he did it."

"So he knew who you were."

"Yes."

"He said he didn't know."

"He's not a bad guy. Fact, I liked him."

Rachel drummed her fingers on her thighs. "What about Jeb?"

"Funny you should ask. I cross-checked our DNA. No match."

"So there was another man."

"Yes." She traced the edge of the remote with her thumb. "Any thoughts on who Sugar might be? I would at least like that piece of my genetic puzzle."

"I don't know. Yet."

"Do you think my biological father killed Annie?"

"In her last letters her tone grew threatening. Maybe he got worried and wanted to put an end to it."

"But they're fake."

"Maybe he didn't know that."

"Who would forge letters from Annie and then create the illusion she's demented?"

"That I do not know. But the letters are important to someone."

"That's why you were attacked."

"And Lexis killed."

Georgia pressed a trembling hand against her forehead. "This needs to be untangled."

"I know."


A ring at Rachel's door had her lifting a tired gaze from a brief. She checked the clock and realized it was after nine. Rising, she moved toward the door and peeked through the peephole. Deke Morgan.

She opened the door, ready for him to rail on her for giving the tape to Georgia. "This is a surprise."

No traces of humor or welcome softened his flinty features. "Why didn't you tell me about the video of Annie at Rudy's?"

Matter of time before he found out. The Morgan clan was a tight-knit bunch. "I'm defending a client. I have a right to protect what evidence I find. And I'd planned to drop off a copy with you in the morning."

"Then why give the CD to Georgia?"

She folded her arms and drummed her fingers against her forearm. "A moment of weakness. I thought she'd like to have it."

He didn't make any attempt to pretend. "How'd you figure it out?"

Rachel cocked her head. "Once I heard Georgia and then Annie sing I wondered. From there it was a matter of putting pieces together."

Silent, a small muscle tensed in his jaw as he seemed to chew on his next words. "She's watched it about twenty times. It means a lot to her."

Unexpected emotion tightened her throat. "So you'll admit that good came out of my nosing around?"

He shook his head as if he'd rather eat dirt than agree. "The DNA came back."

She drew in a breath and stepped aside so he could enter. "And?"

"Jeb's DNA did not match."

"Really?" Her heart raced as her mind ran through the possibilities. It was hardly a slam dunk but it was enough to get the case reopened.

"I can hear your mind working."

"Over the sound of my thundering heart? And what is it working on?"

A half smile tweaked the edges of his mouth. "You want me to formally reopen the case."

"For starters. Then I want Jeb out of jail."

"My brother is working on the case. He's digging through it."

A laugh escaped. "He's hardly partial. I'm filing a motion in the morning."

"I'd like you to hold off."

"Why?"

"Rick knows about the DNA. He's digging into the case and I'm hoping he finds evidence of another killer." He met her gaze. "This isn't about Annie anymore. It's about three women who were killed in the last week."

That caught her short. "You believe the cases are connected?"

"I do."

She stepped back from her excitement and studied the big picture. If days could catch the man who'd killed Lexis, she had to give him those days. "I'll give you three days. Not a minute more."

"Understood."

"I was about to make coffee. Would you like some?"

"I'd love a cup."

They crossed the large open space and moved behind a partition to the industrial kitchen. She took two mugs off a shelf, filled the coffeepot reservoir with water and loaded coffee in the machine. She hit brew.

"Did you watch the CD?" she asked.

"I did."

"I studied it a dozen times searching for some glimpse of someone that might have been the killer."

"Great minds think alike. I didn't see anyone that caught my attention."

"She mentioned Sugar." She sipped her coffee.

"Too bad she didn't offer up his real name."

"You know Sugar is likely Georgia's biological father."

"It's crossed my mind."

"Has Georgia met Margaret?"

"Georgia knows about her but she's not made contact. She's nervous."

A need to disclose again to the enemy rose. Maybe she was losing her touch. "I met with Bill Dawson."

"You get around."

"He said . . ." She paused and fought the urge for honesty before saying, "He said that Annie made him swear when she was pregnant that he'd never leave the baby alone with Margaret."

Deke frowned. "Why?"

"Annie never told Bill. But he remembered her warnings clearly." Rachel sipped her coffee. "Keep the fact in your back pocket."

"I will." A deepening frown suggested this effort at candidness wasn't a natural for him either. "When it comes to Annie she can be nervous."

"Lots of emotions there, I suppose."

"Yes."

"Georgia aside, I will be in court in seventy-two hours."

His quick laugh was unexpected and had a rusty quality as if he'd not laughed in years. "Would expect nothing less, Ms. Wainwright." He gulped more coffee. "By the way, Oscar McMillian's bail was revoked and he's now charged with assault."

"I contacted the court and told them I'm off the case."

"Just wanted you to know, he won't bother you."

"Thanks."

A silence settled and then he rose. "I should go."

Disappointment flared. "Sure."

He moved to the door. "I'll be in touch."

She followed. "Why would someone fake those letters?"

"My guess is someone wanted to get between Annie and her lover. If the lover thought she was unstable then he'd be more inclined to break it off."

"They were written by a woman." She arched a brow. "No doubt a woman who loved Annie's lover as well. Did the DNA say whether or not the second blood sample was male or female?"

The question gave him pause. "A woman."

"A woman killed Annie?"

"Maybe. Or Jeb killed two women with that tire iron."

Rachel considered the theory and dismissed it immediately. "What woman hated Annie more than any other?"

"A lot of women didn't like Annie. Many saw her as a threat." He paused, his hand on the doorknob.

"The woman would now have to be in her late forties at least." She spoke the first name that came to mind. "Margaret."

"Possible. She would have been sixteen at the time of Annie's death. And she's still fit."

"She adored her sister."

His eyes flashed with a savvy knowing of a cop who'd seen too much of the dark side of humanity. "There's a fine line between love and hate."

"You'll need more than that in court."

"I'll figure this out."

"Whoever killed those women and attacked me was strong. Quick."

"The element of surprise offers an advantage."

She turned the idea of a female killer over and over and the more she did, the greater sense it made. "Lexis might have been tossed off guard by a woman. She'd have delayed before acting and that delay cost her."

"Help me figure this out?"

The question mark didn't hide the command woven around the words. "Me? But I'm the enemy."

The intensity in his eyes softened a fraction. "Perhaps not as bad an enemy as I first thought."

Electricity snapped between them and a force she'd never known tugged at her. Suddenly, she wanted to touch him. To feel the rough stubble of his chin under her fingertips and against her cheek.

*Jesus, Rachel, really? He's the last guy you should—*

Rachel silenced the warning. "Thanks."

Deke's gaze ignited with an intensity that nearly took her breath away. She felt devoured by his gaze and he'd not made one step toward her.

He was a man who'd lived his life apart. Out of necessity yes, but also maybe a little out of fear. She understood that fear. The fear of feeling too much. Their kind of emotion was a double-edged sword that cut easily.

But in this moment consequences hovered on a distant horizon far out of sight. She had only now and the tension pulling her toward him.

She took one step. "Stay."


Nikki's head pounded as if a hammer clattered against the inside of her skull. She rocked back and forth in her bed, cradling her skull in her hands. She moaned, wishing the pain would stop.

"The pain is back?" Rudy's voice rumbled like gravel but it soothed her to know he was close.

She glanced up, tears streaming from her eyes. "It hurts. Worse than ever."

Glass of water in hand, he sat on the side of the bed. "I know it hurts. I know it does. I've your medicine."

She threaded her fingers through her hair, clutching handfuls as if to get a handle on the pain. "It makes my head fuzzy."

"Fuzzy is better than pain and the anger." He unfurled a fist, revealing a calloused palm and two pink pills. "Take your medicine like a good girl."

She released the clumps of hair, took the pills and popped them in her mouth. Like a child, she took the water glass and swallowed a healthy gulp.

Rudy watched her swallow and then took the glass from

her. "It won't be long now before the pain stops. Now lie back and close your eyes."

She eased back against the pillow, wincing when her head touched the sheet. "It hurts."

He settled the glass on the nightstand, but kept the pills in his pockets. Once in the beginning, he'd left them behind and had come in to find her ready to eat the entire bottle. "I know. But it will stop."

Watery eyes stared up at him. "Why does it hurt?"

"It always does." He tugged the blanket up from the foot of the bed and covered her, tucking the end under the mattress.

"But why?" Hers was the voice of a child.

There'd been a time when he'd tried to explain about the headaches and why she could get so angry, but his explanations had left her confused and upset. So he'd stopped answering and let the pills simply do their job. "Doesn't matter why, Nikki. Just matters that I can take the pain away."

She looked up at him, her gaze not focusing on his face. "Thank you."

His bushy mustache twitched over yellowed teeth into a smile. "Sure. Anything for my girl."

He sat on the edge of the bed, took her hand in his as he had a thousand times before and waited silently until her breathing slowed and the tension eased from her brow.

Only when she'd fallen into a deep sleep did he rise and move to the door. His gaze lingered on her sleeping form; a long time before he shut off the light.

For so long he'd never questioned what he'd done all those years ago. However, age and time had stirred up doubts that haunted him. What if he'd made a terrible mistake?

*April 1*

*I scare you, don't I? I could see the way you slide me those looks when we meet in public. We don't exchange a word, but there is fear in your eyes. Good.*

*A.*

# Chapter Eighteen

*Thursday, October 20, 9:30 PM*

The look in Deke's eyes told Rachel she'd effectively jumped out of the frying pan and into the fire.

He released the door handle and cupped her face in his hands. Slowly, he smoothed his thumb over her jawline. The touch sent a shock through her body.

He leaned forward and kissed her on the lips.

*Don't be a fool!*

Ignoring the warning, she relaxed into the kiss, savoring the sensual explosions. Her hand pressed to his chest and she realized this was the moment to choose. Jump or dive. Stop thinking and simply feel. She chose to dive into the emotions.

She fisted his shirt in her fingers and pulled him closer, allowing herself this purely carnal pleasure. He wrapped a strong arm around her and pressed her body against his. She arched into him as his hand trailed up under her shirt and cupped her breast. When he fingered her taut nipple she moaned.

He pulled back and stared into her gaze, searching.

She moistened swollen lips. "The bedroom is upstairs."

His gaze darkened as she took him by the hand and led him to her bedroom. He kissed her as he backed her up toward the bed. When her legs bumped the edge of the mattress, he reached for the hem of her sweater and tugged it over her head. A dark smile curved the edges of his lips as he stared at round breasts swelling over lace cups.

He removed his shirt as she kicked off her shoes and loosened the side zipper on her pants. When the zipper released, the pants slid over smooth skin to pool around her ankles.

His chest bore several tattoos. Tribal markings covered a right bicep in a half sleeve. Latin words scripted across his lower belly read *Veritas, justitia, Libertas* and translated into truth, justice, and liberty. A thick scar slashed across his bicep. All told a story that stirred questions she'd likely never ask.

Naked, both kissed as he eased her to the bed. He smoothed a rough hand over her flat belly. "So soft," he muttered.

She pushed against him encouraging him to explore. His eyes darkened as his hand traced under her small breasts. When he cupped her and his callouses rubbed the soft skin of her nipple she hissed in a breath. He loomed over and kissed her lips. She threaded trembling fingers through his short hair and arched into him.

Even as desires grew from embers to flames, the drumbeat of warnings sounded in her head. She didn't know how to give and then walk away. But to expect more than this moment was begging for heartache.

The worries were drowned out by a new wash of desire as he settled between her legs.

The next few minutes were a haze of sensation as he touched her, kissed her bare skin, and coaxed her carefully veiled emotions into the light. She'd not allowed herself this kind of pleasure for a long, long time and realized she was half-starved for touch.

Rachel smoothed her hands over his muscled back, feeling him tense to her touch. When he entered her, she sucked in a breath as flesh expanded. He hesitated, watched her gaze, as she slowly adjusted to him.

"You okay?" he whispered.

She moistened her lips. Touched his face. Smiled. "Yes."

He waited an extra beat, giving her one more instant to reconsider second thoughts, and then kissed her on the lips and began to move inside her.

As much as she wanted the desires to build and to know a release, she didn't want to rush this moment. So much of her life was a *rush, rush, rush* from one crisis to another. No time to think. No time to feel. But not now. She wanted to feel and savor every moment.

His body snapped with tension as she wasn't the only one familiar with deprivation. He moved faster and faster and despite her wish for a slow ride he swept her up along with him.

When climax overtook both of them, tears pooled in her eyes. So long since she'd felt any type of connection. He collapsed against her, his heart beating hard and fast. She closed her eyes, savoring the connection. She understood it wouldn't last but she was used to temporary.

He rose up on an elbow, in no rush to break the skin-to-skin connection. He captured a tear with his thumb. "You all right?"

"Yes." Her voice sounded hoarse and rough. She'd devoured him but knew she'd soon be hungry again.

"You're upset."

"No." A winsome smile flickered and faltered. "Just overwhelmed."

He smoothed his hand over her hair. He traced her jawline. "Really? I didn't think that was possible."

That enticed a throaty laugh. "It happens on rare occasions."

He traced deepening worry lines in her forehead. "You don't like to be overwhelmed."

"I didn't mind it." A faint smile teased the edge of her lips. "But you better take a picture. Won't happen again for a while."

He stroked his hand over her collarbone. "Sounds like a challenge."

"No challenge. Just a fact." Again she couldn't keep the candor silenced. "Moments like this are rare. As much as we want them to last, they don't."

"They do sometimes."

"Not for me. Not for you."

He traced his hand along her arm. "Maybe before, but now—"

"Don't." Just the implication of a promise was more than she could handle. Better to savor what was and not expect more.

A muscle flexed in his bicep. "Don't what?"

"Make any promises."

His marriage history rebutted any promises of tomorrows even before he could speak them. "Fair enough."

She stared at him silently, savoring the warmth of his naked body against hers, not willing to dream beyond now.

He kissed her gently. "I like the way you challenge me. Not many people do that these days."

She ran her tongue over her lips, savoring his taste. "I thought I annoyed the hell out of you."

"You do. You can be a real problem. But I'm getting used to it."

"I'm difficult. Hard to live with. I drive people away."

"Then maybe we are suited."

In this unguarded moment, she spoke her mind. "You'll leave. Work will pull you away. I know that because we are a lot alike that way." Gently she stroked the side of his cheek, kissed him, and imagined how she'd like to make love to him again. She wiggled out from under him, coaxed him on his back and climbed on top.

He cupped calloused hands on her hips. "You've got me all figured out."

"Doesn't take a rocket scientist. Two divorces under your belt are warning enough." She moved against him, smiling as he hardened. "But I don't want forever. I want now."

His hands trailed up her arms to her shoulders. He pulled her toward him and kissed her hard on the mouth. He hadn't disagreed with words but his kiss had a possessive edge that said otherwise. He rolled her on her back and entered her again.

She hissed as her body fired to life again. However passionately Deke kissed or made love, he wasn't going to hang around. And that was okay. It was.

She kissed him on the lips and felt his body respond. This taste of sweetness would leave her craving more.


Baby stood in the new chapel, hands prostrate, staring at the simple white cross hanging above the altar. Hands clasped tight, tears welled. "Lord, let him change his ways. Let him see that he's a sinner and make him the man he needs to be."

Two bodies should have been lesson enough. What would it take to get him to really stand up and do the right thing?

"Who's there?" Pastor Gary's voice echoed in the empty chapel. He wore khakis, a white shirt buttoned to the second to top button and simple brown shoes.

Baby burrowed deeper into the folds of the hoodie. "Pastor Gary."

A smile deepened the creases around his eyes, which conveyed surprise more than welcome. "Baby, I thought that was you. I got your message.

"You said there was a problem. Are you having a bad time?" Pastor Gary shook his head as he approached, a warm smile softening his gaze. "Remember the first time I called you Baby? You couldn't have been more than two."

The gentle tone of the pastor's voice softened some of the hate in Baby's heart. The Pastor Gary standing here now was the man so many people loved. "I don't remember the first time. But I can't remember a time when you didn't call me Baby."

Pastor Gary was silent for a moment. "Why are you here?"

"I come here sometimes when I'm troubled."

He stood silent and tense. "Why are you troubled?"

Baby shrugged. "I'm troubled with too much temptation."

Pastor Gary's gaze roamed, taking in faded jeans, sweatshirt, and loose jacket. "We are all tempted."

Baby's head cocked with curiosity. Fingers slid to the .38 tucked in the folds of the hoodie. "Have you been tempted?"

He cleared his throat and glanced around the arena sanctuary. He saw no one but lowered his voice. "Of course."

"Why do you give into temptation?"

"I pray to God when the devil beckons. I pray for help and guidance."

That wasn't true. He ran toward temptation with open arms. And until now, Baby had forgiven him. "But do you sin?"

Pastor Gary cleared his throat. "What's all this talk about sin, Baby?" He moistened dry lips. "What have you done?"

"Lots of things." No hint of regret darkened the words.

A frown furrowed Pastor Gary's brow as he clasped his hands in prayer. "Baby, you were one of the nicest people I knew. I'd have known if you did bad things."

"Would you?" Baby wasn't sure. "You've never really paid attention to me."

"I'm always paying attention." The confidence humming under the words spoke to his pride. He prided himself on knowing his congregation's sins and secrets, hearing their confessions and knowing the bleakest part of their souls. However, he didn't know Baby's secrets.

The need to confess and maybe even pride pricked at Baby. "You received my warnings, didn't you?"

"Warnings?"

Baby squared broad shoulders. "Dixie. Rebecca."

Pastor Gary frowned, his pale eyes reflecting fear. "What did you do, Baby?"

Baby's right hand remained on the gun, fingering the cool metal. "I took out the trash."

He frowned as if a memory flickered in the shadows. "Someone else said that to me once."

Baby nodded. "So you do remember?"

Pastor Gary took a step back. "Who sent you to me?"

"No one. I decided to come on my own." A shrug lifted square shoulders.

"What do you want?"

"It annoyed me when you stopped coming around to visit. So I sent you the first warning with Dixie."

His face paled as if he recalled the news accounts of the singer's death. "I don't understand."

Laughter bubbled. "We both know there are two less sluts to tempt you."

His unnaturally smooth skin strained against a frown as the weight of the words settled. "Who else knows about this?"

Baby savored his discomfort. "You look pale, Pastor Gary."

"Dear Lord," he muttered. "You and Rebecca . . ."

"I took care of her, too."

Horror gave his eyes the wild look of a caged animal. "You need help."

"Maybe I do. I've sinned, but you've sinned more, haven't you, Pastor Gary?"

He glanced around the sanctuary, cringing. "I've made poor choices."

Baby tugged at the cuff of the hoodie rescued from the church's goodwill bin. Waste not, want not. "You are ashamed?"

He shoved manicured hands into his pockets. He jangled loose change. "I have asked God for forgiveness."

"Is that all it takes? If I were to ask God to wipe away my sins would that be enough?"

"Baby, you hurt those women."

"Hurt, no. Killed, yes. And I liked it."

Color drained from his face. "My God, Baby."

Baby raised a finger to smiling lips. "It can be our secret."

He straightened his shoulders, clearly already assessing the fallout of this confession. His eyes sharpened with ambition. "You expect me to keep this secret?"

"I've never told your secret. Lots of times I could have told but I never did. Reasonable you can keep mine."

"Baby, I can't keep this quiet. I can't." His hand trembled when he shoved tense fingers through his hair. He took a step back. "Why?"

"To punish you. To show you who is really important to you."

Disgust contorted features made smooth by Botox. "I don't want anything to do with you."

"I don't believe you." Baby had expected him to be

upset. No one liked to be punished. But this punishment was in his best interest. Soon he'd see and he'd be grateful.

Revulsion darkening his features, he pointed a finger trembling with retribution. "You are the devil."

His anger wasn't unexpected. "You gonna tell?"

"Yes."

He'd never tell. He didn't have the nerve to risk endangering his empire. "The world will find out about you."

"So be it."

"You are Satan!" The hatred and conviction resonating from the pastor's voice stung like rejection. Baby's heart constricted with sadness and anger. "You never really loved me, did you? You called me your Baby but you didn't really mean it."

He jerked as if backhanded. "God loves all sinners, but I cannot accept what you've done."

The hate twisting around Baby's heart tightened its stranglehold. "Did you ever love me?"

"You are a monster. How could I love that?"

"I'm not a monster! You are the monster!" Shock and sadness pulsated under the words. "*Sugar.*"

He flinched. "Don't call me that!"

His fear offered some solace. "But you like the name."

"Stop!" He backed up several steps as if all the secrets of his past had scurried out of the darkness like rats and swarmed at his feet.

Baby's hand tightened on the handle of the thirty-eight. "Don't walk away from me!"

"We are done!"

Fury had Baby's index finger sliding to the trigger of the thirty-eight revolver. "I thought you'd see who truly loves you. I have your best interests at heart!"

He shook his head as he slowly turned to face Baby. Tears glistened in his eyes. "You are insane."

Baby removed the revolver and stared at it as if it were

strange and wondrous. "I'm not a monster. I'm not insane. You love me. You are glad I showed you your sinful ways. Say it."

Gary held out his hands, his gaze riveted to the gun. "Baby, where did you get that?"

Baby pointed the gun at his chest. "Doesn't matter, does it?"

"Give it to me," he said, his voice clear and direct as if he were the one with the gun.

"No." Baby pulled back on the trigger and the gun fired, striking Gary directly in the heart. Crimson bloomed on his white shirt and he stood for a moment, stunned. He dropped to his knees and then fell face forward on the floor. Blood pooled under his chest and oozed out onto the carpeted floor.

Baby pocketed the gun and for a moment stared, dumbstruck as if watching a movie. "Pastor Gary?"

When he didn't move, Baby's anger melted into puddles of regret. "Pastor Gary, I didn't mean to shoot you. You made me mad. You can get up now. The punishment is over."

A small gurgling sound emanated from his chest as the last breath he'd ever take seeped from his lungs. "Pastor Gary?"

Baby's hand trembled as tears welled. "Wake up!"

Pastor Gary lay lifeless, the gurgling fading to silence. Baby wept.

*April 15*

*Sugggar,*
    *Twinkle, twinkle little star . . . I wish you could love me. Twinkle, twinkle little star . . . I wish I didn't hate you.*

                    *A.*

# Chapter Nineteen

*Friday, October 21, 6 AM*

Deke parked behind the three marked cars with flashing lights on Taylor Road, bordering the Cumberland River. Trucks backed up to bays loaded with dirt and gravel and beyond that a ribbon of trees buffered the property from the river. A long brick building was located on the property next to an abandoned field and a metal shed had long ago collapsed under the weight of age and rust. A peeling blue water tower stood tall, empty.

At the crime scene, Deke strode toward the uniform. "Deke Morgan. Why the call?"

The uniformed officer's crisp brown shirt accentuated a long lean build. "Found the body of a CI that might be of interest to you."

"Who?"

"Max Quincy."

Deke drew in a breath. "Where?"

"The body is by the river."

Dirt and crushed stone crunched under his feet as he followed the uniform toward the green brush. They picked their way through thick underbrush, the scent of the river growing stronger as they travelled. The woods stopped feet from the muddy shores of the Cumberland. Yellow crime-scene tape blocked access to the final remaining feet. Max lay on the shore, faceup, eyes open and his blue mouth agape.

He pulled rubber gloves from his back pocket. The scent of death was foul, as it often was with victims pulled from the water.

"Where is Forensics?"

"On the way. It's been a crazy morning and they are scrambling. And this guy, well, he wouldn't be the first drunk to end up in the water."

Deke studied the configuration of the body, which had all the hallmarks of a body adrift in the water. "Any sign of trauma?"

"I checked when I first arrived. No gunshots or ligature marks. I pulled up his rap sheet on my computer. He was released a couple of days ago from jail. His latest arrest was for drugs. My guess, he either stumbled too close to the water and fell in or pissed off the wrong person."

Deke would have agreed with the scenario a week ago. But Max had been his father's CI and he'd been the key witness in the Jeb Jones case. He was another severed link to the thirty-year-old murder case. "Call Forensics and have them get here sooner rather than later."

The uniform rested his hands on his hips. "What's the rush?"

The skin on the back of Deke's neck tightened as it had during his undercover days minutes before a buy went bad. Something was off about this. Wrong on more levels than he could articulate. "This guy didn't fall in the river or screw up a drug deal. He's linked to the Annie Dawson case."

His cell rang. "Morgan."

"Deke, it's Rick."

"What do you have?" A man of minimal words, his brother called when he had real news.

"Digging through those files and saw the name Beth Drexler. She was Annie's roommate. She died in a car crash ten years ago."

"Okay."

"Her first husband was Pastor Gary Wright."

"The boyfriend who had a crush on Annie?"

"So it seems. Beth was also the sister of Kate Tilden, his secretary for the last thirty years."

His mind wove connections. "Gary could be Sugar."

"He's the right age. He also had a lot to lose if the affair with Annie was discovered."

"Beth or Kate could have forged the letters. But only Kate could have sent them to Rachel."

"Kate's pretty ill. My money is on her daughter, Brenda."

Tumblers clicked, puzzle pieces fell into place. "Brenda Tilden?"

"Yeah."

"Brenda Tilden has been dating KC since late summer." A thick silence filled the line. "This isn't good."

"No, it is not."

"Where you headed?"

"To see Brenda and Kate."

Squirming memories in Nikki's head felt like snakes newly hatched under her skin. Crawly and slithery, they nipped at her nerves and her tendons. She put her mop and bucket away and instead of going up to her room to watch television, like Rudy had told her, she walked into the bar and stood in the empty room. They'd not open for hours and the place stood silent as if it dozed before the next shift.

She liked this time. Quiet. Simple. Not the buzz, buzz of the people talking or the music blaring so loud it cracked and splintered her head into pieces.

She moved to the bar, skimming her hand over the polished wood. Rudy liked the bar nice and neat. Start clean, end clean. He said it all the time.

She nibbled her lip as her gaze roamed over a stack of morning mail. The mailman left it here a lot. He knew Rudy and Rudy knew him. They'd been friends forever. Chapped, cracked fingers skimmed the stack covered with words and letters that jumbled and danced whenever she tried to read. She'd like to be able to read. Rudy said she'd once been able to. But now the words were locked up as tight as the liquor in the storeroom.

Sometimes she would hold up a paper and stare at it as if she understood. Rudy often watched, saddened, not amused by her display. She pushed the letters around on the bar until a colorful picture drew her gaze. She stared at the face of the smiling man who stood in front of a large cross.

"Cross." The man's smiling face drew her, holding her attention tight as if he'd reached out from the page and grabbed her face.

Memories rooted deep and dark in the shadows swirled in her brain, but as much as she coaxed them into the light, they refused. Frustrated, she crumpled the flyer in her hands. Her head pounded. Pictures and sounds pounded in her head making her head throb. She squeezed her eyes shut, and took a deep breath to calm the pain. When her heart slowed, she cracked open an eyelid and peered at the image of the man.

The man.

She knew him. Carefully she opened the second lid and touched the image, gently tracing a fingertip over the full smiling lips and even white teeth. He was a pretty man. Soft. Smooth. Not like Rudy. Gruff. Angry. Smelling of cigarettes and beer.

More images flashed in her head. A man smiling at her. Touching her face. The smell of a sweet scent . . . roses. She studied the man's face. More images flashed. Did he have the key to her brain?

She moved behind the bar and found the tip jar. Shoving her fingers in, she fisted a thick handful of bills in her hand. Grabbing the picture of the man, she walked outside to Broadway. The bright sun made her wince and cringe and the sound of passing cars revved her heartbeat. She looked back at the doors and fearing a mistake moved toward them. She didn't go outside often and when she did it was after dark with Rudy.

One step back toward home and more images flashed. A bottle of perfume. A locket. The smiling man. Music.

She squeezed her eyes shut, her pulse racing hard to make her veins explode. For several seconds she rushed to catch her breath. Finally, her breath slowed. The noises around her calmed, allowing her to shove aside fears and turn toward the street. On the corner sat a yellow car. A man got out and handed the driver money.

She glanced at the money clenched in her bony fist. She didn't know how much she had, but hoped it was enough as she walked to the yellow car and shoved her money and the picture toward the car's driver.

The driver looked at the picture and the rumpled bills scattered over his lap. "You want to go to the church?"

Words swirled in her head like buzzing flies and it was hard for her to know which ones to grab and use and which ones to let fly away.

She swallowed the rising panic as the sun glared in her face. She nodded.

The driver studied her with squinting, leery eyes. "The church. You want to go to Pastor Gary's church?"

Pastor Gary. That sounded right. She didn't know how, but she knew. "Yes."

The driver eyed her. "How much money you got?" He counted the bills and then after he'd arranged them into a neat stack, he nodded. "Enough to get you there at least."

She waited, not sure what he meant.

Frustrated, he raised a brow. "Okay. Get in."

She studied the door handle and for a moment had to think about how it worked. It was simple to work, wasn't it?

Trembling fingers slid over the metal handle and then slid under it. When she pulled up, the door clicked open and she sighed, relieved. She slid into the backseat and pulled the door closed. The cab smelled like the bar—cigarettes, booze, and bad perfume—and strangely it lulled her against the cracked warm leather seats. When the cab lurched into traffic, she straightened and curled her fingers into tight fists held against her thighs.

Time rarely meant much to Nikki. There were days it passed fast and other times moved at a snail's crawl. Rudy often yelled at her when she lost time. Daydreaming, he'd say. Crazy as a shit-house rat, he'd say.

She stared out the window and watched the buildings on Broadway pass as they moved over a large bridge and toward green trees. Rudy wasn't a bad man. He could get mad. Yell. But he'd never hit her. And when he'd come upstairs at night, he always checked in on her and made sure her head wasn't pounding or she wasn't thirsty or hungry.

The car stopped, jerking her from her thoughts.

She glanced through the glass at the driver.

"We're here. The New Community Church like you showed me in the picture. That's thirty bucks."

He counted out money and then shoved the balance back at her through the opening in the glass separating them. She took the money, knowing Rudy always talked about getting money. He would be glad she took it.

She glanced at the door, reached for a handle and pulled up. It didn't budge. Getting frustrated, she tugged harder.

"Wait a minute. You're going to mess up my door," the driver said.

He got out, came around and opened her door. Simple. Just like that.

Glancing at the door, she stepped away from the cab, sorry to be away from the smells.

"Do you want me to wait?" the driver asked.

She would have worried over the question if she'd not glanced up and seen the white chapel.

It ate up the land and reached so high, she imagined it touched the sky. Large colorful windows stretched and caught the light. So beautiful. Drawn, she moved to the large doors and into the building.

"Suit yourself," the driver said. The wheels of his car squealed as he drove away.

Nikki pushed open the doors. Cool air greeted her and the tension banding her chest eased. Rows and rows of seats lined up on either side of a red-carpeted aisle that led to a large stage. Behind it hung the biggest cross she'd ever seen.

Nikki walked down the aisle letting her fingers skim the tops of the polished wood seats. She moved to the stage and stared back at the room. A familiar jolt of nerves tugged at her but it wasn't a bad feeling. Standing here felt good.

She touched her fingertips to her hair and brushed the gray strands over the indentation in the side of her skull. She smiled and imagined the sound of people clapping.

More images flashed in her head. This time they came in rapid fire making her head pound. Noises popped and exploded in her head, drowning out her thoughts and making it nearly impossible for her to stand. She pressed her hands to her ears and staggered away from the edge of the altar.

Scared now, she crept behind the altar, ready to hide and wait for the sounds to go away. She wasn't sure how she'd get back to Rudy. She didn't know how to call and feared asking more strangers. Rudy had said strangers were dangerous and bad.

But as she moved to hide, she saw him. The man with the smiling face. He lay on his back, eyes open and glazed as he stared at the ceiling. His shirt was stained red but his face, well, it looked perfect and peaceful.

She knelt beside him and for a long time didn't dare touch him. She half expected him to reach out and grab her.

When he didn't touch her, she grew braver. With trembling fingers, she touched his jaw. Cold and smooth. Rudy's face was warm and rough.

She poked him. He didn't move; in fact, there was a stillness that frightened her. She backed away and then slowly rose. Terrified, she turned, fearing if she didn't hide something bad would happen.

A door came into focus and she hurried toward it. With a jerk of the door she found a cool, dark closet. Grateful for the small, safe space she scampered inside and closed the door behind.

When Rachel's door all but burst open, she glanced up from a court brief she'd been writing. Georgia stood in the doorway, her face pale and worried.

Rachel had seen Georgia several times under stressful situations but never once had she seen her upset. She rose. Her thoughts went to Deke who'd left her bed early this morning. He'd kissed her, made no promises to return, and left. "Everything all right?"

Georgia closed the door behind her and crossed the office. "I received a call from Margaret."

"Annie's sister."

She nodded, rolled her eyes and sounded as if she couldn't believe her own words. "My *aunt* called me. Margaret Miller."

Rachel hesitated. "How did she find you? Your adoption was closed. Did you contact her?"

Georgia ran a trembling hand over her hair. "No. I've thought about it but I never really summoned the nerve. I don't know how she found me."

"You spoke to her."

"Yes."

"What does she want?"

"She wants to meet me. Says we need to talk. About Annie." Georgia flexed her fingers. "I'm scared."

Rachel remembered Bill Dawson's warning about Margaret. "You don't know her. That's reasonable."

"I know she's family. I know I shouldn't be freaked out over a simple call, but I don't like surprises. And I'm really worried about what she wants to tell me."

"Did you ask her what she has to tell you?"

Georgia rolled her eyes as if to say she might be rattled but she wasn't a fool. "Yes. She refused to tell me over the phone."

Rachel's legal mind calculated the pros and cons. "Does Deke know?"

"No. He'd try to be cool about it but every time I see him I see Dad and I feel like I'm betraying Buddy and Mom."

"You should tell him."

"I know. But he will want to be there and I can't do this with him watching."

"Okay."

She folded her arms, but restless energy had her dropping them by her sides. "Margaret wants me to meet at Pastor Gary's chapel."

The skin on the back of Rachel's neck prickled. "Why there? That doesn't make any sense. It's under construction."

Georgia shoved her hands in her pockets, removed them and then dropped them at her sides. "She said she'll explain when I get there."

"When?"

"A half-hour." She shoved out a breath. "I don't want to go alone. Come with me, please."

The woman's desperate plea surprised Rachel. "You don't know me that well. Don't you want someone that's closer to you?"

Fear and nerves all but radiated off of Georgia. "I want a neutral party with a sharp mind. I clicked through the short list of the people who know about my adoption and Annie and your name rose to the top of the list."

Being dragged into Morgan family business would only complicate whatever she had or more likely didn't have with Deke. As much as it made sense to say no, she heard herself say, "Sure, I'll come."

A grateful smile broadened her face and she grabbed Rachel's hands. "Thank you! I really could use backup."

Rachel tugged her hands free and reached for her purse. "I'll drive."

"I'll owe you the biggest of big favors when this is over."

"No, you won't. This one's on the house."

In Rachel's car, they merged into traffic as Georgia drummed her fingers on her knees, not stopping until they pulled up to the church.

Georgia stared out her window at the white building. "This place gives me the creeps."

"It's one of the biggest churches in the area."

"Maybe, but I don't like it."

"It's okay. Relax." Rachel got out first. Georgia lingered in the car a moment longer and then with grim set to her jaw, followed. "She said the new chapel."

Rachel offered a smile. "It will be okay. This is just a meeting."

Georgia chewed her bottom lip. "I hate not knowing. I like having all the answers."

"Well, you might have more soon."

"Yeah."

Rachel attempted a smile. "Where is the confident woman who runs her crime scenes with an iron fist?"

Helpless laughter rumbled in her chest. "I don't know but if you see her would you let me know?"

"Sure."

They entered the chapel, quiet and dark.

"Hello," Rachel said.

No answer followed.

"We are late, but I thought she'd wait." Her voice trembled with disappointment and hope.

Rachel dug her phone from her purse. The quiet didn't set well with her nerves. "She called you. Said she wanted to meet."

"Yeah."

"She'd cut you a little slack and hang around for fifteen minutes."

"You'd think."

Rachel tightened her grip on her phone. A thick scent of sick-sweet rust caught her attention. She stopped and so did Georgia. Rachel had smelled a similar smell the day her mother had died.

"That's death," Georgia said. "I know that smell."

"This is not good." Rachel dialed Deke's number. "Get back, Georgia. We need to get out of here right now."

The phone rang once and Deke picked up. "Detective Morgan."

"Deke, this is Rachel." Her tone didn't invite a soft response.

"What's the matter?"

"Georgia and I are at Pastor Gary's chapel behind the main building. Something is wrong. It smells like death here."

Instead of a barrage of questions about what had brought the unlikely pair to the church, Deke all but shouted in the phone. "Both of you get the hell out of there. Now. I'm on my way."

"Right." Rachel grabbed Georgia by the arm as she clicked the phone off. The sound of footsteps caught her attention and she turned in time to see a tall form rushing them. Rachel spotted a long metal rod swinging toward Georgia. She pushed Georgia aside in time for the blow to catch her on her tender shoulder. She screamed and fell to the floor.

A second swish of the rod struck Georgia across her thigh. She screamed and Rachel looked up to see Brenda Tilden glaring at Georgia. For a split second Rachel's mind didn't connect Brenda with the attack. Brenda. She was the woman with the warm smile. The woman who loved KC. However anger in Brenda's gaze distorted that warmth into something twisted and frightening.

Before Rachel could assemble words or right herself, Brenda fumbled handcuffs from her hoodie pocket and handcuffed Rachel's wrist and pulled. Rachel screamed.

"Move toward her."

Pain cut through Rachel. When she hesitated, Brenda fished a .38 revolver from her pocket and pointed it at Georgia.

Staring down the barrel of the gun freed Rachel from her confusion. Whoever Brenda had been didn't matter. What mattered was now. "Brenda, what are you doing? I don't understand."

Brenda shoved out a breath. "Shut up. Shut the hell up."

Georgia winced as she sat straighter, confusion making her gaze look a little wild. "Brenda? Is KC with you?"

Brenda sneered, hate dripping from her words as she spoke. "He's gone. He's like the others. Loves me but doesn't really love me. Said it was too soon to meet his boy."

Rachel searched for her phone and found it inches out of reach. She shook off the remnants of surprise and grabbed onto logic and facts. "Brenda's mother worked for Pastor Gary. Her aunt Beth roomed with Annie."

Georgia shook her head. "Your mother knew Annie? What does that have to do with me?"

Brenda laughed. "I'm not stupid, you know. Everyone thinks I'm stupid but I'm not. I know who you are."

Georgia's gaze hardened. "Who am I?"

Brenda cocked her head as if she were speaking to a child. "You are Annie's daughter."

"How do you know that?" Georgia demanded.

"I figured it out, stupid," she hissed.

"How?"

"Wouldn't you like to know?" She jabbed the gun at them both. "Both of you get up. Now. Mother is waiting."

Rachel and Georgia rose, both lumbering under the weight of their injuries. Georgia struggled to stand strong but had to lean on Rachel.

"Your mother is sick with cancer. Why would she care about us," Rachel said.

"She's dying. And your deaths will be my final gift to her."

Nikki had heard the voices and when they'd drifted out of the church she sensed she had to follow. She eased out of the closet and did her best not to look at the man as she quickly rushed down the center aisle and out the door.

*April 20*

*Sugar,*
   *I had that dream again. You ended up dead, dead, dead.*

                    *A.*

# Chapter Twenty

*Friday, October 21, 5 PM*

Calls to KC went unanswered as Deke raced to the New Community Church's chapel, lights on top of his car flashing. He'd called dispatch and ordered marked cars to the scene. Shit. His skin itched as it did before an op went sideways. More times than he could count the sensation had stopped him from walking into an ambush. Shit. He'd seen Rachel early this morning and loved the way her body cuddled against his as he'd clung to reasons why they could work. And Georgia. He'd seen her yesterday.

Life could unravel slowly, or with lightning speed. His marriages had disintegrated with a painful silent slowness whereas Rick had nearly lost his life in an instant.

His grip tightened on the wheel and he pressed his foot against the accelerator. There'd been a lot of times when life had shredded around him but he would not, would not, let it happen tonight.

When he parked his car in front of the large white building that housed the New Community Church, the uniforms were seconds behind him. Out of the car, he unholstered his gun and dashed up the front steps. The front door was ajar.

Deke shoved it open and met with a deadly silence. "Rachel! Georgia!" His answer was his own echoing voice. Grim-faced he glanced at the uniforms behind him. "Search every inch of this place."

The officers disbanded and with guns drawn moved into the sanctuary, two fanning left and two others to the right.

Deke drew in a breath. Searches in buildings could be the deadliest. Too many hiding places. Too many opportunities to ambush.

Gun drawn, he moved toward the altar, his gaze sweeping from side to side for any sign of movement. When he stepped onto the platform he spotted the blood pooling around the edges. For a moment he hesitated, fearful that he'd find Rachel or Georgia dead.

Gritting his teeth, he moved the remaining steps and saw Pastor Gary's body. He closed his eyes and tipped his head back, allowing the relief to wash through him. He cleared his throat. "Rachel, where the hell are you?"


Rachel's shoulder throbbed as she and Georgia walked through the woods with Brenda pointing a gun behind them. Rachel had heard the shrill of sirens as had Georgia and Brenda. Deke was coming, he was close, but would it be fast enough? She had to buy time until he found them.

"He won't be here in time," Brenda said. "He will find you soon, but soon it won't matter. You'll be dead."

Limping now, Georgia balled her fist as if ready to turn and strike. But Rachel shot her a warning glance, begging her to stand down. Now was not the time for Georgia's directness.

Rachel turned her head slightly back. "Brenda, why are you doing this? You didn't know Annie."

Brenda jabbed her gun, a silent order for Rachel to keep

moving. "My mother knew her. That bitch made her life hell and robbed me of more love than I can measure."

Rachel's anger burrowed to the deepest and coldest part of her heart, the place it needed to stay so she could think. "Love from whom?"

"Pastor Gary. My mother. He was obsessed with Annie and all women who looked like her. He could never love my mother. She was so focused getting him to see her, she never saw me."

"Why would Pastor Gary care about Annie?"

"Because he loved her. Adored her. Could never stop thinking about her. Every woman since Annie is a replacement."

"Dixie and Rebecca."

"His wife. His other whores. All Annie."

Georgia glanced at Rachel, her eyes wide with worry. She'd discovered the identity of her birth father and she was reeling. "Where is Gary?"

"At the chapel," Brenda said.

The scent of death. Rachel couldn't bring herself to ask. Georgia did. "He's dead."

Brenda hesitated, frowned. "No. Yes."

The twisted path in the woods opened into a clearing. In the distance, headlights shone on Kate in her wheelchair. With a blanket wrapped over her knees, her form looked fragile.

Rachel and Georgia stopped feet from Kate who stared up at them with dark, piercing eyes. Disease may have robbed her of strength but the fire burning in her gaze told Rachel it had not softened her obsession. "Didn't take much to get you here. Grateful for small blessings, I suppose."

Georgia rubbed her cuffed wrist. "What is this about?"

Kate's glare soaked in Georgia. "You don't look like her. Maybe a little around the mouth but that's about it. You look like," she hesitated as if emotion clogged her throat. "You look like Gary, your father."

Georgia raised her chin a notch. She looked brave and strong, but Rachel felt, rather than saw, a bone-deep vulnerability. "Pastor Gary."

Kate smiled. "You're smart like he is."

The cuff holding Rachel and Georgia tightened, as Georgia fisted her fingers. With her free hand Rachel grabbed Georgia's wrist as if to steady her.

Kate shifted narrowing eyes toward Rachel. "You are good at sticking your nose in where it doesn't belong."

"It's a talent." The sharpness in Rachel's tone was designed to draw fire and anger. If they were focused on her maybe Georgia could somehow escape this nightmare.

Brenda shoved Rachel hard against her tender shoulder, making her wince. "Shut up."

Pain bulldozed through Rachel's body forcing her to take deep breaths. She righted and glared back at Kate. *Let's see who's running this show.* "What the hell is her issue?"

Brenda raised her hand as if to strike Rachel when Kate shouted, "No!"

Brenda lowered her hand but clearly she craved any violence she could rain on Rachel.

Rachel kept her gaze on Kate. She might be physically weaker but she was the one in control here. "You had Brenda kill Dixie, Lexis, and Rebecca. Why?"

Kate moistened pale thin lips. "It's complicated."

"We've time."

A smile quirked Kate's lips. "Not much time. I heard the sirens as well as you. But we've a moment or two."

"Why?" Rachel persisted.

Kate arranged the folds of her blanket on her lap, enjoying this moment of control. "You know why Lexis died. That was your fault."

Rachel shoved aside the guilt. "The letters."

"I knew she would figure out that the last letters were forgeries. I knew she'd know that Annie hadn't written them all and that would raise questions. I couldn't have any questions that might lead back to Pastor Gary."

Rachel gritted her teeth. "If you knew they were a problem then why send them to me?"

"I didn't." Kate looked past her to Brenda. "She did. She thought they'd make Pastor Gary nervous. Brenda wanted to punish him."

The release of the letters had been a mistake, a miscalculation. A laugh tumbled out of Rachel. "She didn't tell you what she was doing?"

Kate shifted in her chair. "Not until after. Not until the damage had been done."

"I did my best to clean up the damage," Brenda insisted.

"Too little, too late," Kate said.

Brenda shook her head. "I was thinking about you, Momma! I wanted him to come see you and make you feel special but he wouldn't. I had to make him squirm."

To split these two vipers' alliance, Rachel had to stoke Brenda's fears and dig into Kate's weaknesses.

"Well, you helped me. Not too smart. You've given the police the weapon they need to prove that Jeb didn't kill Annie. Did you know the DNA came back? Showed a woman killed Annie."

"Shut up!" Brenda shouted.

"Thanks to Brenda, the cops have forgeries which they will eventually trace back to Kate. Dying or not, she'll go to jail."

A glance from Georgia revealed understanding. "My partner identified the forgeries immediately."

"Why go after KC?" Rachel asked.

"He was nice enough and I knew if I had a contact in the police department I would know what they knew once I started doling out my lessons." Brenda laughed. "KC is a fool. He was far too easy to pump for information."

"How'd you meet him?" Rachel asked.

"Gary's prison ministry. It's also where I met Oscar McMillian and gave him your card when he needed a lawyer. One look at him and I knew he'd be hard for you to handle."

Rachel studied Brenda's face contorted with anger.

Under her scrutiny, Brenda's scowl deepened. "If Rachel had given all the letters to Lexis this would be over."

"But she didn't give them all over," Kate said. "You never think it through, Brenda, and you always underestimate."

Brenda's eyes widened with hurt and then as quickly narrowed with anger for Georgia. It would take little to make her fire the gun.

"Kate, why did you write the fake letters?" Rachel asked.

"Gary came to me when he realized Annie was pregnant. Beth would have seen to that. He was in a panic. His new church would have been ruined if people learned he'd gotten a singer pregnant. I told him I'd handle it. And I went to Annie and told her I'd find her a husband if she'd stay away from Gary."

"Is that when she agreed to marry Bill Dawson?"

"She didn't agree right away. But I told her Gary would never marry her. Unless she wanted a bastard child she better turn her magic on Bill, who was like most men in the church. Half in love with her. I set them up on dates and within two weeks he'd proposed. They married a week later."

"Gary married them," Rachel said.

"The last letters made him realize how much trouble she could be. He saw past her smiles to the problems that waited for him if he stayed with her. He married Annie and Bill and was willing to walk away."

"What happened?"

"He couldn't stop thinking about her. He confessed to me several times that he still loved her. He married Beth but was ready to leave her and toss away the church for Annie."

"So why kill Annie?" Rachel asked.

"I went to see Annie after the baby was born. She and Bill had had a bad fight. He'd figured out the baby was not his. She was going to go to Gary and tell him she still loved him. I begged her not to but she wouldn't listen." Kate looked at Georgia. "I didn't go planning to kill her."

Wind rustled through the trees. "When did you figure out Georgia was Annie's child?" Rachel asked.

A satisfied smile teased Kate's lips. "The church held a community fund-raiser last year. She came as a representative from the police force. The minute I saw her, I saw Gary. And then I saw her name tag. Morgan. Buddy Morgan, big-time cop. Didn't take much checking to figure out that the Morgans' adopted a daughter right about the time Annie died. Buddy Morgan. Got the press and the force to hide the fact that he took Annie's baby. I should have seen it years ago but they kept their baby girl off the radar for a long time." Kate shook her head. "I wanted you, Georgia. I wanted to raise you as my own. I had dreams about raising you with Gary."

Brenda's frown deepened as if Kate twisted a knife in her side. "All she did for him and still he was a faithless man. He had his whores and he refused to come see Momma."

"He couldn't help himself," Kate hissed. "He couldn't help himself."

"Brenda, you did the killing this time," Rachel said.

A wide proud grin spread across her face. "I did."

"You knew KC worked Annie's case?"

"I did. He likes to talk. Sweet man. All I had to do was ask a question here or there and then listen."

A sigh shuddered through Kate. "I thought if she took care of Dixie, Pastor Gary would understand that he was on a dangerous path. When it comes to the flesh, he is weak and he never understands how much he can lose if the world figures out his weakness. The public forgives much but not a beloved pastor cheating in such a depraved way."

"But he didn't learn, did he?" Rachel asked.

Kate shook her head. "I love him. I wanted to teach him a lesson for his own sake."

In the distance by the church, Rachel saw the lights of the cop cars flashing. They were so close, but time was draining away. "You framed Jeb."

Kate glanced past Rachel to the lights of the cop cars. She could end this all now but as if giving her last confession said, "It was easy to do. I saw him staring at Annie. He was the perfect criminal."

"And you took her body to the woods?"

Kate stared at Rachel a long moment. "No, I did not. I didn't take her body away."

"What do you mean? If you didn't take the body, then who?"

Kate shook her head. "I don't know. I always thought it might have been Gary. He'd been obsessed with seeing the baby. After I killed her, I ran. Later when my thoughts cooled I came back to make sure she was dead and the baby was all right. Lord, I couldn't believe I'd left that baby alone. The cops were there but there was no body."

Rachel studied Kate's face closely. "Did you ask Gary about Annie's body?"

"No. No. I thought about it a million times but I came to see he must have hid her to protect me. He never said the words but I could see it in his eyes."

Rachel's heart ached for Annie who'd gotten caught up in a hell greater than she'd ever imagined. "You must have loved Gary very much."

"I still love him," Kate said. "I will love him until I draw my last breath."

Rachel sensed Brenda's growing tension. Kate did not know Gary was dead. "So you didn't kill him?"

Brenda hissed in a breath. "Shut up!"

Kate's head tilted. "Why would I kill him?"

"He's dead," Georgia said. "Shot in the chest. He's lying in the chapel."

Kate's gaze shifted to Brenda. Hurt, betrayal, and anger combined. "You killed Gary?"

For the first time, Brenda's confidence wavered. "I didn't want to kill him. I wanted to talk to him. I wanted to know that he loved me, too."

Kate looked at her daughter as if seeing her for the first time. "Of course he loved you."

"Not like I needed him to. Not like a father loves a child." Brenda pointed her gun at Georgia. "Not like he would have loved her."

"He's her own flesh and blood!" Kate shouted.

"But I loved and served him all my life. I'd have done anything for him."

"Blood is thicker than water!" Kate wailed, tears glistening in her eyes. "She'd never have killed Gary!"

"No!"

Kate swiped away a tear. "God, how could you?"

Tears welled in Brenda's eyes. She shook her head as if she fought back all the anger and hurt surging in her. She jabbed the gun into Georgia's back, her gaze carrying the pain of a life lived in the shadows. "It's her turn to die."

Nikki had followed the sounds in the woods, the sound of women fighting. One step at a time, she'd cut through the woods. Closer. Closer. The sounds grew louder until she reached the edge of a clearing where she saw the four women. Her head pounded with a fierce pain. She pressed her hands to her ears and prayed for the pain to leave. She breathed deeply to calm her racing heart.

All this talk, talk, talk. She didn't understand what they were saying but the words made her head hurt. She didn't like them. She didn't like any of them. And she wanted them to shut up so she could get back to Rudy.

The cops were searching the church but there was no sign of Rachel and Georgia. Deke's impatience grew and he found his gaze drawn to the woods behind the chapel. The church owned an enormous amount of land and it would take hours to search. He stepped outside. "Where the hell are you, Rachel?"

He dug his phone from his pocket and dialed dispatch. Once he identified himself he said, "I have a cell number I want you to locate. Owner is Rachel Wainwright." He rattled off the number and prayed she was close.

"You're not going to kill her!" Kate said. "I want more time with her."

"Why do you want more time with her?" Brenda shouted. "I'm your daughter. She is that whore's daughter."

"She's Gary's flesh and blood!" Kate shouted.

Through the thicket of the woods, Rachel saw the flash of lights. The cops had made it to the edge of the woods. Closer and closer.

"You killed my mother!" Georgia shouted.

Kate looked at Georgia. "I didn't want to. I wanted her to listen and to leave town. And I told you when I calmed, I came back to the house to get you. I knew you were in your crib alone and I came back to rescue you. I'd have raised you like my own. I'd have been a good mother to you."

Georgia stood silent, stunned.

It was Brenda that wailed, "I'm *your* daughter. Why not love me! I've done everything that you've ever asked. I can't help the fact that I'm not Gary's flesh and blood."

Kate shook her head. "I thought Brenda was Gary's when I carried her. We were kids ourselves when we were together. I was married, but Gary was the most beautiful boy in town. We had one night, but I hoped. But after she was born, I saw that she wasn't his, but my husband's. It broke my heart to know I didn't have Gary's child to suckle. That's why I wanted you, Georgia. I thought you'd fill the hole in my heart."

Rachel listened to it all, twisting her wrist while the women were distracted. The cuff was loose enough to work her hand free but tight enough that it tore her flesh as she did. Georgia, realizing what she was doing, shifted to hide Rachel's hand.

Cringing, Rachel jerked her hand free.

"I should have been enough!" Brenda shouted.

Brenda glared at Georgia. She raised the gun. "I hate you!"

Kate leaned forward in her chair. "Brenda, no!"

"Why should I listen to you? You don't love me. You are like Gary. I'm nothing but a convenient servant."

A woman's howl shot out from the woods distracting Brenda who had leveled her gun on Georgia. Rachel threw her body toward Brenda throwing the brunt of her weight into the woman. The shot fired wild. Brenda punched Rachel's gut and broke free long enough to right herself.

Brenda stood over Rachel, her gun trained and ready to fire. "I'm going to enjoy this."

A ghostly wail echoed again from the woods. They all froze seconds later when a tall thin woman emerged from the edge of the woods. Gray hair framed a narrow face, badly contorted. Hatred burned in the gaze now nailed to Brenda.

The woman screamed and ran toward Brenda. She threw her body into Brenda and the two fell hard against the earth. Brenda dropped her gun. The banshee woman balled up her fist and struck Brenda hard in the face. Brenda coughed, spit blood, and crawled toward the gun.

Rachel cradled her broken arm and crawled toward the gun, but a winded Brenda rose and scooped it up. Brenda leveled the gun on Georgia.

"Don't!" Rachel shouted, dread and loss washing over her as Brenda pulled back the trigger.

The ghostly woman rose and lunged toward the gun. The gun went off and the woman clutched her chest. Blood bloomed. She fell to her knees and then facedown into the dirt.

Kate's pale face dimmed as she stared at the woman. "Annie?"

Rachel stopped, her gaze narrowing on the figure who looked more specter than human.

Georgia, in shock, stared at the woman, this last bit of news overwhelming her.

Brenda stared at Annie. "I thought you killed her."

"I did," Kate whispered.

Rachel scooped a handful of dirt and lunged toward Brenda, tossing the dirt in her face. The woman's shock distracted her just enough for Rachel to smack her squarely in the face. In panic and confusion, Brenda pulled the trigger and fired her gun. Rachel grabbed hold of Brenda's hand and wrestled the gun free.

Georgia blinked and moved to Annie and rolled her on her back. Brenda's bullet had caught her squarely in the chest.

Nikki/Annie looked up at Georgia, her eyes panicked and lost. "Where's Rudy? He takes care of me."

Georgia smoothed her hand over her hair, knowing the injury was fatal. Her expression pained and panicked, she smoothed trembling fingertips over thin gray hair.

"He's coming," Georgia said. "He's coming."

Kate pulled a gun from her blankets and leveled it on Rachel as Deke burst through the line of woods. He instantly assessed the scene. His gaze zeroed in on the threat: Kate's gun.

"Drop the weapon!" he shouted, his voice cutting through the air.

Kate didn't respond.

Deke fired. The bullet struck Kate in the chest, and she fell back, dead.

"Momma!" Brenda wailed.

He quickly cuffed Brenda as more uniformed officers burst through the woods. He looked to Rachel, who cradled her arm, and then Georgia. "Georgia, are you all right?"

Georgia wept. "This is Annie."

"What?" Deke asked.

Georgia stroked the woman's hair. "That's what Kate called her."

Rachel hugged her injured arm, wishing she did not want Deke to hold her. She understood Georgia needed her brother and, in this moment, she was alone.

Deke looked at the dead woman, his anger clear and cutting. As uniformed officers burst into the clearing he said, "Get Georgia away from here."

Georgia tensed. "I can't leave her like this."

Rachel moved to Georgia and said softly, "She's gone. She's gone."

Georgia glanced up at her with red-rimmed eyes all but jumping off her pale face. Deke wrapped a strong arm around Georgia and helped her stand. As they moved away from the bodies, more uniformed officers gathered. A screaming Brenda was hauled away and EMTs summoned.

Deke wanted to pull Rachel in his arms but he'd never seen Georgia so weak and rattled. A uniformed officer approached Rachel. He couldn't hear what was said but watched as the officer guided Rachel away.

He'd made a connection with her. He'd imagined with Rachel the future might be different. But the job had tugged at the fragile connection until it frayed. In the past, he'd have let the threads unravel but the thought of it now made him hollow and aching. "Georgia."

Tears welled in her eyes as she raised her chin. "Go to her. I'm fine."

"You aren't."

She closed her eyes, hesitated and then looked at him. "I can survive a few minutes alone. Go."

Deke touched Georgia's face and then turned and jogged to Rachel as the EMTs readied to raise her stretcher into the ambulance. He cupped her face, staring into dark eyes already dulled by painkillers. "Rachel."

"Deke."

He leaned forward and kissed her on the lips. "You're going to be all right."

Rachel squared her shoulders but the act of bravado cost her pain. "I'm always all right. Bouncing back is what I do." The loneliness coating the words tore at him. She'd lived apart and alone too long.

"I'll be there for you."

Her head tilted as she searched his gaze. "You said being there is not your thing."

He traced her jaw with the calloused edge of his thumb. "Not this time. This time it is my thing."

# Epilogue

*Six weeks later*

A special day should be filled with bright sunshine. It should be warm and the birds should have been singing. It's how Rachel had always imagined the day when her brother would have been released from prison.

But that day had never come and this day was gray and cold as the granite walls of the prison. Rachel sat in the car, watching the rain droplets slide down the windowpane.

Rachel shifted in her seat as her shoulder throbbed. It had been four weeks since her surgery and her arm still ached on cold and damp days. The doctors had said it could take a few more weeks before she was up and running and they'd advised her against the trip. But she'd refused all advice and concerns.

She peered from the dark SUV, staring at the gates of the prison. She could have gone inside but Kirk Jones had asked if he could go in and get his father, Jeb. Happily, she'd agreed.

Seconds ticked, as she watched the gates and when she thought they'd never move, they opened and Kirk Jones walked out with his ailing father at his side. Jeb could barely walk these days and required a wheelchair but he'd insisted on walking out of prison.

The old man raised his face to the gray sky and closed his eyes. There wasn't much sun to be had today but Jeb lapped it up as if starved. Kirk opened the car door of the Jones garage truck. Jeb looked past the car to Rachel, raised a trembling hand to her and smiled. She smiled, raised her own hand and watched Jeb get into the passenger seat.

KC had been devastated by Brenda's lies. And when Deke had talked to him, he'd admitted he'd met her in the prison. When Brenda had made a move on him, he'd been so damn flattered he'd not questioned her or the affair. Weeks before the vigil, he had complained to Brenda about Rachel's DNA request. He'd also admitted to Deke that he'd shared with Rudy case information on Annie Dawson's case.

Rudy had been arrested after Annie's identity had been confirmed and he'd confessed that he had found Annie soon after Kate had beaten her so badly. He'd not called the cops but had taken her back to his bar and nursed her. He admitted that he'd always loved her and had wanted her for himself.

Annie had never really recovered from her head injury. Her memories had been destroyed and her thoughts never able to focus again. But Rudy had resolved to take care of her. For weeks he'd kept her in the second floor of his bar, tending her as cops and patrons flooded the downstairs bar.

When KC came into Rudy's all those years ago, unburdening himself with the details of the Dawson case, he'd never realized Rudy had known all along where Annie could be found. As the weeks passed Annie started to improve some. She would never be the same but now was a little harder to handle. With cops refusing to let go of the case, he'd feared it was a matter of time before Annie was found. Rudy realized he needed a body to get the police to stop searching. He'd found the body of a dead prostitute who resembled Annie in height and stature. He'd beaten the body postmortem, removed the head and hands and left it in the woods dressed in Annie's bloodied clothes and necklace. When he was sure the remains could not be identified, he'd called in the tip.

Kate had believed Gary had guessed her terrible secret and that he had taken Annie's body and hidden it to protect her. When the remains had been found, she'd feared for him so she'd hidden the tire iron in Jeb's car, found Max and given him the tip. The discovery of the body and the tire iron had ensured Jeb's conviction.

Rachel's thoughts skittered to Luke, whose nagging voice had been silent for weeks. Maybe he was at peace now? Maybe she could live a more normal life.

*Let me go. I am free.*

Tears glistened in her eyes. "I hope so."

"Hope what?" Deke asked as he came around the car.

She swiped away a tear. "Just talking to myself."

Deke leaned against the car on her good side, so close his shoulder brushed hers. For a moment the two just stood close, absorbing each other's energy. "You must be proud."

Rachel rarely celebrated victories. There'd just never seemed to be enough time for accolades. But not this time. This time, she would celebrate. "Sometimes, life tosses out a real special moment. As rare as a blue moon, they do happen."

Deke faced her, wedging her body between his body and the car. "Only on blue moons?"

The heat of his body warmed her. "It's not like I said never."

He traced her jaw with his finger. "Blue moons come

every two or three years. I'm thinking we can do better than that."

They'd been seeing each other for weeks. No promises of forever. No lifetime plans. Just fun and a gradual peeling away of all their protective layers. It would take time. But it seemed there was no real rush. "Maybe a little bit more often than that."

Deke laughed and skimmed his hand up over her hip and cupped her waist. "I'm thinking there could be many great moments."

She cocked a brow. "Sounds a bit like a commitment. I thought we weren't doing that."

Smiling, he kissed her. "Don't look so rattled, Wainwright."

Rachel wrapped her good arm around his neck. It felt so good to hold him close. "You can't rattle me, Detective."

"Ah, that's what I like about you, Rachel. Always a challenge."

Please turn the page for an exciting sneak peek of
Mary Burton's next romantic-suspense thriller,
BE AFRAID,
available now!

*Monday, August 14, 4:30* AM
*Nashville, Tennessee*

Reason and Madness, like Jekyll and Hyde, were two sides of the same coin. One worshipped peace, the other devastation. One told the truth. The other, rule breaker and thief, always lied. Once again, a war raged between the two.

The cell phone on the granite kitchen counter buzzed with an incoming call. A glance at the display revealed Sister was calling again. This was her sixth call in the last two hours. Sister could see past the smiles and the assurances. She sensed when meds had been skipped and Madness regained control.

Ignoring the call, Madness reached for a half-full tumbler of whiskey and held it up, letting moonlight illuminate the honey brown liquid depths. A quick toss of the glass, and the whiskey slid down a parched throat, soothing tense muscles and pushing aside all thoughts of Sister's call. It wouldn't do for Sister to know about tonight's endeavor. Tomorrow Sister would get a visit. There'd be lots of wide smiles and a box of her favorite chocolates gift-wrapped in a bright blue bow. Blue was her favorite color. They'd play the question and answer game for a time. She'd be satisfied and then shift talk to regrets and the what-should-have-beens.

Madness washed the glass in the sink, careful to dry it with a paper towel before replacing it in the cabinet. A few wipes of the cabinet knobs, the faucet, whiskey bottle, and the surrounding area erased all fingerprints. Some might consider the action overkill but attention to detail was key to a successful performance. Madness had learned well from Reason.

Down the dimly lit hallway carpeted in neutral beige, Madness admired the new coat of antique white paint. Fresh paint was a wonder. One swipe of the roller eradicated dirt, grime, and shadows of framed memories that no longer mattered.

A few more steps toward the master bedroom and the scent of paint gave way to the aroma of diesel fuel. This room—center stage for tonight's performance—was painted a pale yellow with white trim. A tasteful landscape of the Smoky Mountains hung on the wall by the door, a gilded mirror topped an oak dresser displaying strategically placed crystal perfume bottles, a new hairbrush, and a tiny camera displaying a bright red RECORD light.

In the center of the room was a four-poster bed. On the bed lay a woman, the actress in this play. Her near naked body nested in twisted sheets damp with sweat and flecks of blood. Ropes lashed manicured hands, nails painted a soft pink, to the headboard and feet to the baseboard. A river of mascara-stained tears trailed down pale cheeks and duct tape–covered mouth.

Carved in the headboard above her was the word FAITHLESS. Madness thought it a fitting tribute to another woman, Sara, who'd plagued them during their youth.

As Madness approached the bed, green bloodshot eyes alert with panic darted from the man standing in the shadows back to Madness, the night's true master. Her wide pleading gaze reflected panic and desperation. Good. She understood who was in charge.

The man in the shadows, Jonas Tuttle, stepped forward, his large, calloused hands wrapped tightly around the grip of a forty-five caliber handgun. Tall and broad-shouldered, he stood over six feet. A man's man, some might say. But fear all but vibrated off every inch of his muscled body. "We've been waiting for you. I need you to tell me what to do next."

The warmth of the whiskey kept anxiety at bay. "Patience, Jonas. Patience."

Jonas, the bloodthirsty and angry hero tonight, had nurtured a murder fantasy since he was a young boy. Careful observation of Jonas over the last six months told a lot about the man. His likes. Dislikes. Fears. Wants. Needs. Stalking the stalker.

Jonas's murder obsession had stalked him most of his life, his fantasies playing over and over like a worn record. As much as he craved killing, he also feared the cops and prison. And so, he'd bottled up his wants and needs for years. Madness had found this want-to-be killer ripe for guidance in a bar six months ago washing frustrations away with whiskey.

*"I can show you how to kill," Madness had whispered.*

Jonas's gaze had danced first with hesitation, then interest and finally excitement.

Madness had taught Jonas how to stalk, to watch and to plan. Madness worked with Jonas for months, priming him for this kill.

Now at the brink of the grand finale, Jonas oozed desperation and need. Nervous energy buzzed around him as if live wires zapped his nerve endings. This was the moment he'd dreamed about a long, long time.

One nod and he would fire.

Instead of giving permission, Madness shifted attention to the woman. Pretty and slim enough, the woman, Kelly Smith, until hours ago had been dressed well and had walked with confidence. She, no doubt, had caught the eye of many men. She liked rich, buttery Chardonnays paired with a creamy Brie or goat cheese. She liked good conversation and old movies. Reason might have befriended her if not for Madness.

In this macabre scene, Madness, not Reason, was the ultimate authority. Madness chose the staging, the casting and, of course, the final execution. Moments like this thrilled because it gave Madness the one thing he could never sustain. Control.

"Can I do it now?" Jonas's timid voice had a familiar, annoying ring.

"Savor the moment," Madness rasped.

Jonas's hunger was sharp as a razor and, of course, the woman's senses had never been so acute. Being this close to death made everyone in the room feel alive.

Kelly's watery gaze was a mixture of terror and confusion. *How could this have happened to me? I'm careful. I play by the rules.*

Madness saw the question flash. A soft chuckle rumbled. "But you didn't play by all the rules, did you, Kelly? In fact, you like to break them every so often. Not too much. But once in a while, you enjoy a walk on the wild side."

Kelly shook her head as tears streamed down her cheeks.

Gently, Madness approached the bed and sat. The mattress sagged. Kelly's black hair was plastered to her forehead by sweat. "Didn't you ever hear that cocaine is a bad habit? If not for that little quirk in your personality, you'd have been fine." Jonas had lured her out of her car with the promise of coke. "You'd be on the other side of that door right now sitting in your living room watching that cooking show you enjoy so much. But you couldn't control it and now you must pay your toll."

She closed her eyes and shook her head, a soft moaning rumbling in her throat.

"Maybe it's not a crippling compulsion, but it's there nonetheless." Madness continued to stroke her hair, so soft and dark. "You're not different than me. Once in a while, I get the cravings. I can ignore them for a time. But the more I deny them, the more they grow until one day I just must have one little bite." A snap of even white teeth close to her ear made her flinch. "You're my bite."

She closed her eyes and wept.

Drawing in a deep breath, the scent of her fear smelled sweet. Deliciously intoxicating.

"Now?" Jonas asked.

The world and the people in it were in such a rush. "In a moment."

"I can't wait! Why do I have to wait?" He pressed the handle of the gun to his head as if trying to soothe the pounding behind his eyes. *Bang. Bang. Bang.* The tantalizing promise of release was painful.

"Anticipation is the sweetest part of dessert." Madness patted Kelly on the arm, rose, and moved to the back corner of the room by the dresser.

Madness double-checked the camera's angle and then hefted a red can of diesel fuel and jerked off the cap. Slowly, deliberately, a tip of the canister splashed the fuel on the gray carpet, over the blue bedspread and up sheer white curtains that blocked the light of the full moon.

Jonas shifted from foot to foot. "Haven't you spread enough of that stuff?"

"Never can be too careful." Diesel burned longer but didn't have the initial combustive power of gasoline, which could spread too fast or burn out.

The woman twisted at her bindings. She rolled her head from side to side as if willing this nightmare to end.

They were all suffering with anticipation.

Backing up to the room's threshold, Madness stood silent, savoring the scene one last time. Finally, Madness retrieved a box of matches from the deep pockets of a blue Windbreaker and struck a match. The flame danced and swayed as if begging to be sent out on stage. A breeze caught the flame and blew it out.

"What're you waiting for?" Jonas asked.

One. Two. Three. Savor. Savor. Savor.

"Okay, Jonas."

"I can shoot now?" Excitement and fear rumbled under the words.

"Yes."

Kelly's muffled scream rumbled in her throat as Jonas raised the gun. She jerked at her bindings until her wrists bled.

Jonas pulled on the trigger and, as the gun fired, he closed his eyes on reflex. The bullet hit the woman directly between the eyes. Her body jerked as blood splattered and her eyes rolled back in her head. In one second she was gone, dead.

Jonas opened his eyes and looked at his gun in shock, as if the entire moment had been lived by another. He pressed the gun to his chest, cradling it close. "I killed her! I finally did it."

Madness pocketed the camera. "Yes, you did. You did it just right."

Jonas studied her. "She's so still."

"Yes."

Seconds passed as Jonas stared at the carnage. Slowly the brightness in his gaze dimmed. The near bursting bubble of anticipation had popped with one sharp prick of a bullet.

"You're feeling let down," Madness soothed.

Jonas looked at the gun and the woman. "How did you know?"

"Because I feel it too. All the planning, thinking and dreaming. All gone in an instant."

"Yes."

"And just like that, it's over." The snap of two fingers echoed in the room.

Jonas flinched. "I thought it would last longer."

"It never does. It's always over in a blink."

Jonas shook his head. "I thought there'd be more."

"I told you, anticipation trumps the moment." Breathe in. Breathe out. "That's why I made us wait."

"I can't believe it's over."

A clap of hands made Jonas start and look up. "Time to go. Time to destroy the evidence."

Jonas sat on the bed and took the woman's cooling, still hand in his. "I won't see her again."

"No."

"Can't we just stay a little longer? I don't want to leave her."

Madness moved toward Jonas and gently pulled the gun from his hands. "We have to go. We need to destroy this evidence and leave."

Tears welled in Jonas's eyes. "I don't want it to be over."

"No one ever does." Taking Jonas by the hand, it took little strength to disarm him and guide him toward the door. One last glance back at the room, the strike of another match, a quick toss and the room immediately was ablaze. Quickly, the flames generated white, then gray billowing smoke that thickened and blackened to a dense inky shade. Smoke and flame moved up the walls, over the ceiling and back down to the floor again in a deadly whirlpool.

If they stayed, they'd see the flames devour the floor, walls, ceiling and, of course, the woman. It all would be reduced to cinders in fifteen minutes. There'd be some forensic data to retrieve, but not much. The body, perhaps, and the bullet. But not their DNA.

Out the front door, they moved into the darkness toward Jonas's car, a station wagon. The actors always drove to the scene, never the master, in case a witness happened to look.

Jonas fired up the engine, revving the accelerator.

"Remember, drive slowly. We don't want to be noticed."

"Right." Jonas gripped the wheel and drove.

The rearview mirror gave a perfect view of the flames consuming the house. In the distance, fire engines wailed. Someone had already called 9-1-1.

"Is that the cops?" Jonas asked.

"No. The fire department." They rounded a corner and the fire faded from view.

In silence, they drove for several minutes before Jonas gripped the steering wheel tighter. "Can we do it again? I want to do it again!"

"Not right away. We have to wait." Anticipation burned under the yoke of Reason's screams to be freed.

But like Jonas, Madness didn't want to wait. Madness had been starved for too long and would not allow Reason to dictate terms.

Lights from Broadway in Nashville's music district flashed across Jonas's face as they made their way toward the crowds of tourists. "I don't want to wait."

"Let's get a drink."

"There's no parking this time of night."

"I know a place. An alley."

Jonas frowned.

"You've trusted me this far. Have I ever let you down?"

"No."

"Then trust me."

# Connect with

Visit us online at
**KensingtonBooks.com**
to read more from your favorite authors, see books
by series, view reading group guides, and more.

for sneak peeks, chances to win books and prize packs,
and to share your thoughts with other readers.

facebook.com/kensingtonpublishing
twitter.com/kensingtonbooks

*Tell us what you think!*

To share your thoughts, submit a review,
or sign up for our eNewsletters, please visit:
**KensingtonBooks.com/TellUs.**